Magoonagoon

Magoonagoon

ASHLEY HOVATER

This is a work of fiction. All of the characters, lands, and events portrayed in this novel are products of the author's imagination or are used fictitiously, and any resemblance to actual persons, living or dead, events, or locales is entirely coincidental.

Magoonagoon. Copyright © 2012 by Ashley Hovater. All rights reserved. Printed in the United States of America. No part of this book may be used or reproduced in any manner whatsoever without the prior written permission of the copyright owner.

Illustrated silhouette drawings and map of Magoonagoon by Ashley Hovater, are courtesy of his own personal collection. Copyright © 2012 by Ashley Hovater. All rights reserved.

"It's too late"
Words by Ashley Hovater. Copyright © 2012 by Ashley Hovater. All rights reserved.

ISBN-13: 978-1475236606
ISBN-10: 1475236603

This book is dedicated with love to
Audra,
my princess

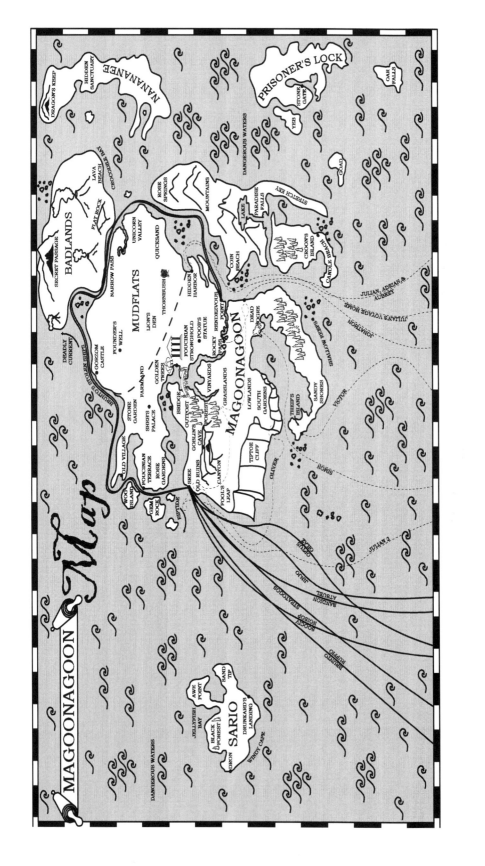

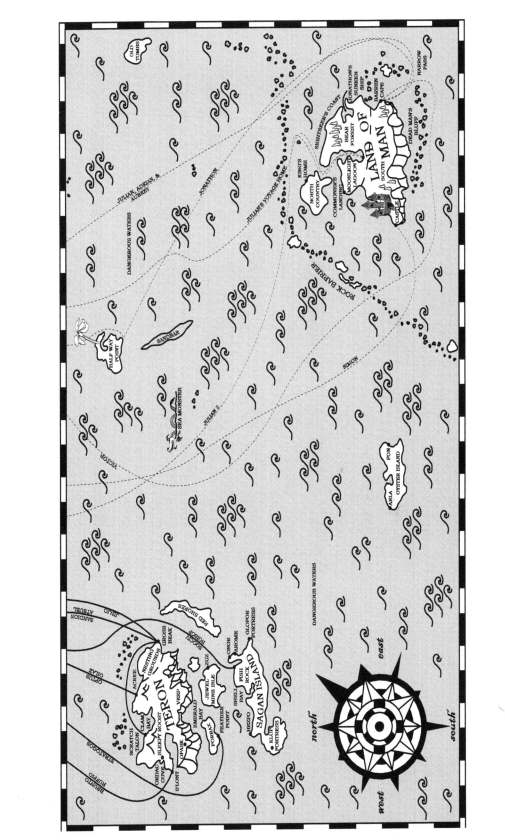

Magoonagoon

CAST

Brunto	**THE DESTROYER**
Victor	THE BURLY MAN OF WAR
Oliver	THE SORCERER
Sapsoon	THE PROUD PIRATE
Prince Marion	HIS MAJESTY THE PRINCE
Julian	THE MERCENARY
Emery	SON OF JONATHON
Ruffio	BROTHER OF BRUNTO
Jonathon	THE OLD WHALER
Aubrey	THE LEGIONNAIRE
Sandion	THE OLD FEMALE
Oilaz	THE EMPEROR
Wrothor	THE OGRE
Simon	THE SERVANT
Booballet	FOUCINIAN CHAMPION
Atsuel	THE RUTHLESS MURDERER
Felix	SON OF JONATHON
Wolneas	THE EVIL FOUCINIAN
Silas	BROTHER OF PERCIVAL
Stratogos	THE JUGGERNAUT
Soociv	DASTARDLY BLACK FEATHER
Amelia	DAUGHTER OF VICTOR
Godwin	THE DAUNTLESS
Premo	FOUCINIAN LEADER
Princess Penelope	HER MAJESTY THE PRINCESS
Cassereen	THE ADVISOR
Ubis	THE GOBLIN
Eescas	FOUCINIAN SCOUT
Warren	THE PHYSICIAN
Vindeen	LOYAL FOUCINIAN
Norion	THE EVIDENCE
Percival	BROTHER OF SILAS
Iipkam	NAKED BUZZARD
Noisop	SHIP CAPTAIN
Kounjab	THE HULK
Zannasor	THE GIANT BLACK FEATHER
Gonee	THE FATHER OF BRUNTO
Jinjo	THE WISE OLD VETERAN
Serpano	THE HEAVYSET HUNTER
Zinder-faso	MASTER OF THE NET & PITCHFORK
Atlas	THE QUICK STRIKER
Hawasaw	FOUCINIAN WATCH
Silstra	THE MAN-EATER
Optus	THE CAPTURED
Moojan	THE ROYAL GUARD
Komoras	SAGAN DOCTOR
Philip	THE PROTECTOR
Old Hob	THE DRAGON
Adrian	THE BROTHER OF JONATHON & VICTOR

"It is my war now," mumbled Simon.

Magoonagoon

CHAPTER 1
Unexpected Guests

It took ten strong Foucinians to drag the body of the slain giant from their stronghold to the sea. The ropes were strung so tight they looked as though they would snap under the strain of the tension. The Foucinians had looped and tied thick and heavy ropes around the long, slender neck of the huge Sagan. The knots slipped ever tighter as the hairy beasts pulled and tugged their way to the ship. The remains would be loaded without delay, for departure would be forthwith.

The feathered carcass slipped over the sand and the tracks

that followed in its wake drew a dreadful profile. When the Foucinians reached their lengthy ship, they pitched the ropes aloft onto the planks. The ropes landed in the middle of the deck where they were quickly retrieved by the crew. The massive body lay there lifeless as the hairy Foucinians scurried about. All at once and all together the host began to pull the giant aboard.

That old Sagan was Norion, one of the biggest and most powerful leaders. He had been slain by Booballet, the Foucinian champion. Norion would be the evidence, the proof that the humans would demand. The giant Sagan would no doubt encourage the humans to join the Foucinians as allies. The truth remained and was known to all, if the Foucinians fell to the crushing Sagan army, the humans would soon suffer the same fate.

The hairy beasts finished loading the ship with gold, the bounty that would persuade the most daring men to come at once. Those Foucinians who would make the journey stayed aboard, and the rest helped to shove off the vessel. In a moment's time, the ship departed and headed out to sea. It was the first time in a thousand years that a Foucinian had left the shores of Magoonagoon. The waves battered the ship and rattled the cargo. To the foreign shore they pressed so urgently to find an ally.

For many days and nights they followed the old charts and maps that had been recorded by the ancients. The giant Sagan had already begun to rot under the scorching sun of the day, and the spray of the ocean had made its slimy skin sag. When the agony of the sea had drained them of all hope, they growled and gnashed their teeth. Still, the crew sailed the ship onward, disgruntled and annoyed. Desperation plagued them—

until land could be seen in the distance.

Into the shallows they raced, approaching the shore. The ship was spotted by a small boy who was walking on the coast. The fellow looked upon the Foucinian ship with amazement and wonder. When he saw who was at the helm, the boy ran to tell his father. He passed over the dunes and ran inland to the nearby village. When the fellow reached the town his voice rang out cries of alarm.

"The Foucinians are here!" shouted the fellow.

The boy raced ahead to his home, warning people all the way. When he passed by the village, the boy shouted in the window to alert his kin. His uncle, who was working, stood to his feet in astonishment. Quickly, he ran to the door and moved into the street where he might speak to the lad.

"Here! Emery? What did you say?" asked the man.

"Uncle Victor, they're coming! Foucinians! I have seen them! They're nearly ashore!" said Emery.

Victor watched the boy run down the street and out of sight. Victor stepped back into his shop and grabbed his sword and looked at it. He looked into the shiny steel and remembered the time he served in the army. The sword brought back memories of anguish. So he decided to lay it back down and grab his trumpet instead. With a twist he returned to the street and followed the crowds to the coast. Hundreds of men and women passed over the dunes and gathered on the beach to greet the visitors. The people could not believe their eyes as they watched the vessel crawl ever closer. They all wondered if there would be trouble. With urgency, Victor spoke to another youngster that had followed the crowd.

"Amelia! Go and get Julian!" said Victor.

When the ship drew near, the men realized the urgency of the situation. They saw the hairy Foucinians on the deck of the craft and listened to their dreadful rumbling. Never before had any of them seen such ghastly creatures. Only in legend had they heard of the Foucinian beast. Some of them wore armor, which made the situation seem dangerous. Some of them carried weapons, alarming the men who waited nearby. Those that dipped the oars wore tunics and cloaks. The rest of the horrid creatures were bare and exposed. When the rowing ceased, the unexpected guests prepared to come ashore.

The men braced for the worst as the Foucinians washed into shouting distance. The scary beasts could be seen working away at something aboard the ship as their sullen leader snarled and growled at them. The storytellers of old had mentioned how dangerous the hairy Foucinians could be. Since the men were unarmed, many wondered if they should flee. They were mere moments away from that point when Jonathon arrived. He and Emery made their way through the crowd and the sight of the man settled the nerves of many. Yet a great many of them still thought about leaving. Then Silas rushed to the front, giving the host a little more confidence. Still, the multitude began to scatter, and the bulk of them would have fled had not the prince arrived.

Prince Marion came onto the scene with his soldiers and stirred the hearts of them all as he passed by. Julian, the mercenary, one of the greatest warriors in all the land, marched beside the prince. Amelia followed them closely and bathed in the glory of their shadows. The young girl dreamed as if she were the one the crowd warmed to.

So there the men stood as the defenders of the realm. Upon the shoreline they waited to make contact with the Foucinians. Without delay the ship moored into the sandy bottom and stopped in the shallows. The Foucinians splashed over the side and trod through the surf carrying thick ropes. They heaved and pulled the craft out of the water. They tugged it further and deeper onto the beach with their hairy backs trembling from the tension.

When they reached a certain point in the sand, the leader snarled and moaned at them. When they heard the order they dropped the ropes and stood by. Others leaped down from within the ship until a great multitude of Foucinians collected there in front of the men. On the beach they hunkered and bellowed out snorts through their black snouts. They hissed and moaned out obscenities and vaunts at the men, until the leader scolded them.

All at once many of the creatures climbed back aboard the ship. Those who massed on the ship's deck collected near the body of the giant Sagan. The Foucinians grabbed the twisted body of feathers and heaved it over the side. The heavy monster fell to the sand with a thud, and the sickening sound of snapping bones cracked in all their ears. When the body came to rest, some of the loose feathers broke free from the decaying skin. The men gasped at the sight of the extra-large monster.

Then the leader of the brutish bunch moaned once more. He barked an order or two, and from the crowd he came with an escort of soldiers. His thin black legs looked as though they were under heavy burden, for they supported his hefty hips. He walked within speaking distance of the men and blew out of his black trunk. A rumble and a bit of spit leaked out of his snout as he exclaimed.

"You are in great danger! Do you see this wretch here? Dead he is! But there are a thousand more like him," said Premo.

"Who are you and why have you come?" asked the prince.

"I am Premo. Foucinian! These are my own troops here who have battled the sea and tempted death to show you of the peril beyond the waves," said Premo as he pointed at the dead Sagan.

"What the devil do you want with us? We have no quarrel with those monsters," said Jonathon.

"Oh? But you will! If we do not stop these murderous Sagans, their thirst for conquest will surely lead them here. I have come here to collect reinforcements. We only need those with enough courage to battle giants," said Premo.

The men glared at each other in wonder and suspicion. After all, they remembered the tales of old about the Foucinians. They knew of their barbaric ways and had learned from their ancestors to fear them, for the travelers of old swore that Magoonagoon was a wonderful place, but the creatures in the land were to be feared. Only the sailors who had returned from the land with the gifts of splendor had spoken of it. Still others never returned from the island.

"Come and see! All of you! See this pile of bones in the sand!" shouted Premo.

Seeing the hesitation, the large Foucinian leader tried to quell their fears by kicking the giant creature in the ribs. The swift kick shook loose several more of the black feathers as the body jiggled. Then the Foucinian looked down his snout at them as if to gesture and laugh at cowards. Premo decided to use another tactic to reason with the men. The hairy beast filled his lungs with air and spoke to the men once more.

"We have brought a fortune in gold to be paid to those who will return with us. Fetch the chests! Bring me the riches! Is there a man in this land who will come? I wonder? Is there a man here now?" asked Premo.

It was at this moment, and after those words, that Aubrey entered with a congregation of the bravest men in the land. They rushed onto the beach with unsure expectations, for they had never seen a living Foucinian. Shouts of warning came from the throats of the beasts as if to scare some of them away. Like dogs they barked and taunted the procession as they approached.

At the front of the cavalcade, near Aubrey's side, came Godwin and Jonathon's youngest brother, Adrian. The group ran onto the beach with their weapons drawn and settled next to Jonathon and Victor. There they huddled on the dunes and waited for a decision to be reached. It was Adrian who spoke to his brothers first.

"Are they looking for a fight?" asked Adrian.

"No. They have come in peace. They wish for us to join them as allies against those," said Victor, pointing to the remains.

"Dare I say the quest would be foolish! We are no match for those monsters!" said Jonathon.

"We may be no match for them alone, but we will not be alone. Those beasts you see there will be more than help. Look at their size. They are giants to us, and they will be at our side," said Julian.

"Ah! Julian! No match for you! We are not mercenaries. You have made a fortune of wages. Wages for combat! There are many of us who have never been to war. Allow us to make the right decision here," said Jonathon.

"He's right! What chance does a man have against a Sagan?" asked Godwin.

"None!" shouted Philip as he made a motion with his hand across his own neck as if to say they would slit his throat.

"Let the prince speak with them. There is no need for us to deal with them," said Victor.

"Jonathon! You have battled whales upon the sea. Do not be afraid of these beasts or that pile of bones that lies before them. Come with me if you will, in close to the host, and I will speak to them," said Julian.

"Afraid I am. Not of these beasts! Not of that dead thing over there. I fear war! A war that cannot be won. That dead Sagan standing would be more than twenty feet tall. Imagine the possibility of trying to fight that hulk. Even with weapons to distance yourself from its long reach…a normal man would not be able to counter a defensive," said Jonathon.

"Your majesty! What shall we do?" asked Victor.

"Hear me. Let us think for a moment here together before we rush across to join them," asked the prince.

"Which one of you has enough courage to leave with them today? I for one say that man would be a fool!" said Jonathon furiously.

"Come now, Jonathon!" said Julian.

"Let them kill one another! It is not our concern! Send them away before their money tempts your better judgment," said Jonathon.

"Maybe Julian is right, Jonathon. Let us not jump to conclusions. First let us approach their ship and hear the story," said Victor.

"My own brother defies me? I warn you all. This is nonsense. Those who rush ahead with these beasts without careful planning will be doomed. So be it. I have warned you," said Jonathon as he walked away.

"Do not be so rash, Jonathon. Let us hear them out. Come and see! Let us see what they have to offer," said Prince Marion.

"I will tell you what they have to offer. Death! Stay away from them!" said Jonathon as he disappeared over the dunes.

Magoonagoon

CHAPTER 2
A Few Brave Souls

With Jonathon's warning and scoff, he left them standing on the beach, making it clear that they should beware. While the beasts waited in the distance, the rest of the men looked to Prince Marion and waited on his decree. They knew that he would be the only one to make any kind of decision. There was silence for a moment until the prince gave out an order.

"Anyone who is brave enough, follow me," said Prince Marion as he began to walk toward the Foucinians. The crowd began to stir with emotion and the confidence gave others enough courage to join him.

So the congregation trekked across the sand with Prince Marion in the lead. When they reached the Foucinian ship, the large Sagan guarded the way as it lay stretched out on the sand. Its huge talons appeared razor sharp, and its beak looked like it could tear through flesh with ease. Its long arms lay there with a loose, lifeless demeanor. The Sagan's posture was terrible with a dreadful hunch in his back.

The men looked at the giant up close for the first time with trepidation. Emery picked up one of the huge feathers that lay near the giant's side. He held it by the translucent quill that used to be buried deep in the skin. The long and silky black feather was almost as tall as him. They could tell that the Sagan was flightless and its body appeared considerably sluggish. Yet the creature gave the men a sense of fear that they had never felt before.

Seeing the Sagan at a close distance, many of the men agreed that this monster was way too big to be fought alone. When Aubrey bent down to see the huge mass of skin and bone, one of the Foucinians let out a rumbling roar. The shout caused many of the men to flee. The Foucinians all laughed at the gesture and mocked the humans with obscene gestures. Only a few brave souls had remained. The two young cousins, Emery and Amelia, raced away.

Aubrey was not moved by the shout. He merely stood to his feet with his hand on the hilt of his sword. Prince Marion and his guards had shifted back a short distance, but they had not turned to flee like so many others. Aubrey, Adrian, Godwin, Julian, Victor, Philip, Silas, and his brother Percival had held their ground, but the rest of the crowd had run off the beach in fear. The long laughter turned to silence when Julian volunteered to join them. He spoke with a bellowing voice that every man and beast could hear.

"I will join you! For gold and silver! I have many troops that will join me, enough to fill your ship. But my price is steep. All the treasure in your ship! All in advance! This is the price I demand!" said Julian.

The Foucinians looked at the man, stunned and disbelieving. Premo scratched his wooly face and pondered the thought, then he stepped near to the man to test his courage. In close, the giant treaded with his long legs and nimble strides until they almost touched. Premo bent down and put his snout in Julian's face. The beast was way too close for comfort and everyone wondered what would happen next.

Premo's glossy black eyes stared right through the man. He had two sets of glassy marble-sized eyes that were embedded in his hairy face. Under his snout, yellowed teeth and fangs dripped with saliva. The hair stood up on the back of the beast's neck as he drew a great breath. Then he lifted his head up to the sky and shouted a roar. His roar was followed by other shouts and vaunts behind him. Then, after the shouts, Premo welcomed Julian and the deal was done.

"Unload the lot! Give every bit to this man! There will be other ships full of gold here soon. Enough for a chest of treasure for each man who will come! Is there another? One with enough courage to come with this man?" asked Premo as he looked at the prince.

"I can see why these men are hesitant to join you. These here are the bravest in the land and if they are hesitant, I dare not go. What say the rest of you?" asked the prince.

"My prince, I do not wish to race off to war with these beasts. I have been to war and I have battled men, but never have I battled something as great as that lying there. My brother spoke the truth. This I know. I do not want to travel to Magoonagoon," said Victor.

"We all know of its dangers. It is an unknown land with strange creatures. As you can see from the look of that heap of feathers," said the prince.

"There may be several reasons not to go. If there is a man so daring, I revere his decision. Let me choose to stay behind in respect for my brother and his wishes. This should not stop any of you," said Victor.

Victor spoke his farewell to Julian and wished him luck on his journey. The burly man started to walk away when his younger brother Adrian volunteered. Victor stopped in his tracks and turned in an instant with shock. He could not believe his ears, or for that matter, understand why the youngster would want to go.

"He will not go! Do not go!" shouted Victor as he grabbed hold of Adrian's arm.

"I am old enough to make my own decisions. Let me be!" said Adrian.

"Do not defy both of your brothers and spoil your youth with these beasts. I beg you! Come back here," commanded Victor.

"I will watch over him, Victor," said Julian.

"He is no mercenary, Julian! Adrian! Do as I say and let's go home," shouted Victor.

"I am going. There is nothing you can say to make me change my mind," said Adrian.

At that moment Victor was ready to go on the ship after his younger brother. If the eldest, Jonathon, had not already left the beach, he would have entered the ship to retrieve him. However, Victor took a different approach as he fell to his knees in the sand. The man clutched his hands together and began to plead for his sibling. As wet tears poured down his face, he shouted for his brother to listen to his wish.

"Hear my plea! Adrian, come back here! All the gold in their ship is not worth your life! Please stop! Please come back," cried Victor.

So hearing the man's sincerity, Aubrey, Victor's closest friend, moved to his side and tried to speak to him. Kneeling at his side and clutching his wrist, he looked straight into the man's eyes and honored him with the suggestion that he might go to protect Adrian. Victor thought for a moment as he shook his head. Finally, he agreed and decided that it would be best if Aubrey would go and watch over him. Into the ship the man went without hesitation or thought of his own life. Like a true friend he showed his devotion.

As the ship heaved back into the ocean, Victor almost joined them. He started to rise up from the sand, but his knees shook beneath him. The men who were left watched the ship fade away. Never before had any of them seen such gallantry in the face of danger.

Magoonagoon

CHAPTER 3
A Shadowy Figure

One year passed without so much as a word from the three men. Then one day, out of the blue, a Foucinian ship was spotted off the coast. Word traveled over the land and soon there was a great gathering on the shoreline. As the slender ship churned through the surf, a shadowy figure stood upon the bow. They could tell from the shore it was a man, but what man they knew not.

The figure stood with one foot on the rail and a slumping posture. He appeared to be wounded as he held his hand on his back. The man was wearing a helmet and a cape. The cape was draped over his shoulders and made him look as though he weighed a ton. When the ship crawled in close, the sun revealed the man's handsome face. It was Julian underneath the helmet. He had returned from Magoonagoon.

The people on the shore searched for the other two. Their eyes darted all over the ship hoping to catch a glimpse of Adrian or Aubrey. When the ship touched bottom, the Foucinians leaped out just as they had done the year before. With their ropes they tugged and pulled the craft in until it rested high on the beach. Julian urged the Foucinians to stay back and allow him to speak with the men alone. Then he sluggishly leapt down from the ship and was greeted by the welcoming villagers.

Victor clutched the man's wrists and the two rejoiced for a moment. Jonathon had the look of curiosity and suspicion on his face as he received him. Silas and Percival acknowledged the man with jubilant praise. Godwin also hailed him with cheers of admiration. Then Julian removed his helmet and pitched it to the ground. He moved to speak directly to Victor and address him with sensitivity.

"Victor. I have terrible news. It has burdened me deeply. Your brother has been killed by those villainous Sagans," said Julian and the crowd gasped.

Victor fell to the ground and pulled on his hair as though he wanted to scream out. Jonathon grit his teeth and tried to hold back tears. The others began to question Julian with disbelief. It was at this moment that Victor cried out with a moaning and eerie voice.

"It is to my shame that I did not stop him! I can see it as clear today as I did a year ago! I pleaded for him to stay! I begged him not to go!" Victor cried aloud.

"Oh! How can this be?" asked Philip.

"I warned him! Trouble yourself not. It was his choice to join them," said Jonathon.

"Please, my friends! Hear me out! Adrian's death will be followed by countless others if we do not act accordingly. His death was not in vain. No, he fought against a rising evil that if not stopped will spread to this land. Please, my friends, you must understand, the danger is worse today than ever before," said Julian.

"What do you expect us to do? You have brought us news of Adrian's death. Are we to follow? I do not see Aubrey. Where is he? He has not returned to this land," said Jonathon.

"Aubrey lives! He has sent me to gather the support of others. He has specifically asked for you, Jonathon," said Julian.

"My brother is already dead from those giants you speak of. Many more will meet the same fate if they choose to embark on this journey. I said it a year ago and I will say it again today, forget this talk and allow yourselves to live," said Jonathon.

"We are all responsible for this tragedy. Do you not see that we should join them? Everyone here would like to forget the danger and continue on with our lives," said Victor.

"Julian is a man of his word. I know this to be true. I would not dare say he was lying. The hurt of our brother's death pains me. Still, I warn you and anyone else who dares to sail. Mark me! The evil that is across the ocean will forever remain. It cannot be defeated, and soon after you will be fighting a two-front war against those beasts behind you," said Jonathon.

"My friends! I am so glad to be home. I never want to

leave this land again. Every moment in Magoonagoon is misery. I have killed so many of those giants, but there are thousands more. The land near the stronghold reeks with the rotten carcasses of those I have laid down. I do not wish to return, but I must go back. Aubrey needs us! He has asked specifically for Jonathon. We cannot leave him abandoned and alone," said Julian.

"Listen to him Jonathon. Aubrey has asked for you," said Victor turning to Jonathon.

"You don't want to hear what I have to say," said Jonathon.

"Everyone here knows that you are the one! The one we need to turn the tide against the evil villains," said Julian.

"Please be reasonable. Fight!" insisted Julian.

"I will not! I have warned you, just as I warned Adrian. Do not make the same mistake," said Jonathon as he walked away.

At that moment the host began to break up and scatter in all directions. Victor began to shake his head in disbelief and ponder the idea whether or not to heed his brother's warning. He scratched his beard and then rubbed his forehead with his huge hands. Then he looked at his friend dead in the eye and searched for the right words to say. When the thought came to him it was clear, and so he filled his chest with a breath of air and placed his trumpet to his lips. With a blast that carried across the land, the man blew. Without a doubt the signal proclaimed a call to assemble.

Magoonagoon

CHAPTER 4

Fortify Ourselves

"Summon every able man! Send for those brave enough to fight! Send for the craftsmen as well. We need carpenters and blacksmiths to build the ships," said Prince Marion.

"We need weapons. We are not fighting against a mere man! The armor we have is not good enough. Where will we get the equipment we need to face those giants?" asked Philip.

"He's right! We need to move quickly to construct a foundry! We don't have a lot of time. We must start at once to fortify ourselves with armor and weapons," said Julian.

"I want every man to have a helmet on his head and a

sword in his hand. Each man should have three javelins and a shield. You will have long spears to distance yourselves from those killers," said the prince.

"Someone needs to go and get Oliver. He must go with us even if we have to tie him up and make him," said Godwin.

"He will come. Silas will go and speak with him," said Percival.

"Summon all the tailors and seamstresses in the land. We need sails for the ships. I want them here to sew cloth. I want uniforms for each man," said Prince Marion.

"We need food rations as well. We cannot depend on those hairy beasts to supply us," said Percival.

"The Foucinians have promised to send ships back here full of wealth," said Julian.

"When they arrive with the amount owed to me, I will use it to pay for as many provisions as its worth. You will have barrels of wine, grain, bread, fruit, nuts, and cheese," said the prince.

It was not long after when the shipbuilders began to construct the warships. Each would hold seventy strong men armed with weaponry. Other ships would be built to house the horses and chariots. There the fine rigs and swift stallions would be stored as desperately needed cargo. Within a month the progress was substantial, and the plans were well on their way to completion.

The army grew more plentiful each day, and supporters came from every corner of the land. Prince Marion appointed qualified men to be captains and officers. He picked those who had experience in previous campaigns. Volunteers were split up into squadrons and they camped near the ship of their captain. The prince set up his tents down at the shore and greeted the new recruits as they arrived. The recruits were sent to vacant spots according to the space allowed on the ships.

Each of the captains trained their men. They learned signals and memorized the different sounds of the trumpet. They conditioned themselves and made ready for war. Giant targets were built that looked like the huge Sagans, based on the single corpse they had seen and on Julian's descriptions. The men practiced day after day, attacking the targets and honing their battle skills according to Julian's instruction. Nevertheless, all the courage, devotion, practice, confidence, and training could ever prepare them for Magoonagoon.

Magoonagoon

CHAPTER 5
Treasure

Late one evening when the sun was changing from orange to pink, the Foucinians returned as promised. When they were spotted, a runner sent word to the leaders. Everyone gathered on the beach just as they had done twice before. The men and women waited for the Foucinian ships to crawl into the shallows. Godwin sped from the beach and headed toward the castle. The fellow ran as fast as he could to reach the fortress. When Godwin reached the castle walls, he shouted to the watchman on the wall.

"Tell the prince that the Foucinians have returned!"

shouted Godwin as he approached the tall ramparts breathing heavily.

"What?" questioned the watchman.

"Tell the prince that the Foucinians have returned!" shouted Godwin.

"They have returned? Did you say the Foucinians have returned?" asked the watchman.

"Yes! Tell the prince!" shouted Godwin.

The prince overheard the announcement from his seat in the garden. Prince Marion stood to his feet and walked into the clearing to confirm the message. The watchman quickly ran down the steps of the tower and entered into the courtyard where he found both the prince and princess.

"Your majesties! They have returned!" said the messenger.

"Who has returned?" questioned Princess Penelope.

"The Foucinians your grace. They have returned as promised," said the watchman.

"Tell them that I will be there shortly," ordered Prince Marion.

"Your chariot awaits your majesty," said one of the footmen.

"Marion, must you go?" asked Princess Penelope.

"I must be there to greet them," said the prince.

"No. I mean why must you go to Magoonagoon?" asked the princess.

"My darling. These men need the prince to lead them. We will make quick work of those creatures and be back in no time," said the prince.

"Marion. Its too dangerous. I don't want to lose you. Appoint someone else to lead them," suggested Princess Penelope.

"Don't think about it anymore tonight. I will be back later and we can talk about it. Don't be troubled," said the prince.

"I still don't understand why you don't ask my father to join you. He has legions of troops," suggested the princess.

"Northerners! Ha! We don't need them. I have told you before, these men are the bravest in the land," said Prince Marion.

"You are forgetting that you and I were married to obtain peace. The king had your army surrounded," said Princess Penelope.

"Is that why? All this time I thought it was because of my charming good looks," said the prince.

"Oh Marion! Don't go!" said the princess.

"Penelope my darling. You must not worry," said Prince Marion as he kissed her on the cheek.

The prince left the courtyard and he and his soldiers raced to the beach. They arrived at the water's edge just as the Foucinians had finished mooring the ships. The prince moved to the front of the congregation and waited for the Foucinian leader. Premo was at the helm of the command ship. The men heard him barking out commands to his soldiers. The hairy beast ordered some of the Foucinians to retrieve a wooden chest. They unloaded the box and carried it to shore. When they reached dry land they lugged it right up in front of the men. They threw it down at Prince Marion's feet and spoke to those standing there.

"I have returned as promised! Here is the treasure! The

ships behind me are full of chests just like this one!" said Premo as he flung open the lid.

The men could not believe their eyes as they looked inside the chest. They gazed upon the jewels and coins with wonder. The silver, gold, and precious gems sparkled and delighted the spectators. Victor stood at the box and studied the contents for a brief moment.

"There are seven hundred boxes. One for each man," said Premo.

"One for each man?" asked Julian.

"Do you not have seven hundred men willing to go?" asked Premo.

"There are eight hundred and ten men who are trained and ready to go," said Victor.

"Choose for yourselves! Seven hundred is all we have!" said Premo.

"Unload the ships. Stack the chests here on the beach where I can count them. After the count is finished, we will take them to the treasury. Then, let every man go to his home. Say goodbye to your wives. Tomorrow we go to war!" said Prince Marion.

Magoonagoon

CHAPTER 6
The Princess Penelope

    Later that evening, Prince Marion was setting in his garden alone. He was thinking of the dreadful task in front of him. The prince was not looking forward to the journey. He was fearful of what he might find in Magoonagoon. He was uncomfortable with the plan to join the Foucinians. On top of that, just the terrifying thought of having to face the Sagans left the fellow troubled.

    The young man shook his head when he thought of leaving his castle. He looked around the garden with all its spleandor and wondered why anyone would ever want to leave the luxury and comforts found within.

While the prince stared off into the flowers and roses he heard a lovely voice singing to him. As he looked around the wondrous garden for the sound, his eyes met his darling princess singing.

> *Hold me for a moment.*
> *Kiss me for a while.*
> *Tell me that you love me. Say it with a smile.*
> *Put your arms around me and never let me go.*
> *I'll be your's forever, please tell me so.*
> *Its too late, too late, you stole my heart away.*
> *It's too late, too late, for me to try and get away.*
> *I knew it from the start. I knew you would win my heart.*
> *It's too late. It's too late.*

Princess Penelope walked tenderly through the beautiful flowers and came over to the prince. Her lovely hair sparkled in the sunlight and her long dress made her look so splendid. As she touched the prince's face, the man gently spoke to her.

"My darling. What brings you out here?" asked the prince.

"I have been looking for you," said the princess.

"You should be getting ready for the banquet," said Prince Marion.

"Oh! Marion. Why must you go?" asked Princess Penelope.

"Penelope my darling, it won't be for long. Soon things will be just as they are now," said the prince as he reached out for her.

"How can you leave? I don't want you to go," asked the princess.

"I don't want to go. I fear that the men don't want me to go anyway. It's just a terrible mess. There is so much arguing and fighting among the men. Oh! How can they even join together to fight?" asked the prince.

"Oh! Marion! Let's just go! We'll sneak away! Let's get out of here. Let them go without you!" suggested Princess Penelope.

"That sounds so wonderful. We could leave at once. We could disguise ourselves and slip out. We'll go to the country," said the prince eagerly.

"Oh Marion! Do you mean it?" wished Princess Penelope.

"You know I can't. I am the prince you know. It is my duty to go with the army. I desperately want to stay here with you my darling but it is just not possible," said the prince.

"I just can't stay here alone. This castle will be so lonely without you," said Princess Penelope.

"Why don't you go to your father's? You will be around people you love and the time away from me won't seem so long," suggested Prince Marion.

"If I go to see the king without you…there will be a war here at home," said the princess and they both laughed.

"Your right. You couldn't explain anything to the old man. He would flip his wig," said the prince.

"Oh! Marion! Stay here with me! Please stay here!" said Princess Penelope as she held him tight and started to cry.

"My love. Keep me in your prayers. I will return. So wait for me. One day I will return and we will rejoice. We will be like kids again. You will see. Soon you will see," said Prince Marion as he squeezed her tight.

Magoonagoon

CHAPTER 7
The Stowaway

As soon as Amelia heard that her father was headed to war, the girl started planning a way to go with him. She knew that Victor would never let her go. Still, she had the courage and willingness to go with them. Amelia would visit the soldiers every day. She wandered around the ships and looked for a great place to hide. Amelia had made up her mind; she was going with them to Magoonagoon.

Each day she would walk along the ships thinking and studying all the preparations that were being made for the journey. One day she noticed that two of the ships were being built completely different from the others. So she moved in closer to the construction and spoke to the ship's carpenter.

"Why are these two ships different than the others?" asked Amelia.

"That one is for the horses and the other one will be for the chariots," said the carpenter.

Then and there Amelia knew that she had found a hiding place. Still, somehow she would have to sneak aboard and hide herself from view. The girl continued to walk down to the ships every day. When they were close to being finished, the men began to load crates and boxes aboard. She noticed that some of the boxes were large enough for her to fit inside them comfortably.

The thought came to her instantly. Her plan was to go down to the ships during the night and hide herself in a box that was going to be loaded into one of the boarding ships. Late that night, she waited until things got quiet and found a chest that was the perfect hiding place. The box was filled with blankets for the horses. Amelia rushed back to her house and packed a sack of food. She made sure to pack enough to last her for the journey. She gathered some raisins, a small wheel of cheese, some bread, and a jar of juice. Amelia knew that she would have to get far enough away from home that the men would not turn around and bring her back.

Early the next morning just before sunrise, the men were in their homes making final preparations for the journey. Many of them were enjoying the last moments with their families, some were packing up the remaining provisions they needed, and others were sitting quietly awaiting the call to assemble. They were all anticipating the sound when they heard the trumpet blast. The hum was eerie and the note was long. When the tone stopped the people knew to make their way to the shore. The men, women, and children entered the streets and walked to the coast. Amelia kissed her father goodbye from the edge of her bed. He patted her on the head and walked over the doorway. There in the doorway he stood and spoke to his daughter.

"Remember to lock this door. You know where the sword is. Don't be afraid to use it. I love you," said Victor.

"I love you, father," said Amelia.

Victor left the house and joined the multitude to journey to the ships. Before the door had even shut, Amelia sprung out of bed to carry out her plan. She slipped into her clothes and grabbed her pack that was filled with supplies. The girl joined the crowd and quickly made her way to her hiding spot. Amelia walked right to the crate she had picked out the night before and slipped inside the box. No one had noticed the girl because they were all focused on their goodbyes. Just moments after she shut the lid, two men picked up the crate and took it aboard.

Prince Marion arrived just as the sun began to rise. At his arrival the captains immediately gave orders to their troops commanding them to board. The men were forced to let go of their wives and children as they marched up the gangplanks to enter the ships. From the decks the captains gave out orders for the launch just as they had practiced. Those who were staying behind waved and called to their sons, husbands, fathers, cousins, and uncles.

"No matter what happens, I love you, son," said a man's voice.

"Father! Over here! Goodbye!" said another.

"Be sure that I love you, son! Hurry back!" said a mother with tears in her eyes.

"Put into practice what you have learned. Be brave and courageous!" said someone from the crowd.

"We will rejoice on the day when you will return home!" said a new bride waving to her husband.

"Remember, soon you will have your reward when you return home to us," said another.

"Long live the prince!" yelled Princess Penelope from the crowd, and all the people cheered!

The men on the decks looked back at their families and wondered if they would ever see them, or their homeland, again. The prince waved his hand in the air at the crowd and blew his princess a kiss. She waved back at the man with tears in her eyes. The crowd stayed on the beach waving and cheering until the boats drifted out of sight.

Out in the ocean the captains and leaders encouraged the men to tend to their duties and get them under way. When they all worked together they moved further out to sea. The men unfurled the sails and captured the wind.

Amelia rested on the journey beneath the thick comfortable blankets. She kept quiet for two seemingly endless days and nights. When she could not take it any longer, Amelia came out during the dead of night while everyone was asleep. She wanted to stretch her legs and get a cool drink. As she walked on the deck, the stowaway was spotted by the watchman.

"Hey! What are you doing? Who said you could be back there?" asked the man, but Amelia gave no answer.

"Who goes there?" asked another man.

"You're a girl! What are you doing on this ship?" asked the night watch.

"I am following my father. You should probably let him know that I am here," said Amelia.

"Who is your father?" asked the man.

"Victor," said Amelia.

When news reached the command ship, Victor was so furious that he demanded that a ship to turn around and take her home. However, the captains and leaders talked him out of doing something so rash. They convinced the man that they were past the point of no return. When Victor and Amelia were reunited, the little girl stood in front of her father with tears in her eyes. When Victor finally looked at Amelia, his anger melted away. The girl was so beautiful and delicate, who could ever be cross with her? Still, the man spoke to her with correcting words.

"You should not have come. Why did you come? Magoonagoon is no place for you. It is a place full of danger," said Victor as he embraced her.

"I wanted to be with you," said Amelia.

"How can I continue my duties as a captain now? I cannot watch over you and guide my troops," said Victor.

At once, Victor convened with Prince Marion and tried to step down from his position. The prince refused to let him quit, citing that he would continue to be a commander. Still, Victor pleaded his case that the girl would be helpless when they went to war.

"How can I leave her behind when I rush off to battle? I will not leave her at the ships. What then do you propose I do?"

asked Victor.

"I will assign a man to guard her," said the prince.

"No. I will not let her out of my sight. I would not ask another man to guard her. I will keep her with me at all times. I must resign. Please, my prince, I will not take her to war," said Victor causing a man to speak up from the crowd.

"I will personally protect your daughter. She will be under my watch at all times. I will defend her with my life," said Philip.

"If this man will take a vow to defend her with his life, how can you turn him down?" asked the prince.

"I cannot argue with you, my prince. Please, it is not his place," said Victor.

"I will take the vow," said Philip.

"Then let what has been said be done," said Prince Marion.

Magoonagoon
CHAPTER 8
Victim to Sleep

The days passed and time brought the army of men close to their destination. However, thirst cracked their lips and dried up their skin until each man began to doubt if they would ever see land. After seven miserable days, word came from the watch on the command ship.

"Ho! Men! Land!" said the watch.

The men lowered the sails to grab the oars. Each man took hold of a paddle and heaved the smooth ships closer to land. The ships slid in on their bellies in the shallows and Prince Marion commanded them all to drag the vessels ashore. So each man followed the orders and moored the ships high up on the sand. They pulled on the huge ropes and tugged with all their might to bring the boats aground, for they had reached the land of Magoonagoon.

Victor helped heave the vessels ashore himself, for they needed his strength. He bruised his hand when two of the mighty sterns buckled together against the waves. But through the pain he helped pull each craft ashore. The mooring of the ships took every last ounce of their energy, for their journey had been long and the distance was hard to endure.

To everyone's surprise Aubrey was waiting for them there on the shore. He was standing on top of the largest rock overlooking the beach. The men were so glad to see the fellow and they were so relieved to be on dry land again. Julian was the first to speak to him as he yelled to the peak.

"Aubrey! I have returned as promised!" shouted Julian.

"I am glad to see you and I am glad to see you have brought all these soldiers with you!" shouted Aubrey.

"Come down here, my friend!" shouted Julian.

As Aubrey made his way down from the peak, the men moved up on the beach picking out spots to rest. Silas and his brother Percival were the first to lie down near the tall palms to relax. Others followed their actions and lounged in the sand. However, Prince Marion gave out strict orders for each man to arm and gather up the bright weaponry. As they began to set up camp on the shore, the prince gave a decree.

"The first man to kill a Sagan will become the leader of the army!" said Prince Marion.

But the men defied him, for they were tired and sleep was

the only thing on their mind. The exhausted troopers collapsed onto the sand. The fools paid no attention to the leader, and each one laid down to rest for they knew not of the danger. Even the prince and his guards fell asleep on the sandy ground.

The sun continued to climb throughout the day until it was high overhead. Aubrey made his way over to the ships and climbed aboard to inventory the supplies. Down the beach, no more than a stone's throw away, one of the captains kept watch as he clenched his teeth in anger. Like a huge boulder that could not be moved, Victor kept watch with his trumpet as he sat in the hot sand. In deep distress he guarded the front like a true sentry; for his eyes were heavy as well. Still, the man fought sleep for he knew that in this strange land there was great danger. He peered across the landscape with a squinting brow until he too fell victim to sleep.

Then the attack began. The Sagans came on in swiftness and haste to kill every last one of them with the points of their deadly swords and spears. An entire detachment of Sagans descended upon the beach where the men lay in sweet sleep. It was the Brown Sagans, veterans of combat with a bold leader named Brunto marshaling them.

The clang of their armor gave away the element of surprise and Victor awoke from a deep sleep. The hero opened his eyes to see a large foot with giant talons near his face. Fear gripped his limbs and the hair on his neck rose as it had never done before, for he had never seen a creature so big at such a close distance. He kept still and peered upon the huge foot in front of him. As Victor lay there on the ground he thought to himself.

What is he waiting for? Why didn't the creature stab me? thought Victor.

The Sagans wisely crept into the camp in silence with the intentions to kill every last one of them while they slept. The old man thought to leap to his feet and cry out a warning, but austerity was near to him with peril so close. Nevertheless, the stake was not so great that he might not warn the others. So Victor gathered up the courage to roll away from the danger. Then, like thunder rumbling and lightning that cracks, the man rose up and took to fighting in his fine sandals; he overcame the fear of the feathered giants and moved in close, hand to hand.

With a blast like a spirited lion that casts out a terrible roar, so too the man warned the others with his trumpet. The Sagans answered with battle cries of attack, and strife began among them close to the ships. Prince Marion's guards were the only other men who had weapons in hand. They kept their weapons with them at all times to protect the prince. With their swords in hand the men encircled the prince and kept the Sagans at bay.

Unarmed men were left to fight with bare knuckles and clenched fists against the foe. However, the Sagans were covered in heavy armor and each boasted bright weaponry that held the upper hand. The prince ordered three of his soldiers to go and defend the left while Victor spearheaded the right. Each man tried to block the way, but the guards were too inexperienced against such a large opponent. It was not long before the Sagans took their first victim.

A spear point slammed into the poor man's hip and drove him to the bright sand with a thud. There the feathered giants leaped upon him with their quick swords and hacked away his life. It seemed as though it would be a slaughter, for the men could not compete bare-handed with the enemy. Many of the men retreated to the sea and plunged into the surf for safety.

Without the spears to distance the fighting, the men began to fall like drops of rain to the sand. However, Victor held his own and protected a great host of them with their backs against the ships. With one thrust of his sword, Victor became the leader of the army as the first Sagan fell dead in front of him. He rushed to the left and then to the right countering their moves and breaking their lines. Victor killed another giant in front of the rocks and moved farther out on the dunes to fight. He battled to give others who had gone to gather arms time to return from the hulls of the ships.

Other brave men came on to drive away the foe as the Sagans began to burn the ships. Hearing the commotion Aubrey raced to wake Oliver, who was asleep in the hull of one of the vessels. When he found him, Aubrey quickly spoke to the sorcerer.

"Wake up you fool! They are all around us!" shouted Aubrey.

The sorcerer yawned and stretched out his arms. He calmly stood to his feet and stretched some more while the legionnaire pleaded for him to help. Oliver slowly knelt down and picked up his prized winged helmet. After he carefully placed it on his head, the wizard walked over to Aubrey and patted him on the shoulder.

"You just can't rush into these sorts of things," said Oliver.

When it looked as though all might die, the wizard emerged out of the ship. He leapt down from the bow of the ship and landed in the sand on both feet. While the old magician surveyed the scene, Aubrey rushed to aid Victor against the attackers. Then the wizard began to use his powers. He slapped his hands together and with the clap sprayed white light. The sparkles leaped from his hands into the air. With a twist the magician became a tornado of sand to ward off the Sagans. Seeing this, the Sagans began to retreat. It looked as though the sorcerer would end the battle as quickly as it had begun. However, the bold leaders of the feathers paraded in to sway the outcome.

Great Sagans, that were legends of their time, marshaled into the contest. Perhaps the greatest of them, Brunto, moved against Victor and Aubrey as they matched other Sagans back to back. The giant attacked the pair as they fought along the dunes. Oliver began to tire and his powers relinquished after the spell drained his energy. The Sagans returned with their shouts and calls, hoping to destroy the men. With Oliver's stamina expiring, the Sagans had time to take the offensive once again.

Brunto swung his sword around and took a stab at them with his long wooden spear. The iron tip of the pike grazed Aubrey's shoulder and spun him around to the sand, spilling his blood. There he sank deep in the grit where the coarse sand covered his knees. Seeing the man plummet, Brunto moved to strike the wounded challenger. The Sagan took back his spear behind his head and swung the wood with great force to destroy Aubrey as he tried to stand up.

The end of the rod smashed down across the man's

helmet and Aubrey fell back to the sand upon his handsome face. The sword that was clutched in his grasp fell loose. Seeing this, Victor leaped to protect his friend as Brunto moved to finish the legionnaire with his deadly sword. However, Victor blocked the killer's strike with his matchless strength. As the metal struck, the sound echoed like a scream through a deep canyon. They held the blades together and pushed upon the swords. Victor slipped in the sand as the huge killer pushed on him with his strong back. His fine sandals lost traction on the sandy beach.

Additional Sagans moved to kill Aubrey, just as other sturdy men moved to protect him. As he lay still on the beach, Silas and Percival ran from the water with heavy feet to protect the fellow. The two came just in time to save him from death. Like two pillars holding up a sturdy roof, so too did the brothers restrain the foe, unyielding and solid.

Nevertheless, the waves of Sagan fighters grew exceedingly difficult to defend, and the Sagans moved to set fire to the fast ships once more. They lit torches and threw them upon the planks and the fires spread deep in the hulls. With the men outnumbered, fatigued, and unarmed, the outlook appeared grim.

When it seemed all of those left might be killed and every ship burned, the Foucinians came on in attack. They poured onto the sand like wine spilled from a pitcher. Their hairy backs took to fighting and soon they turned the tide against the Sagans. Boasting long spears, they chased the Sagans off the coast and into the wastelands where they continued to battle. Casting smooth spears and javelins, the Foucinians rushed ahead of the men. From their black trunks, the Foucinian battle cry cast a loud rumble across the land and brought fear to the hearts of both man and Sagan.

With them came a great ogre, standing shoulders above the rest. Mighty, tall, green, barbarous, and riddled with scars and old wounds, a veteran of combat, the ogre was the last of his kind. He was such a big target among the horde of Foucinians that many of the deadly volleys from the Sagans were cast his way. The ogre smashed a Sagan flat with his huge hammer. After letting out a blaring roar, the green giant drooled and licked his lips as he peered upon the men.

Magoonagoon

CHAPTER 9

A Trophy

Victor ran with the pursuit matching them step for step in quickness. Unwavering, the man continued to attack as he gauged his range and struck their flank. The Sagans retreated further away from the coast and the Foucinians stopped attacking to return to the water's edge. However, Victor continued fighting them until he was all alone. The Foucinians ran away like cowards after throwing their volley of spears. The heavy footsteps of the ogre ceased when his allies retired. Still, the man fought on among the giants without fear of death.

He had wounded many and laid a few of them down to

rest with his silver sword. But the Sagans were no longer on the run and the old man debated whether or not to flee. For the Sagan warriors had turned around and were now advancing on his position. The deadly throng moved to surround the man slashing their swords. In that instant, the tide turned when Brunto attacked. Just as he had snagged Aubrey so too did he disable Victor as he knocked free the sword from his grip. The blade fell from Victor's thick wrist to the sand where he could not reach it.

Victor fell back and scurried away from the killers and he blew the trumpet for help. He called for Julian at the top of his lungs with every ounce of strength in his chest. But no man came to his aid as the Sagans advanced upon him. He called out again for Percival, who was second best among them. Still, no one came as he dodged their jabs and throws. The man kept up his fists and dared them to get within his range. His hip was struck with an arrow as he taunted the host of feathered monsters.

Other Sagans moved in close to attack the man, like the mighty Kounjab who stood eighteen feet tall. Before others marched in, Brunto kicked the man in the ribs, sending him to flight. Victor flew off the cracked ground and rolled to a stop with a hard landing. The roll snapped off the tip of the arrow deep inside his body. Victor called out once more for help. He yelled at the top of his lungs for Silas to save him. As the killers closed in, Brunto spoke with a deep voice.

"Stop!" said Brunto and the Sagans obeyed their commander and waited for his orders.

"Ha! Fool! Did you think you could match us all? I have never seen such courage from one being! Do not kill this goat! We will keep him as a trophy!" said Brunto with an evil grin.

So they moved in close to take him, but their plans were canceled when other fine men raced onto the scene. Others—including Silas and Percival, who were dashing fighters, rushed in to protect their captain. Racing at the front came Godwin and Eugene in outfitted gear with shields on their arms. They moved in close to protect their comrade and they circled around him.

Victor stood to his feet and quickly gave out commands to steer clear from Brunto. They did so, restraining the Sagan out to their left. However, the force was too small to continue their assault against the huge detachment. As he retreated Victor tripped and fumbled about on the ground. He picked up a rock he found lying there, and the captain took it back away from his body. He cast the rock at the heads of the giants near him. The stone sailed straight and true and struck a tall killer in the cheek, smashing the beak. Now the time was exceedingly dangerous, and the moment right for retreat, for the bulk of the Sagan division closed in upon them.

Seeing this, Victor had to run straight at the charging enemy to retrieve his trumpet. He had dropped it during the skirmish when he had been hit by the arrow. When he picked it up, he blew the trumpet and signaled the retreat. Oliver arrived just in time to use his magic again to hold the Sagans at bay. The old sorcerer held off the assault from the rear as they retreated with quick steps.

The men ran back to the safety of the Foucinian force. When the Sagans were out of sight and range, the men rejoiced to be alive. The doctors tended to Victor as he congratulated each man and thanked each one with praising words of gratitude. As the men passed by the Foucinians, the beasts grumbled and glared at the group.

    Back at the ships, those who had stayed behind tried to put out the fires that burned, but the flames grew intense. The flames cooked the fine chariots that sat in the smooth hulls, for they had not been unloaded. When the group of captains reached the scene, they moved to their men and urged them to salvage what they could from the smoldering mess.

Magoonagoon
CHAPTER 10
Offer a Truce

The hairy Foucinians kept their distance from the men and stood atop the dunes like something out of an eerie dream. Victor moved to check on Amelia. The girl was found being tended to near the ships. She was wounded on the ankle and shook up from the jump she had to make from the burning ship. Victor sat down beside her and took hold of her hand. Amelia acknowledged her father with a strong hug, and the two rejoiced as the doctor attended to them both.

"I saw this man kill the first Sagan with my own eyes. Here is the leader of the army," said the prince pointing his finger at Victor.

Then, like a great quake, Victor stood to his feet upon fine sandals and held his fists tight. His chest stuck out like a proud champion, and he gathered up the warriors who had come to his rescue to approach the Foucinians. They grouped together on the center of the beach while the rest salvaged the spoils from the smooth ships. The prince stood among them with his hands on his hips. Then the commander moved to speak to them all.

"Sheath your weapons and approach these beasts with me. Do not fear this pack! Let me do the speaking and keep your tongues behind your teeth," said Prince Marion.

The captains put away their weapons and approached the Foucinians, leaving the safety of their force behind. The beasts began to fidget back and forth between their columns and lines. The men walked behind their leader with long strides. Prince Marion moved to the front where the Foucinians stood fast, snorting through their long snouts and grumbling at the approaching group. There the commander searched to find the officers and pacesetters of the Foucinian force. He looked for Premo but the beast was nowhere to be seen. Surveying, he spotted the biggest of them that carried a large spear in one hand and a smooth round shield in the other.

When their eyes met, the prince knew he had found the one. Upon seeing him, the beast threw down his weaponry and strode out to meet them. It was Booballet, the Foucinian champion and commander of the forces. Prince Marion told the procession to stop and hold their ground, and they obeyed him without question. Then he ordered Victor to walk with him toward the gargantuan beast.

The prince, his guards, and Victor walked in front of the band of men just out of the reach of their ears. There they strode like legends, and when they drew close, Booballet was the first to act. He swept his foot and kicked up some sand across Prince Marion's feet, which is customary of the Foucinians. In greeting, this was traditionally how the Foucinians would welcome a guest. From behind and in unison, the prince's guards drew their swords to attack. The prince felt offended by the gesture, but he quickly spoke to them before they proceeded.

"Stop! Put your swords away!" said Prince Marion. Fortunately the group was able to stop before they were in striking distance.

The shock of the men drawing their swords sent a stammer over the dunes where the Foucinians stood. At the prince's command, the soldiers stopped dead in their tracks and returned their swords to their sheaths. After Prince Marion looked down at the dust covering his feet, he walked ahead of his men right up to Booballet and stood before him without fear. The prince took his foot and raked it across the ground and kicked some sand back at the champion, inviting disaster.

A sulk came from one of the largest and was followed by murmurs that seemed to share his opinion. The host began to call out slogans of abhorrence and degradation from their black snouts. The horde commenced in kicking sand in the direction of the humans. Still others mocked like dogs barking at a stranger, leaping out away from the crowd and taunting the men. Seeing this, the prince moved to speak with words of compassion.

"So this is how you treat those who have come to your aid? Kicking sand on my feet?" asked the prince.

"No! This is how we greet a friend. But your actions defile the greeting. For my troops saw you kick the dirt in return. There is much grumbling behind me," said Booballet.

At that very moment, at that time of serious side effects, the mercenary strangely appeared out from the Foucinian lines. Shockingly, Julian burst to the forefront, wearing his dazzling armor. At his side hung the diamond blade, a sword hewn by the ancients from a single stone. Its color was of brilliant blue and the sheen was impeccable. The sword was a true trophy of fortitude.

There publicly before the commission, he campaigned to make things right. The man approached the duo and moved between them to settle the matter. There in the middle, he held out the palms of his mighty hands to invite negotiations. With the cavalier attitude, Booballet was first to address the situation.

"What advice would you offer, Julian?" questioned Booballet.

"Offer a truce! It would be a fitting tribute to our new allies!" proclaimed Julian.

Feeling the heat and tension at the forefront, Booballet had no other choice but to agree with the man. The beast scratched his chin and thought for a moment for the decision he would make could bring about backlash. Then he rallied to speak with the men.

"What we do now will be done under oath. For I will move to discredit the shame you brought upon me. Kicking the sand back at me was foolish!" said Booballet.

"Mind your tongue! This is no ordinary man! This is a prince, you fool!" said Julian, and Booballet grumbled at them all.

"I could not expect you to know our ways and traditions. Therefore I consider it annulled. For I have seen your courage. Let us make amends," said Booballet as he turned to one side and waved his hand in a way to ask them to follow. The prince started to follow the beast, but the monster corrected him quickly.

"Not you!" said Booballet, looking at Prince Marion.

Victor looked to the prince for direction before he proceeded. Prince Marion gave Victor a nod as if to tell him to go ahead. Julian continued forward, but Victor stood still in his tracks and waited for the prince to speak. The prince noticed that Victor would not go without orders from him so he commenced to speak.

"Go," said the prince sternly, and Victor did just that walking right past the Foucinian.

Then Victor walked further out toward the Foucinian legion. This made the other men feel uncomfortable and they grumbled from behind. Even the great sorcerer, Oliver, was hesitant to let Victor go on his own. Nevertheless, Julian was right there at the man's side and that made it permissible. He was a true chaperon. In war or delegation, Julian could hold his own with any adversary, whether they were friend or foe.

So Victor and Julian strode toward the Foucinian lines and Booballet moved to correct the prince's mistake. The Foucinians snarled at the men as they approached and they raised their swords against them, but Booballet held them back and quickly gave out commands for the Foucinians to set down in the ranks. Hearing the orders, the Foucinians sat down for they feared their leader. After each one had sat down, Booballet spoke to the crowd.

"Listen to me! If you value your life you will not speak until I am finished. That man over there knew not the custom. For he is not of this land. His views are different from ours," said Booballet.

Then Booballet moved to make things right again. He asked Victor to call his men in close, and Victor went and got the army. The man returned with the multitude, and they shuffled in close where all could hear. Booballet called for his spear and the Foucinians pitched it to him. The beast caught it in air then he held it up high over his head before the crowd. After they looked upon it, he took the wood down to his knee and snapped the spear in half. The wood splintered as it broke over the hulk's thigh. He held the two pieces up for everyone to see.

Then he handed Victor one of the pieces of the broken spear and Booballet kept the other for himself. Booballet strode down the lines holding the tip up for all to see. Victor did the same in front of his men, showing everyone the same gesture. Each man stood tall and poised for whatever was to come next. Booballet walked over to Victor's side and moved to speak.

"Now from this day forth let it be known that we are allies. Let our swords point in the same direction, against the same enemy. Let us look into the storm and prevail as one. I will carry this broken shard with me always as a reminder of this oath," said Booballet and Victor humbly presented the second shard to his prince.

"I will do the same!" said the prince and everyone saw the prince place the stick in between his linen garment and golden belt.

The silence was broken when Booballet commanded his troops to march off the beach. All the Foucinians stood to their feet and each one marched out in line and column. The men watched the beasts leave the site and the crowd began to murmur. Amelia looked up at Philip and questioned him.

"Where are they going? Why have they left us?" asked Amelia.

"Julian, what are they doing?" asked Philip.

Magoonagoon

CHAPTER 11
Exiled

The men watched the Foucinians leave them behind. They all stood still for they had not been given the command to march. Victor convened with the captains who sat there among the ranks. Each one informed him of the damage sustained to the ships. Learning of the terrible loss, Prince Marion hung his head and shook it sorrowfully. Then the prince put his hand to his chin and thought for a moment. He knew the decision that he was going to make would be difficult for the troops to endure.

"We will abandon the ships for a safe place," said Prince Marion.

"My prince, the ships are all we have! If we leave them we won't be able to return home! We will be exiled!" said one of the captains.

"Do as he says! Enter the surf! Scavenge everything that can be used! Gather up the equipment and weaponry and bring it up on the beach!" shouted Victor.

Hearing these orders, the men wet their feet and carried the equipment to the center of the beach. They brought out two chariots that escaped the flames. They saved thirty horses from the deep hulls and tied them to several hitching posts that they drove in the sand. Then they hauled in the weapons and chests that carried their fine armor. After they brought them ashore, Prince Marion again gave strict orders to arm and prepare to march. This time no man hesitated to arm and each one covered their chest with protection.

They left the burning ships behind as they marched inland to seek refuge near the Foucinians. Aubrey had regained his strength and caught up to his friends at the front. When his eyes met Julian's he rushed at his friend. They clenched wrists and met with watery tears. There the friends moved with freedom to speak.

"I am so glad you are still alive! I feared you would not last until I returned. I feared the worst. I thought I would never see you again," said Julian with glee.

"Julian! It is good to see you. It is good to see all of you again!" answered Aubrey.

"Aubrey! You must be a very rich man by now," said Victor.

"The labor and the scars of battle have earned me a

sovereign ransom. Crowns and roses are my trophies. I have more money than I could ever spend," said Aubrey.

"Thank you for your help back there, Julian," interrupted Prince Marion.

"My friend! You are their only hope. They must have an alliance with you. I did nothing but calm the beast down. Come. Let us go now to a place of safety, where your men can rest and regain their strength," said Julian.

Victor blew his trumpet and gave the command to march. As the congregation departed, Victor picked up Amelia and began to lead the host of his raiders inland. Aubrey and Julian served as point men of the force, guiding the way with experience. Their helmets sparkled in the sun. They marched the soldiers away from the shore and over the high mounds that blocked the way to the beach. They entered the grasslands, and Victor called for a chariot. When the chariot was collected, Victor sent the brothers, Silas and Percival, ahead of the force to scout out the terrain. The two men entered the chariot and sped away whipping the horses.

They rode across the grass and found the road cut by the Foucinians. There at the road, Percival took the reins and Silas gripped the javelins to protect them. They accelerated down the road far from the safety of the army. The horses began to stretch their legs and stride long over the journey. Percival spotted the Foucinians entering the forest ahead of them, and he slowed down the pair of swift horses.

While the two men waited for the rest to catch up, Silas stepped down out of the chariot and walked among the trees. He looked for any signs of danger or trouble. Seeing the pair, Victor waved his hand for them to proceed on in front of them. Given the signal, Silas climbed back in the chariot and gripped the rail. The horses leaped forth and carried the men down the trail.

Through the forest they traveled among the tall trees following the tracks of the Foucinians. Silas peered under the visor of his silver helmet with straining eyes as Percival steered the team. In a flash, the two rolled out of the wood and into the grasslands with great acceleration. The Foucinians headed left away from the cracked ground with quick steps. Percival held the reins tight and forced the horses to circle. Again, the scouts waited for the men on foot to catch up as the horses churned up dust.

While they waited, Percival challenged Silas to test his arm at a target. Percival pointed out a target in the distance that happened to be a hefty tree. Silas readied his hand by taking back the javelin behind his ear. Percival ushered the horses up to attack speed. When the carriage came around, Silas let loose of the pike and it leaped forth from his hand. The wooden spear flew straight and true as it drove into the tree.

"Ha! Ha! Percy! How do you like that?" asked Silas.

"A fine throw, my brother!" said Percival as he slowed down the horses.

In the woods, Victor called for the soldiers to quicken their steps and each man followed the direction. The men trekked after their commander who led the way and they struggled to keep up. When Victor exited the woods, he motioned for Silas and Percival to proceed. After Silas collected his spear he leaped back into the chariot and the two traveled on. They chased the fleeing Foucinians who scampered in the distance; they spotted the Foucinians crossing a viaduct that stretched over a mighty river. As these supposed allies poured over the stone bridge with its fine abutments, Silas spotted some Sagans in the distance. Quickly he pointed them out to Percival and spoke words of warning.

"Percival, look over there! The Sagans are advancing toward the bridge," said Silas.

"I see! We should warn the others!" said Percival.

The man tugged on the reins to turn the pair and they responded with loud whinnies. The wheels spun as the horses tracked back toward the army of men. Silas watched the rear as they sped away and looked on with wide eyes. They raced to warn Victor and the army of the danger with fleeting steps. When they reached the leaders, Percival spoke to them with urgent words.

"Victor! Up ahead on the trail! A different group of Sagans! At least a hundred troops! Thirty or more on horseback!" said Percival.

Victor thought for a moment to devise a plan. He commanded Julian to trade out with Silas and Percival, for the mercenary was an excellent charioteer. They did as they were bid and Victor leaped into the chariot himself. Then he pointed to Philip and gave him strict orders to protect his daughter.

"Get her out of the way! Get to a good hiding place and stay there," said Victor.

"Don't leave me! Father!" cried Amelia.

"Go!" said Victor harshly, and Philip took the girl by the hand. They took off into the woods. After Victor sighed and shook his head, he called for Godwin. In moments, one of the soldiers returned with Godwin and the dauntless fellow spoke to the crowd with self-confidence.

"What is the plan?" asked Godwin.

"Lead the men back into the trees! Hide in ambush! Wait for me to return!" said Victor.

The army followed Godwin back into the woods. In the forest they hid among the branches and foliage. There they concealed themselves to make preparations for war.

Magoonagoon

CHAPTER 12
Ambush

Victor looked at Julian and gave him a nod to proceed. The old man lashed the reins and the horses leaped forth. The two traveled out ahead toward the danger where the Sagans were advancing. It did not take long for the horses to carry the two men into close range, but Victor commanded Julian to keep a safe distance.

The Sagans moved on the bridge with speed and valor for at the helm was their emperor. He rode at the front on the back of two mighty horses joined with one saddle. It was Optus, the emperor that led the feathered Sagans here to this foreign shore to wage war. They converged on the Foucinians and broke their lines at the bridge. The Foucinians repelled the attack with their huge wooden spears, but many of them fell to their deaths over the sides of the massive bridge.

The Sagans continued to attack despite the deadly volley of javelins. Optus held the lines of Foucinians in check with his huge sword for they cowered away from him. One of his advisors, Oilaz, who matched him in size, strode beside him. The Foucinians began to retreat and each of them fell back toward the forest.

Victor and Julian watched from the hilltop as the battle traveled their way. The men waited to see if the Foucinians could reverse the toil. As the battle came near, Victor encouraged Julian to drive them back to the wood. The mercenary lashed the reins and propelled the horses. The chariot sped to the tree line where the men hid beneath the foliage. When the two reached the woods, Victor jumped down off the chariot and gave clear orders to every man.

"Men! Use the trees as your ally! Stay out of sight and wait for my signal! When you hear the trumpet, attack them with all you've got! Do not be overcome with fear! Stay hid among the brush while the Foucinians run through. Philip! Keep Amelia out of sight and away from the danger," said Victor.

After he finished, he ordered Eugene to hide the well-made chariot and cover it with branches, and the man did just that. His men untied the horses and forced them to lie down. Just as they finished, the Foucinians began to rush into the woods, running for their lives. The swift feet of the Foucinians carried them safely into the trees. The Sagans followed boasting shrieks and calls. The most dangerous division of the Sagan army came slamming into the tree line with the emperor at the helm.

The men kept low, out of sight and in ambush, until a host of the enemy had entered. Then Victor rose from the brush with his trumpet in hand and gave a mighty blast. Hearing the call to battle, every man came into sight with ready weapons and attacked. The shock took the Sagans by surprise and a multitude of them fell among the trees. Victor rushed to the right and tackled a huge feathered monster as he buried his sword deep in its ribs.

Aubrey moved to the center where he planted a javelin square in the back of a killer. Julian ran a Sagan through with his diamond blade as a giant approached him. The experience was devastating for the Sagans as the men attacked. Seeing the Sagans topple caused the Foucinians to regroup. They returned to the edge of the forest and joined the men. The hairy beasts clobbered the Sagans and together the allies surrounded them among the trees. The Sagans became encompassed from all angles and directions. Many of the Sagans turned back toward the men and buckled their lines. They charged straight toward Aubrey and Julian, who held down the center.

The enormous Sagans engulfed them and forced Aubrey to retreat. All alone, Julian had no other choice but to follow him out of the way. Many of the Sagans escaped out of the woods, including Oilaz, the emperor's advisor. Victor moved to seal the wound in the lines and he handpicked a team to follow him. He found Eugene and Godwin and ordered them to follow his lead. They raced on his heels and ran toward the gap where the line broke. However, before the group had time to seal the crease,

Oliver used his magic. The wind began to whip and the trees started to pop as the man held his arms out wide. In a moment's time, he raised his hands to the sky and gave out an order. The very trees bent and slumped from their towering heights, and all at once the mighty branches intertwined to form a great barrier. The wall of foliage blocked the Sagans' escape.

Aubrey and Julian joined him to trap the remaining Sagans inside. There at the forest edge, Victor blew the trumpet and signaled a charge. Both the men and Foucinians closed in and the Sagans began to fall. The huge emperor, Optus, was knocked from his horses and the Foucinians moved to kill him. They leaped upon his body with spears and held him down in the brush. The rest of the Sagans were slaughtered.

Booballet, the Foucinian champion, moved to subdue the emperor with his huge hands. The beast gave out strict orders to his soldiers not to kill him. As the beasts held the huge emperor down, the Foucinian defender moved to speak with words of revenge as he stood up on the Sagan's chest.

"Optus! Death is upon you. You have been conquered!" shouted Booballet.

Then he commanded the Foucinians to pull on the Sagan's strong limbs, and they pulled until his bones snapped loose. As Optus begged for his life, Booballet took the point of his knife and drove it down into each of the Sagan's eye sockets. The emperor's eyes were put out of his head, rendering him blind. The huge Sagan let out a wail of pain as the blood ran forth from his head.

Magoonagoon

CHAPTER 13
The Celebration

    The men watched the Foucinians drag their trophy out of the forest. Optus pleaded for the Foucinians to spare his life as he wailed out in pain. The Foucinians began to bellow and snort to each other. They danced and congratulated one another as they cut off the heads of their enemies. It was at this very point the men all began to wonder what sort of creature they had befriended.

    Victor ordered his men to file out of the wood and they marched hastily to the clearing. He gave commands for each of the men to sit down in the ranks and wait for him to return. After

Victor finished, he quickly moved to speak to Booballet with a sense of urgency. He found him celebrating with his captains and leaders near the center of the wood. So there the man tracked with long steps, right through the middle of those dangerous Foucinians. He was filled with courage as he approached the group.

Near the celebration, Victor was stopped by the second-in-command, Wolneas, who put his hand on Victor's breastplate and shoved him down. Victor was caught completely off guard. The man landed hard on his backside and toppled back flat on the ground. The shove was so hard and unexpected that Victor lost his breath. In chorus, the Foucinians burst into laughter.

"That is where you belong! Down in the mud beneath my feet!" shouted Wolneas.

"Look here at this one! He has been conquered!" said Vindeen as he laughed.

Victor became so angry that his eyes almost popped out. As he climbed back to his feet, he brushed the soil from his hands. The man gritted his teeth and glared at the Foucinian with a look of hate. Victor reached to his belt and pulled his sword to fight. Seeing this, Wolneas addressed the fellow a second time.

"Ho! Foucinians! Look! This fool wants to die!" mocked Wolneas and the congregation laughed Victor to scorn.

Victor's eyebrows plummeted down to his nose. The man stepped toward Wolneas to kill him, but before they fought, Booballet moved in between them with quick steps, to draw clear lines and set things straight.

"Get back! Put away your sword! Hear me out! The work you have done here will not go unrecognized. Without your help we could not enjoy this victory," said Booballet with wild eyes that lusted for carnage.

Victor lowered his sword and waited. His temper cooled when Booballet scorned Wolneas and sent him away. Then, Booballet pulled Victor aside and the two walked away from the crowd. The gargantuan beast put his arm around the man's shoulders and spoke with him privately.

"Pay no mind to these fools. They have no say here. I am the leader. Forget these words they have said," said Booballet.

"That one, that one there, he is dead. He is dead already," said Victor as he pointed at Wolneas.

"Listen to me. Forget what these have said and listen. Assemble your troops! Get them ready to march at once! You and your troops will seek refuge inside our walls! Behind the tall battlements! Within the safety of the Foucinian stronghold!" said Booballet.

Straightway, the trumpet blast moved the marching men as they jostled on toward the stronghold. Julian acted the part of the helmsman leading them across the land while searching the horizon for danger. The men had the sense that the enemy was all over them, all around them. They followed the Foucinians toward the stronghold. At the rear, the ogre marched sluggishly longing to snatch a weary man for a meal. The green slob lazily towed his huge hammer as he hobbled behind. He drooled at the thought of gobbling down one of the men for a tasty treat.

They journeyed over the viaduct where the Foucinians had battled the Sagans earlier that day. The short spans of the bridge supported the massive structure over the vast river, and the piers towered from the water at great height. The Foucinians had set a swift pace and all of the men struggled to keep up. Throughout the crossing, the nimble horses clamored and bellowed. The two chariots rolled proudly at the front of the mass; with each turn of the wheels they declared superiority.

In one of the carts rode Amelia, who had been wounded in the initial skirmish. The girl had regained her strength and stood with a firm grip on the rim. Philip drove the team of horses and escorted the damsel safely across the void. The small girl began to realize that she never should have traveled to this land.

The Foucinians led the men across the lowlands, past the skeletons that lay there: huge bones of the barbarians that lay tangled in dry dust. Prince Marion peered over the lowlands, his hand near his face to shield the sun as he surveyed the landscape. The prince never batted an eye or seemed to alter from the course.

Near the evening hour, they saw something in the distance that caught their eye. The newcomers looked upon it with wonder and astonishment. There on the horizon stood an immense structure of sound architecture. As they drew near, they began to pass the abandoned shelters which once served as homes to many—except now the houses were in chaos, wrecked and destroyed. The great statues that once stood at the entrance to the city had been toppled. The fine gardens where the beautiful fountains once sprang clean gushes of water had been smashed. As the columns and lines marched onto the streets, the group gazed around in wonder. Long ago the place must have truly been a city of beauty. Now toppled statues and idols covered the ground. Broken pieces of marble and rift lay in ruins.

When they reached the ancient walls of the stronghold,

they were spotted by the Foucinian watch atop the high battlements. Word of their arrival reached Premo, and he rushed to greet them at the magnificent gate. The mighty stone gate rumbled and cracked as strong Foucinian warriors took on the heavy burden of opening it. There Premo ushered the men through, offering them welcome and praise.

Inside the tall walls they found the world of old. The men discovered what had been protected. Grand palaces and fine homes that lay in ruins outside were unscathed within. Between the green gardens and fountains they stared at decadent mansions. The men caught the scent of flowers as they walked on the marble streets. Vast columns supported great roofs and magnificent monuments anchored the thoroughfare. It was like entering into paradise.

Upon seeing the men, the Foucinians grumbled and their heads shook. Wet creatures stepped up out of the warm healing pools to catch a glimpse of their new allies. Out of the tall palms the hairy beasts came on guard and watch. Around the waterway that flowed slowly through the plaza, and under the ancient walls, they stood, with an evil eye on the crowd.

A fight very well could have broken out over the visit and things would have turned ugly, if not for Booballet, who came to the rescue. The bold ruler strode to the center of the court and moved where he could see each and every eye. The place he found to speak happened to be in the center of the shallow waterway, and he sloshed through the meandering stream. The gargantuan beast spoke to them all.

"I have not only offered a truce to these men, but also refuge from the enemy. For we cannot have our entrusted allies outside our walls. Let them walk about freely. We have a truce. An oath which was sworn. A promise to keep," proclaimed Booballet.

"They do not belong here inside our walls! Let the rabble fend for themselves outside the gates!" shouted Wolneas.

"We should have never agreed to this!" shouted Vindeen.

"What you and your pack have said has brought shame and discredit to my command, Wolneas," shouted Premo.

"Is this the way you would have me treat an ally? Make room for these men in your homes and offer them food and drink. Without them our outlook is grim. If anything is to be done, it will be to bring more of these men here to Magoonagoon!" shouted Booballet.

"Get out of here Wolneas!" shouted Premo.

Wolneas shrugged out of sight and those who agreed with him fled also. Still, there were others who honored Premo and Booballet which bid the humans welcome. They took them into their homes and fed the hungry and gave water to those who were thirsty. Prince Marion and all his captains moved into the splendid house of Julian. There they found luxury and riches that appeared whimsical to the senses.

Gold lay carelessly strewn about on the ground, jewels were flung into the corners as though discarded trash. Silver cups and monetary coins had been pitched to the ground as if worthless junk. The vast valuables covered every space of the house as though it were a vault of a rich treasury. Marvelous seating and spacious chambers brought each man his own sense of comfort.

Julian invited them to his table where they had their fill

of food and drink. As the servants scurried to and fro carrying delicacies of delight, others scampered at Julian to take off his armor and help him wash for supper. The man did nothing for himself; the servants catered to his every wish. After each man had partaken of the food, he bid them to rest. Then Julian departed from the house and he traveled alone to meet with Premo.

Magoonagoon

CHAPTER 14
The Toast

The mercenary entered Premo's house and the servants directed him to make his way up the steps to the top of the roof. There he found Premo seated at the rooftop table. Upon seeing the man, Premo invited him in to sit down in the well-made furniture. There the two shared a drink of wine and joyfully spoke of the new allies.

"Are you sure these are the most daring men in your land?" asked Premo.

"Yes. These are the ones you want," said Julian.

"Good, Julian. Good. I just want to make sure that all of

them are here?" asked Premo.

Julian paused for a moment to give a definite answer. He knew that Jonathon had not come over with these men. The man knew there were great warriors back in the land of man. Still, Julian held his head high and looked at Premo dead in the eye to answer him with confidence.

"Yes. Every man with a backbone is here. You have them all and you even have the prince," said Julian.

"What about those fools that came with you before?" asked Premo.

"Adrian and Aubrey? Adrian is dead. Aubrey is so stupid I did not have to kill him. There was no reason for me to kill him. He is so oblivious. He has no idea why he is even here. Aubrey doesn't know anything about our plan and he never will," said Julian.

"I don't think you give him enough credit. He is still alive isn't he? And he has been here just as long as you have," said Premo.

"If you are that concerned I will go and slit his throat," said Julian.

"No. No. No. Don't worry about him. He is just a boy," said Premo.

"I have done what you have asked. Now I am going home. I shall leave at once," said Julian.

"Ha! What?" asked Premo as he spewed out the wine.

"I am going to go back at once. I have done what you wanted. Everything has gone according to your plan. The bravest and most daring men are here at your complete mercy. Their ships are destroyed. They have no way to return home. It worked out perfectly; Booballet arrived just in time to save them from annihilation. They have no provisions. No reinforcements. You have them just like I said you would," said Julian.

"Yes. Yes. You have kept your end of the bargain. Now you want me to honor mine. Why so soon? Don't you want to look at the faces of all these men you have betrayed?" asked Premo in surprise.

"These men have doomed themselves. It won't be long until you meet the same fate. Time is on the side of the Sagans. I have led these men to a quick death. Now, they are here. I brought them here as you wished," replied Julian.

"What would you like me to tell them before they die? Will I say the great mercenary betrayed them only to bring them to their deaths? Oh, Julian! You are a cruel man. Can you live with this burden?" asked Premo.

"I can live as a rich man! My ship may sink with all the treasure you have paid me! These men mean nothing to me. But if I were you, I would use them for a while. You heard Booballet…he said that if anything we need to bring more men to Magoonagoon. Use them! You can postpone your doom for a little while. If you kill them now, you won't have anyone to throw at the Sagans," said Julian.

"You're right! Well then, what will I tell them when they ask me what happened to the great mercenary? What shall I tell them when they ask where you have gone?" asked Premo.

"Tell them that I am going on a mission of great importance. Tell them that I am traveling back home where I can recruit other men to fight. These fools will believe anything. I do not care what you tell them. Tell them they will all hang!" said

Julian.

"You've gone mad!" said Premo.

"I am through here. Finished I tell you! I have done what you have asked," said Julian.

"What will you do when we come to your land and destroy everything in our path, taking slaves, burning down your houses, and destroying all?" asked Premo.

"I will take my chances," said Julian.

"Take your money and go then! Eat and drink up this money for blood!" mocked Premo.

"Do not mock me!" replied Julian with an angry glare.

"Come now, Julian! I was only joking. Drink up, my little friend. This is not the time to be so serious…you have done very well for yourself. You should rest for your journey. Let me trouble you no more. I will approach Booballet and tell him of your leave," said Premo.

"No. He does not need to know of this," stated Julian.

"Go as you wish then," said Premo.

"Very well! I shall assemble my men. I am leaving tonight," replied Julian.

"Tonight? Now I know you are mad. Many have already retired for the evening. Tonight? Must you go now?" asked Premo.

"Yes. The darkness shall cover our maneuvers," stated Julian.

"Go then. It is a journey that I cannot keep you from," said Premo.

"I shall never return to this land of death," said Julian.

"These fools are daring! So courageous! The rest of them

will be mud beneath our feet. You have done well, my friend. Let us drink to that!" replied Premo as he raised his cup.

Julian drank to the toast, and then he quickly departed. The man ran down the steps and moved to find the leaders of his squadron. He found them asleep in their fine homes and palaces. He woke each of them with the motivation of a traveler journeying back home. Silently they gathered up every coin, every last piece of treasure, all the jewels and all the precious stones, and stowed them away in sacks and bags. Like thieves in the night they swept the whole house clean while the others slept. The prince and his men were so tired that they never heard Julian and his soldiers as they scurried about.

They left the comforts of the stronghold to embark on a great journey over the ocean. To the seashore they went, where the sleek ships were moored high on the sand. Onto the ship they raced and boarded like true sailors. In a moments time they disappeared in the night, protected by the darkness.

Magoonagoon

CHAPTER 15

Come Closer

The next day Prince Marion and his captains awoke to an empty house. All the treasure was gone and the house was deserted. The men wondered where Julian and his soldiers had gone and they questioned one another about their whereabouts. Some of them went outside to see if they were in the streets. Those who were curious searched the entire morning and returned without finding a soul.

Victor told his men to enjoy the time of peace and to make themselves at home in the palace. The fellows wandered through the courtyards and meandered down the marble streets.

They were hypnotized by the tranquil sound of the fountains that splashed and sputtered cool water. The gardens had the beautiful scent of flowers that smelled of expensive perfume.

There were flowers everywhere. On nearly every corner stood a fig tree or some sort of fruit-bearing tree. The courtyard was filled with pecans, almonds, apples, and peaches. Near the city gates grew the creeping vines that held clusters of grapes. The giant magnolia trees were in bloom with beautiful white blossoms. Lavish bricks, cut stones, and painted tiles decorated the walls and trim. The walkway was accented with jewels that were dazzling to the eye.

Victor had gone to inquire about Julian. He had left Philip to chaperon Amelia, but the fellow laid down to rest and fell asleep. The girl decided to explore the stronghold on her own. She left Julian's estate room and exited the fine house to take to the streets. There she studied the tall buildings and marveled at the pristine homes. Amelia scaled the tall steps and climbed up to the top of the perimeter wall to take a look around.

The girl gazed over the land that stretched as far as the eye could see, then she walked down the steps beside the healing pools that bubbled hot gasses out. She followed the water duct that fed the spa, and it took her by the statues of the ancients. She slipped past many Foucinians on her journey, but they paid the youngster no mind.

When Amelia came to a great rosebush that must have had a thousand blooms, the damsel sat down to rest. Amelia studied the Foucinians that passed by and watched as if she beheld a parade. Then, the most magnificent place caught her eye. The maiden stood up and walked over to the huge wooden door that towered above her head. Amelia studied the size of the opening and wondered if a giant Foucinian had once lived there. Her curiosity made her investigate further, and the girl entered through the garden gate. In the garden, the youth stepped in a huge track that had been planted in the mud.

The girl's tiny body could have fit inside the print easily. Upon seeing the footprint, the little one instantly knew that she was at the home of the evil ogre. Amelia gasped in horror as her heart began to race. Her mind told her feet to run, but her limbs were petrified. The girl was so horrified by the shock that she could not move. Just as Amelia was going to flee, she heard a dreadful voice call to her.

"Come here, little one!" said the ogre and Amelia just stood there trembling.

"Never!" said Amelia as she made a horrible face and shook her head.

"Get in this house! I have a terrible itch in my ear, and I need your tiny arm to reach in and scratch it," said the ogre to the damsel.

The ogre pleaded with the girl and tried to make a deal with the maiden. The giant slob moved closer to the girl and grabbed a purse from off the table. He raked his large hand across the tabletop and dragged some coins to the edge, then carefully swept the coins down into the sack and let them jingle.

"Here is a bag! A bag full of gold! Please! If you will only scratch inside my ear! Here! Here is all the food you can eat!" pleaded the ogre but the girl never flinched.

"Look here! Look at these!" shouted the ogre.

Amelia shuffled far enough through the doorway to see

what the giant was holding. Inside his hand, he held a few teeth that had been pulled out by the root. Amelia looked at the teeth only for a moment and fixed her eyes back on the dangerous ogre.

"Come closer and look! These are dragon's teeth! They have magical power! Come here and take a look! I pulled them out of old Hob's mouth myself. Come here and I will show you!" said the ogre.

Although the girl was skeptical, she did creep a little further to see some magic. The ogre closed his fingers around the teeth and shook his fist as if they were dice. Then, the giant pitched them to the ground and they rolled over to the girl's feet. As the girl watched the teeth topple to rest, the ogre took in a deep breath and blew the door shut. The wind caused the door to slam behind Amelia and the ogre spoke once more.

"Come here, child, and I'll crush your bones!" growled the ogre as he tried to snatch the girl.

Amelia screamed out for help at the top of her lungs. She ran around the room dodging the giants reach. The ogre knocked over some of his furniture as he tried to catch her. He smashed a chair with his huge knee and cornered the girl in the kitchen.

"I have you now!" said the ogre.

"Help!" cried Amelia.

Just down the street the sound found its way to the ears of Oliver. The sorcerer leaped to his feet and raced toward the shout. He flew in the air over the houses searching for the voice. When he heard the cry a second time Oliver feared that he might be too late.

The wizard entered the garden and rushed to the aid of

the endangered. The ogre had both hands on the child. His mouth was open wide, his intention clear. When Oliver saw the girl in the grasp of the monster he called out with a voice that would have killed the fainthearted. The shout caused the ogre to drop the maiden from his clutches. Amelia scurried to the side of the sorcerer and clung to his cape.

"Curse you! You stole my breakfast! I'll get you for that! Be certain!" said the ogre.

Oliver thought for a moment to kill the slob. But knowing the damage it could bring to the newly formed alliance, the sorcerer only thought to ridicule him. He pulled Amelia back and put the girl behind him to give these words of warning.

"If you dare look upon a human again with the thought to kill, you will be sorry! Your life means nothing to me! Know this, if you cross me a second time, you will wish you were dead," said Oliver and then he and Amelia left the house.

Magoonagoon

CHAPTER 16
A Scheme

    The next day everything remained quiet. Late that evening it was so quiet that the men began to feel troubled. They patiently waited for Julian and his men to return. Even the servants had disappeared from the house; no one was around to even question Julian's whereabouts. Victor had returned from his meeting with Booballet without any knowledge of Julian's location. Booballet had no idea where the mercenary had gone.

    Later that night, in the ballroom of Julian's fine home, Victor was wide awake and troubled. He began to wonder if they were on the right side. The thought, though dreadful, gave him an idea and a sense of compulsion. He walked in the darkness to the room where his captains lay. As he crept into the room, he looked for the magician. Oliver was laid over a table with his head down. His arm was stretched out as if he were reaching into a dream. Victor calmly touched the hair on his head to wake the man. Then he softly spoke to him.

"Sorcerer. Come with me. I have a task for you," said Victor.

The magician quietly stood to his feet and picked up the narwhale tusk that lay at his side. It was a long spiral tusk that was taken from a great whale's upper jaw. Some said it held magic and others said it was just a trophy, still none dared to touch it in fear of its power. They walked along the corridors of the mansion and traveled to a place where they could talk privately. In the plush gardens the two stopped. As the great fountain gurgled out fresh water, they whispered to one another.

"Oliver. You must promise not to disappear or change your appearance with me until we have rightly spoken," said Victor as he looked at the man with deep concern.

"Fine! I will not disappear," said Oliver.

"I am serious. For what I am to tell you may quicken your heart and change your mind," said Victor.

"I will not flee, Victor," said Oliver.

Victor grabbed the man's arms to hold him with a powerful grip. He held him so tight that the strength of the embrace hurt the sorcerer, but Victor knew the grip was necessary to keep the magician from disappearing. With watery eyes Victor began to speak.

"You know that you are dear to me. All these years you

have been at my side. That is why this will be so difficult. That is why it must be done," said Victor.

"What, Victor? What?" asked Oliver.

"It will all be an act, of course. We must have an argument in front of the others. Not just a regular spat. We must part. You will see to it to dissolve our ties. Our bond must be broken to the point where the troops will turn on you. It must be a believable show. For if you still had any connection they would wonder why you wouldn't help them in the fighting," said Victor.

"Not help them? Stop fighting? Are you mad?" asked Oliver.

"The men would not understand if you were to just leave on your own," said Victor.

"Leave?" asked Oliver with a look of astonishment on his face.

"Yes, Oliver. They would spurn you if they knew you willingly left. That is why you must do something so rash that they will drive you out," said Victor.

"But why?" asked Oliver.

"I need you to use your magic for a secret mission. A mission so dangerous and menacing that a mere man could not manage. You will go to the Sagans. Without fear or hesitation. For your magic will sustain you against them. There you will become a spy and learn about the Sagans. I am wondering if we are on the right side," said Victor as he released Oliver from his grasp.

Oliver's hands began to tremble as he touched his face and rubbed his tense neck. He shook his head and wrung his hands nervously. The wizard almost disappeared in the night, for his backbone jittered so. He dropped his head and gazed at the floor as though he drifted off to another world to ponder the idea. Still, Oliver looked at the ground for only a moment more. When his eyes rose up from the floor the magician was prepared.

"Victor. What you have asked of me will be done. You must know! What you want me to do can never be reversed. The others will never forgive me. Let it be done soon or I will lose the courage," said Oliver.

"Wait until the morning. That will give you time to come up with a scheme. It will give you time to make the drama believable. For now let the others rest," said Victor.

Victor put his hand on the man's shoulder and motioned for him to follow. They walked back to the room where the men slept, and they found a place to recline. It was not long before Victor fell fast asleep in the comfortable place. There in the presence of the captains, Oliver pondered in the darkness. His eyelashes never batted in the night as he worked out a plan. When the idea came to him, a tear trickled down his face.

Magoonagoon

CHAPTER 17

Trickery

The morning came quickly to those that slept and the men woke to the sounds of the Foucinians. The bustle of the workers in the courtyards brought the captains to life and they moved to the fountains to wash their faces. Each man splashed the sleep from their eyes as they grumbled hellos to one another.

"Has anyone heard from Julian?" asked Silas.

"He and his troops have vanished," said Godwin.

"Victor? Where is Julian?" asked Eugene.

"Who knows? I have not seen him. Perhaps he has left," said Victor.

Oliver kept to himself while he fitted his limbs with armor. He put on his gleaming silver helmet which had wings soaring from the sides. As the sorcerer stood to his feet, he shuddered away, trying not to make eye contact with any of the troops. The man walked over to the fountain to get a drink with his eyes fluttering nervously.

He caught sight of Victor washing his face as he splashed the cool water and it dripped from his husky beard. With clear eyes the two looked upon each other and realized the day; the time had come and the plot would now unfold before them. Victor scratched his beard and thought for a moment, and then he gave out rude commands for his officers to ready the troops.

They filed out of the room and headed to round up the legion. Oliver pulled the whale tusk from his belt and stepped out to direct his troopers. When all the warriors were gathered in the street, Oliver mustered up the courage to pick the fight with Wolneas. Oliver then unveiled his trickery in front of the audience of spectators.

He deliberately smashed the point of his whale tusk down against the toe of the Foucinian as hard as he could press. With a stumble and a bump, he progressed to make it appear accidental. The giant Foucinian went mad and hurled obscenities at the wizard. Then, just as the man had planned, Wolneas struck him with the back of his hand. The sorcerer pitched over backward and landed on his face. As quick as he fell, the man returned to his feet and summoned up magic to battle.

Oliver slid the spiral whale tusk back into his belt and steadied his feet like a boxer in the ring. He held his arms out and spread out his fingers to cast out a spell. A thousand hornets flew from his palms in attack. The bees raced to the fur of the Foucinian and there they began to sting. Wolneas dropped to his knees and bellowed out in agony. The Foucinians moved to surround the wizard as he continued. However, Prince Marion called for Victor to correct his man.

"Victor! Put an end this foolishness at once!" commanded Prince Marion.

"Oliver!" shouted Victor.

Oliver paused only for a second and then proceeded to conjure up even more supernatural powers. He motioned his arms back slowly and shook his hands with a tremble causing the hornets to fall to the ground as if they were dead. There they lay still for a moment until his hands stopped shaking. The sorcerer stood motionless like a cobra ready to strike. Then, with a nod and a wave, the very ground began to shimmer and shake.

The base beneath the beast turned to quicksand, devouring the Foucinian. As he sank beneath the surface, Victor approached to discipline his man. With quick steps the burly man reached his side, and with a shove he crippled the magic spell. Wolneas stumbled and climbed to his feet. Upon being free, the beast fled to the safety of the Foucinians. When the skirmish was over, Oliver moved to speak to Victor.

"How dare you touch me, Victor!" shouted Oliver.

"You would have killed him! I swore to kill that dog myself!" whispered Victor.

"I could have saved you the trouble! He deserves to crawl beneath the ground like the worm he is!" shouted the magician as he drew the whale tusk from his belt.

Oliver then held the tusk up for all to see and pointed it at the cowering Foucinian. Wolneas hid behind some of his comrades like a weakling. A loud noise cracked their ears as the magician summoned his powers. A spark of light leaped from the tip of the tusk like a bolt of lightning. The jolt made its way to the body of Wolneas as he crouched behind his confidants. The Foucinians looked upon him in surprise. The beast appeared to be fine, until his friends around him began to notice the vile smell that came from his fur.

"Enough of this! Oliver! Go! Back to the house!" commanded Victor with a stern look.

"Victor. Do not cross me. You dare not command me. This is between me and that maggot. It would be better for you to fall on your own sword than to cross me," said Oliver.

"Go! Go to the house or I will have no other choice, but to place you under arrest!" shouted Victor and the shout startled the men.

"Very well, cross me then! It is your undoing!" shouted Oliver as he returned the whale tusk to his belt.

"Arrest him!" shouted Victor and the command shocked the men and made them murmur.

When no one moved, Victor drew his sword from his belt and stepped toward the man to chastise him. Only, the magician had one more trick to try. Now the magician moved to set his plan in motion, so he closed his eyes and reached out his hand with his fingers cupped as though he were holding a sword. This caused Victor to stop in his tracks with a jerk. Then, the illusionist assumed control of Victor's body, like a puppet master who gracefully controls his marionette.

Oliver forced Victor to turn the sword at himself and grip

the hilt with both hands. Victor strained to avoid the spell and his muscles began to jolt and jiggle. The sorcerer mirrored his movements and held him there. As Victor stood in a trance, all the others watched close in anticipation. Shouts came from the crowd of warning and desperation. Then, the magician moved to speak to both the men and Foucinians as he struggled to hold Victor in place.

"I warned him! I told him! That it would be better for him to fall on his own sword than to cross me!" shouted Oliver.

"Stop, sorcerer! Turn him loose! Or you will surely die!" shouted Aubrey.

Others moved to save Victor, but the powerful spell prevailed. Victor thrust the sword into his own belly. The sword ran deep and spilled forth the blood. When the sword found its final place, both men fell to the ground. Victor gurgled in blood as the men rushed to his aid. Others moved to kill the sorcerer, but the man could not be killed.

"Chain him!" shouted Aubrey.

"Send him down to old Hob!" shouted Wolneas.

"Yes, feed him to the dragon!" shouted the Foucinians.

"Get the surgeon!" shouted Prince Marion with urgency.

So they apprehended Oliver and moved to bind his limbs while his powers were drained. The Foucinians chained his arms and legs with the powerful irons. The beasts tried stabbing him with their swords, but the sorcerer's skin could not be penetrated. Unable to kill him, they arrested the wizard and showed no mercy as they beat him savagely.

Magoonagoon

CHAPTER 18
You Cannot Escape

Oliver had pulled off the illusion without any difficulty. It was so believable that it seemed real to everyone. In the chains, the Foucinians dragged the man to take him to prison, but with every step the enchanter regained his powers. When he had enough strength to transform, the magician changed. Oliver turned himself into a snake and slithered away from their grasp. The strong chains could not hold him and he slipped free.

The Foucinians hacked at him with their swords and knives hoping to split him in two. With a flash, he changed into a rabbit and whisked away from their jabs and slashes. After he had moved a good distance away, the magician transformed back into his old self. The Foucinians cursed at him as they chased on his heels. Oliver ran until he faced the others longing for revenge. There he heard the shouts of his old comrades.

"Oliver! You fool! Look what you have done!" shouted Aubrey as he pointed to Victor's bleeding body.

"Save him! Save him! We know you can!" exclaimed Godwin.

"He is going to die, Oliver! I cannot stop the bleeding!" shouted Warren.

Oliver paid no attention to them, for he knew the man would not die. The men could not see through the illusion as well as the magician could. So he ran further away from the sharp points of the Foucinians. Seeing the sorcerer, Aubrey attacked. The legionnaire ran after him wishing to wound him with his sword. They tracked down the street with shouts and Aubrey dared Oliver to turn and fight.

Soon they had reached the outer wall and the Foucinians shouted for the sentries to be ready. With fast steps he cleared a wide space between them, and when Oliver drew near to the wall he leaped into the air. He spread out his arms in flight, and the man transformed into an eagle to soar out of their reach. Over the wall he flew as they threw spears and derogatory words at him. As he left the stronghold, Aubrey shouted at the sorcerer.

"Old man! Do not dare to come back! If ever I see you again, you will surely die! I will find a way to kill you!" shouted Aubrey.

As Oliver touched down on the other side of the wall as his old self, the man wept in heartache. Still, from the tall battlements they launched spears and arrows hoping to wound him. The magician took to running once more away from their efforts to kill. When his energy redeemed to full strength, the man transformed into a swift stallion.

He galloped from the wall and distanced himself away from their reach. There the man thought the chase had ended and the deed done. As he ran, Oliver used the last bit of his powers to heal Victor. Warren, the physician, was amazed as the wound sealed up before his eyes. Many captains of the legion saw the miracle as well, but they never dreamed it was all Oliver's doing.

They continued to chase Oliver through the ruins and out of the territories, gaining on his every step. The sorcerer began to panic as the group closed in on him. Exerting so much power, Oliver was dangerously drained to the point where he was vulnerable to attack. So the man changed his image back to his own body and ran in sandals. The swift charioteers and horseman came at him with great speed. Nearly out of breath, the man rushed onward toward the South Gardens. He ran in the open with fleeting steps until he heard the cries of his old colleagues.

"Stop where you are, Oliver, and surrender to us!" shouted Silas from the chariot.

"You cannot escape! For we will hound you until the end of our lives if it so demands!" shouted Percival.

"Your powers are dwindling! Soon you will give in or die!" shouted the dauntless Godwin.

Hearing these threats the old sorcerer grew even more grief-stricken, for these men were his dearest friends. When they drew near, the magician had to transform once more to widen the ground between them. He turned into an elk and leaped away from their range. The transformation drained him of every last bit of supernatural strength. But the swift legs of the elk took him far away from the aggressors until the magician could go no more.

Oliver had reached the edge of Tiptoe Cliff and had no choice but to stop at its towering peak. The pursuers continued as the trickster converted back to human form. They lashed the horses and drove the teams ever faster to encompass the man. As the group closed in on the sorcerer, they moved to block his only escape. Tears filled the eyes of the old man as he watched his comrades move on him. The feeling of the betrayal was nearly enough to kill the sorcerer. In his last moments the legionnaire spoke to him.

"We warned you, old man! We will not endow you time for your powers to restore. You will surely die," said Aubrey unaware of Victor's miraculous healing.

The magician backed further away from the hunters until his foot slipped off the cliff's edge. The small pebbles that broke loose skipped and pitched to the mighty ocean below. Without his powers, looking down, the man felt frightened, an emotion he had not perceived since he was a small child. For three hundred years the man had lived without this mantle of mortality.

Fear gripped him as he gazed down at the waves that slammed into the stony rocks below. The legionnaire advanced upon him with fleeting steps yearning for revenge. Oliver held out his hands as if to beg for life as he cried aloud. Aubrey would have killed him as he drew back to strike, but the old man leaped off the cliff to escape. His old body dropped straight down and splashed in the sea as the others watched from above.

Magoonagoon

CHAPTER 19
Washed Up

Under the water the magician sank like a heavy stone to the bottom. Aubrey and the others watched in disbelief as the man sank beneath the waves. They half expected Oliver to transform into some sort of a winged creature at the last moment. Silas and Percival peered down on the waves in bewilderment. Seeing the old man hit the water caused them to shake their heads in wonder. They thought Oliver to be invincible. Godwin gritted his pearly teeth as he looked on in astonishment. The group lingered, befuddled, for a few moments before deciding to return to the safety to the stronghold.

Beneath the waves the sorcerer swam. He had survived the dangerous fall and moved away from sight under the dark ocean. With the first part of his mission accomplished, the clever sorcerer moved to complete his task. When he had swum a great distance the man surfaced as a dolphin to breathe a short breath of air. With his powers barely regenerated, the man moved to finish his venture. In the water he journeyed around the island of Magoonagoon to find the Sagans. As a dolphin he leaped around the coast.

Oliver dangerously pushed his powers further than he had ever before. In the shallows, Oliver was caught in the current as he pitched beneath the waves. He could not battle the riptide and the sea got the best of him. The wizard washed up on the shoreline in his original form, the form he was in when he received his powers. His body had returned to the figure of a scrawny child. The tiny body settled face down in the sand on the beach. Oliver lay there for a short time before he was discovered by one of the Sagans. Kounjab, the huge hulk, scurried over to the boy and picked him up by his ankle. The brave Sagan, as proud and jubilant as he was, spoke to his comrades.

"Look what I have found! A meal fit for a king!" shouted Kounjab as other Sagans approached with curiosity.

"Kounjab, you fool! Why would you want to eat human flesh when we still have goat, swine, and oxen to eat?" asked Brunto.

"Do you not tire with the same old food?" asked Kounjab.

"See if he is still alive. He may be rotten," replied Ruffio.

Kounjab tossed Oliver down to the coarse sand and he landed with a thud. The thump caused the water in his lungs to come forth, and the boy choked for breath. When his chest was filled with air, Oliver leaped to his feet with his small fists up and dared them to approach. This shocked the group of Sagans to see such courage in a little fellow. After they had a good laugh, the paramount Sagan spoke to Oliver.

"Ha! Ha! Little fellow! Which one of us would you like to battle first? Or will you take us on all at once?" mocked Brunto as the Sagans surrounded the lad.

The host moved closer to the sorcerer and made plans to eat him. Oliver wiggled his fingers and caused a disturbance in the ocean behind him. The Sagans would have taken the fellow, but the sorcerer's magic saved him again. The Sagans' eyes caught sight of a slender sea snake slipping ashore. The big Sagans sniffed and drooled with open mouths as the snake slithered past them. A frenzy ensued as the giants chased the viper to and fro. They dove at the serpent yearning to taste its flavor, hoping to snatch the prize, for snake was their favorite dish of all.

All the commotion may have saved the sorcerer. The brutes continued to chase the quick snake until Brunto snatched him by the tail. As he held the viper tight, he was struck several times on the wrist and forearm by the sharp fangs. However, the giant was unscathed by the poison and he quickly gobbled him down. Still other sea snakes came ashore and the Sagans feasted on the opportunity.

After each Sagan had partaken of the delicacy, they wondered if the boy could have been the reason for the good fortune. The biggest of them, Brunto, moved in close to the youngster and lowered his long neck down to see. The great Sagan looked him in the eye and smiled at him with glee. Then the vast Sagan spoke to the sorcerer like a friend.

"It is good fortune finding you. You brought us a great treasure. You must have been sent to us by the gods!" said Brunto as he sniffed the lad.

"He is sent from the gods! This is true!" shouted Ruffio.

"Yes! And I am the one who found him!" said Kounjab.

"You were going to eat him!" said Ruffio.

"Yes! That cannot have sat well with them, my friend," said Brunto.

"We will keep him then?" asked Kounjab.

"Yes! And you will protect him with your life, Kounjab. If you wish to offset this dishonor," said Brunto.

Late that evening when the tide was coming in, the winged helmet and the whale tusk both rolled up on the shore. Oliver had been watching closely to see if the tide would bring them in. When he saw the objects, the boy sprang to his feet and chased after the articles. When the wizard grabbed the whale tusk he felt relieved. The riptide tried to take the helmet back out to sea, but the fellow snagged it before the waves could pull it away.

Magoonagoon

CHAPTER 20
The Truth

The men who chased Oliver all the way to Tiptoe Cliff returned to the walls of the mighty stronghold. When they entered the mighty gate, they proceeded to the place where Victor was kept. There in the great palace, Victor had fully recovered from his wound. They approached his side with quick steps and heavy hearts for their captain. When they reached the place where he lay, Aubrey gripped his arm and moved to speak.

"It is done," said Aubrey with a racing heart.

"What is done?" asked Victor.

"He is dead. The sorcerer is dead," said Godwin.

"Dead?" asked Victor as he tried to lift his sore body.

"Yes. But not by our hand. He leapt to his own death

from the cliff," said Aubrey.

Victor collapsed back to the spot where he lay and began to moan. Then he rolled over away from the men holding his stomach. There in agony, the man tossed and turned, crying aloud. Audibly Victor sobbed for the loss of his friend, for he thought Oliver was dead. Then he sent everyone away but the legionnaire. At his side, Aubrey stayed and Victor told him the truth. He told him of the facts that were kept in secret, and when he heard these things he too grieved in anguish.

Nevertheless, Oliver lived. Among the Sagans he toiled. There embedded in their force he became a spy. The sorcerer lived with them and prepared to fight with them as if he were one of them; for if the men were to prevail they must know how to combat the foe. So the magician, Oliver, infiltrated the Sagan camps in sleuth. The great sorcerer had tricked them all once more.

Magoonagoon

CHAPTER 21
Brunto

The Foucinians kept their watch from the mighty walls of the stronghold. They summoned archers up in the towers and lofty battlements to keep the Sagans at bay. In those days, the multitude of Sagans was great and the peril imminent. However, the safety of the mighty walls around the Foucinian stronghold kept them free from attack.

Among the host of the magnificent Sagan legions, there rose up a new emperor. An emperor, who as legend had it, usurped the throne. After the great Optus was captured, Oilaz crowned himself emperor and no Sagan dared to question his authority or challenge the decision at that time. However, Oilaz did not have favor with all the clans, and many of the Sagans became angry with his rise to power.

Thus, the host wanted another to lead them, for the morale was weak. A forerunner who would turn the tide against the Foucinians needed to come forth. A pacesetter who would help them to regain the momentum, a trophy the Sagans once held and revered. Late one night, the commanders and chief warriors from each of the divisions met secretly.

The clans were represented by leaders and lords from three of the four tribes. The cruel and dastardly Black Feathers, as they were known, cast an evil shadow in the house. Their leader, Soociv, had the reputation for being a cold-blooded killer and a war-loving mercenary. Members of the clan still loyal to Optus came in numbers to join the coup. This group of Sagans became known as the Loyalists, true even to the end to their marshal. Those Sagans that considered the matter to be treasonous became known as the Royal Allegiance and remained ignorant of the secret meeting.

The Sagans gathered in a secluded place down by the sea where their talks could be held in private. There they would pick the one who would stand for them all, who would make a challenge and duel for the crown. Among them was the leader of the third tribe, the Brown Sagans from the land of S'Lont, the huge warrior called Brunto. The tall warrior listened to their discussions and held back his tongue. Brunto heeded as the elders spoke of the emperor's plan to retreat. When he heard these words, the Sagan wailed aloud in the night.

"Must we set here and wait for this fool to send us back

to Teron? Do we want to retreat for home in disgrace? This is an outrage! Who among you will support me to challenge the emperor?" asked Brunto. Not a sound was made until a strapping fighter stood to his feet in opposition.

"I for one will not see you die!" said the Sagan.

The multitude of warriors burst into laughter mocking the giant, and Brunto grew angry and impatient in their company. Outrage crept into the Sagan's chest and the pain of humiliation went to his head; for Brunto was the youngest of them and he lacked their patience and ability to be tolerant. Quickly he moved to speak interrupting their laughter.

"Let me test my strength against the coward and I will conquer the stronghold. There is no one here who could match up with me," said Brunto.

Hearing these words, the others shook their heads and scoffed. Among them sat a giant who was both powerful and knowledgeable. He was the most outspoken Sagan at the meeting, but he had ties with many of those loyal to the emperor. Protecting his honor, the giant Zannasor, moved to ridicule the youngster with words of pity.

"Ha! Ha! Brunto! Mighty warrior! Is your strength greater? You are so fat and clumsy! The robust fighter does not always prevail. I know you will greet a fast death…if you decide to rival with Oilaz," said Zannasor.

The congregation laughed once more, interrupting any reply from Brunto. Still others moved to speak for Zannasor, and they chose his side in the matter. They were all unaware that the comments had scarred Brunto's heart. From that point on he became enemies with many of them. Nevertheless, on his behalf, one of them spoke with words of wisdom.

"I say let Brunto make his stand. For he has the courage that most lack. He is capable of the test," said Zinder-faso.

"Ha! Do not be foolish! Your old feathers forfeit proper judgment," said Zannasor as he scorned the leader.

"Zannasor, if any Sagan should lead us into battle, let the most powerful of us call for the duel," said one of the Sagans.

"Tell us then, who will it be? Who will stand against the emperor?" asked Zinder-faso.

"Let it be the one that is most skilled in weaponry," said another.

"Yes, if my word has any say in the matter, let us call for Soociv. For none of the host can match him in combat. Not with the sword or the spear, nor can they match him with the javelin's point," said one of the Sagans.

The Sagans all squawked together in the old Sagan tongues. Then, they began to whisper in secret. This chattering only fueled Brunto's rage, and the words pricked him like thorns causing the giant to panic. Finally, Brunto defended his honor.

"Silence, you fools! I am a champion! Each of you know this! I will make the challenge! I do not need your support. I will find backing among the ranks of my own soldiers," said Brunto.

But the war lords and leaders ignored the youngster to continue their discussion. A cold look came upon the long face of the tall champion. Out of the house the brown feathered Sagan stormed with rage in his eyes. His armor of polished gold reflected the stars of the twilight sky. He mounted his fast black horse and headed down the coast for his iron-tipped spear and heavy golden shield. When he reached his long wooden ship, the nineteen-foot Sagan dismounted from his horse and spoke to his own soldiers who greeted him on arrival.

"I will call for the challenge!" said the powerful Brunto.

"They picked you, brother?" asked Ruffio with excitement.

"They decided you must hurl your spear?" questioned another Sagan.

"Is there any doubt? I knew you would be the choice. There is no other who can match the power and strength of my older brother," said Ruffio.

"Who among you will support me in the duel?" asked Brunto.

"I will carry you into battle," said the swift charioteer.

"I pledge my support and loyalty to Brunto! Everyone else would be wise to do the same!" said the hulk Kounjab.

"I will be beside you," said Ruffio.

"My bow will protect you, my friend," said the deadly archer and after much discussion, Brunto timidly addressed the group.

"Is there a Sagan here under my command that will have the courage to take the message before the emperor?" asked Brunto.

Brunto looked around the gathering waiting for a volunteer to step forward. However, the great host of them stood still without enough courage to respond until a shout came from the rear. Then Oliver pushed his way through the crowd. He walked beneath their huge legs and skipped over and across their sharp talons. When the youngster had reached a clearing, he addressed them all.

"Not a Sagan…but a man! I will bear the news," said the young lad Oliver, as most of the group began to laugh.

"Oliver, you have unrivaled bravery among us. But you are not one of us. You are just a boy," said Kounjab.

"Oh! Little fellow! You have the fortitude of a lion," joked Brunto as he looked down at the lad.

"Your courage is greater than most. You are indeed favored among our gods," said Ruffio.

"Yes, you're right, Ruffio! He shall be the one then. Take my word of challenge before them and speak with a clear voice. Let the coward know that he will soon find the cold hand of death upon his neck tonight!" shouted Brunto.

Though they thought him to be only armed with courage, Oliver hastily mounted a horse and headed inland for the emperor's home. Brunto gathered up his weaponry and put on his helmet, then draped the fine sash indicating his rank around his shoulders. The rest of the company mounted their horses and headed out to the valley. However, only thirty Sagans out of the sixty fighters under Brunto's command pledged their support. Many of them had made the choice not to join the band of adversaries.

Magoonagoon

CHAPTER 22
A Mirage

When the Brown Sagans reached the cracked earth of the dry lowlands, they saw a strange image in the distance. The patrol rode further into the desert void to see the blurred reflection. It appeared to be a mirage or something out of a dream, and the image drew the Sagans' curiosity. The group quickly armed and made ready to go to battle with whatever was in front of them by drawing their weapons. The escort approached cautiously to find the likeness of a Sagan crawling on the ground. The comrades rode in formation right up to the being, poised in attack and ready to battle. The squadron surrounded the crawling creature as it stretched out its arms for help.

"It is a Sagan!" said one of the soldiers.

"He must be a deserter," said Ruffio.

The Sagan was without his horse and was crawling on his hands and knees. He had been stripped of all his armor and was left naked. The fair feathers that once covered the tall Sagan's body had been plucked out. The skin of the Sagan was burned red from the heat of the day. He was close to death, in and out of consciousness, and confused. The Sagan had been battered beyond recognition. Brunto jumped down from his gold chariot to meet the pitiful Sagan. The great taskmaster then spoke.

"Pick yourself up from the ground," commanded Brunto as the woeful Sagan slowly rose to his feet.

"What tribe is he from?" asked Kounjab.

"He is a traitor, Brunto. Let's leave him here to die," said Ruffio.

"Yes, the Foucinians would have tortured and then killed him," said a Sagan.

"No! My comrades! Hear me! I was captured! The Foucinians let me go!" said the Sagan, causing the gang of riders to burst into laughter.

"Kill this traitor!" commanded Brunto and one of the Sagans quickly got down off his horse and moved to kill him.

"No! No! I beg you. Let me tell you the truth," said the battered Sagan as the soldier drew back his knife.

"Wait! Tell us the truth then! Tell us why you are here crawling like a worm on your belly! But choose your words carefully and do not lie to us again!" said Brunto.

"They let him go, Brunto! Look at him! He has been tortured by those dogs!" shouted Kounjab.

"They did! They let me go last night! I had been tortured for three days. They ripped my feathers out of my skin. I thought that I would die in their prison! I thought they were going to feed me to the dragon, but they took me out to the desert and left me for dead!" said the exhausted Sagan.

"Enough! You fool! There is no way they let you go!" said Brunto.

"It is a disgrace to get captured! You are a coward! You should have died with honor on the battlefield," said Ruffio.

"No! My horse was killed in the battle and the rest of my company fled. I was left behind in the woods. The next thing I knew I was surrounded," said the weak Sagan.

"You should have fought until death," said Ruffio as Brunto approached the weak and battered escapee with heavy steps.

"You lie!" shouted Brunto as he gave the Sagan a swift kick in the stomach.

"Do not touch me!" yelled the former captive.

"Why have you been spared? Are you favored among the gods?" asked Brunto in a loud voice as laughter broke out among the warriors behind him.

"Please! Give me a drink of water!" requested the featherless Sagan on his hands and knees.

"Tell us the reason or we will slit your throat," said Ruffio with his hand upon his sword.

"We do not bargain with cowards!" shouted Kounjab.

"Alright! Alright! I'll tell you! I have a message for the

emperor," said the Sagan.

Brunto wailed to the sky in anger. The tall commander walked over to the Sagan, and punched the former prisoner in the face, knocking him on his back.

"I knew he was lying! There is no escape from the stronghold!" said one of the soldiers.

"What is the news for the emperor?" asked Brunto.

"The Foucinians want all of this to end. They want to bargain! They want to put their best champion against ours!" said the pale-skinned creature, gasping for breath.

A distraught look came over the face of Brunto as he learned of this strange destiny. His heart sank and the news came at the Sagan like a charging bull. It was as if Brunto had stepped out of his own skin. For the moment called for change of action. The plague of cowardice crept into his heart, and seemed to change his mind. He thought to himself.

I will not only have to fight Oilaz. I will also have to battle Booballet the Foucinian champion. Who am I to fight two titans back to back? thought Brunto.

With this news it was going to be difficult for Brunto to follow through with his own challenge. Brunto knew that he should do something quickly and he would have to come up with a scheme to get out of this mess. From this very point Brunto decided to cower and shun the task of becoming the alpha ruler. After the wise Sagan thought through a plan he moved to speak and compile information from the traveler.

"What is your name?" asked Brunto.

"Iipkam," said the battered Sagan.

"I have heard of him, Brunto. He is an old veteran of

combat," said Kounjab.

"We will take this Sagan and hide him in our ship. He is not to deliver this message! Do you hear? Not a word of it!" shouted Brunto.

"My brother, what about your challenge?" asked Ruffio.

"Yes. The boy is on his way to see the emperor now. What will you do?" asked another.

"You cannot back down now!" said Ruffio.

"I will not back down!" shouted Brunto.

"Wait! Who has made the challenge? Ha! One of you will challenge the emperor? I know there is no Sagan here that can defeat Oilaz," mocked Iipkam provoking one of the Sagans to kick the loner in the side, wounding him in the ribs.

"Brunto, the most powerful among Sagans, has challenged him," said one of the soldiers causing Brunto to wail.

"Brunto? The son of Gonee? I saved the neck of Gonee many times. He was a weak fool. No son of his could ever be emperor," laughed Iipkam.

Brunto took his mighty spear high over his head and reached back to swing. He slapped the side of wooden spear right against the Sagan's throat. Iipkam groaned and fell on his face as he choked for breath. Then Brunto drove his long spear deep in the ground and marked his challenge.

"I will soon be emperor, and among you I will choose my council," said Brunto pointing to his warriors.

"Yes! At last!" shouted one of the Sagans.

"Here is where I will make my challenge," said Brunto pointing to the ground.

"Do not make the challenge. The emperor will find death

against Booballet the Foucinian champion. Then we will head for home, back to the shores of Teron," gasped Iipkam.

"Shut your mouth, coward! Or I will ram my knife into your chest," said Ruffio.

"If any Sagan is to fight Booballet, then let it be me!" shouted Brunto, thinking only of his plan.

"Ruffio and I will wait here for Oilaz. All of you leave us and take this Sagan back to my ship. Gag his mouth and do not let this message from those Foucinians leak out," said Brunto.

"We will stay here with you!" shouted one of the Sagans.

"No. All of you go. For there is a slight chance that I may lose. If that were to happen, you would all be killed as supporters. I am confident that I will be victorious. Still, if that fool was to get lucky, I would not want to see any of you dead for my sake. Stay there and guard the camp. For I will make quick work of this self-proclaimed fool!" said Brunto.

The Sagans wondered why Brunto insisted that they all to go to the ships. Still, they carried out the order without question because they knew the danger of the repercussions. One of the Sagans pulled on the reins of the gold chariot to turn the fast horses around. Then another proud fighter ran over and jumped onto the swift carriage. The Sagan raised his bow high over his head and gave out his battle cry. The Sagans rode back to the ships, churning up dust behind them.

Magoonagoon

CHAPTER 23

Ruffio

Away from the valley toward the mighty ocean the newfound emperor of the Sagans, Oilaz, met with his chief advisors. At dusk, in the twilight hour, under a small grove of palms the captains gathered in the shallows of the warm healing pools. When talks of strategy and tactics were just getting underway, the news of the challenge came.

As a small boy, the brave sorcerer rode his horse right up to the trees with no fear of the emperor's royal guards who lurked in the shadows. The emperor's guards raised their spears and stopped the magical messenger before he could reach the group. The guards grabbed the reins of his spirited horse and brought him to a stop.

"Dismount from that horse at once, boy!" commanded the guard.

"I have a message for the emperor!" yelled Oliver as he stepped off the horse. Hearing this, the emperor and his advisors stood from the pool to see what the commotion was all about. Oliver brought the announcement after he dodged a swipe of a sword.

"A challenge has been made!" said the young boy.

"What? From who?" questioned Cassereen.

"Yes! From Brunto! He is waiting for you out in the valley!" shouted the magician.

"Seize him!" commanded the emperor.

The soldiers ran at the boy with heavy steps to catch him. Oliver then cupped some sand from the ground, and as the soldiers tried to apprehend him, he tossed it into the air over his head and disappeared. To the Sagans' astonishment, the boy vanished before their eyes. The bewildered host quickly made preparations to arm and seek out the challenger. Oilaz growled and spit on the ground.

"Arm yourselves! Ride with me to the valley and watch me kill this laggard! Bring me my best spear and shield," commanded the emperor.

The emperor's servants quickly gathered up the battle armor, his iron-tipped spear, and battle-hardened shield. They strapped on the wide chest plate covered in battle scars. Then they placed the crocodile skull on his head that gleamed pearly white. Its jagged teeth gave the emperor's head a fearsome look.

Last but not least they draped the emperor's back and shoulders with the long red sash that signaled his title. The servants handed the tall emperor his weapons.

Oilaz then mounted his two best horses to ride out to meet the challenge. The two of them were joined by one huge saddle. His captains and elite guards surrounded him carrying their spears and the flags of the legion. High on their horses they rode to the lowlands.

Back out on the desert wastelands, Brunto had mounted his horse and began to get nervous while waiting for the emperor to arrive. He pulled on the reins of his horse and drove her in circles anxiously. After Brunto had made a pass around his brother, he spoke to him.

"My brother, I fear I have made a terrible mistake," said Brunto.

"No. Soon you will be emperor and I will be your advisor," said Ruffio.

"Let's flee while we still can!" said Brunto as Ruffio groaned and shook his head.

"Take courage, Brunto! You can defeat him! He is just another Sagan and he has not engaged in combat since we have arrived. He is bound to be rusty. No other Sagan can match your strength. There are few Sagans left with your might. Don't be gutless!" said Ruffio.

"We will hide in the desert. The emperor will soon forget about this misunderstanding," said Brunto.

"No! You will be called a coward! They will kill us both! Face the fool! Thrust your spear into his chest and claim the throne!" said Ruffio as Brunto pulled hard on the reins of the horse.

"Come on, let's get out of here before they see us," said Brunto.

"I will not run away! Go without me. I will fight the emperor for you!" said Ruffio.

"Do not be stupid. The emperor will not accept a challenge from you. Your rank is too low! The emperor's royal soldiers will kill you as soon as they arrive," said Brunto.

"Run and hide in the desert. I will stay and make the challenge," said Ruffio.

"Don't be ridiculous, Ruffio! You cannot defeat Oilaz. Get on your horse. Let's get out of here! They are coming. We must hurry!" said Brunto as he started to ride away.

"If you go, do not ever return! For no brother of mine would run away from a fight!" yelled Ruffio as Brunto kicked his horse in the sides and rode away.

"Come on, Ruffio!" yelled Brunto once more as he rode further.

Ruffio realized he was in big trouble. The way Ruffio saw it, he only had two choices. He could join his brother in flight or he could wait for the emperor to arrive. His only real chance to live would be to flee.

Forlorn and abandoned, Ruffio stood on the windy lowlands. In the distance he could hear the emperor and his soldiers approaching. As the sound of the hooves grew louder so did the beating of his heart. When they crept closer, the Sagan's knees began to shake, and a breath of wind or a falling branch might have made him flee into the night.

Magoonagoon
CHAPTER 24
Oilaz

    Ruffio stood there alone and worried that he would soon be dead. As Ruffio watched Oilaz and his soldiers approach, Oliver magically appeared at his side. Ruffio was so nervous that he did not even notice that the boy had arrived on the scene. As Ruffio's beak started to chatter, he heard the boy's voice speak to him.

    "Where is Brunto?" questioned Oliver causing Ruffio to scream out in horror.

    Ruffio took his spear and dangerously waved it in every direction that he anticipated an attack. When the Sagan calmed down enough to collect some thoughts, he realized who it was beside him. When Ruffio saw that it was Oliver, he let out a sigh of relief.

"You scared me to death!" said Ruffio.

"I did not mean to frighten you. I have been looking all over for you," said Oliver.

Oilaz and his soldiers rode right up to the challenger with their flags and spears held up high. The metal of their swords clashed against their armor as they fumbled about. The cool air slipped out of the horses' nostrils in puffs of smoke.

"Ruffio? Where is Brunto?" questioned Oilaz.

"I will make the challenge!" said Ruffio with his chest stuck out. Hearing this, the emperor's guards and soldiers began to laugh.

"Where is Brunto?" asked Cassereen.

"I killed him," lied Ruffio with a straight face.

"You killed him?" questioned Oilaz with his hands on his hips. Then the emperor's soldiers laughed again.

"Yes. I will make the challenge in his place!" said Ruffio.

"You cannot challenge me!" said the emperor as he laughed.

"Is it because you are afraid of me?" asked Ruffio foolishly.

Oilaz let out a loud wail that pierced each of their ears. Then the emperor dismounted his powerful horses. The pair of stallions let out a sigh of relief as the heavyweight stepped off. The emperor pushed the guards around him away in anger to express his dominance. Then the huge killer snapped his beak at them and groaned at them with warning calls. The bulky hulk moved to give out orders and commands to the others.

"Form the circle!" commanded Oilaz.

The soldiers got down off their horses and formed a vast circle around Ruffio. The twenty-foot-tall emperor walked out to the center where Brunto had jabbed his spear into the cracked earth. There the giant relieved himself as he urinated on the base of the spear. The soldiers burst into laughter at the sight of it, and this marking disgraced Ruffio. The challenger had been belittled and this proved he was inferior. Should Ruffio's supporters have been there things might have been a little different. Since he was alone there was nothing he could do. Then all at once the emperor's soldiers wailed and squawked as they prepared for the challenge.

Ruffio's legs trembled as Oilaz let out a loud shrieking wail. The emperor then raised his own iron-tipped spear high over his head and drove it hard into the ground right next to the other spear. The emperor could see the fear in Ruffio's eyes as he trembled. Then Oilaz began to speak.

"Brave Ruffio. Your brother left you here. A shame. I don't blame the coward. He was a wise Sagan. Smarter than you, I believe," said Oilaz and the emperor's soldiers began to scoff in the old language.

"My brother is dead. Killed by my hand," fibbed Ruffio.

"I can't believe the fainthearted Sagan ran away after making this boastful challenge. You, however, his dear brother, have stayed to make the test of strength," said the emperor, hissing at Ruffio and the boy.

Oilaz stepped real close to Ruffio. The emperor took his fingers and felt of Ruffio's sash. Ruffio tried to keep his distance from the emperor and crept back out of the way with wide eyes. The young Sagan's sash was decorated in green with gold stitching. The sash he earned early in the fighting, the rank given to him from Optus. But now Optus was no longer the emperor and the rank could be dissolved if Oilaz so chose. Still, Ruffio wore the colors with pride for himself, and he wore them to honor his squadron. The soldiers began to wail and groan as Ruffio embarked on a course to back away from the emperor in fear. Oliver disappeared as the Sagans began to snap their beaks at Ruffio. The Sagan encountered an enemy everywhere he turned. It looked as though the emperor was going to let his soldiers kill the challenger. When they reached out to grab Ruffio, the emperor spoke.

"Wait! Brave Ruffio. You cannot challenge me! Your rank is too low. I should let my guards tear you to pieces. However, for your courage I will permit you to challenge for a higher rank," said Oilaz, pointing to his guards.

The emperor moved to pick out a warrior that would enter the challenge, and Oilaz selected one of the best of them who happened to be the warrior called Zannasor. Zannasor was stunned with surprise. He pushed through the crowd to the center with an angry head and stepped out of the crowd with heavy feet. He raised his neck high into the air and let out his battle cry.

Zannasor began to beat his chest with his huge fists and let his presence to be known. Then the feathered serpent walked out to the center of the ring where Ruffio stood. Ruffio kept his distance in a poised position ready to strike.

"Let the challenge begin!" commanded Oilaz, lifting his left hand. Then the Sagans all cheered. After they had finished, the emperor's counselor moved to speak.

"Bring me each sash!" commanded Cassereen.

Magoonagoon
CHAPTER 25
The Floating Sword

The two challengers walked over to Cassereen and each handed over their finely tailored silks. After handing Cassereen his sash, Zannasor quickly slapped Ruffio with the back of his hand, knocking him to the ground. The emperor's royal soldiers started to laugh and seemed to enjoy the bully's gesture. While on the ground, the brave fighter picked up a round stone and slowly climbed back to his feet. But before Ruffio had a chance to retaliate, the emperor moved to speak.

"Enough!" said Oilaz.

"Take their armor and weaponry!" said Cassereen.

The emperor's soldiers quickly surrounded the two warriors and began to strip them of their possessions. The Sagans looted the two challengers, taking everything they had on their bodies. The group of Sagans began to punch and kick Ruffio as they stripped him of his armor and belongings. In the skirmish, Ruffio moaned from the pain and dropped the round stone that he had picked up before.

The soldiers gave the two Sagans some space and drew their sharp daggers and swords at the boundary. Then the soldiers began to squawk and cheer on the fighters in the ring as they waved their weapons about. The host of guards and soldiers began to reach into the circle and use their weapons to slash at the competitors. They stood firm and poised, ready to use their daggers to hack away at the two challengers if they got close to them.

Ruffio moved closer to the center, away from the angry Sagans. However, Zannasor failed to move away from the edge in time and was cut on the shoulder by one of the soldiers. Zannasor let out a loud moan and snapped his beak at the crowd as he lowered his long neck. He raised both his arms and gave his battle cry, then clenched his fists and began to beat his broad chest again.

On the emperor's signal, the two warriors scrambled to the center for the spears. The two spears had remained in the pool of urine that Oilaz had left marking the challenge. Zannasor arrived there initially and wisely took both weapons. The tall hulk held the spears over his head and boasted arrogantly to the crowd. Zannasor stuck out his tongue and gave the crowd a hiss.

Zannasor continued to raise the spears into the air,

boasting that he had already won the test. The tall hulk pulled one of the spears back past his beak to take aim at Ruffio. Ruffio moved as far away from Zannasor as he could without catching a knife in his back. Zannasor was known to be one of the best spear throwers among the Sagans. He steadied the spear and closed one eye zeroing in on his target. The strong mammoth hurled one of the spears into the air. The long wooden spear whisked by Ruffio's head and stuck into the throat of one of the emperor's warriors, rendering him dead.

The two challengers circled the small arena, being careful to watch their backs. One of the emperor's soldiers sliced the ankle of Ruffio when he backed up too far. Ruffio's heart began to beat hard in his chest as Zannasor held the other spear high over his head gesturing and pointing at Ruffio. Zannasor coaxed the other spear back over his shoulder and took aim once again. When the Sagan was ready, he heaved the spear into the air toward Ruffio. Disappointment came to the crowd when the tall Sagan missed his mark again.

"I fear that Zannasor will be dead at the end of this challenge!" shouted the emperor.

"Give me a sword! Who will give me a sword?" asked Zannasor.

"You cannot have my sword," said Oilaz with a grin as Zannasor appealed to Cassereen.

"Cassereen! Give me your sword!" said Zannasor.

Cassereen put his hand on the handle of his sword and started to take it out of the sheath. After careful consideration the advisor put the sword back at his side. Zannasor then began to panic anxiously, waiting for someone to give him a sword.

"Lend me your sword!" said Zannasor, looking at Sapsoon.

"Ha! Ha! Ha! You want my sword! I should stab you with it. You had two chances with the spear!" said Sapsoon, gritting his beak.

"Give me a sword…and I will not fail," said Zannasor. Then the arrogant pirate took out his sword and threw it on the ground in front of Zannasor.

Zannasor grabbed the sword and quickly turned to face Ruffio. Then he raised the sword and began to boast to the crowd. Ruffio began to ask for a sword, but looking at the crowd, he could not see anyone who would be willing to lend him a weapon. Ruffio's cowardly brother Brunto had sent all his supporters back to the ships, and there was no one there to help him.

"I do not have a sword. Lend me a sword!" said Ruffio, patiently waiting for one of the Sagans to offer their sword.

Just when the Sagan had given up all hope, the wizard, who brought the message to the emperor, came to the rescue. Oliver had been watching the fight from a safe distance. The sorcerer scurried between the host looking for something he could find, anything that could be used as a weapon. He used his wizardry to slip through them unnoticed and with ease.

Just in time, he found a sword and snatched it from the Sagan's belt. The fearless Oliver magically disappeared and it looked as though the sword floated in air. Oliver ran over to Ruffio and to the crowd it appeared that the floating sword flew over to the Sagan's hand. Ruffio and the other Sagans all gasped in fear as he gripped the handle.

Magoonagoon

CHAPTER 26

Race to the Ships

All the Sagans stood in bewilderment of the floating sword. They could not believe the sword had magically floated into Ruffio's hand. The only Sagan that did not remain in shock happened to be the brute Ruffio was fighting. Zannasor attacked Ruffio with two hands on the handle of his sword. Ruffio blocked the powerful hit, and the two opponents fought with great skill. They battled back and forth with their swords exchanging hard crashes. Still, the fighters took nicks and cuts from the emperor's soldiers as they fought around the circle. The test of might seemed to change hands several times.

However, Ruffio's stamina slowed, and the Sagan felt weak. The mighty strength of Zannasor almost prevailed. Zannasor lunged at the Sagan and the shock of the defense jarred Ruffio's very bones. There the contest might have ended, and Ruffio destroyed, if not for Oliver. The sorcerer snapped his fingers and a gust of wind rushed like never before. The wind whisked at their shoulders and changed the momentum.

The challenge ended in a surprise to everyone, as Ruffio's sword went bluntly through the stomach of Zannasor. Even the emperor was astonished to see the giant fall to the dusty ground. One of the Sagans quickly scrambled to pick up Sapsoon's sword, but the old pirate met the Sagan with his powerful fist. The warlord knocked the scavenger back ten feet, then took the sword from the land and returned it to his leather belt. So the emperor spoke with strong words.

"Give Zannasor's sash to Ruffio and take Ruffio's and place it on the boy. The rank goes to the Ruffio for his victory, and the young fellow will take the other for his courage," commanded Oilaz.

"You cannot give rank to a human!" shouted a voice from the crowd.

"It is done," said Oilaz with a stern look that could not be questioned.

"I also want Zannasor's horse," interrupted Ruffio, and the emperor turned his head in surprise.

"Do not get too greedy, Ruffio. You may have his saddle. I will keep the horse," said Oilaz as everyone listened. Then Oilaz held his hand up to make a decree.

"Race to the ships, and board them with our horses first

and load the hull down with all your weapons. Pack your armor and equipment tightly in the wooden belly. Do not leave anything of importance behind for the Foucinian dogs! When you see my ship start to tread out into the sea, leave the rest on the sand. Go aboard the ships! Raise our flags and dip the oars into the foamy sea. Tonight we will sail for Teron!" said Oilaz and all the soldiers cheered and squawked.

What? Sail for Teron? wondered Ruffio as Oilaz walked over to him accompanied by Cassereen and Sapsoon.

"Ruffio! Victor of the challenge! I have big plans for you and that fearless boy," said Oilaz with an evil grin.

What does he want with me? thought Ruffio.

"It is widely known that you are a skilled navigator, and I have a mission for you. I want you to accompany Sapsoon on his ship," said Oilaz.

"I have a ship of my own and I will be guiding it home," said Ruffio.

"Yes, that is exactly why I need you to oversee a very important task," said Oilaz.

"Very well. What do you need?" asked Ruffio.

"I need you to navigate Sapsoon's ship south through the rock barrier to the land of man," said Oilaz.

"Man? Never! Never! I will never go back! What would I want to go back there for?" asked Ruffio.

"Ruffio, permit me to tell you. We need them to aid us in the fighting. We will make them row our ships and carry our equipment. Of course we will train some of them to fight. Just look at that daring boy there! Furthermore, if we run out of food, we may eat them," said Oilaz with Sapsoon and Cassereen joining in the snickering.

"But I thought you said we are going home," said Ruffio.

"Well, some of us are going home. We need to resupply and bring back reinforcements. You will accompany Sapsoon and his squad as they travel to the land of man," said Oilaz.

"I am not going with him and those pirates," said Ruffio.

"Oh! It won't be for long," said Oilaz.

"What does he need me for?" asked Ruffio.

"You safely navigated your ship through the treacherous rocky shelf at the bottom of the ocean floor. I trust you remember where the passage is?" asked Oilaz as Ruffio nodded his head and frowned.

"What if I do not want to go?" questioned Ruffio.

"Oh! You will go. You do not have a choice. You will go or die," said Oilaz.

"Who will captain my ship and lead my soldiers?" asked Ruffio.

"Let the boy captain your vessel," said the emperor.

"They will not follow him. He is a human," said Ruffio.

"It does not matter. Get on your horse and ride to the coast with the rest of us. Tell no one about this mission. Just tell your soldiers you will be sailing with Sapsoon. Order them to load your ship and get things under way. Let the boy captain the vessel if you want, but you will be sailing with Sapsoon," said Oilaz.

Ruffio mounted his horse and did exactly as the emperor said. Along the way he tried to think of what to do with Iipkam, the featherless Sagan, and wondered if he should let the others know of the Foucinian challenge. The Sagans raced for the ocean where their fast ships waited in the harbor. When they reached the sandy beaches, the soldiers spread the word to those that had stayed behind. Ruffio went to speak to his squadron near their ship. The Sagan took off his helmet and entered into the tent.

"Load the ships. We are heading for home," said Ruffio.

"Are you giving out commands now, Ruffio?" questioned one of the soldiers.

"He is in charge now," said Oliver.

"How dare you speak, human!" shouted one of the Sagans with an angry expression.

"Have at you! This boy outranks you all!" shouted Ruffio to the host.

Then the group noticed the boy's sash that draped his frail stature. The host looked upon the boy with bewilderment. Their eyes could not believe that a human could don a banner of rank. They closed in on the magician and hissed in the old Sagan tongues. The clicks and clucks aroused chill bumps on the boy's arms. As the crowd drew near, the brave brother of Brunto spoke to them.

"For bravery!" shouted Ruffio as he pointed to the sash.

"How dare you! A human should stay in its place!" shouted a Sagan as he gestured with his arm and motioned to the ground.

"This boy saved my life! You will revere him as you acclaim me!" shouted Ruffio.

"Acclaim you? What happened to Brunto? Is he not still lord here?" questioned another.

"I took his place. He is dead," fibbed Ruffio.

"Are you serious? Brunto dead? Sailing home? Who

makes these foolish allegations?" asked a soldier.

"Do not question his command. Just load the ship and put the horses on first," said Oliver.

"See here, boy!" shouted a Sagan.

"Where is the Sagan called Iipkam?" interrupted Ruffio.

"He is tied up in the belly of the ship," said another.

"The boy will captain the ship home. Obey his every command," said Ruffio.

"Are you not going home?" asked Oliver.

"I am traveling on Sapsoon's ship," said Ruffio.

"He has gone mad! Sapsoon's ship?" asked one of the Sagans.

"Who cares? We are going home you fools! Load the ship!" said another inciting the rest to cheer.

Magoonagoon

CHAPTER 27

Iipkam

Ruffio put his helmet back on, entered the surf, and waded out to his ship. He then climbed up the rope net on the side of the boat, boarded the serpent of the surf, and walked along the long wooden deck. The Sagan opened the doors to the galley with haste and went down the stairs to find Iipkam.

Ruffio found the weary Sagan asleep on the floor. Iipkam still had his mouth gagged just like Brunto had ordered. Ruffio drew his knife and placed it to the neck of Iipkam. Startled by the cold blade, Iipkam awoke in horror. Then the brother of Brunto moved to weave his web of deception. He started by telling a lie to make his plan work.

"If you wish to live, listen, and listen well. Before the challenge, we were attacked by the Foucinians and my brother was left behind. He is still alive. If you wish to live, you must find him and help him survive. You must promise to find him," demanded Ruffio as he took away the muzzle.

"Please! Let me live! I agree to your demands!" said Iipkam.

"Very well! All of this must be done in confidence," said Ruffio as he took the knife away from Iipkam's throat.

"I will find him! It will not take long, you will see!" said Iipkam.

"Yes. Brunto is not far from here. He is in the desert, near the canyon," said Ruffio as he untied Iipkam's restraints.

Ruffio knew he could not tell the weary Sagan the truth. He would have to make up a tale, something the fool would believe. Brunto could live for a while on his own, but without help he would soon be caught by the beastly Foucinians. In order to save his brother, Ruffio continued to stretch the truth further.

"You will sneak ashore, being careful not to be seen. There is not much time," said Ruffio.

"Please, I am very weak. Give me a drink," said Iipkam.

"We leave for Teron in a few days and we are already packing up the ships. My command keeps me from helping you in the search. I cannot spare any of my soldiers to help you. I need all of my soldiers available to load the ship," said Ruffio.

"I will find him," said Iipkam.

"You must hurry. If you are not back in time, I will have to leave you both behind," said Ruffio, knowing that these were his very intentions.

Ruffio gathered up some food and water for Iipkam. He hunted for a cape or some sort of garment to cover the featherless Sagan. He found a dark cloak with a hood and placed it on the Sagan's shoulders. He gave Iipkam a map of charted land and a helmet for his head. Into the surf they jumped with a splash. Ruffio then took the Sagan ashore being careful to keep him out of sight.

"You can take my horse, but you must start your search right away," said Ruffio as Iipkam mounted the horse and rode away.

The rest of the Sagans loaded down the fast ships with the spoils of war. When the emperor's ship hoisted its huge anchor and began to tread out to sea, the wizard used his magic to sneak aboard Sapsoon's ship. There he could keep an eye on Ruffio and better serve his fellow men. The sorcerer moved to trump them with his magic in additional espionage. Oliver knew that if there were Sagans going to his homeland, he had better go with them.

The Sagan warriors turned to sailors as they tracked out to sea. Each of them grabbed hold of an oar and pulled the wooden frigates away from the island. Slowly the ships crawled out of the shallows and into the deep. When the fleet passed the hard current they raised the sail and tied down the rigging to bank off the wind. The Sagans had left Magoonagoon.

Magoonagoon

CHAPTER 28

Devastation

Across the foamy sea the Sagans sailed in their fast ships back to Teron. With every pull they moved further away from Magoonagoon. They dipped their oars into the black ocean, and when they reached the halfway point, Sapsoon's ship turned south. Most of the ships followed Oilaz on his way to Teron, but two came behind Ruffio, the steady navigator, toward the land of man. Just as the Foucinians before them, the small force traveled there to hunt down and capture new recruits to aid in the fighting. However, the Sagans were going to use a different approach to persuade the men.

The sea lions leaped and pitched in the waves in front of them as they traveled. Within days, the great ships had slipped through the narrow rock barrier to the island where the humans resided. They scooted through the shallows and slipped right up on the shore without being seen. There the strange nightmare unfolded, as a lot of shrieking and gawking in the old Sagan tongues was broadcasted.

"Gather as many prisoners as the ships will hold!" shouted Sapsoon as he rallied his pirates.

One hundred Sagan troops ran aground, carrying swords and spears, capturing as many humans as they could, turning them into slaves, and taking them into bondage. Some they killed on the spot for sport, others were beaten and left for dead. They swept the countryside marching on farm towns, searching for weaklings to do their labor. In their well-made uniforms trimmed with steel and mail for protection, they began the hunt.

Foot soldiers followed the chariot riders down the dirt roads, ravaging and destroying the people. With their armor clashing they marched relentlessly and callous, dispersing judgment to those in their path. Sapsoon and his pirates embellished the rear with the most elite soldiers on horseback.

The people in the villages scurried after their children and hid out in the fields. Some of the people in the small towns took up swords to defend themselves. Others were caught off guard, and those unable to fight were quickly killed or chained to the slave-hold. As they passed through, the fields were set ablaze. Many people were killed in the burning and devastation. All of those unfortunate enough to be caught were marched to the ocean.

Back at the ships, Oliver emerged from hiding. The long rest he got during the voyage allowed more of his powers to return to him and the sorcerer felt a burst of energy as he stretched his little legs on the ship's deck. Oliver leaped off the deck and flew through the air. In flight, the sorcerer quickly moved to find Jonathon and tell him everything.

Magoonagoon

CHAPTER 29
Emery and Felix

Out in the fields working, Emery, one of Jonathon's sons, spotted some smoke in the distance. The boy jumped up on the plow to mount the high back of his horse. Seeing the fires, he quickly untied the stallion from the plow and rode to tell his mother. On the way to his house, he spotted his younger brother, Felix, who was chopping timber.

"Brother quick, let's go! We must ride and tell mother! The field is ablaze!" said Emery, reaching out his hand.

Felix grabbed his brother's hand and they rode as fast as they could toward their home. The horse strode long and swift, taking them down the dirt path. Ahead on the path the boys spotted a tree down across the road from a great storm.

"Don't try it! She will never make it!" said Felix. The adventurous Emery did not slow down the horse. Instead he nudged the horse in the side, encouraging more speed.

"Slow down, we are too heavy! We will never clear the tree!" said Felix once again, but it was too late.

The horse jumped as high as it could with Emery and Felix on its back. The front legs of the horse cleared the tree with ease, but the back legs were clipped by a branch. When the back legs hit, it sent the two boys tumbling into the air, and they both landed hard on the ground. The fall did not hurt Emery, but it hurt Felix's arm. The boys were both shaken and the horse was lame.

"Are you all right?" questioned Emery as he gazed back at his brother and witnessed the tears trickling down.

"No, my arm is injured," said Felix, knowing they were still miles from home and a long way from help.

"Oh! What do we do?" questioned Emery.

"Go ahead and tell mother. I'll stay here," said Felix with tears in his eyes.

"I am so sorry, brother. I'll be right back to get you," said Emery.

Emery ran down the path as fast as he could and dashed for a shortcut through the woods. He could see his home in the distance. As he drew near, the boy saw his brother's horse behind the fence. It happened to be the fastest horse his father owned. The young boy called for it.

"Come!" shouted Emery, and the pony came to the gate.

The horse came running and dancing to him.

"Go and get Felix. He is just down the road. Go on!" said Emery.

The horse obeyed the boy and ran down the path. Determined to get help, Emery continued to run home as fast as he could. His swift feet carried him though the fields and across the land in haste.

Magoonagoon

CHAPTER 30
Stature

When Oliver's feet touched down on the shore of his homeland, he wept. The wizard buried his knees in the sand and rejoiced. After praise and thankfulness was expressed, Oliver headed inland to find Jonathon. In the distance in front of him, Oliver could hear the rolling wheels of a chariot approaching. He hid in ambush down in a shallow ditch as the chariot came near. When the cart passed by, the sorcerer arose from the ditch with the whale tusk drawn. Oliver gave out orders for magic to leap from the tip of the tusk.

A burst of energy thundered from the tusk. The powerful

burst blew a mighty wind gust. The Sagan that held the reins flew off the back of the chariot and tumbled down the road. His body skipped on the ground and rolled with speed. The poor Sagan was soon swept out of sight; his body bounced and whirled away in the wind.

Oliver quickly caught the reins of the team of horses and steadied himself inside the chariot. With a flick of the wrist, the wheels continued to turn. The sorcerer coaxed the horses up to speed as he traveled down the road. When they began to stretch out their legs, Oliver spotted some Sagans ravaging a group of people up ahead of him on the trail. The wizard pulled the whip from the rim of the chariot and encouraged the horses to accelerate.

When he reached the crowd, he pulled a javelin from the rack on the cart and spoke a magic spell. The tip of the pin ignighted and burned and the magician threw it into the Sagan closest to him. The creature's body was engulfed with flames and in seconds the charbroiled Sagan fell over dead. Other giants moved toward the chariot in attack. He pulled the straps of the rig and forced the horses to stop. Oliver leapt out of the chariot and advanced in the direction of the foe without fear. As the band of Sagans ran toward him, Oliver summoned up more magic. He waved his hands and moved his fingers back and forth. All of the sudden his body began to grow.

Oliver's stature shot up to the sky and the wizard towered above the enemy. As an enormous giant, he looked down on the frightened Sagans and smiled. The sorcerer waited only for a moment, and then the hulk began to defeat them. With his right hand, he smashed one of them down into the ground with his huge fist. With his left hand, he squashed another in his powerful grip. As the squadron began to retreat, the wizard smashed a couple more of Sagans with his foot. Oliver looked like a boy who was playing too rough with his toys.

When they had all fled, the sorcerer returned to the size of a young boy. The people thanked him for saving them and cheered for the victory. They did not understand how he was able to transform into a giant and defeat the Sagans, but they were glad to be alive. When the emotions settled, the sorcerer moved to speak with the group.

"All of you! Come with me! We are still in danger!" shouted Oliver as he leapt into the chariot.

"Where will we go?" asked a voice from the crowd.

"We will go to the castle! It's the only place where we can be safe," said Oliver.

"Julian has taken over the castle. His guards will not permit us to enter," said a woman's voice.

Oliver twisted his lips into a snarl and turned his head to answer the plea. When he discovered who it was, the fellow jumped down out of the chariot and fell to his knees. There the sorcerer stayed with his head bowed until the voice spoke to him again.

"We are desperate. Everywhere we turn there is danger. Please help us," asked the woman.

"Your majesty! I will surely help you. You needn't worry about that. I am so glad to see you alive and well," said Oliver as the crowd sighed in wonder.

"Rise to your feet young man. None of these people know who I am. How is it that you know me?" asked Princess

Penelope.

"Your excellency! It is I! Oliver," said the sorcerer.

"How is it that you are so young?" asked the princess.

"I was submerged beneath the waves in Magoonagoon and drown. Somehow I came back to life. How I do not know. When I awoke this is how I looked," said the sorcerer.

"Please. What do you suggest we do?" asked the princess.

The boy stood to his feet and quickly returned the whale tusk and winged helmet to their place. When he had placed the helmet back on his head and tucked the tusk down in his belt, he began to walk away from the crowd. As he climbed back into the chariot, he called to the princess.

"Come on let's go," said Oliver inviting the princess to ride with him in the cart.

Magoonagoon

CHAPTER 31

Hurry, Brother

On the other side of the island, Emery had reached the walls of his home with swift legs. He had ran as fast as he could to get there and was breathing hard. The boy dashed beside the wall and around the entrance where he slowed down to turn the corner. There the little fellow stopped in his tracks. At the entrance to the city gate stood a marching party of Sagans. The gathering of creatures cast an evil shadow on the wall.

Emery could hear the screams of the people inside. Short of breath, the lad peeked around the corner of the wall to see the danger. As soon as he did this, the young boy was sighted by his mother, who was watching for her sons to return. She had hoped to warn them. His mother's eyes grew wide and she tried to get him to run. Unintentionally, she gave away his position.

"Get him!" said the soldier, pointing for two Sagans on horseback to ride.

"Run! Emery! Run!" shouted his mother.

In an instant, she was stabbed by the Sagan soldier and knocked to the dusty ground. Emery had witnessed his mother's murder and stood there in emotional pain. He was so grief-stricken that he was not sure what to do. However, as the danger progressed, the boy let instinct drive him. Emery bolted out of sight and moved as fast as his legs allowed him toward the fields to hide. The soldiers on horseback gained on him directly. The boy entered into the tall cornfield and advanced back in the direction of the fallen tree. He reasoned that if he could get the soldiers to try and jump the fallen tree, they would never make it. Emery ran for the trap, but he had been running for such a long time at a very fast pace. He knew he could not continue on much longer and he knew that they would soon catch him.

Emery hit the road as if he were a chariot team on the last lap of a race. The skinny boy could see the tree and he could see his brother getting on the very horse he had sent to retrieve him. Emery's heart was filled with joy when he saw his brother on their fastest horse. Behind them the soldiers came beating their mounts. They saw the boy dive under the fallen tree and neither of the Sagans slowed down. As they pressed on, Emery called for his brother who had started to ride away.

"Felix! Felix! Let me ride!" said Emery.

Felix heard him shout and came riding back to greet his

brother. The Sagans were getting close to the tree. It seemed as though they were going to take the bait and fall into the boy's trap. With weary steps the lad reached out to his brother in desperation.

"Hurry, brother! Hurry!" cried Emery.

Felix rode the swift horse as fast as he could to get his brother. As the two Sagan soldiers jumped the tree, the legs of both horses were clipped. Emery's plan had worked just as he had expected. Now, all he had to do was get on his brother's horse and ride to freedom. The lad tried to climb onto the tall horse, but his first try was unsuccessful. His exhausted legs had given out.

"Hurry, brother!" cried Felix.

"I can't get on!" shouted Emery.

The two Sagans were not hurt, just shaken up a little. They both came running after Emery yearning to snatch the lad. Felix had to hold the pony beside Emery, for she was fidgety around the predators. Then the young lad tried once more to jump up on the back of the animal, but he could not reach. Emery's skinny legs could not hold him any longer. The boy was out of energy and time. He needed a boost for the soldiers were almost upon them.

"Give me your other hand!" cried Emery.

"I can't! It's hurt!" shouted Felix.

Felix reached out with the injured arm to try and pull Emery up. Emery took hold of his brother's hand in desperation. Felix pulled with all his strength and screamed from the intense pain. No matter how hard Felix tried he could not pull Emery up because of his injured arm. Tears filled their young eyes, for they knew that at very moment they would be separating. Emery gave his brother one last look with a tear streaming down his face. It was clear from Felix's expression that he knew what Emery was thinking.

"No! Brother. Come to the other side and try! You can make it!" said Felix but it was too late.

"Do not look back, brother!" said Emery as he looked over his shoulder to see the Sagans. Seeing that they were too close, he gave the horse a smack on the rear, allowing Felix to escape. Emery thought of what was best for his brother and not himself.

"We have you now!" said one of the Sagans as he grabbed the lad. Then the two Sagans began to beat the young boy with their huge fists. After they finished, they dragged him back down the road to the village.

Magoonagoon

CHAPTER 32

The Mercenary

In the meantime, Oliver and the refugees traveled over the land with fleeting steps and drew near to the castle. The group was greeted by the watch as they walked up close to the towering castle walls. Outside the tall city wall, Oliver stopped his chariot and pressed a spear into the ground. There he tied the horses and proceeded on foot, leaving the safety of the chariot.

"Go away! Get away from here! You will not be permitted to enter!" shouted one of the guards.

"We mean no harm! Open the gate!" shouted Oliver.

"Move back away from the walls or I will be forced to

summon the archers!" said the watchman and Oliver walked back and encouraged the people to move as the guard had directed. When they had all moved a safe distance away, Oliver spoke to the group.

"Wait for me here. I'll go inside and see what is going on," said Oliver.

Then the fellow turned himself into a pigeon and flew up over the castle. From the sky the sorcerer studied the positions of the guards and thought of a plan. As he soared through the air an idea came to him. With a clever plan in mind, Oliver swooped down to the courtyard and landed in the shadow of the wall unnoticed. Oliver changed his image back to his own and waited there in the shadows for his powers to fully rejuvenate. As he hid, the fellow took a look around to see what sort of challenges he might have to face.

When he felt enough power return to him, the sorcerer made a bold move. Oliver changed his appearance to the spitting image of Prince Marion and stepped into the courtyard. He walked with the same confidence as the prince and moved quickly to address the guards.

"You there! Why are you not at your post?" asked Oliver disguised as the prince.

"Oh! Your excellency! Forgive me!" said the guard as he fell to his knees.

"Where is Julian? I must see him at once!" shouted Oliver just like he was the prince.

"Your majesty. He is upstairs in the palace," answered the guard.

"Get back to your duties!" demanded Oliver pointing his

finger.

The guards quickly moved out of sight and Oliver walked on past the sentries that blocked the doorway. They each bowed down low as the fellow passed thinking he was really the prince. Oliver waltzed into the room just like the prince and scurried into a hiding place. In the hiding place, Oliver transformed back into his own image to let his powers refresh. When they had fully restored the sorcerer pressed on.

Oliver traveled up to the top of a grand staircase, and then he walked down an immaculate hallway to find Julian. When he peeped into a giant room filled with art and pleasure, Oliver found the mercenary. Oliver took a deep breath and transformed his image back into the prince once more. He walked into the vast room and felt strange spirits in his presence. The feeling gave him the sense to be apprehensive of his fellow man. He noticed something lying on the floor that sent chills to the very bones. There in the middle of the great room lay a large black feather. This was no ordinary feather but one of great length and width—one that could only be found on a war-loving Sagan.

Seeing the piece of evidence, the wizard clutched the hilt of the whale tusk to be primed. Even the whale tusk was disguised to look like the prince's sword. The sorcerer squinted his eyes and proceeded on without fear of the danger. Notwithstanding, Oliver had already walked into a trap. He had no idea that Julian had been secretly paid off by the Sagans! Julian stood to his feet in shock and horror when he saw what he thought was Prince Marion. With a shaking lip the mercenary spoke.

"My prince! What brings you here?" said the mercenary.

"Traitor! I am here to kill you," said Oliver confidently, and the crowded room gasped.

"Oh no your majesty! Let me explain!" pleaded Julian as Oliver swiped at him with the sword.

"You betrayed us! You left us to die in Magoonagoon! Now you sit here in my castle while the Sagans are killing our people," said Oliver as though he were the prince.

"Look, Marion. I am no traitor! This castle is the only safe refuge in the land!" said Julian.

"I don't know why you wish to die, but the words you are speaking lead me to believe you want to commit suicide," said Oliver as he took another swipe at the mercenary.

Julian began to panic and became angry from the reproach. He moved behind a large table to distance himself from the attacker and anticipated his next move. As he shuffled around the table to avoid the prince, he realized that the prince was outnumbered. After all, the men standing in the room were his own. At the realization Julian began to laugh and spoke once more.

"We have you surrounded! You have no one to protect you. Throw him out the window!" said Julian.

The soldiers in the room all drew their weapons and closed in on the fellow. Oliver took three quick steps and sprang up into the window. Oliver turned to face the collaborators in the windowsill and changed back into his own image. He stood there as a small boy with the whale tusk pointed at them. They men had paused for a moment to try and understand the change and the pause gave Oliver time to speak.

"Julian! It is I! Oliver!" said the small boy as he curtsied.

"Oliver?" questioned Julian.

"Yes. It is I," said Oliver.

"What are you doing here? Why have you come?" asked Julian.

"I had to see it for myself! I did not want to believe it, but now I know," said the sorcerer.

"I don't know what you mean. What have I done?" asked Julian pretending not to know.

"You have betrayed us all! You left us behind. You left us alone to die! Oh! Wait until I tell them, I found you hiding here in the prince's castle," said Oliver.

"No! No! That's not it at all! Let me explain," said Julian as he bid the wizard to come down from the windowsill.

"It's too late! I will return to Magoonagoon and warn the prince and the others!" shouted Oliver.

"No! No! My friend! If Victor and the others are waiting for me I will return and support them. Please. Honor me with a pardon so I may prove to you my word. I will dispatch my troops immediately," pleaded Julian.

"Traitor! You will hang!" shouted Oliver.

"Seize him!" commanded Julian.

As the soldiers attacked, Oliver leapt from the window and dropped from the great height. In midair the sorcerer transformed into a hawk and landed outside the walls. The wizard moved with a sense of urgency and importance as he tracked away from the castle walls.

"After him! He is not to leave this land," said Julian to a group of his soldiers.

Out from another room the nineteen-foot-tall Sagan,

Soociv, walked out to battle. He wore his battle armor and carried his bright shield and sword. His brilliant-colored sash, the grand treasure, endowed his shoulders and stood for him as a symbol of fortitude. There on his beak were the large scars from the campaigns. The scars across the Sagan's face and beak looked so fearsome that it would take a commoner's breath away. The black feathered Sagan walked over to address the mercenary, but before he could speak, the Sagan was interrupted.

"Get on your horse and ride after him! Take fifty of my troops with you! Bring me the head of that boy. Go! Before that fool gets away!" said Julian provoking the Sagan to wail and the high-pitched noise forced the man to cover his ears.

"Don't tell me what to do," said Soociv.

"Very well. Do what you wish. I just thought that you might want that fellow as a trophy," said Julian.

"Anger me not, old man, or I will put my spear in your neck. What do I want with a boy?" said the glorious Sagan Soociv as he looked out of the window.

"He is no ordinary boy. That was the sorcerer. That was Oliver," said Julian.

"Ha! Oliver is no boy! You have been deceived," said Soociv.

"I will get the fool myself then. In my own fashion! Go! All of you! Go and get him!" said Julian to the rest of his soldiers in the room.

Outside, Oliver had heard the high-pitched shriek and became even more alarmed. As Oliver ran toward his chariot, he began to feel troubled. Soon the wizard noticed that he was being followed. The guards were scrambling behind him and they moved with intent to kill. Near his chariot, Oliver was stopped and quickly surrounded by guards bearing swords and spears. The magician drew his weapon in defense and waited for them to attack.

"Put down your weapon," commanded the head guard.

Surrounded by the small force, Oliver was in a stalemate. He stood there poised and ready to strike. To the guards he appeared easy prey, just a very nervous kid who knew nothing of combat. Since Oliver had spent so much time in the castle, the princess had commanded the people to move to a safer place. The group had already moved a great distance away from the chariot when they heard the commotion behind them. They watched from the distance as the standoff progressed. Sensing the danger, the crowd decided to flee.

Magoonagoon

CHAPTER 33

The Myriad

Near the castle gate, the sorcerer and the guards faced off. Surrounded by sentinels, Oliver had no choice but to use magic to get out of the ambush. A man came at Oliver with a small dagger, but before he had a chance to use the blade the guard was pierced through by the flames from the whale tusk. After that first strike, others attacked and many more fell to the ground dead. The guards attempted to fight him, but they were no match for the magical fellow.

The skirmish had begun with Oliver outnumbered twenty to one. However, the tiny boy held his ground and fought against the myriad. As he fought through the crowd, the wizard perceived the time to run. For every man Oliver laid down, two more sprang up in his place. If the sorcerer was to prevail, he would have to hurry.

    Oliver bolted toward the chariot. Spears came whistling past his ears thrown from guards at every angle. A spear-man hit his mark as he struck the arm of the great wizard, spinning him around violently. Oliver was knocked from his feet as he spun around in agony.

    The whale tusk slid across the ground and out of his reach. When the rapier found its final resting place, it was collected by one of Julian's servants. The servant bent down and gripped the whale tusk and in that moment, Oliver realized that the tusk was lost. The sorcerer slammed his fist on the ground and sent a pulse that blew back his attackers.

    Oliver gathered his thoughts from the lapse in hostility. The boy then pulled the spear from his arm with wrenching pain. This was the first time the wizard had ever been wounded. The servant who had grabbed the whale tusk wishfully pleaded for them to end their barrage.

    With fury boiling inside his heart, Oliver moved to fight them without clear thought or sound judgment. The wizard held the spear that he had pulled from his own flesh tight, and threw it hard at an attacker who stood between him and the chariot. The spear drove home, hitting the guard right in the face and rendering him paralyzed.

    Oliver reached the chariot and tried to jump in. Incidentally, one of the soldiers grabbed hold of Oliver's fine cape as he leapt. His little body was jerked to a halt when the slack of the cape stretched tight. Oliver fumbled to untie the fine cape from his beautiful garments as other soldiers ran to stab him. As they approached, he quickly tried to loosen the cape from his neck.

Oliver was fortunate to have such a long cape, for its length was enough to save him from the first man's deadly bayonet. He tried to unbuckle the golden clips but they would not budge. At the last possible moment, the cape came loose to free his neck. The guard who held on to the fabric fell to the ground when the cape was set free.

Then, with a turn and a leap, Oliver twisted around to see his chariot waiting in front of him. But to his dismay, he beheld more assailants heading straight for him. The boy ran as he never had before to reach the war cart. He longed to attain the weaponry inside its rims, the sharp javelins, the principal tools of war. Within the chariot, he would find a surplus of daggers and darts to counter their charge.

Spear after spear rained down from the observers high atop the castle walls. The sorcerer picked up one of the spears and headed for his chariot. Oliver quickly felled a horse and rider with one blow. While he sprinted, another came at him with a heavy spear and knocked him off his feet. The boy was struck on his chest with a smooth stroke. The hard lick was precisely placed by the smooth swing of a spear. Guards came running at him with swords and shields hoping to take the boy down. Oliver scourged them back with magic and leaped into his carriage with a skip.

Now and always a charioteer, the boy grabbed the reins of the powerful horses to run. With the flick of his wrist the wizard urged the pair forward and toward the sea. However, the relentless patrols gave chase mounting their stallions.

Peering from the top of the castle wall, Julian and Soociv watched as the boy escaped. Julian growled and leaned on the handrail while he shook his head in disbelief. The mercenary could tell that Soociv disapproved of the way things were handled. The large Sagan placed his hands on his hips and dropped his head.

"He is going to get away," said Julian.

"I'll get him," said Soociv with a snarl.

Magoonagoon

CHAPTER 34
Soociv

Soociv walked down the stairs with a certain quickness in his step. The tall Sagan held tight the handle of his sword as it clung to his side. The Sagan's eyes grew wide from the excitement of the chase ahead of him. When he reached the bottom of the steps, he quickly gave out orders.

"Bring me my horse," said the tall Sagan.

His servants quickly went to get the black steed and his saddle. They led the horse into the courtyard. In the atrium, Soociv mounted the magnificent horse with one step. The vast Sagan made the muscular horse look like a small pony with the giant on her back. Nevertheless, the mare was no pony. She was seventeen hands tall and covered in muscle, the finest of all animals, with strong shoulders and strapping knees.

"Open the gate," commanded Soociv.

As the gate opened a gust of wind blew Oliver's torn cape on the ground. The Sagan champion burst out of the gate on his swift horse in pursuit of the sorcerer. Ahead of him, Oliver continued on his way to the coast, easily outrunning the guards giving chase behind him. Their horses were no match for the fast chariot. The wooden wheels zipped down the dirt road churning up a cloud of dust in their tracks. Yet Soociv was gaining fast on the swift chariot with his super horse.

When the Sagan was within range of the boy, Soociv gave his battle cry and Oliver turned around in horror. Blood dripped from the hip of the black horse where Soociv was whipping her. Oliver could see a ship in the distance that gave him a glimmer of hope and he coaxed his horses to go faster. Soociv continued to thrash his horse until he was on top of the chariot. There the Sagan drew his weapon to kill the boy. With each stride, his mare brought him closer to the boy and within reach of his deadly cutlass.

Oliver looked back to see how imminent the danger was, and he was surprised to see the feathered killer so close. The Sagan was in striking distance and ready to kill the boy. Oliver quickly ducked to dodge a swing and pulled the reins to the right just in time, avoiding the sword of the killer. The chariot turned sharply and almost tipped over from the swerve.

A cloud of dust went into Soociv's face as he tried to recover, and the debris choked his wind. Oliver quickly turned the horses back on course toward the coast as he steered them to the left. He lashed the team to encourage more speed. In the distance, his eyes caught a glimpse of a ship he recognized, a ship he knew well. He could see Jonathon and the whale hunters ahead of him on the beach. They gave his spirit a renewed sense of hope.

"Get to the ship! Get to the ship!" yelled Oliver.

Jonathon and the sailors strained to see who was hollering at them across the distance. When they heard the muffled warning and noticed a Sagan approaching they knew to be alarmed. Soociv ushered his mare back to pursue the boy and quickly caught up with him. As they raced for the coast, the vast Sagan swiped at the sorcerer with all his strength, hoping to strike his flesh. Oliver ducked beneath the hull of the carriage and it was another narrow miss. Then the wise Sagan moved to cripple the boy with his next blow. Soociv took his sword and struck the wheel of the chariot. The blow crushed the wooden wheel and sent it flying off in wobbling tracks.

The chariot wrecked and tumbled over and over as it beat against the ground. Oliver was sent flying out of the wooden vehicle and landed hard on the gritty terrain. The horses came loose from the hitch and they slowly trotted back toward Oliver as he lay there still. Soociv jerked the reins of his horse back, bringing the mare to its knees with a violent stop. The glorious Sagan put his feet down and nudged the animal to get back up off the dirt. The black mare struggled back to her feet from the shock of the stop.

He galloped the smooth creature back to the wreckage. As he laughed at the boy, Soociv romped the horse around the rubble. The famed Sagan's helmet glistened in the sun as Jonathon and his men looked on in disbelief. Oliver lay face down on the sandy ground without a budge. The great sorcerer opened his eyes as he felt the cool ocean breeze pass over his neck. Oliver tried to rise up from the hard dirt, but his limbs would not obey. Though the sorcerer could hear the tranquil sound of the crashing waves in the distance, he could not reach their safety.

"It looks like you have finally met your match, Ah! The sorcerer! I have been anxious for this hour," said Soociv as he stepped off his horse.

Oliver began to crawl toward the horses near the broken chariot. Bleeding and hurt, the sorcerer knew his only chance was to grab the reins of the powerful team and let them drag him away. Soociv reared back his massive sword high over his head to chop the injured boy. Just in time, Oliver grabbed hold of the broken wooden wheel with both hands. In an instant, the boy rolled over and blocked the strong forward thrust of the giant Sagan's sword that would have chopped him in half. The metal blade of the sharp sword cut right through the wooden wheel and smashed down on Oliver's chest. An impression of the great sword cut across the skin. The mark stretched from hip to armpit and stung the boy with a sharp bite. Oliver gasped for air as he crawled away from the giant's reach.

Soociv began to boast and gloat of his victory with a deep voice, loud enough for Jonathon and his men to hear. Oliver continued to try to crawl away from the massive feathered champion on his elbows and heels. The Sagan began to vaunt and swell in front of the boy in the old Sagan language.

"Nothing can save you now…you are dead…the sorcerer is lost! Forever! Look across at those cowards. They dare not venture beyond the safety of the ship. Your death will be a laurel in my honor," said Soociv with an evil grin.

Just as the words left his mouth, an arrow fell from the sky and struck the Sagan in the shoulder. The point buried deep in the Sagan's flesh where it met the bone. Soociv let out a wail that was heard all over the land. Seeing his chance to flee, Oliver crawled over and grabbed hold of the reins of the swift horses.

Anger flamed in the eyes of the Sagan champion as he pulled the arrow from his shoulder. Soociv immediately moved to strike and drew the sword back once more to end the life of the famous sorcerer. Just in time, Oliver used his magic to lash the powerful pair, and they drug the injured fellow out of the reach of the blade. Soociv's sword nearly took off the boy's feet as he slipped away. The horses drove Oliver to the beach where part of the ship's crew attended to him.

Magoonagoon

CHAPTER 35
Abandon Ship

Jonathon quickly put the wounded sorcerer into the small wooden craft. They dipped the oars of their small boat into the surf, casting off to the bigger whaling ship waiting out in the deep. Jonathon gave out commands for the crew to row as quickly as they could. Just as he spoke the rest of Julian's men arrived. They dismounted on the sandy beach and began to hoist their spears in the air at the boat. One of the slender wooden spears hit its mark, striking the back of one of Jonathon's men.

"Row! Row for the ship!" shouted Jonathon.

Soon the little vessel was out of the range of Julian's

men. They continued to paddle to reach the curved ship that waited in the deep. Soociv kept his distance from the stinging arrows of the talented bowmen and decided to return to the castle, for instinct honed by training and experience protected him. Wisely the black Sagan decided to end the chase.

Julian's soldiers went down the coast and boarded some ships to continue the chase. Just as Jonathon and his sailors were getting under way, more trouble came from around the bend of the island. Two of Julian's ships were fast approaching with dead aim of their rudder.

"We are being followed!" said Jonathon.

"We are doomed!" said one of the sailors.

"Here they come again! Tell the men to get us under way!" said Oliver.

"Get us out of here!" said Jonathon to the orator down below.

The men heaved the oars back and forth with their strong backs and spirited will. As they churned up the sea foam, the ship began to gain speed. Unrelenting, Julian's vessels came on to continue the chase.

"We will never outrun them. They are war ships. They are built for speed and in the open ocean we will surely die," said Jonathon.

"Raise the sail. Head for the nearby coastline away from the danger," said Oliver.

"Who are you?" asked Jonathon.

"It's me! Oliver," said the fellow.

"Oliver? The sorcerer? Who are you trying to fool kid? Oliver is an old man," said one of the sailors.

"You're going to get us all killed. Why are they chasing you?" asked one of the sailors.

"If you don't believe me, I guess I'll just have to show you who I am!" said the boy confidently.

Oliver got up from where he was sitting on the side of the ship and used his magic to buy them some time. He closed his eyes and lifted the palms of his hands up, then made a motion to the sea. The sea began to rumble and the surface danced with bubbles. All at once from the depths fish began to leap up out of the water. They covered the planks of Julian's ship. There were so many fish that they threatened to capsize the boats. Fish continued to leap up out of the sea until Oliver's powers relinquished and the boy passed out on the deck. Jonathon's sailors were inspired by the magic and turned the oars even harder. The weight on the decks of the enemy ships made the planks bend and pop. Julian's men worked quickly to clear the surface of the fish so they could get back underway.

"He's who he says he is! I know it now! It's the magician!" shouted Jonathon.

Jonathon quickly gave out orders for the men to head for the sand like Oliver suggested. Behind them the warships of Julian were closing in. Steadily, the speedy ships gained on them as they bored through the water. They caught up with Jonathon's men at the brink. One of the sailors held Oliver and helped him come to.

"Use your magic to buy us some more time!" said the sailor who was aiding him.

"I can't, the last trick took all I had. We must abandon ship," said Oliver as everyone on board looked at him as though he were crazy.

"He's crazy! Abandon ship?" asked one of the sailors.

"If we get any further out to sea, we will not be able to make it back to land. Here at this point is where we must abandon ship. Those war ships will crush us out in the deep if we don't," said Oliver.

"Do what he said! Row with all your might! Until I give you the command then swim for shore. We will all make it," said Jonathon.

The craft moved in for attack. To war they went to encounter man against man. The ax-shaped bow was only yards away and approached fast.

"Turn the ship starboard," said Jonathon.

Just in time, the ship avoided being ripped in half. They could hear the enemy cursing and yelling at them as they passed. It was a narrow miss, and short-lived, for the second ship was right on course to hit. Fiery arrows came aboard and landed on the planks. The second ship did not miss—it slammed home, breaking the large timbers.

"Abandon ship! Abandon ship!" shouted Jonathon.

Into the surf the men dove, plunging themselves into the black sea. Julian's troops stormed aboard the ship, killing part of the crew that did not make it off the deck in time. Jonathon was knocked overboard and sank under the surface. Beneath the surging waves, Jonathon was able to swim back toward the shore. In a different direction, Oliver swam toward the opposite beach. It seemed as though the two of them were the only survivors to make it to land.

The ship sank there in the shallows. Sadly, Oliver

watched from the shoreline as Julian's men shot arrows into the sailors who remained. They executed Jonathon's sailors as they treaded water among the wreckage. The sorcerer hung his head with disappointment from the devastation. As he looked across the sea at the opposite shore, he caught a glimpse of Jonathon climbing aground.

When Oliver saw Jonathon, the optimism helped him to regain his strength. The wizard headed off the beach and into a wooded forest. When he reached a dirt road, Oliver spotted a rider approaching at top speed on a very fast horse. The sorcerer hid in the thick brush nearby and waited for him to pass with caution.

When the rider came near, he noticed that it was a young boy. The boy flew by Oliver on the swift horse. The horse pumped its neck and legs in rhythm as its hooves kicked up clumps of dirt. Oliver immediately recognized that the boy was Felix, one of Jonathon's sons. Then he learned the reason why Felix was traveling so fast. He was being chased by two Sagan soldiers also on horseback.

The wizard picked up a branch that was lying there in the woods. Oliver watched the boy go by and then stepped out into the road in front of the soldiers. Oliver held the limb out like it was his own sword and decided to use a little magic. The soldiers pointed their weapons to attack and raced toward the wizard with fury. Oliver bent down to press the limb into the ground. As he waved his arms a huge tree sprouted up from the tiny branch. The tree instantly knocked the rider on the left off his horse with one decisive blow. However, the other rider was able to dodge it and ride past the wizard to continue chasing the boy.

Oliver ran to mount the fallen Sagan's horse who struggled to his feet. The sorcerer quickly leaped on the back of the horse and also gave chase leaving one of the Sagans behind. Both Oliver and the Sagan ahead of him chased Felix, but neither seemed to gain any ground on the swift horse. However, Oliver caught up with the Sagan soldier and used some more magic. With the wave of his hand, Oliver turned the Sagan's horse into a porcupine. The Sagan landed on the quills and slid to a stop. The sorcerer continued riding after the boy, leaving the Sagan behind.

"Felix! Wait!" yelled Oliver. The boy looked back but continued to ride. Finally he observed that the soldiers were not there, and only a boy followed him.

"Slow down, boy!" said Oliver as the youth started to slow down.

"Stay where you are!" said Felix, commanding the wizard to cease the chase. With these words, they both came to a stop.

"Who are you and why are you chasing me?" asked Felix.

"It is me, Oliver, the sorcerer," said the wizard.

"You cannot be Oliver! Oliver is an old man," said Felix.

"I do not look the same as I used to, but I assure you I am he," said Oliver.

"I don't believe you! How did you get here? You are supposed to be in Magoonagoon!" questioned Felix.

"Your uncle asked me to spy on the Sagans and I ended up here. Just moments ago I was with your father when our ship sank. I was walking from the sea and saw you ride by. Then I saw those soldiers chasing you," said Oliver.

"Why should I believe you? My father is out to sea. He has not returned," stated Felix.

"We don't have time for this. Your father is here. There are Sagans all around us. We must go and find him," said Oliver as Felix rode his horse up beside him.

"If my father is here, he will be searching for me," said Felix.

"We will find him," said Oliver.

Magoonagoon

CHAPTER 36
Come Aboard

Back in the village, the Sagans were having a wonderful time wrecking, destroying, and creating terrible chaos for anyone who got in their way. The Sagans took some of the prisoners to the top of the cliff near the city and threw them off for fun. The Sagans enjoyed watching them hit the rocks below. They continued until late that evening when it was time to leave with those souls destined for Magoonagoon. Down on the beach, there in the shallows, the glorious boats were anchored side by side.

Sapsoon turned up a bottle of wine. The red wine poured into the Sagan's beak until he had drank every last drop. When he finished, he tossed the bottle down against the ship and it smashed to pieces. With his hands on his hips the pirate laughed at the cowering men as they came aboard. The people were chained together in small groups and were pressed through the surf by the crack of a whip.

"Come aboard! Come aboard!" shouted Sapsoon.

Emery was pulled toward Soociv's ship. As he dredged through the shallows, the boy was violently pushed in the back of the head by one of the Sagans. There in the surf, Noisop handpicked who would come aboard his ship. Noisop just happened to turn his head and look away when the boy ducked under the water. Emery passed by the large Sagan and walked up the gang plank. On the way up the plank to the deck of the mighty ship, Emery and the others were informed of their duty. In front of them, at the entrance to the boat, the division leader branded the men with the mark of the Sagans as they came aboard.

"Listen, you fools! You will live only to serve us! You will serve us or be served as our dinner! If you are not willing to fight, we will eat you!" shouted Sapsoon.

"Oh! Give me death! Give me death!" cried one of the men and Noisop granted his wish with his sword. Afterwards, he noticed that it was slowing down the progress of the chain gang trudging through the shallows. Seeing his mistake, Noisop cut off the dead man's foot to set the body free from the shackles. For fun, the Sagan tossed the foot aboard the ship and laughed. Through the crying and screams, Sapsoon spoke to the crowd once more.

"Here is some hope for you! See here! The first man to

kill a Foucinian I will set free!" shouted Sapsoon.

After Noisop came aboard, he looked over the men. He lowered his long neck down and glanced into the eyes of his captives. The Sagan walked among the men checking them for any threats. He stopped in front of a short fellow who had an angry expression on his face. Noisop pulled his knife from his belt and took the opportunity to make an example out of the man. The giant grabbed the man by his head and slit his throat.

"Throw this dog overboard! Oars...oars...Get the rest of these fools below and hand them all an oar," said Noisop.

The Sagan started to walk away, but he noticed someone who looked out of place. Noisop was puzzled about what he saw and he turned his head around to take a second look. The Sagan thought his eyes might be playing tricks on him. After seeing the proof, Noisop walked over to the small fellow and studied him close. When the Sagan reached Emery, he pointed his sharp talon down at the lad in anger.

"This one does not belong here. Who brought this boy onto my ship?" asked Noisop and no one uttered a word. The Sagan wailed and continued.

"He is too young to fight! He should have been placed on the slave ship. Get him off my ship!" said Noisop.

A Sagan came running up to get Emery. The Sagan jerked the boy up and proceeded to take him toward the plank. However, the Sagans had already removed the ramp and they were making preparations for the launch. Soociv walked over to the lad and bent down to take a good look at him. The giant sniffed the boy and shook his head in disappointment.

"It is too late. Take him down below!" shouted Soociv.

Another Sagan grabbed him and down they went into the dark cold underbelly of the ship. Emery was pulled down the steps to the entrance where he would pull the oars.

"Get down there boy," said the Sagan, tossing him down the hatch.

"Get in your place, boy!" shouted the pace striker, pointing to an empty spot.

On the deck, the Sagan soldiers began to hoist the massive anchor from the dark surf. The dreadful noise of the chain being hoisted up sent chills up and down their spines. The men waited for orders and Soociv wailed at them.

"Prepare to launch!" said Soociv.

"Get us out of here!" shouted Noisop.

Magoonagoon

CHAPTER 37
The Goblin

Alone, but resolute, Brunto searched for a place to hide in his solitude. He walked along the delta leading his pony. He staggered through the wastelands, longing for food and shelter. When he entered the canyon, he tracked hopelessly through the ravines, searching desperately to escape the heat of the sun. In the shadows of the gorge, the giant found refuge. A great cave in the mighty wall of the tall canyon had its mouth opened wide. The cool place bid him to enter, and the Sagan drug the horse in with him.

The pony stamped its hooves and shook its muscular

neck as the Sagan pulled on the reins. The horse could sense the danger inside the cavern, and as they walked in Brunto perceived the fear. Still, the tall Sagan pressed on. Brunto pulled the horse behind him as he stepped in the moist dirt. Suddenly, the ground turned to mud and the sediment beneath them mired. The sludge oozed between his toes and a flickering light in the distance revealed an underground lake.

Seeing the water, Brunto freed the pony and rushed forward to get a drink. He collapsed on his fat belly and submerged his head beneath the water. Then the Sagan gulped and swallowed as much of the cool water as he could. The horse wanted to flee, but knew better than to leave the side of its master. Instead, the pony trotted up next to Brunto and lapped the fresh fluid. It was then when the scratchy voice called out.

"Who dares to drink from my lake?" echoed the voice, and the sound rose the feathers on Brunto's neck.

The giant stood to his feet and drew his sword to defend himself. Brunto lowered his neck and squinted his eyes to peer across the lake. In the distance, he noticed a flickering light and watched closely to see any shadows. The Sagan's heart began to race and thump in his mighty chest. Fear gripped his knees as he heard the sloshing water in front of him. The horse bellowed out in horror, as she shuddered and quivered. Then, once again, the voice exclaimed.

"Who dares to drink from my lake?" repeated the scratchy voice.

The giant struggled to speak and waved the sword in front of him recklessly. Every noise amplified and every movement loomed as an enemy. As his beak began to chatter, the giant's back shook from the suspense. As the sloshing ceased, the dumbstruck Sagan prepared for the worst. On the edge of the muddy bank he awaited the voice from the other side of the lake. However, to his surprise, the voice came from behind him.

"Coward! Have you no backbone?!" said the voice as Brunto turned to answer.

"Who goes there?" asked Brunto.

"It is your worst fear! The sinister evil that haunts you!" said the voice.

"Now you have made me mad!" said Brunto.

"Good! Anger is good for cowards!" said the voice.

"Perhaps you should show your face!" shouted Brunto with a trembling hand.

"It looks like you could use a little courage. Your fears haunt you! Look into the light and see for yourself!" said the voice as he lit a torch. The light illuminated the cavern and the torch glowed bright.

"Ahhhh!" shouted Brunto.

"Ha! Ha! Ha! Here I am! A goblin!" said the voice.

Brunto stepped back into the lake and almost fell flat on his back. The goblin continued to laugh as he moved forward with his torch. As Brunto sloshed around in the water, the goblin pulled out a dagger and hissed at the Sagan. The dreadful hiss exclaimed over the crevices of the cave and echoed throughout. Brunto looked upon his ugly head and shuddered from his countenance. The evil booger stood poised to strike the Sagan with his little dagger. He was hunched over at the waist and his posture made him appear even tinier than he was. His green skin reeked from stench and his yellow teeth grinned an irrefutable wickedness.

Then Brunto grit his beak and shook the water from his beautiful feathers. Embarrassed by the goblin's trick, he moved to scold the evil creature. With one mighty step he cleared the wake and the Sagan stood in front of the vile critter. Brunto drew back his sword and almost attacked, but before he struck the little demon spoke.

"No! Wait! Do not destroy me!" begged the goblin.

"A vile goblin you are! You are doomed! You have played your last trick!" said Brunto.

"Please! Have mercy!" pleaded the goblin.

"It is too late! After I kill you, I will throw your body into the lake!" said Brunto.

"No! I beg you! There are many things I can offer! That is if you let me live!" said the goblin. Brunto shook his head and snarled at the small demon.

"There is nothing you have to offer that I want," said Brunto.

"I can offer you many things! Things you desire and need!" repeated the goblin.

"Dare you trick me again! I will not fall for another trick! Besides, I already have everything I need!" shouted Brunto.

"Oh! This comes from a giant who is afraid of his own shadow!" said the goblin as he laughed.

"Afraid! Not I!" shouted Brunto.

"Oh? We'll see about that!" said the goblin.

At that moment the goblin snuffed out the candle that he held in his hand and once more the cavern grew exceedingly dark. Brunto swallowed a lump in his throat and shivered once again in fear. He swung his saber at every noise and whisper, for fear had consumed his body and spirit. The Sagan tried to reason with the little goblin.

"All right! You are right! I am afraid! Show yourself, you vile goblin!" said Brunto with desperation in his voice.

"Pity on him! Ha! You are a giant and I am only a mere sprite!" said the goblin as he slit the ankle of the big Sagan with his small dagger. Brunto wailed from the pain as the goblin laughed.

"I beg you! Show yourself!" pleaded Brunto.

"Did I not beg you? Foolish Sagan! You no longer wish to live!" said the goblin with an evil snicker.

"I yield to you. Please! Show yourself!" shouted Brunto. Then the goblin slashed the Sagan across the knee.

"You sniveling snot! Take courage! That is one thing I could have offered! You are a whelping, weeping dupe," said the goblin as he laughed once more.

"Very well! Do your worst and be doomed!" shouted Brunto, emboldened by the threat.

"That's the spirit! You need a dose of fortitude," said the goblin.

At that moment the goblin lit the torch. The light blinded the giant and sent him stepping back away from its splendor. The goblin smiled at the giant, and the creature urged Brunto to calm his rage. For the moment, the feathered Sagan stood still and waited for the goblin's next move. The little creature walked past the Sagan without any fear or reservation. Then he invited Brunto to follow him. They moved to the other side of the lake where the goblin lived.

As they approached the goblin's house, the creature reached into his pouch that hung from his belt and took out a fine powder. The goblin then pitched the resin into a woodpile and a luminous fire surged forth. Brunto leaped back away from the heat and shook once again from the onslaught. The goblin shook his ugly head at the giant and snickered aloud. Then he walked over to his abode, and passed through a tiny hole that served as a door. The opening glowed with light and the illumination made Brunto curious. The big Sagan knelt down to see, but the hole was too low. So Brunto moved back a short distance and tried to peer into the house. The goblin reappeared and spoke.

"Come closer," said the goblin and the giant approached with caution.

"I cannot enter into this place for the doorway is too small," said Brunto.

"Lie down and stick your head into this house for I have something to show you," said the goblin.

"Ha! I am no fool! You cannot trick me into that! For what reason should I look in?" asked Brunto cautiously.

"Have courage! I am small and you are huge! Take thought of that! There is something inside that I want you to see!" said the goblin.

"Bring it out here! There is no reason for me to lie down in the grit. Bring it forth so I may see," said Brunto.

"If you do not have the backbone to lie down and gaze into my house you will not see," said the goblin.

"Then I will not see!" said Brunto with an evil tone.

"Very well! But I warn you! What you see in the house may change you forever. You may find the answers to what you are looking for," said the goblin as he hobbled at the entrance.

Brunto shook his head furiously and kicked some sand toward the house. As he grit his beak, the giant had an idea to smash the house in and reveal the luminescence, but his curiosity prevailed. So the giant laid down on his huge stomach and crawled near the entrance. He slid his long neck through the small hole with caution and his eyes grew wide from the glowing light. When his head reached the room he could not surmise the splendor.

He looked into the immense room and stared upon the troves of treasure. The trap was sprung and the goblin ensnared the giant with a rope around his neck. He tightened the noose down and cinched the rope firm to his anchor point that happened to be a large wooden beam supporting the structure. Brunto struggled to free his powerful neck, but there was no use. The Sagan was enslaved by the goblin who had tricked him into the trap. So crippling his movements, the evil goblin moved to speak.

"Ha! Ha! You fool! Now I will feast for a year on your flesh! I will pick your bones clean and enjoy every tender morsel!" said the goblin.

Brunto struggled to free himself from the noose as he shook and rocked his huge body. The goblin approached the giant's head with his knife drawn, ready to swindle his life from him. Brunto snapped at him with his beak and warned the goblin away with cursing vaunts. However, the evil little monster relentlessly scurried forward to find a way to slit the Sagan's throat. Nevertheless, the giant placed his arms firmly on the ground and gave a push that might have lifted a mountain.

The mighty bones of the titan shimmered and shook. The wide back of the Sagan trembled as he constricted his muscles. The house began to rumble as pebbles and debris fell from the roof. All at once a fracture cracked across the ceiling, and the force from the Sagan quaked the house. Then, with the strength of ten Sagans and fifty men, the giant brought down the house. The vaulted ceiling fell and the place collapsed on top of them.

With his arms free, Brunto moved to untie the noose from his neck. In a flash, he was free from the binds and he scrambled to grab the goblin. Brunto found the goblin pinned under a heavy stone at the back of the dwelling. The little sprite was half way beneath a huge rock that had fallen from the roof. When the dust settled Brunto spoke to him.

"I will leave you here to be pinned under this rock for all eternity!" said Brunto.

"No! Please! Do not leave me here! You must save me! I can help you if you save me!" said the goblin.

"Ha! You said you would help me before! If I would only stick my head into your house!" said Brunto.

"This is no trick! I will help you! Please free me and you shall see!" said the goblin.

"I know the legend! If you save a goblin, he must offer you a wish in return!" said Brunto with wide eyes.

"No! Help me first! Then I will give you anything you wish!" said the goblin.

"Ha! You're not in a position to negotiate! You are at my command! Do as I say or I will leave you here beneath this rock!" said Brunto.

"Very well! What is your desire?" asked the goblin.

"I wish to be invincible!" exclaimed Brunto.

"I cannot give you that power, but I can offer you something that you need. You need courage. I can offer you fortitude and valor. If it is your desire? Turn me loose and you will see!" said the goblin.

"I told you! You will grant my wish first or you shall stay beneath this boulder," said Brunto.

"If you wish to have courage, reach under this stone and grab my pouch. There you will find a magic powder. Hand it to me," said the goblin. Brunto reached under the stone and took the pouch, but instead of handing the pouch over to the goblin he spoke.

"Ha! Now I have your powder and you are doomed! What do I need you for?" asked Brunto.

"No! What are you doing?" questioned the goblin as Brunto started to walk away.

"I will leave you here to die!" shouted Brunto.

Brunto then took the magic powder out from the sack and dusted his own head. The powder covered his mighty head and sparkled and glistened down his back. Then the giant shouted out a spell to help himself.

"Fortitude and might with the courage to fight!" said the feathered giant.

As he said those words his body changed, and his demeanor changed as well. In his heart the fortitude embraced his spirit, and in his soul the power of might bestowed the Sagan with an embodied supply. The vast Sagan shouted out with glee. The shout echoed in the cave and the rumble shook the whole cavern.

Magoonagoon
CHAPTER 38
Where Are They

After several days of peace, Eescas, a Foucinian scout, was sent to the shorelines of Magoonagoon. There the beast would check on the Sagan invaders. Trained in stealth the hairy warrior had no problem passing through the narrow canyon with its many different caverns and caves. He rode his brown horse across the desert wasteland and over to the coastline to the Sagan camps. He traveled to his usual spot high on top of the rocky cliff where he had spied on the enemy many times before.

On the way to the top, Eescas noticed that the beach was deserted. There was no sign of the Sagans around the old abandoned homes of the Foucinians. As the scout rode further, he noticed that the fast ships that once moored on the sand had vanished. There were still some tents and equipment on the sandy shore, and many of their campfires still puffed black smoke. Eescas took a second to make sure that this was not some sort of a trap. Then he swiftly turned his horse around and headed down to the beach to check out the spoils they had left behind.

Brunto had been out in the canyon hiding from Oilaz and his soldiers. The Sagan had regained his courage and was on his way back to the Sagan camps to meet his brother. Made bold by the magic dust from the goblin's pouch, the barbarian was filled with bravery and moved to challenge the emperor right away so that he might reclaim his place. Brunto had left the goblin under the stone and was now empowered with a sense of fearlessness.

The feathered warrior's horse was weary, she needed water and rest. She struggled along the way with the heavy titan on her back. Even though Brunto himself was tired he wanted to regain his honor and dignity. Once a coward who ran from his destiny, he was now a valiant and daring creature with the tenacity of a czar. Brunto returned to the camps with euphoric delight.

Eescas and Brunto came into the camp at the same time. The Foucinian entered from the left and the Sagan came from the right. Their eyes met with surprise, and Brunto wailed his loud battle cry. Eescas's heart began to race, and the hair on the back of his neck stood up when he saw the nineteen-foot-tall Brunto draw his saber. A chase commenced between the two enemies. Eescas raced down the sandy coast on his pony trying to avoid any confrontation. His duty was espionage and only to report troop movements.

The pair of combatants raced down the beach with fury. Brunto kicked the sides of his horse to urge her closer to the Foucinian spy. Brunto's horse carried him close enough for him to take a swipe at Eescas. Only the mare was too fatigued to carry the heavy Sagan on her back at full speed. She galloped as far as she could, but soon her legs gave out and she slowed to a trot. In the blink of an eye, Eescas was out of sight and far away from the brown monster. Eescas never looked back as he rode his horse as fast as he could toward the Foucinian outpost.

Brunto dismounted from the horse he was riding and took hold of the bridle. He wailed out in anger and shook the horse's head because the mare had let the enemy get away. She jumped away in fear and snorted at him audibly. The tall Sagan led the horse back into the camp to look for some food and water. When he got there, he noticed to his disappointment that all of the fast ships that once rested on the shore were gone. He began to look around for anything he could use to help him survive. Brunto found some small plums and a canteen of fresh water. Before he took a drink, his eyes sighted a large barrel of wine. Brunto laid his head down under the tap and opened it up to drink. The wine poured into his beak and he drank as much as he could. Afterwards, he sat down in the sand and admired other things he could use.

Where are they? Have they gone home? wondered Brunto.

The Sagan warrior ate and drank as much as he could while he peered out at the equipment. As he ate, the hulk strode along the beach looking at the discarded treasure. After he had finished eating, Brunto took out his sword and smashed open an iron lock that protected a strongbox. Then the feathered soldier ripped the lid off the wooden chest to find a great bounty. The hulk took two small daggers and a round wooden shield out. The Sagan threw a purse of coins haphazardly over his shoulder that he found deep inside the chest. Brunto also found a long wooden bow and many steel-tipped arrows lying on the ground.

Surely these things were left in the scramble…for their worth is far too great to have left behind, thought Brunto.

He loaded the equipment into a painted wooden chariot, no doubt left behind by the fleeing Sagans in their eagerness to leave. A mistake easily made in the commotion, for the chariot was worth a king's ransom. After Brunto had given his horse some food and drink, the Sagan fastened the stallion to the carriage. Then he loaded the cart down with provisions and weapons. When he was finished, Brunto led the horse back to his hideout deep within the canyon walls.

Magoonagoon
CHAPTER 39
The Destroyer

Eescas fled as though a thousand Sagans were lurking behind him and ready to ensnare him. He bolted toward the other side of the canyon. As he dashed through the narrow passages and corridors, he stumbled upon another Sagan warrior mounted on a fine horse. Eescas pulled hard on the reins of his swift horse and came to a halt. In front of him, the Sagan warrior pranced his horse back and forth mocking the Foucinian.

"Ho! Foucinian! Have you ever been so foolish to venture so far from safety?" asked the Sagan.

"Naked buzzard! So foolish! It is you who have the look

of a buffoon! Pray for your feathers to grow back! Ha! They never will!" shouted Eescas.

The Sagan was Iipkam, the featherless, former prisoner of war, sent to search for Brunto. The wayfarer had ended up in the canyon. Now, the Sagan blocked Eescas's only way out of the gorge. Even though the two appeared to be evenly matched, Eescas wanted no part of the featherless creature. As the Foucinian looked over his shoulder to plan his escape, he spoke once more to the Sagan.

"Were you marooned on this island to die? Forsaken by your comrades! Or even now do you seek them? Ha! Say you chose to stay here alone! Tell me! Will you toil with all my brethren by yourself? If so, you are the most foolish being to have ever lived!" asked and stated Eescas.

"I will tell you this! Alone I may be! Revenge is what I seek! Staying behind will bring me pleasure! For every warrior must have his first victory, and my first triumph will be over you!" shouted Iipkam wanting nothing more than to put his javelin in the back of the Foucinian scout.

Eescas drew his wooden spear back and hoisted it toward the featherless Sagan. The iron tip of the spear whistled through the air as it sped toward Iipkam's head. However, the spear missed its mark and fell to the ground back behind Iipkam.

"Ha! Ha! Ha! Now you will die," mocked Iipkam as Eescas spun his horse around and retreated from the Sagan.

Iipkam gave his horse a kick in the side and gave chase. Soon the featherless Sagan caught up with the spy in a long straightaway. The Sagan let his spear fly and the javelin drove deep into hind quarter of Eescas's horse. The horse fell hard to the ground churning up the dust as it rolled. Eescas tossed forward and flipped three times as he came to rest on the dry ground of the canyon floor.

Iipkam brought his horse to a stop back from the wreckage and peered down with his long neck hung low. He then climbed down off the fast horse given to him by Ruffio. Iipkam clutched his fists tight and let out another wail to prepare for combat. Eescas jumped to his feet to battle the Sagan. The muscular Sagan struck first by punching the hairy beast in the throat.

Eescas was not stunned and returned with a hard blow of his own. He reached back and punched the Sagan in the face with all his strength. Iipkam was knocked to the ground and ended up next to the wounded horse. With stars in his eyes he shook away the pain as he sat on the gritty silt. The spit dripped from his beak as his head bobbed about. The old Sagan wiped away the spittle with the top of his forearm and in a flash he was back on his feet.

Iipkam quickly scrambled to pull his spear out of the horse and face the Foucinian. The Sagan gripped the spear tightly with two hands and pivoted around to swing. The spear smashed across the skull of the spy and sent him crashing to the ground. The hard force of the hit broke the spear in two.

"How did that feel?" questioned Iipkam with a snarl.

"You will pay for that!" shouted Eescas as he jumped to his feet with his hand on his head.

Iipkam tossed the splintered handle of the spear aside and clinched his fists once more. Eescas filled his chest with air and let out a low grumbling noise. This grumble was meant to call for help. The Foucinians could communicate over long distances and he knew that his companions would soon be in the area. Without a weapon to face the feathered attacker, Eescas was outmatched.

As he crouched with poise to make a move, Iipkam held out his fists and shook them at the Foucinian soldier. The strong Sagan warrior then let out his battle cry with open jaws. Eescas took the opportunity to run and headed for Iipkam's horse. However, he did not get past the Iipkam with ease, for as he fled, the beast met the razor-sharp talons of the Sagan. The nails gnashed down the Foucinian's left side and brought forth the blood. The swift-footed Foucinian quickly mounted Iipkam's horse and began to ride away. The hairy beast rode the horse over to the spear that he had thrown earlier. Being sure to hold onto the leather reins, Eescas jumped down off the horse and picked up the wooden javelin.

"Come back and fight, you coward!" shouted Iipkam.

Eescas mounted the horse and turned it around to face Iipkam. He held the spear in a position to throw next to his brawny face. The scout then kicked the horse in the side and charged in attack as he lowered the spear to joust the Sagan. Eescas gained speed and headed right for the Sagan with intentions to kill. Suddenly, the scout pulled hard on the reins of the horse, jerking its muscular neck. The spy brought the horse to a rapid stop, buckling the knees of the stallion; he could not control the fear in his heart as he dropped the wooden spear.

Brunto appeared from the rock walls behind Iipkam. His wooden chariot made the turn on one wheel and settled down as it headed into the straightaway. Brunto raised his sword in one hand and pointed it toward the sun as the horse pulling the cart pumped its muscular neck. Then the massive feathered creature gave his famous battle cry that echoed through the canyon.

    Eescas quickly jumped to the ground and picked up his spear with his knees quaking. Without taking good aim the spy hoisted his javelin into the air. The wooden pike carried through the sky and whisked past Brunto's head. Eescas jumped back on the stallion as fast as he could.

    Eescas managed to turn the horse around and the chase began. He kicked his horse in the sides and took off down the canyon. Brunto raced past Iipkam and gave chase to the wanderer against the backdrop of the orange stone. Desperate and terrified, the Foucinian scout began to beat his horse on the hind quarters to urge more speed, but the wheels of Brunto's chariot turned faster and faster as he steered.

    Soon the feathered monster caught up with Eescas and swiped at his neck with his sword. Brunto swung with so much power that the force lifted the chariot off the ground. When the wooden carriage landed, it headed on a course to hit the rock wall. The chariot ran into the rocky side of the cavern. The wooden spokes of the wheel scraped and dug into the stone as Brunto fumbled to get hold of the reins.

    The Sagan almost dropped his sword as he tried to regain control over the speedy coaster. Eescas looked back in desperation hoping that the giant had wrecked. To his disappointment, Brunto continued to chase close behind. In a flash, the nineteen-foot-tall Sagan was back on the heels of the scout. With fleeting speed he had managed to bridge the gap between them and close in on the beast.

Eescas dodged another attack from Brunto as his sword slashed near his arm. Brunto rode up beside Eescas and busted him across the chest plate with his sharp sword. The harsh blow knocked Eescas clear off his horse and down to the rocky dirt in a cloud of dust. The feathered monster rode a little further and slowed his horse to a trot. He grabbed the reins of Eescas's horse as he came to a stop. Brunto quickly fastened the other horse to his chariot as he mocked Eescas.

"I am going to run you over!" shouted Brunto.

He tied up the hitch and knotted the leather straps. Then he made sure the reins were secured before he jumped back on the chariot. Now with twice the horse power the carriage became more than worthy of battle. Jubilant with glee, Brunto extended his neck and let out an ear-piercing wail of victory.

The son of Gonee whipped the reins and sped toward Eescas, who lay just ahead in the dirt, still unconscious from the previous attack. Brunto took the horses up to a gallop as he rode right over the fallen enemy. The carriage took a few ruff bounces as it mangled Eescas's body. The racing wheels then smoothed out after they passed over the speed bump.

"Ha! Ha! Ha! Your days of spying are over!" mocked Brunto.

Then the destroyer rode past the body and slapped the reins to bring the chariot up to full speed. The charioteer then pulled exceedingly hard to one side forcing the horses to turn around. The chariot slid behind the horses with agility and they continued their pace galloping back to make another pass. On his way the Sagan spoke to the dying Foucinian.

"Your brother cannot save you this time," said Brunto.

The swift racer gave a long smooth lash of the reins and launched the horses back toward Eescas a second time. The carriage churned up dust as it sped toward the injured Eescas, who had wakened in pain and tried to crawl for safety. The Foucinian struggled to lift his heavy body from the canyon floor, and as he trudged on, Eescas surrendered to his own immutable conclusion. The wheels of the chariot rolled over Eescas, crushing his body. The ruthless Sagan never slowed down as he passed across the carcass. The second pass brought an end to the famous Foucinian scout. Brunto looked back over his shoulder to assess the damage of his attack. Then the tall Sagan pulled hard on the reins to slow down the horses. The white-and-gold-painted chariot came to a halt a short distance away. Booballet's brother was dead, killed by the destroyer.

Magoonagoon

CHAPTER 40
The War Machine

Brunto began to beat his chest and gloat about his victory in the old Sagan tongues. He stepped down off the chariot and raised his arms toward the sky. His celebration was loud and boisterous, echoing through the deep canyon walls. Brunto began to look over his new carriage with its proud ponies. After he tightened down the hitch, the Sagan climbed back aboard the war machine. Brunto turned the horses around, and they began to prance down the dirt track.

In the distance, Brunto began to hear the thundering hooves of the Foucinian patrol. In the background the sound of a battle cry of bone-chilling volume rang through the sky. Brunto recognized the call, a voice that he had heard a thousand times before. It was one that he knew well. The shout was from Booballet, the best of the Foucinians, the brother of the fallen Eescas. The footsteps of the horses grew louder as they rumbled the small stones on the ground. The Sagan had won the small battle just in time to bathe in its glory.

As the riding party of the Foucinians approached, Brunto turned the horses around as fast as he could. He smiled ear to ear as he prepared for their arrival. The hulk knew that this would be his moment to shine and restore his name to greatness. In preparation, Brunto parked the chariot so he could make a fast getaway. He waited for the soldiers to come around the bend. Then the Sagan picked up the bow that he put in the chariot and threaded an arrow on the line. When the riders made the turn, they brought their horses to a stop. As soon as they saw the giant, the warriors drew their swords. Booballet, the nineteen-foot-tall Foucinian, immediately spoke with harsh words.

"Foucinians! Look at the foundering oaf! Have any of you ever seen such a harlequin?" shouted Booballet to them all.

"Ha! Ha! Beg for your lives while you still can! Foucinian dogs!" shouted Brunto.

"This is a fitting place for your corpse to rot! Here in the canyon! This place is proper enough for your blundering bones!" shouted Booballet.

"Look here at your brother! Soon you will lie next to him in the dirt!" shouted Brunto.

"Eescas? What have you done with him?" asked Booballet.

"Ha! Ha! Ha! Come and see the body of your brother, Booballet! Come and lie down beside him with my spear in your gut!" yelled Brunto.

"No!" yelled Booballet as he kicked his horse in the sides and went after the Sagan alone.

"Booballet! Do not rush against him alone!" shouted one of the Foucinians.

"Doom you then! If ruin is what you so wish! Let him go! He will fare well against that monster," mumbled Wolneas to the others as he grinned.

"You do not wish for him to die?" asked one of the Foucinians.

"Fool! I heard you! I will not hear of this treason!" shouted Vindeen as he rode off.

"If the fool wants revenge, let him be satisfied with his own death!" shouted Wolneas.

"That talk is treacherous, Wolneas!" shouted one of the Foucinians as he departed to accompany Booballet and the others.

In front of them, Brunto drew back an arrow on his line and let it fly from his bow. The wooden arrow jetted through the air and struck one of the Foucinians. The arrow killed him instantly, dropping the hairy rider to the ground. The others kicked their horses and began to pursue Brunto through the canyon. Brunto placed the bow down inside the carriage, and slapped his horses with the reins, launching them down the dirt path away from the foe.

Brunto steered the painted chariot over the body of Eescas one more time as he traveled away from the Foucinian riders. Booballet gave up the chase and dismounted where his brother lay dead. One of the powerful guards and comrade of Booballet, stayed behind to watch the champion's back. The other two backers followed after the nineteen-foot-tall Sagan with ready weaponry. They raced through the canyon running the shoed horses down the path. The Foucinian horses pumped their necks and stretched out their long legs, but they could not gain any ground on the fast chariot.

When Brunto had traveled a short distance, he looked over his shoulder to see if the two warriors had given up the chase. There was no sight of the pair as the Sagan made the turn of the canyon. After he had driven a short distance away, he slowed the horses down to a gallop. He opened his canteen and took a drink of water. After he wet his throat, he heard a voice up ahead.

"Brunto!" shouted Iipkam and Brunto was filled with excitement because the voice sounded like his dear brother, Ruffio.

Ruffio has come back for me, thought the giant.

With his eyes open wide, Brunto rode ahead to meet the cry. He ushered his team up to battle speed as he traveled the canyon course. When he reached the area, he discovered with dejection the Sagan that he had passed earlier. Disappointment filled his heart, and he addressed the featherless Sagan with heavy words.

"You! I told my soldiers to gag your beak and put you in the belly of my ship," said Brunto.

"Your soldiers obeyed your orders. They did as you told them. I was taken to your ship and stayed there until Ruffio came to see me," said Iipkam as Brunto's eyes grew wide with excitement.

He's alive, thought Brunto.

"You spoke with my brother? Explain yourself! Why did he want to see you?" asked Brunto.

"He told me to find you and bring you back before the ships departed for home," said Iipkam.

"They are already gone and may never return," said Brunto.

"Yes, I know. The ships departed the very night he told me to find you," said Iipkam.

"So they left us behind?" asked Brunto.

"I was tricked! Ruffio told me that they would not depart until you and I returned," said Iipkam.

"Are you calling my brother a liar?" questioned Brunto as he put his hand on his sword.

"No! No! I am only saying that he left me with the intentions to help you," said Iipkam.

At that very moment the Foucinian riders came riding around the corner. One of them pointed his long broad sword at the two Sagans and let out a loud rumbling roar. Seeing the adversary, Brunto spoke to the featherless Sagan.

"Well, here is your chance to help. Grab a sword from the chariot and prepare to fight," said Brunto.

Iipkam ran to grab a sword. The featherless Sagan chose a curved blade with a sharp tip that had the look of a cutlass. Brunto took hold of his shield and drew his strong blade from his leather belt. Vindeen rode into the Sagans slashing his sword. The steel blades clashed as many blows were traded.

Brunto used the shield to block many of the hits from Vindeen's comrade. The warriors churned up dust as they battled in the dried-up riverbed. Brunto had enough of the fool he was fighting, and his reckless style of combat. The Sagan blocked one of his blows with his shield and put his sword into his ribs. However, Iipkam was in trouble and beginning to tire from the intense fighting he received from Vindeen.

Brunto watched Iipkam battle Vindeen for a moment. He wanted to see if the Sagan could hold his own in a fight. Instead of jumping in to help Iipkam, Brunto looked over the spoils. The victorious Sagan quickly snatched the reins of the dead Foucinian's horse and fastened them to his chariot. Now the chariot had three powerful horses at its prow.

Iipkam began to fight back, as he deposited three hard hits on Vindeen's sword, sending it flying into the air. Vindeen pulled hard on the reins of his horse and blocked Iipkam's attack. In a flash, Vindeen had the fast horse turned around in retreat.

"Ha! Look at him run! Come back you coward! I want that horse!" yelled Brunto.

Vindeen never looked back and rode his horse out of sight. The warrior rode through the canyon and headed back to meet up with Booballet. He passed through the narrow rock walls that reached for the sky. When Vindeen reached the pair, he dismounted from his horse.

"Where is your comrade?" asked one of the Foucinians.

"Dead!" interrupted Vindeen.

"Now three are dead because of this murderer," said another Foucinian.

"What do we do now, Booballet?" asked Vindeen.

Booballet got so angry that he cursed and kicked some dirt. He picked up the body of his brother Eescas and rose to his feet. Booballet laid his brother across the horse of the Foucinian that was killed by the arrow. Then the beast turned to speak.

"Take Eescas home. I will take care of this murderer," said Booballet as the other Foucinians jumped on their horses.

"Vindeen does not have a sword," said one of them.

"Go with him and protect him," commanded Booballet with a cold glare.

"Are you sure? Let me help you," asked another.

"Go!" yelled Booballet in a voice that could not be questioned.

Good! You do not need help! Go alone and be doomed! thought Wolneas to himself.

The Foucinians parted and headed for the stronghold just outside the canyon. Booballet rode his horse violently, gnashing his teeth as the hooves of his strong horse pounded the dirt. He held his black trunk to the sky and trumpeted his warning. The black snout rumbled a shout that echoed to the heavens. Nevertheless, Booballet rode all the way out to the coast but found no sign of him.

When he reached the sandy shore, he noticed that all the Sagans were absent. There was no sight of the fast wooden warships either. The beast galloped down the coast and found the equipment that was left behind. After he looked over the spoils, the hairy barbarian rode down to the end of the rocky coast. There the cliffs tower over the ocean's edge and the waves thundered down below.

He raced around the hills outside the canyon looking for

any sign of the chariot. He rode the horse near the edge so he could peer down into the deep gorge. The Sagans had vanished into hiding without a trace. Booballet stopped at the long straightaway and looked down where his brother was killed. The hot sun burned over head in the sky, for it was the season of prevailing heat.

    The sturdy giant tried to think of a spot where they might be hiding. He pulled the reins of his white horse and headed for the rocky cliff that overlooked the sea. When he topped the hill, he looked for tracks of the chariot hoping that it might have left behind as a clue, but there was no hint or trace of it anywhere.

    The general foraged the island, and desperately devised a plan all the while to evoke his revenge. He scrutinized every track of land on the island. The beast explored in the high mountains and the valley where the mighty river flowed. Booballet pursued Brunto until his horse collapsed and died.

Magoonagoon

CHAPTER 41
The Ogre

The next morning, Booballet entered the stronghold and there the Foucinians rejoiced at his return. The men came to see him as well, and they cheered with the hairy horde. Booballet passed by them in the street and encouraged their applause. However, there was one in the crowd that did not delight. The vile ogre hobbled into their presence with an evil swagger. Booballet passed in front of the ogre to reach the fountain. There at the fountain he dipped a gourd into the water and drank.

The ogre stood above them with his vile and putrid skin dripping with sweat. The men were overcome by his stench. The monster looked down at the crowd as the soldiers scurried about in front of him. The green giant laid his massive weapon, the spiked club, down at his repulsive feet. From his imposing nostrils the ogre sniffed, as though he was looking for a meal. At the opportune moment the ogre snatched a helpless bystander as he passed. The ogre lifted the fellow off the ground with both of his foul hands. He wrapped them tightly around the man's waist, and the sheer force of the grip cracked his bones.

Then the ogre did the unthinkable. As the man struggled in the behemoth's grip, the ogre bit off the fellow's head. He seemed to smile as he crunched and chomped at the skull. The crude monster took another bite of the man as he swallowed the head. Silas and Percival were the first to arrive on the scene, as they rushed toward the beast. When they arrived, Silas borrowed a spear from his brother and took to fighting.

The ogre paid no attention to the threat, for his skin was tough as iron. The brute was covered with thick scar tissue and he was rotten to his ghastly bones. He laughed at Silas as he approached and continued to chew on the man. Booballet and the Foucinians ignored the skirmish, for they knew the dreadful manner of the ogre. Some of the Foucinians laughed at the ogre as he continued to crunch away at the man's bones. Silas stood before the evil fiend and cast his spear with the longing to kill him. However, the spear point bounced off the ogre's chest and fell to the ground. As the ogre finished devouring the man, he spoke.

"Fool! Do you not see I am eating?" mocked the beast.

"Murderer! In this instant, let me be the one to put you down! You have sealed your fate!" shouted Silas.

The ogre pinned another man down with a slap from his massive hand and grabbed the fellow tight. The vile creature picked the man up from the ground and bit off his leg. His yellow teeth ripped the leg from the man's body with ease. The man screamed out in agony as the ogre held him by the waist. As the ogre was chewing on the leg the prince gave out an order.

"After him! I want him dead!" shouted the prince.

With the prince's royal command, the men moved in attack. Victor came to the front and pushed toward the slobbering ogre. The ogre used his massive club to mash one of the men into the ground and the impact shook the buildings. The hit completely buried the man beneath the grime. It was then that Victor and the others attacked. Godwin and Eugene jumped at the beast with their swords. Aubrey lunged at the ogre with his spear, and Victor raced at the ogre with his javelins.

In his stride, Victor flung the first of his two javelins. The dart flew at the ogre's head and submerged into his neck. The beast let out a roar that could be heard all over Magoonagoon. The noise echoed in their ears and caused their heads to ring. Following the terrible shout, the monster propelled himself forward to strike back. With a wave, the spiked club in his rotten hand took out seven or eight men. Where those fell, others rushed to take their place in haste and fury.

The ogre strode forward, whacking and smashing as many men as he could. All the while, the captains and defenders worked diligently to bring him down. They surrounded him like hunting dogs that rallied to cripple a huge bear. He barreled out of the massive gate and struggled with them beyond the walls of the stronghold. The Foucinians remained inside the protected walls and elected not to join the men. This left the men in dismay, and once again the Foucinians forsook them.

The men continued their press without them. They bit at his wart-covered back with thrusts from their spears, and they hacked at his shins with their sharp weaponry. The host desired to exhaust the despicable giant with their unavailing assault. The ogre spat on one of the men and the disgusting spit knocked the bystander to the ground. Still, the ogre fought on with derogatory words for his assailants as they climbed on him.

"Ha! Heir to death! I am bestowed with vigor! For your stabs and pricks only arouse my anger! I may be the last of my kind! There is a reason for that! I am the greatest! I have outlived all the rest!" said the ogre with carnage on his mind.

The battle stretched into the lowlands and the ogre killed many of the men with his club. Aubrey surged at the ogre's chest and he thrust his sword deep into the green skin where it remained. Then the ogre reached down to grab at the man as he fell away. There his hand found the burly man of war. Victor drove his second javelin deep into the creature's flesh. The harpoon met the bone of the cursed ogre and brought forth the vile blood. Attaining the point, Victor spoke to the men.

"Beware of the blood from this wretch! It is bubbling poison!" shouted Victor as the toxin trickled out.

Near the outskirts of the wastelands, the men fought on with the ogre. The beast had not tired, and for that matter seemed to have strengthened. He crushed groups of them with each blow from his huge spiked club. The monster gnashed his yellow teeth and called out to them as he fought. Godwin had leaped on his back and rammed his spear point right in his spine. The spear dove to the bones and made the giant's limbs tingle.

Then the ogre flew mad, cursing at the men and urging them to fight harder. He chased after Aubrey, who skipped around in front of him searching for a weapon. His sword remained buried deep inside the fiend. The ogre chased and fought the men all the way to the sea. There near the waves, Victor intensified the quarrel. He was unarmed like Aubrey and they counted on the host of men to defend them. As the ogre lugged his massive club to nettle them, the brothers spoke one to another.

"Give me a javelin! Lend me a lance! I will put him down!" shouted Silas.

At that moment, Percival pitched his brother a lance. Silas caught it in one hand and his spirit soared from his chest. He raced out away from the giant monster and set his feet to make a throw. Just before he threw, he gave his brother a nod and a wink. All the practice and effort put forth in rehearsals delivered. As the javelin leapt from his hand, it bounced in flight. The bolt ripped into the eye of the villain and put it out. Then the ogre moaned a terrible sob and spoke to his attackers.

"You heathen! You have spoiled me! Scum! You have rendered me blind in my eye! I will smash you to bits!" said the ogre whacking his club.

Ahead of them in that forsaken land, Silas scurried away from the ogre to rearm. Silas found his brother again and furnished his hand with Percival's sword. As the ogre rushed at the man, he bent over at the waist with his arms stretched out and his mouth opened wide to devour him. As the giant roared, Silas ran straight for the ogre. When he drew close, the man set his feet firmly on the ground and leaped into the giant's mouth, slipping right down his throat. Inside the ogre's stomach, the man began to cut and hack with his sword. In moments, the ogre collapsed to his knees and began to curse the men as never before. With his last gasp, he moaned hateful words at them.

"Curse you! You vipers! Disdain and death to you all! Down to the depths with you! I hope you are all fitting meals for the Sagans. Curse you! Curse you!" grumbled the ogre.

Then the ogre fell over backwards and lay flat on the ground. He dropped his hammer as his huge hands fell loose. There, down by the waves, the creature died. His huge green body spoiled the coast with his rancid smell.

The men gathered around the ogre in shock and silence. None of them could believe what Silas had done. Percival fell to his knees in anguish and disbelief. As he cried aloud the others tried to comfort him. After the ogre had lain there for a moment, an echoing noise came from his fat belly. A sword pierced through the fat abdomen and began to saw a line. Quickly, the others climbed upon the carcass and tried to help the man escape from inside. They used their spears to pry apart the ribcage and sawed with their knives to free him.

"Be mindful of the poison!" shouted Victor.

Silas surfaced from the depths in affliction, gasping for breath and reeking of bile. After he caught his breath, Silas emerged triumphantly to the shouts and cheers of his comrades. The greatest ogre to have ever lived had faded at the hands of mankind.

Magoonagoon

CHAPTER 42

Sapsoon

The Foucinians began to get comfortable with the idea that the Sagans were gone for good, and it looked as though they would never return. Nevertheless, the Sagan ships were on their way back to Magoonagoon. The slender vessels tossed back and forth in the waves as they challenged the sea. The large red-and-white-striped sails were hoisted to catch the mighty wind. Aiding the sails were the human slaves that were forced to row the mighty oars. Those poor souls were in complete misery. The Sagans jumped at the opportunity to kill anyone who made a mistake. They were constantly beating the rowers and degrading them with foul language. Food was only given to those who were completely focused on their assigned task. No man was able to rest for those who were intended to be reliefs had to take the spots of the dead.

Out in front, on the lead ship, the great Sapsoon rode the waves with his band of pirates. Among the Sagans was the smooth pilot Ruffio, who had steered them past the dangerous rocks a second time. Appreciative as they were, Sapsoon and his soldiers were through playing games and for that matter ready to take back control of the ship. His cavalier attitude could be bridled for only so long and his temper was running hot.

Since the emperor had clearly given Ruffio the command, no Sagan moved to cross him. Throughout the trip Ruffio had feared a revolt, for he was among pirates and barbarians. He would have been wise to restore Sapsoon to power after passing through the rock barrier. Sapsoon stirred up his crew to take back the ship.

"All right! It's time to take back the ship! Take him! Get rid of this fledgling," shouted Sapsoon in the old Sagan tongues.

The Sagans ran at Ruffio with fury. Sapsoon's comrade, pulled his sword to stab the Sagan. Ruffio moved out of the way and the attacker planted his blade into the side of the ship. One of the others clutched his fists to fight the brown navigator. Another Sagan moved his broad shoulders in to smash Ruffio's head. As they laid hands on Ruffio, the cunning navigator spoke.

"Please! No! What are you doing?" asked Ruffio.

"Shut up!" shouted Sapsoon.

"Perhaps I should knock some sense into him," said one of the Sagans.

"Well then! Let's take back control of the ship, mates. Throw him overboard!" said Sapsoon with a grin.

"Seal your fate! Throw me over! If you desire to die…so be it. Brunto will find out what you have done! Then you'll be dead!" shouted Ruffio.

"Brunto? Oh! You simpleton! You said yourself that he was dead! Your cowardly brother cannot protect you!" said Sapsoon as he laughed.

"Brunto lives! He is alive! Soon! He will find you!" shouted Ruffio with fear crippling his knees.

"Throw him over the side!" said Sapsoon.

"This is mutiny! Do you know what you're doing?" yelled Ruffio as the Sagans held him over their heads.

"Wait! Hold him for me," said Sapsoon.

The pirates held Ruffio's arms and legs so that he could not move. Sapsoon walked over to the Sagan and punched him hard in the stomach. Ruffio gasped for breath as he hung his head. Sapsoon then pulled his knife from his leather belt.

"Strip off his armor! What do you think? We should dip our nets into the sea for a catch? We are hungry! Are we not? Should we try to catch a fish?" asked Sapsoon as he sliced Ruffio on the arm.

"Use him as bait!" shouted one of the bandits with glee.

"Put him in the net! You can't be too careful with this sort of thing. Tie his hands and feet!" said Sapsoon as he sliced Ruffio on the knee with his sharp knife. The soldiers all laughed and enjoyed Sapsoon's remarks.

"You will pay for this," said Ruffio.

"Ha! Ha! Ha! Is that so? Well, we had better make sure

that the monsters find you then. We will have to entice them a bit," said Sapsoon as he jabbed his knife into Ruffio's shoulder. Ruffio wailed in pain from the deep wound.

"Throw him overboard!" commanded Sapsoon.

The gang of bandits carried Ruffio down the large wooden deck of the great ship and tossed him into the surf. His body was entangled in the large fishing net. Ruffio's shoulder grazed the rough barnacles on the hull of the ship as he bobbed in the ocean waves. The Sagan's blood spilled out in the salty water as the net bashed against the boat. A host of them held the Sagan under the waves with the long wooden paddles trying to drown him.

"Crank out the boom and drag him for a stretch," commanded Sapsoon.

Two of the sailors turned the crank and moved the net away from the boat. Ruffio struggled to free his hands, but there was no chance of breaking the strong ropes.

"Ha! Ha! Ha! Don't drown him under the waves! We want the monsters of the deep to eat him alive," said a Sagan. At that moment one of the Sagans on the deck shouted to the rest and pointed to the surf.

"Look there is a big one!" said the Sagan.

"Sapsoon, what if he is right? You may be making a mistake," asked one of the Sagans.

"Oh! I hope you are making a mistake! Ha! Ha! Ha! When Brunto finds out what you have done, he will put his spear in your chest," jokingly said Sandion.

"Brunto? That coward is dead. Sent away in shame. We have nothing to fear from him!" yelled Sapsoon.

All the Sagans on the deck pushed to see at the edge. The large monster had reached the net where Ruffio struggled to live. Its huge teeth snapped the line that held the net, setting the Sagan free. When the net came loose one of his soldiers spoke.

"He's dead now," said one of the Sagans.

"It's too bad that I won't get to witness him getting eaten by that monster," said Sapsoon.

Magoonagoon
CHAPTER 43
Booballet

Sapsoon, the old pirate, quickly took charge of his ship. The first thing he did was raid the wine cabinet. Straightaway the Sagan found a bottle of dark red wine and turned it up to drink. Sapsoon drank every last drop and tossed the empty bottle aside after he finished. Then, he opened another bottle and drank it down just like the first. While the crew watched in amazement, the proud pirate stuck out his chest and began to give out commands to the crew.

"Listen, you fools! We will attack tonight! As soon as we land we will head for them! Anyone who wants to go can come along. Let the cowards stay behind and guard the humans!" said Sapsoon as he grinned at the crowd.

When the convoy reached the shallows of the harbor of Magoonagoon, the Sagans leaped over the side and dipped into the sea. The hundreds of warriors drudged through the surf to reach the shore. Then a great host of them joined the human captives to hoist the thick ropes and pull the ships aground.

After the equipment was unloaded, the powerful assault team mounted their horses and gathered at the edge of the beach. When they finally grouped everyone together, the warriors pressed toward the outpost on horseback. Thirty brave fighters rode through the desert sands to reach the high canyon walls.

The band of champions entered the canyon. Sapsoon's chariot raced out in front with the riders close behind. The tassels tied to the horses danced as they trampled down the pass. Stratogos followed the assault team on foot. The juggernaut was too large to ride a horse or fit in a chariot. It was impossible for Stratogos to keep up with the group, but he pressed on to keep from being labeled as a coward.

The squadron exited the canyon and entered the forest that stood between them and the outpost. Sapsoon guided his chariot to the front and held his sharp javelin high over his head. He swung the weapon from his fast chariot and smashed the neck of the Foucinian sentry on duty. Then the group of warriors invaded the outpost. Fierce hand-to-hand combat overwhelmed the Foucinians.

Inside the small fort rested the Foucinian champion Booballet. When he heard the chariots, he leaped to his feet and moved for his weaponry. He had no time to don his bright breastplate, nor did he place his fine helmet on his head. Instead, he grabbed his long spear and took hold of a round shield to battle.

Swords and spears clashed as the battle grew more intense. Sapsoon made a figure eight with his fast iron axle as he lashed the ponies hitched to his chariot. The Foucinians had grown complacent since they had not seen the Sagans for so many days.

They did not expect the attack, and most of them were caught off guard. The gates were open and none of the hairy beasts had put on their protective armor. Heavy casualties were being taken by the Foucinians. The outpost was overwhelmed by the powerful Sagans. Booballet got excited when he saw the chariot racing towards him. The beast's eyes grew wide because he thought it was the killer of his brother, the dastardly Brunto.

The glorious Booballet held out his arms and let out a roar. The beast tossed the round shield to the ground so he could hold the spear in both hands. As he clutched the long wooden spear, he gave his famous battle cry.

Sapsoon quickly turned the carriage toward Booballet. As the Sagan passed, Booballet swung his spear and struck Sapsoon hard near the collarbone. The wood found its mark on the neck of the Sagan with a hard thud. The proud pirate was picked clean off the chariot and rolled backward on the hard ground. The warlord quickly jumped from the dust and chased after his chariot looking over his shoulder with fear. Sapsoon cursed at his horses as he watched them dash out of sight.

Magoonagoon

CHAPTER 44
Swim For It

    Out in the ocean, Ruffio drifted on the current in the waves. The waves took him out to sea and away from the island. Ruffio was able to free himself from the fishing net and get to the surface. He had fought the large monster and won. Ruffio battled the intense sea and kicked to stay afloat. The Sagan struggled to stay above the waves as he paddled and splashed. He swam and kicked until he could touch bottom on a small sandbar. On the tiny refuge the Sagan began to rest. Ruffio was still in shock from his ride in the net, but pondered revenge.

    I will put my sword into the coward's belly and watch

him whimper in front of those slobs. When our soldiers find out what has happened, they will be outraged. Oh? But! How will they find out? There is no one who knows about this. I will walk on this sandbar as far as I can go. When I have gained back my strength, I will swim for it, thought Ruffio as he walked in the shallows.

Ha! I cannot swim that far. It would be suicide. Still, I was very close, when they put me astern. I might only have a few more waves to muster. I will use the hatred to urge me on. I will live only for revenge, thought the Sagan as he picked up some stones at his feet.

I will tie these stones to the large fishing net out in the deep. I will make a throw net to catch some fish. After I eat, I will catch my breath here on this shallow refuge. Then I will swim for Magoonagoon, thought Ruffio.

Ruffio treaded through the sea to the end of the sandbar and swam down to the bottom to retrieve the net. When he reached the clear bottom he used his talons to cut out a section of the net. He slipped his talons into the fibers of the strong cords. Ruffio stayed under the water as long as he could, but had to surface before he finished.

Ruffio returned to the bottom of the clear ocean. Ruffio's sleek feathers clung to his body as they gracefully slipped through the water. On his way down, Ruffio noticed a large school of red fish near the sandbar. At the bottom, the Sagan grabbed the large rope and heaved it to the surface. Ruffio used his powerful beak to saw through the tough fibers. When he finished, the Sagan grabbed the piece that he had cut and bobbed into the shallows. The brave Sagan slipped past the fish and treaded through the water across the sandbar. Ruffio bent his knees and sat down on the shoals of the surf. Exhausted and fatigued, the Sagan gasped for breath.

Ha! You are young. You should have more wind, thought Ruffio.

Ruffio did not waste any time and fastened the stones to the small net. Then he took the rope and divided it into three different pieces. After he separated them out, he tied one of them to the center of the newly made throw net.

"Now I will eat," said Ruffio.

Ruffio took the net under his arm and headed for the fish. When he reached the edge of the reef, he took the ends in his hands and flung the net out into the deep. The net stretched out like a spider's web in midair and touched down gently in the foamy sea. The net swallowed most of the red fish as it sank to the ocean floor. Ruffio had a firm grip on the rope and tried to reel it in.

"I got them!" yelled Ruffio.

The Sagan drug the massive host of fish to the center of the sandy refuge. Ruffio swallowed the first large red fish whole. He tore into the second slimy creature with his sharp beak and left only the bones. Ruffio gorged himself on the catch. After the Sagan had eaten plenty of good fish, he sat down to rest. Then the wise Ruffio pondered his situation.

I will wait for a clear night and map the journey by the stars, thought Ruffio.

Magoonagoon
CHAPTER 45
Now We Have Him

Back at the outpost, Booballet waited for the Sagans to attack him. The squad of Sagan fighters rode away from the mighty beast and gathered a great distance away in a huddle. There the host planned an attack against the loner. Even though they outnumbered the beast twenty to one, they still feared him for Booballet was the greatest of the Foucinians. The squadron of Sagans lined up and waited for the call to attack.

"Ha! The fool is ours!" said Atsuel.

"Yes! Now we have him! Let us take him together or he will pick us off one by one," said Sandion as she stretched out her long arms and showed her sword to everyone.

"Get off that horse!" shouted Sapsoon to one of his soldiers as he joined the crowd.

The soldier quickly gave Sapsoon his horse so the pirate could join in the attack. After Sapsoon mounted the animal, he wheeled her around to initiate a charge. As the Sagans began to advance, they aimed their weapons at the Foucinian champion. Booballet stood there by himself waiting for them patiently. The Foucinian did not turn around to run; instead he lifted his spear to fight. Sapsoon was a little surprised to see Booballet stay since he was clearly outnumbered and outmatched. The Sagan steered at the helm of his fast horse and the mighty warlord became the spearhead of attack. The squadron of Sagans quickly approached the valiant Foucinian as he ran straight for them.

Sandion rode her horse to the front and passed Sapsoon in a flash. Atsuel tagged behind Sandion with his gleaming armor. Booballet wasted no time as he mounted his charge and ran to the left flank of the Sagan force. The Foucinian champion quickly took out two of the Sagans as they passed. However, the convoy was able to wound Booballet as they passed by.

Then the Sagans made a second charge to try and kill the Foucinian fighter. The feathered combatants lashed out with their spears and jabbed at the monster with their swords as they passed. One of the Sagans fell from his sturdy white horse to the dirt with a crash. However, the kill cost Booballet an injury, as he suffered another wound from the bow of the archer. The arrow went in around the shoulder and buried in deep. But the powerful Booballet never slowed down, he moved on the offensive while the others positioned to turn around.

Sapsoon jerked on his leather straps and brought his horse to a halt. The feathered jackal cursed Booballet as he turned around, ripping the neck of the pony. Again the Sagans made another pass and again another fell among them. As the horses ran by, the mighty Stratogos arrived on foot. He had walked all the way from the sea and had finally caught up with the party. The giant wasted no time attacking and wounded Booballet in the side. With only the spear to protect himself, Booballet could not compete.

Stratogos had slammed his javelin through Booballet's shoulder blade. Wounded and weary, Booballet kept his balance and snapped the wooden pike so he could continue fighting. The wood broke and jarred against the bone. As the Sagans regrouped, Booballet caught another arrow in the stomach from the accurate archer.

Booballet staggered about in front of the Sagans as he cringed from all his wounds. He pulled the wooden arrow from his belly and tossed it to the ground with a deep groan. The Sagans turned around again and started to give chase. Before the crew of feathered demons took off, Sapsoon spoke.

"Wait! Put another arrow in the coward!" said Sapsoon.

The archer threaded the line of his bow and pointed the arrow toward the sky. He let the wooden shard fly from his hand. The single arrow climbed to the peak of its arch and slammed down in the knee of the brave champion.

"That will work! Hurry! Let's get him before Stratogos does!" said Sapsoon.

Sandion kicked her horse in the sides and beat its hind quarters with the side of her sword. She knew the next blow would bring down the beast, and she wanted to get there first. Atsuel followed close behind the murderer with his sword in hand. Sapsoon brought his horse up to top speed and quickly caught up with the pair. As the Sagans raced, they watched their comrade Stratogos waddling around Booballet intimidating the beast with roaring vaunts.

Booballet tried to assault Stratogos but only managed to get up to a trot before he collapsed to his knees. Sapsoon flew past Sandion and Atsuel with ease as Stratogos moved in for the kill. Booballet had managed to climb back to his feet and he dared them to come closer. At the last possible moment, Sapsoon darted in front of Stratogos and slashed at Booballet with his sword. The swift move gave the beast a fatal wound.

Still on his feet, Booballet found death from a blow to the chest from Sandion. The female ran him through with her curved sword. The blade was driven deep into his sternum, and Sandion lost her grip of the handle as it clung to the flesh. Booballet fell to the ground with the sword still inside his hairy body. As he fell, Stratogos jumped on him with both feet snapping his bones. It was an immeasurable victory for the Sagans.

Magoonagoon

CHAPTER 46
Take Credit

In disbelief, the Sagans gathered around the body of Booballet as the wind began to blow against their feathers. A sense of pride began to creep within their chests and the spirit grew dangerous. First they babbled in the old Sagan tongues, and then the group began to cheer in sequence. They had killed the best of the Foucinians. Sapsoon held up his arms and was the first to speak with flamboyance.

"I have killed him!" boasted Sapsoon.

"Ha! Sandion made the kill!" said Atsuel.

"No. No. No. It was Sapsoon! Who took him!" shouted

Stratogos.

"Whose sword is in his belly?" asked Sandion, pointing to the sword. Sapsoon grinned with glee and stepped down off the horse and noticed that Sandion was unarmed.

"Oh? It looks like it's mine," said Sapsoon as he pulled the sword out of the dead body.

Sapsoon pointed the sharp blade at Sandion and motioned for Atsuel to move back. Stratogos bullied his way in to the thick of things to join Sapsoon. When Sapsoon saw Stratogos join him he nodded his ugly head and grinned. With a little whirr, Sapsoon spoke to the crowd.

"I will take credit for this kill, Sandion. You will not question it. You will agree with this or die," said Sapsoon.

"Kill her anyway! While she is unarmed!" shouted one of the soldiers.

Atsuel quickly tossed Sandion his sword. Sandion caught the sword with quickness and propelled the group away with a wave from the sleek blade. As they moved back, Sandion moved to sway their opinion. She popped her long neck as she stretched it to the right and left, but before the murderer had a chance to attack, the archer stepped into the skirmish. He pointed his sharp arrow right above Sandion's armor in a vulnerable place.

"It looks like you won't get the chance to use that," said Sapsoon as the feathers on his neck rose.

"Drop the sword or die!" yelled the archer with wide eyes. Seeing the arrow's sharp point, Sandion tossed her sharp sword to the ground.

"That's a wise move, Sandion. But I am afraid it will not save your life. Kill her!" said Sapsoon as he leered at her with wide eyes. Sandion stepped her horse back in surprise.

"You're dead!" yelled Sandion as she jumped down from the mare to reach her sword.

Sandion caught an arrow in the shoulder inches away from her gleaming armor. Sapsoon took hold of a spear and thrust it into Sandion's leg, spinning her around in the dirt. With a leap, Stratogos was upon her with pounding blows. Atsuel dismounted to help his comrade, but the title of hand-to-hand combat belonged to Stratogos. He took Atsuel to his knees with a smooth blow from his fist. Sapsoon grabbed Sandion's horse and dashed out of the way. Stratogos picked Sandion up over his head and threw her as far as he could. Sandion landed with a thud and gave a terrible groan. Then the warlord gave strict orders to the rest of the team with a shriek.

"She is dead! Leave her!" said Sapsoon.

"Grab Atsuel's horse and we will leave him here to die as well. Load up the body of Booballet so we may boast it before the others!" said Sapsoon. Some of the soldiers scrambled to take hold of Atsuel's horse. Sapsoon and his warriors started to ride away, and they laughed as they fled.

Magoonagoon

CHAPTER 47

Oh! You Do Now

As the others rode away, Sandion surprisingly climbed to her feet. The two forsaken Sagans limped their way through the woods toward the canyon. They found their way into the tall rock walls of the gorge. Sandion hobbled on her wounded leg, and with the help from her comrade Atsuel, the two searched for a place to hide. The wind blew against them and the sand burned their exposed skin. As the pair reached the tall walls of the canyon, they began to hear something in the distance.

"Do you hear that?" asked Atsuel.

"Yes. It sounds like it is coming from that cave," said

Sandion.

"Give me back my sword and I will take a look," said Atsuel.

"It's my sword now you laggard! I should stab you with it!" said Sandion as she scolded Atsuel and pushed him away.

"I thought you were injured. You look fine to me," said Atsuel.

"Idiot! Get off my foot!" shouted Sandion.

"I am trying to see!" shouted Atsuel.

"Be quiet you fool! We will go together," said Sandion. The pair climbed up the rocks and peered down into the cave. To their surprise, they saw Brunto and Iipkam beside a small campfire.

"So this is where you have been hiding," yelled Sandion causing Brunto and Iipkam to jump to their feet in shock.

"Oh, don't worry, we are alone. Left here to die," said Atsuel. Sandion staggered down to the fire and flopped down near its warm flames. Brunto gripped his sword tightly and carefully spoke.

"Who left you to die?" asked Brunto.

"Sapsoon and those treacherous pirates! That coward will pay for what he has done," said Sandion.

"I have no quarrel with Sapsoon," said Brunto.

"Oh! You do now!" said Atsuel.

"Why should I turn on Sapsoon?" asked Brunto. Atsuel started to speak, but Sandion stopped him.

"Shut up you fool! I want to lie down here and rest," said Sandion.

"If you wish to stay here, you must obey my command,"

said Brunto.

"Huh! I should spit in your face! Why would I? You have been labeled a coward." asked Sandion.

"Should the head of that female stay on?" asked Iipkam.

"Leave her alone," said Brunto.

"What about him?" asked Iipkam, pointing at Atsuel.

"Ask him yourself," said Sandion.

"Will you be loyal to Brunto?" asked Iipkam.

"I don't have a sword so my answer will have to be, yes," said Atsuel.

"Good! Then tell me the reason why I should have a quarrel with Sapsoon," said Brunto.

"Because he killed your brother," said Atsuel. Brunto wailed in agony.

"Killed him? Why?" asked Iipkam.

"Hold on! He may still be alive," said Sandion.

"What do you mean?" asked Brunto.

"Sapsoon had him thrown overboard on the way back from our journey," said Sandion.

"Thrown overboard? What for?" asked Brunto.

"He was piloting Sapsoon's vessel by orders from the emperor. With you gone, Ruffio is the only one who could navigate the narrow rock passage. Once Ruffio had steered them through, he was of no further use to the swindler," said Sandion.

"Mark my words. That feathered snake will die," said Brunto as he started out of the cave in rage.

"Hold on, Brunto! Do not go after that fool alone. Give us time to recover from our wounds and we will help you," said Atsuel.

"Yes. Let me regain my strength and I will help you kill them all. Every last one of them," said Sandion.

So they made a pact and swore on their own lives. The four of them declared revenge as they sat by the fire. As the night slipped away, they hid in the safety of the cave.

Magoonagoon

CHAPTER 48

The Secret Army

Back in the land of man, Simon, the new owner of the whale tusk, felt burdened. He had watched as Julian's soldiers had chased Oliver out of the palace. He had stood by while they tried to kill the boy. He did not want the fellow dead and hoped that there might be others who had the same feelings. He thought to himself.

Who am I? I'm nobody. What can I do? thought Simon.

Days later, Simon was up on the third story of the castle cleaning the room Julian liked to stay in. After he had dusted the furniture, swept the room, and washed the floor he sat down for a moment to rest. Just as the man had sat down, Julian came into the room and scolded the fellow for not working.

"What do you think you are doing? I don't pay you to sit around. Get up!" shouted Julian.

"I am sorry sir," said Simon.

"What did you say?" asked Julian thinking he said something derogatory.

"I said that I am sorry," said Simon.

"That's not what you said. I heard what you said. Get over here!" commanded Julian.

Simon quickly approached the mercenary. Julian met the man in the center of the room and slapped him across the face. Simon humbly turned his head and waited for Julian's next move. The mercenary waited for Simon to give an apology, but when he did not speak Julian gave him an order.

"Get out! Get out of this place before I throw you out the window!" said Julian rudely.

Simon quickly left the room and headed down the hallway. When he reached the stairs that led to the exit, the man stopped and wondered why this had happened. As he stood there and looked over the great room, something inside the man snapped. He turned his head and looked back down the hallway for the last time. He walked out of the castle and went home.

When Simon got home he went and sat down in his room. As he stared at the wall and thought about what had just happened, his eyes looked upon the whale tusk. It was leaning up in the corner of the room all by itself. The fellow got up from his seat and walked over to the corner and picked up the tusk. The man looked into the whale tusk with all its luster, and when he peered into its ambiance it took control of his thoughts.

You must help him, thought Simon. The whale tusk called to him again and again. It soared into his heart and rallied his spirit to the forefront of courage.

Now I know what to do. No one will ever treat me that way again, thought Simon.

He searched throughout the land and found enough daring men to form a secret army. All across the land there were whispers of a secret army. Rumors spread that a great warrior was headed for Magoonagoon and he was collecting volunteers to go with him. The stories grew and encouraged brave men to come in droves. Simon knew that his reputation as a warrior was fake. He had never been in a battle. As a matter of fact, the only fight he had ever been in was the one with Julian. Still, he dared not tell anyone that he was only a servant.

The rumors reached the ears of the sorcerer. While looking for Jonathon, Oliver found out about the army and soon he and Felix traveled to meet with these soldiers. During the cover of night, they came to the hideout of the secret army. Seeing them at the shoreline, the sorcerer spoke to them.

"Who here on this shore, is daring enough to travel to Magoonagoon?" asked Oliver.

"Who is it that asks? Show yourselves!" asked Simon as the two boys came into the light.

"Let it be said before all! Let it be told for centuries! These before me now are bestowed with the greatest of fortitude," said Oliver.

"He is the one! The one they tried to capture! He has escaped from their clutches! Ha! This is the boy that I spoke of! The one who battled the entire regiment by himself. Ho! Men!

This must be the sorcerer!" said Simon.

"May we join you? We need to get back to Magoonagoon," asked the sorcerer.

"Absolutely! You are both welcome here," said Simon.

Simon's initial thought was to give them food and drink, but he knew what must be done first. The whale tusk took control of his thoughts once more and demanded him to pass ownership back to the wizard. Seeing the sorcerer, Simon moved to transfer the tusk back to its rightful owner. After he handed the whale tusk back to Oliver, Simon brought them to his tent and offered them food and drink.

The two boys ate and rested with the volunteers until late that night. Then Simon offered them a place to sleep down by the ocean not far from the ships. The two boys thankfully accepted the hospitality and slept there through the night. Early the next day, the boys were awakened by one of the volunteers.

"Quick! Get up! They are coming! Get ready to battle. Simon has ordered everyone to arm and defend the boats. An army approaches," said the man.

Just as those words were spoken, a huge army flooded onto the beach. The garrison walked over the dunes and clanged onto the shore. There were so many men with the force that they made the volunteers look like only a handful. Simon and the others realized that they were outnumbered and they thought they were doomed. To everyone's surprise the army stopped when they came into range and the leader of the troops came forward.

"In the name of the king! Her majesty! Princess Penelope! By royal command! Orders the leader of this band to come forward!" shouted the spokesman.

Simon almost swallowed his own tongue. Nevertheless, the man stepped forward and approached the congregation with quick steps. He walked within range of the speaker and told the man that he was the leader.

"I have a message for you sir from the princess. If you are headed for Magoonagoon she wishes that you will see to it that a message gets delivered to the prince," said the speaker.

"I will see that it gets done," answered Simon.

"Good! All these men you see here will be accompanying you on your journey complements of her majesty, the Princess Penelope. They are in your charge until you join up with the prince," said the spokesman and the volunteers erupted into joyful cheering.

Later that day, as the men were fellowshipping together, Julian's men came onto the scene in attack. Heavily armed men rushed onto the beach with swords and shields drawn. They leapt over the dunes and began their assault by racing into the volunteers.

"Felix! Get to the ships!" shouted Oliver.

Felix and many others raced for the ships while the betrayers advanced toward them with their bright weaponry. They marched into the contest with the meaning to vex every last one of them. At the front, men hoisted spears with sharp tips. Behind them, droves of warriors with hard steel darts and daggers clamored and clanged. Then the host of them plunged into battle near the ships. The soldiers rushed before the ships and the armies became tangled together like knotted ropes.

Oliver waved the whale tusk and exhausted many of the

adversaries as they advanced. Beside him, Simon stood defending the ships. Wave after wave of unyielding fighters sprang up; adamant soldiers they were, ready to annihilate everyone in their path. They pushed the secret army and the king's men back to the brink. The number of turncoats grew exceedingly difficult and when it appeared most bleak, the villain himself showed up. As his soldiers engulfed the group of volunteers, Julian gave out commands.

"Bring on the catapults!" shouted Julian.

From the rear came the huge catapults. They rolled through the crowd with their squeaky wheels. The horses struggled to pull the heavy contraptions through the sand. The men tried to encourage the horses to drive the carts within close range, but the sand covered the wheels and buried them deep in the mire. When Julian saw the predicament they were in, he leapt up on a rock and spoke again.

"Clear the way! Help them with the catapults!" commanded Julian. Hearing the command, many of the soldiers rushed to pull the artillery. Within moments, they had them in place and ready to fire.

"They're getting away! Launch them at the ships!" shouted one of the officers.

"Bring me the leader! Bring me his head! I want to see the face of this so called greatest warrior in the land!" shouted Julian.

"Look! There he is!" shouted one of the soldiers to Julian.

"Him? That man there? You've got to be joking?" asked Julian.

When Julian looked at the man, he saw his former servant. He thought at first his eyes were playing tricks on him. Julian could not believe it. The so called warrior was his old servant. When their eyes met, Julian laughed and laughed until his men started to wonder if he had gone crazy. After he quit laughing, Julian angrily shouted to his soldiers.

"Fire at will!" shouted Julian.

The catapults began to hoist their ammunition out into the surf. Shot after shot missed its intended target until one of the ships was struck. The large stone smashed into the ship's side and wrecked the wooden planks. There the ship slowly sank and many aboard were killed. Some of the men had managed to swim to the other ships, but the terrible bombardment of stones made it almost impossible.

Julian's men were relentless as they climbed aboard the ships. On the decks, the sorcerer summoned up more magic and filled Simon's men with courage. When the men's spirits were lifted, they swung the momentum back into their favor.

On the shore, the catapults continued hurling stones at the ships. The deadly stones plunged into the ocean creating huge swells of aftershock. Oliver leaped upon the rail at the bow of the ship and yelled at Julian.

"Julian! You traitor! You have betrayed us all!" shouted Oliver.

In that instant, Felix saved Oliver from falling overboard, as the ship violently pitched in the waves. Oliver would have went over the side had not the fellow grabbed his cape. When the ships moved out of range, Julian's soldiers stopped attacking and they patiently awaited further orders from their leader. From the shore, Julian watched the force creeping out to sea and he debated with himself whether or not to continue the chase. The mercenary only waited a second longer and then he gave the order.

"Let them go! They are doomed anyway. They are sailing right into hell," said Julian.

Magoonagoon
CHAPTER 49
He Goes With You

Weeks later, during the night, Simon and the secret army approached the coasts of Magoonagoon. Near the sandy beaches the oars dipped into the shallows of the mighty surf. The sails had been lowered on arrival to the island. As their ships pitched along, they languished to find their hour, their time of revenge.

Oliver stood on the bow of the lead ship and ate the fresh olives found in the stored provisions. Simon paced back and forth behind him impatiently. Felix, the young son of Jonathon, sat in the shadows in rest. Now they had reached their destination. They had found the land of Magoonagoon.

"Drive the hull clear onto the beach! We will moor the ship on the sand!" commanded Simon.

The men turned the long poles over in the water, pitching the ship forward. The sleek wooden hull glided through the waves with ease. The large flags whipped in the wind above their heads. Oliver leaped upon the bow and peered along the shoreline for the enemy. Seeing the clear beach he directed them in like a true spotter. The sorcerer guided them forward to what looked to be a large rock on the coast. Then the wizard spoke to Simon.

"When we land, I must leave you. I must warn the others and tell the prince about you and your men," said Oliver.

"All right! When we land, go to him. Tell him of our arrival. For now we will unload the horses and set up our camp here on the coast," said Simon.

As the ships approached the beach, the stars in the night revealed the rock on the shore. Simon took out his telescope and scanned the shoreline. He noticed the rock on the empty beach lay stretched out as if it were a giant body. Simon discovered that it was the corpse of the dreadful ogre.

"This boy goes with you, Oliver. I am putting him in your charge. Stay near his side and be ready for anything," said Simon to them both.

"It may be too difficult for him. We will have to cover a lot of ground," said Oliver.

"He goes with you. It will be too dangerous with us. The rest of you be ready and do as I command! Get your swords up!" yelled Simon over his shoulder to his soldiers as the boat came to rest in the shallows.

"Simon! I hold this message for the prince. It is of great importance. It is my duty to deliver it to Prince Marion at once," said the messenger.

"Yes. I know. I have given my word that it shall be delivered," said Simon.

"Oliver. Take this man to the stronghold as well. Take twenty men and go. Go to the stronghold and deliver the message," commanded Simon and he quickly turned to address the others.

"Forward! Into the surf!" yelled Simon.

"Wait here for my return! Do not try to press inland without me. I will return," said Oliver, but Simon shook his head.

Into the shallows the men splashed. Their armor sparkled in the starlight. They clambered onto the beach with fury searching for the foe. There on the shoreline the host began to catch the putrid scent. The carcass of the dead ogre lay in front of them on the sandy beach. His ghastly body gurgled. Its vile stench still lingered around it, and the smell caused many of them to gag. The mammoth still leaked the deadly poison from his veins. Ahead of it in the distance, a group of tents huddled near a fire. Simon and his men plowed into the camp where the tents had been pitched. With ready spears and weaponry they tracked to kill the insurgents.

"The camp is empty!" yelled a man.

"Our advantage is surprise! When they return, we will ambush them!" said another.

Behind the man stood an eighteen-foot-tall Sagan, who had stayed behind to guard the tents from attack. The Sagan quickly snatched the man up by the neck with his strong hand. The tall Sagan picked him up off the ground and flung the man into the air. Seconds later the zip of an arrow whisked into the Sagan's chest. The mighty Sagan seemed unfazed and continued his assault. The powerful giant smashed the skulls of two brave men with his bare hands. Before the Sagan had a chance to kill another, Simon drove his spear into his feathers. The giant paused a moment and fell to the ground with a thud.

"Look how big he is. He is a monster," said one of the king's men.

"Burn the tents!" commanded one of the officers.

"No! I have other plans. Unload the horses!" said Simon.

At that moment the soldiers returned to the ocean and began to strip the ships clean of their equipment. They each went into the water and fetched their horse from the belly of the ships. Many went back into the surf a second time to get the long wooden pikes, called Sagan killers, which they had left behind. After sending the men to the ships, the leaders of the host discussed strategy and tactics.

Magoonagoon

CHAPTER 50
Enemy Territory

Deep inside enemy territory, the sorcerer crept his horse in the canyon. Like a sneaking fox, Oliver and Felix slipped through the darkness with the king's men following them close behind. Under the cloudy cover of night the pair guided the small group through the towering canyon walls with precaution. As they traveled Oliver instructed them all.

"Stay behind me. The Sagans have made a big mistake moving into the canyon," whispered Oliver.

"What do you mean?" asked one of the king's men.

"It is to our good fortune," said Felix.

"We really need to tell the others about this. Quick, hide over there," said Oliver, pointing to some large rocks and the group all hid behind the cover.

"Look at all those guards. This is not going to be easy," whispered Felix.

"It's good to have you along. I need you to create a diversion and get them to chase you," said Oliver.

Oliver grabbed the reins of his horse and dismounted. He handed the leather straps to Felix and the boy tied the two horses together. Oliver and the others hid behind the rocks in a crouched position.

"I don't know about this. What if they don't take the bait?" said Felix.

"Are you mad? In the name of the king! What are you doing? Is this the only way to the stronghold?" questioned the messenger.

"This is just a little detour. That's all. There is no need to get upset over it," said Oliver.

"You are going to get us all killed," said the messenger.

"He may be right Oliver. Are you sure you want to do this?" asked Felix.

"Yes. Don't worry about it. You will be fine. They will never catch those horses. You can out run them. When one gets tired…switch to the other," said Oliver.

"Let me help you battle these cowards. There are enough of us here, let's take them," suggested Felix with a smile.

"It is more important that you lead them away. When they give up the chase sneak around the canyon and hide in the forest. We will meet you there later tonight," said Oliver.

"Give me that small stone lying there," said Felix.

Oliver picked up the stone and tossed it to the boy. Felix gathered up the courage and rode toward the sentries. He stopped near one of the guards and flung the stone into the camp. The stone busted one of the Sagans in the side of the head. Felix then spoke from the saddle.

"Who is keeping watch here? It looks as though many of you are asleep!" yelled Felix. The guards began to come at Felix with their swords and spears. Sapsoon stood to his feet and quickly gave out commands.

"You three! Get him!" shouted Sapsoon, pointing at three of his soldiers.

But before the Sagan soldiers had a chance to use their weapons, Felix turned the horses around and fled. The three Sagans mounted their horses and gave chase. After they disbursed, Oliver and the small band cautiously slipped past the remaining soldiers by staying in the shadows. Oliver's strategy did not work out as well as he had planned, still they hid their swords from the fire's light and listened to the feathered soldiers speak.

"Those humans are so foolish. Why do they want to do things like that?" asked a Sagan.

"Because they are stupid! That is why!" said Sapsoon.

Oliver moved behind one of the Sagans and hunkered down in the darkness. The Sagan basked in the light of the fire as he laid there on his stomach. The other Sagans sat around the flames and drank the dark red wine. They had been roasting the carcass of a large mountain goat and were anxious to eat. One of the fattest Sagans finished gulping down a drink and rudely burped out loud. Oliver was just about to move from his hiding place when another patrol rode up to the dancing fire.

"Get down you fool! You're going to get us caught!" whispered the messenger.

The pack of soldiers drifted into the light and they jumped down off their strong horses. As their faces entered the light, Oliver began to recognize them. One of the large Sagans was Cassereen, the second in command. Cassereen was accompanied by other notables and captains who shoved their way into the light. The emperor's main supporter, the intelligent Cassereen, walked over and claimed his share of the juicy goat.

"Cassereen? Is that you?" asked Sapsoon with surprise.

"Yes. It is I," said Cassereen as he ripped away a piece of meat.

"Get up and salute the second in command! You fools!" shouted Sapsoon.

"What are you doing here in the canyon?" asked Cassereen.

"I go where I wish! What is it of your concern?" asked Sapsoon.

"Shut up you dog! You will soon find out!" shouted Cassereen.

"It's quite unusual to see you away from the emperor," said Sapsoon as he snarled and lowered his head.

"The emperor is on his way. I am here to announce his arrival," said Cassereen.

"What is he coming here for?" asked Sapsoon.

Cassereen paid no attention to the big monster as he concentrated on the piece of goat. One of the Sagans had made his way to his horse. He had sensed trouble from the arrival and made an effort to sneak off. The Sagan mounted his ride and pulled the reins of his mustang to leave the guard post. However, before the Sagan had a chance to get away, another party rode into the camp. The hooves of the horses pounded against the ground as they entered the light of the fire.

"Where is he? Where is the fumbling fool?" asked Oilaz.

The soldiers dismounted and entered the light bearing swords and shields. The swarm of soldiers quickly surrounded Sapsoon and secured the area. Overpowered and outnumbered, Sapsoon yielded to the force. The soldiers subdued him with their sharp weapons. Sapsoon wisely let the force take his sword while Oilaz approached. Sapsoon's soldiers kept as still as they could and listened. They were hesitant to move, fearing death from the guards. The royal guard Moojan held his silver sword against Sapsoon's throat. He dared the hulk to move with his weapon ready to kill.

"How have I angered you my emperor?" asked Sapsoon.

"Whose idea was it to move into the canyon?" asked Oilaz.

"It was my idea! It was time to press forward," said Sapsoon.

"You idiot! I am wondering if you thought this through," said Oilaz

"I am here to fight! We will press on! All the way to the stronghold!" shouted Sapsoon.

"Lift your head to the sky and peer on the peaks of the walls. Imagine for a moment thousands of spears and arrows raining down from those points," said Oilaz.

"We have scouts above the canyon, my emperor," said Sapsoon.

"Your recklessness with your command will cost you. Something has been brought to my attention that you must answer for," said Oilaz.

"What are you talking about? What do you speak of?" asked Sapsoon.

"All right! Tell me why you killed Ruffio?" asked Oilaz.

"Why do you point your finger at me? Tell these goons to lower their swords. This reckless display proves your fear!" shouted Sapsoon. Some of the emperor's soldiers immediately lowered their swords.

"No! Do not lower your defense. He will catch you off guard and take it from you," said Oilaz.

"Tell me the reason for this outrage. Everyone knows Ruffio is of no concern to you or anyone else," said Sapsoon.

"Speak carefully, Sapsoon! I swear to the host! I will order them to kill you," said Oilaz.

"Ruffio deserved to die. He was plotting all our deaths. He had plans to put my ship into the rocks," said Sapsoon.

"I have heard enough! Who will navigate the ships safely through the rock barrier the next time? You fool! Strip off his armor and take him out to the mudflats. A challenge has been made," said Oilaz causing Sapsoon to let out a high-pitched wail and push away some of the guards.

"Combat? Ha! Who has enough gall to challenge me? Who is it? Not one of you has a chance! Atsuel has fled into the desert fearing my hand. Who else could it be? It could only be you, Oilaz. There is no other worthy opponent," said Sapsoon, shaking his fist at the crowd.

"Oh! Don't worry, Sapsoon. I will not kill you in the arena," said the emperor.

"Who will it be then? Who beckons death? Who calls for my sword? There is no reason for fear! I will give them a quick death!" said Sapsoon.

"Before you boast too much, let me say you might have a reason to panic," said Oilaz.

"Well, who is it then? Who am I to fear? Is it Stratogos?" asked Sapsoon.

"Brunto," said Oilaz and chatter arose among the Sagans around the campfire.

"Brunto? He is not alive," said Sapsoon with fear in his eyes.

"He wants to avenge his brother's death!" shouted Oilaz.

"Why do you give him this chance? He is a deserter and an outcast!" said Sapsoon.

"I can answer that!" said Cassereen. Cassereen paused to wait for the emperor's approval.

"Well, go ahead," said Oilaz.

"Right after our ship landed, I was greeted by Atsuel and Sandion. They told me the story of their mistreatment. After you left them for dead, the pair found refuge with Brunto. I told them to fetch Brunto from hiding and take him to the lowlands. He is waiting for you there. You are in a great deal of trouble," said Cassereen.

"Take courage, Sapsoon. I am offering you a chance to redeem yourself. By letting you match with Brunto there is a slight chance you may live," said Oilaz.

"Brunto is no match for me!" shouted Sapsoon at the top of his lungs, and the shout echoed through the canyon.

"Maybe so. We shall see. You're lucky that I don't let Sandion tear you apart. For I will be the first to warn you, she has an evil glare in her eye," said Oilaz.

"Go and get the others!" yelled Sapsoon and one of the Sagans rushed to go after them. The rest of Sapsoon's soldiers climbed to their feet and headed toward the sea.

"Yes! Get them all! They all want to see this!" said Cassereen.

"Bring them to the lowlands!" said Sapsoon as the last of his soldiers left.

"Now you're all alone, Sapsoon. Maybe we should rough you up a bit," said Cassereen walking toward the warlord.

Cassereen drew his knife from his belt and showed it to Sapsoon with a grin. He cut away Sapsoon's armor and pitched it to the ground. As Cassereen pitched the knife, he planted a swift kick in the warlord's side.

"As soon as I kill Brunto you will be next," said Sapsoon, looking at Cassereen.

"Put him in shackles. I do not want this coward to have a chance to run," said Cassereen.

In the shadows, Oliver and the men waited until every Sagan had left. When the coast was clear, the boy walked over to the tasty goat and took a piece to eat. Oliver knew that he needed to warn the others that the emperor and the bulk of the Sagan army had returned. The king's men pleaded with Oliver and urged him to get them to their destination.

"Come on! Let's get out of here!" said one of the men.

"We don't have time to eat! Let's get going!" said another.

"Yes. What if they come back?" asked the messenger.

Oliver knew they were right. Still, he jokingly offered them a piece of the meat, but they frowned at him with glaring eyes. Oliver tossed the goat's leg into the fire. The small band moved with caution out of the canyon and into the forest. They had another close call on the way passing a patrol with many numbers. In the forest, he found Felix. The boy had out run the Sagans and had hid in the forest just as he had been instructed.

The sorcerer and Felix led the group of men out of the forest and made tracks toward the safety of the Foucinian stronghold; they barely took a breath in the cold night in fear of the lurking demons. Everywhere the two boys looked, they saw a Sagan, and every sound had them jumping. To the group's astonishment, the night sky began to glow with beautiful lights of wonder.

Magoonagoon

CHAPTER 51

The Meteor Shower

From the heavens came a beautiful display of lights. It was a magnificent site of bright green, orange, beautiful pink and dazzling red bursts. There were purple streaks, glowing yellow flashes and explosions. The men gazed at the spectacle in amazement. All the while the show grew closer to their positions. A giant ball of fire came roaring and tumbling down out of the night sky and landed a short distance away. The impact was so close to their position that the ground rolled in a giant wave. The group was knocked to the ground and the display grew exceedingly dangerous. It was at that very point when Oliver spoke.

"It's a meteor shower! Run for cover!" shouted the sorcerer.

Oliver and Felix raced their horses in one direction while the messenger and the king's men ran in the other. Giant burning stones came raining down on their heads. Marvelous sparkles and streaks of danger ricocheted off the ground. Oliver dismounted from his horse and used his magic to save Felix. A giant asteroid was headed straight for the boy. The rock was on its way to smash them both, but the wizard had redirected it at the last moment to save their lives. The blast threw Oliver from his horse. The magic saved both the horse and rider, but the shock sent the steed running away in horror.

The messenger and the king's men were hammered by the falling debris. Some of the men were killed instantly while others were wounded. There was no place to hide, nowhere to run from the terror. As it continued to fall, the messenger was struck by a huge meteor. The burning stone slammed him to the ground and paralyzed his limbs. There was no escape. The streaking stones mercilessly dropped from every angle in droves. Oliver's magic was once again pushed to an exceedingly dangerous point where he was so exhausted that he was vulnerable to death. When it appeared that they were going to die, the meteor shower dissipated. The shower had pummeled the king's men. None of them were standing. Without shelter or magical protection from Oliver, the fellows did not stand a chance.

Oliver and Felix raced over to them with the hope that they might still be alive. To their disappointment, they were all dead. Some of the meteors were still on fire and the intense smoke made it difficult to search for any survivors. When Oliver and Felix decided to give up the search, they heard a voice call to them.

"Over here!" said the voice.

The two boys ran to find the voice that called to them. Through the dense smoke they found the man. His poor legs were pinned by a giant stone and his arm was missing. The rest of his body was severely burned. The fellow pointed with his finger and stuttered with dying words.

"There…there…is the…the…message," said the fellow as he pointed to the message box.

Oliver knelt down to comfort the man but it was too late. The one fellow to survive the beating without the help of magic was dead. With his last failing breath he had managed to remind the two boys of the task to deliver the message. Felix went directly to the box and looked on it in amazement. The wooden box was unscathed. It did not even have a burn mark from all the embers. It lay there untouched by all the danger. With a lump in his throat, Felix spoke to the sorcerer.

"Do you think we should open it?" asked Felix.

"I don't know. What do you think is in it?" asked Oliver.

"It's something important," said Felix.

"Let's open it then. I'm not going to carry that box all over Magoonagoon," said Oliver.

"Well you'll have to unlock it," said Felix.

Oliver touched the lock with the tip of his whale tusk and it sparkled blue florescent light. In seconds, the lock fell from the hasp and the lid was opened. The two boys peered inside of the wooden box to see what treasures lay within. To their surprise the box contained a single letter bearing the seal of the king. The letter laid there on the base of the box.

What could be so important about this letter that an entire army of men came to this land to deliver it? thought Oliver.

Oliver placed his hands on his hips and took a second look down into the box. He shook his head in disbelief. The boy made a sigh and pondered some more. Felix waited only a moment longer, then the boy reached down and picked it up.

The sorcerer looked at Felix with uncertainty as the fellow placed his finger near the seal to tear it open. Oliver held up his hand and motioned for the boy to wait. Felix paused at the gesture and questioned him.

"Should I open it?" asked Felix.

"No. No. Don't even think of it. That letter is for the prince. Look how many men have gave their lives to protect it to this point. Honor them my friend by delivering it to the prince," said Oliver.

"I will," said Felix.

With these words the two moved on toward the stronghold on foot. Both horses had fled from the storm and now the two boys were alone. The wind blew and the night grew darker still as the clouds covered the moon. They were still miles away from the stronghold when they heard howling in the distance.

"Did you hear that? What was that?" asked Felix.

"Wolves," said Oliver with certainty.

Magoonagoon

CHAPTER 52

I Mark My Challenge

Out on the delta, Brunto waited with Sandion and Atsuel at his side. The three Sagans stood alone without torches. The trio kept their guard by the light of the stars, more celestials in the night than could ever be dreamed; many of them twinkling like flickering flames. They stayed in the saddle as they anticipated the arrival of Sapsoon and his soldiers.

Brunto decided to leave the comfort of his iron-axle chariot back in the confines of his cave. The Sagan did not want to make a triumphant return in his painted chariot so he traded the fast war carriage for the hard leather saddle. At least for this fight he had made a wise decision. For his return was one of controversy among the host.

In the distance, the trickling torch fires of the mob came into sight. The fires shimmered in the night poking holes in the blackness. After a few moments the pounding hooves of their horses caught the attention of their ears. Brunto felt a little nervous but showed absolutely no fear. Anger and revenge crept into the heart of the four-hundred-pound Sagan. The wooden spear in Brunto's hand began to pop and crack from his tight grip.

"Let's go!" said Sandion to Atsuel.

"Where are you going?" asked Brunto.

"To get your soldiers. They await our return on the coast," said Atsuel.

"Some of them will not join me," said Brunto.

"You will be surprised," said Sandion.

The pair galloped off toward the sea to rally the others. Brunto kicked his horse in the sides and raced to meet the multitude. He cut across the desert to meet up with the horde. The horse ran in perfect harmony stretching out his powerful neck. Brunto brought his horse to a stop in the direct path of the thundering herd. Brunto paused for a moment and then gave his famous battle cry. Instantly the mass of soldiers slowed to a gallop and approached the shadow with caution. Holding the spear over his head the feathered monster and his horse stood firm like a huge cornerstone on a great building.

"There he is! There is the coward who calls me to fight. All I want is to reach his heart with my spear," said Sapsoon as he wrestled in the shackles.

"Brunto! I did not figure you to show. However, your challenge will be recognized, and if you slay Sapsoon, you may rejoin us," said Oilaz.

"Dream that dream while you still can, Brunto! Because the nightmare will unfold before your eyes as I turn you cold," said Sapsoon as he almost fell off the horse.

"And…you, Sapsoon? If you topple Brunto? You will be restored," said Oilaz.

Brunto dismounted from his horse that he took from the Foucinian warrior Eescas. The constellations above them glowed with luminescence. The tall Sagan walked toward the procession of warriors and lifted his spear into the air once more.

"I mark my challenge!" shouted Brunto.

"You have marked your end. You will not die with honor Brunto. I will see to that," said Sapsoon.

Brunto reached back and drove the spear deep into the ground. Sapsoon shrieked with anger as he fumbled about on the horse. He struggled to free his hands so he might evoke his dreadful anger toward Brunto.

"Untie my hands! You fools! And give me a spear! I'll kill him! Let me end this weakling's life! You will soon find the same fate of your brother!" said Sapsoon.

Sapsoon jerked and tugged with his wrists to break the binds. With all his might he pulled on the thick chains. In an instant the giant fell from the mighty horse that carried him.

"I will have my vengeance! Curse your face!" shouted Brunto.

"Hold on! This contest should be even. Do you not all agree?" asked Cassereen.

"Oh! I don't think so. Sapsoon has been loyal to the army. He deserves a slight advantage," said Oilaz. Sapsoon's soldiers all cheered and raised their swords.

"Here! Here!" they shouted.

However, Sapsoon paid no thought to the speech. He staggered to his feet and pulled tight on the thick shackles until they broke. The warlord stretched out his muscular arms and shrieked his battle cry. Sapsoon, the proud pirate, did not wait for the ritual of the challenge. Instead the Sagan charged at Brunto with his fists. The two Sagans fought with fury, unable to conquer the skills of the other. Their feathers waved smoothly during the battle as they shifted and pitched their weight around.

Soon the older Sapsoon began to tire, but with a last effort he used the chains to plant some hard blows on Brunto's face. The hits knocked Brunto from his feet. Stunned at the power of the punches, Brunto moved back away from the red feathered Sagan. As chains met bone and the battle slowed, the old warlord spoke.

"Pick yourself up!" shouted Sapsoon. Just at that moment, a regiment of Sapsoon's soldiers rode up to the fight. One of the Sagans had obeyed the commands of Sapsoon and returned with all the ranks.

"Kill him! Kill him!" shouted one of the soldiers.

"Toss me a sword and I will kill him now!" shouted Sapsoon. Sapsoon turned to his soldiers and flexed his might.

"Not just yet!" shouted Oilaz, holding up his hands. Everyone stopped to hear the emperor speak.

"Take his armor off him!" commanded Oilaz.

Some of the soldiers hastily moved to strip the powerful

Brunto of his armor. It took twelve fully grown Sagans to hold him down. After they peeled away his breastplate, they pulled off his gleaming helmet. They tugged and ripped away some of his beautiful brown feathers. After they finished roughing him up they hastily retreated. The defenseless champion managed to grab one of the soldiers as they parted.

    The powerful brown Sagan tackled him to the ground and began to pound the soldier to death. After he finished, Brunto struggled to his feet and gasped for breath. The short moment of rest gave Brunto a regained strength. Then he quickly claimed the attention of all the soldiers by hoisting the dead Sagan over his head.

    The monster bent his knees and pitched the heavy body forward high into the air. The pounds of mass landed among Sapsoon's soldiers, knocking many to the ground. Brunto arched his back and began to beat his chest with his large fists.

    "Your poor old body is in a great deal of trouble, Sapsoon," said Cassereen.

    "Bring each sash here to me!" shouted Oilaz. The soldiers grabbed the tailored sashes made from fine silks and took them to the commander. Then the powerful Sapsoon began to speak to his soldiers.

    "Why do you set back away from the fighting? Is there not one among you with enough courage to lend me their spear? Or will the host of you flee like cowards in the night?" asked Sapsoon.

    "Oh! Sapsoon, you will not fight without a spear! I am not a coward!" yelled one of the Sagans as he tossed Sapsoon his long spear. Sapsoon caught the wooden javelin and spoke to his friend.

"I knew you would be the first soldier to come forward. Mark these words…your courage will not be forgotten," remarked Sapsoon.

Sapsoon turned around to see another procession of riders carrying torches. The leaders of the host rode right into the arena between the two challengers. Out of the darkness came the angry Sandion and her comrade Atsuel. Sandion rode right up to Sapsoon and pranced her horse around him. The red Sagan pushed Sapsoon with her powerful horse and gave him an evil stare.

"Curse you, Cassereen! Did you plan to start without us?" asked Atsuel with a snarl, twisting his neck into Cassereen's face.

"Oh! No! Atsuel! We want all of you here," proclaimed Cassereen as he laughed.

"That's good! Because all of Brunto's soldiers have journeyed here from their ships! They wanted to see for themselves their leader reborn," said Atsuel.

Sandion, the old female, continued to harass Sapsoon with her strong horse. She awkwardly forced the muscular horse to push on the big warlord. The powerful hooves and iron shoes stepped dangerously close to Sapsoon's feet. Sapsoon then began to speak to his guards.

"Guards! Get her away from me!" commanded Sapsoon.

The guards moved. Sapsoon held his ground and watched his guards scurry toward the female. No sooner than the small force got started, they were on the run again after Sandion warded them off with her powerful sword.

"For Ruffio! You will pay, Sapsoon! And we will not stop with just you. Your crew of pirates will also pay!" said one of Brunto's soldiers as he pointed across the way.

"Ha! Ha! Ha! You fool! After Brunto is dead where will you belong? Your words have marked your allegiance as well as your death!" shouted Sapsoon.

"What shall it be? Spears or swords?" interrupted Cassereen.

"Let us use knives and I'll slit his throat," said Brunto.

"Since Sapsoon has shown loyalty to the army, he will have the advantage. His craft is with the sword so swords will be the weapon," proclaimed Oilaz.

"Ha! Lucky for you, deserter! That means a quick death for you! No one can match my skills with the sword! I will cut him to pieces!" boasted Sapsoon.

"Let the challenge begin!" shouted Cassereen.

There was no time to form the circle so the boundary was not marked off. Their torches gleamed in the night and the soldiers chanted and squawked. They waited anxiously to slice and stab at the challengers. Brunto and Sapsoon turned to face each other in combat.

"You're dead!" shouted Sapsoon.

Magoonagoon

CHAPTER 53
My War Now

That same night, Simon sent scouts out to find the enemy while his secret army waited there on the coast. One of the scouts had ridden out to the wastelands and noticed the commotion of the fight between Sapsoon and Brunto. He could see the bright torches in the distance and knew from the squawking that it was the Sagans. So the scout turned the horse around and returned to the coast to alert the others.

When he reached the sandy shore, Simon and the other captains were there to meet him. Simon lifted his head from drawing in the sand and looked in surprise to see who had returned so quickly. The scout rode up to Simon and spoke.

"I found them! They are out on the mudflats. Not far from here," said the scout.

"This man will show us the way, let us make preparations for a night attack," said Simon.

"Oliver said to wait for his return," said one of the men.

Simon slapped the man across the face and shocked everyone in the gathering. The crowd gasped at the harshness of the correction and they murmured at the amendment. In that moment, Simon realized that he was acting just like Julian. The man thought to himself.

I am no better than Julian. What have I done? Still, I cannot show any sign of weakness. If I do, I will lose control of these men, thought Simon.

Simon quickly commanded a group of men to lay down wooden planks over the venom soaked sand where they could reach the ogre. The men carefully handed the boards to one another and they made a bridge over the smoking venom. When they had made a clear and safe path to the dead ogre Simon spoke to every man.

"Hear me now! Dip your spears and weapons into the ogre's carcass and spare not an inch! For it may save your life! For in the vile stench lies a coat of deadly poison that is lethal to the flesh," said Simon.

Just as the man commanded so they obeyed and heeded to the orders. They dipped the tips of their swords and long spears into the poison. After they finished, all the men mounted their horses and followed the scout away from the coast into the lowlands. They rode in silence and without their fires lit, for the stars shown so bright they did not need them. The men could see the challenge in the distance.

The humans could see the torches burning and they could hear the skirmish. Simon commanded his troops to move into formation and get ready for attack. He rode in front of the lines with his proud armor ahead of the host. Without fear or caution the dashing man led them toward the foe.

Simon then drew his sword out of the sheath and pointed it in the direction of the glowing fires. Other men on faster horses sped out ahead of him with fleeting strides. Without saying a word he kicked his horse harder and lashed the steed unsparingly. The man passed all the others and rode headlong toward the Sagans. The mighty procession of men followed the great leader in attack. They lowered their pikes and charged into the thick of feathered enemies. Many of the Sagans were caught off guard and fell by the hand of man. Before the Sagans knew what was going on they suffered many losses. The Sagans were run through with the wooden pikes that were covered in poison.

In the thick of the fighting, Sapsoon had his hands full with Brunto. The powerful champion began to slow down. Brunto climbed up on the ribs of a dead horse and gained some ground on the older Sapsoon. He took his sharp talons and dug them into the horse. Perched atop the high ground, Brunto took the advantage.

At the same time, Oilaz caught up with Simon. The tall emperor clipped him off his horse by denting his breastplate with his wooden javelin. Simon fell to the earth gasping for breath. The man peeked up to see the big talons on the emperor's massive foot. After gathering his thoughts he quickly jumped to his feet with a sword in hand. Seconds later, he found himself on the ground again after Oilaz cracked his ankle with the pike.

"You have shown a lot of courage! Attacking us with such a small force. Why have you come? This is not your war!" questioned Oilaz.

Simon started to speak but was interrupted by Oilaz's fist. The man was knocked several feet into the air and landed hard on his back. After the man slid to a stop, Oilaz walked over and placed his foot on the man's chest and put his weight down. The sheer force caused Simon to give up his sword. The big emperor reached down and grabbed the man by his ankle. He lifted Simon into the air and laughed.

"Answer me! Dog!" shouted Oilaz.

"It is my war now," mumbled Simon.

Magoonagoon

CHAPTER 54
Even Up the Odds

Oilaz called for the attention of his soldiers speaking in the Sagan tongues. All the Sagans stopped what they were doing and the war came to a hault. No doubt, the men had already been defeated. After they lost the element of surprise, the humans suffered tremendous losses. Sadly there were only a few humans left alive.

"Tell them to throw down their weapons and surrender," commanded Oilaz to Simon as he held him upside down by the ankle.

"Give up your weapons!" shouted Simon.

"Save this one only! Kill the rest!" yelled Oilaz with a grin and then he walked over to the battle between Sapsoon and Brunto.

"Can one of you not conquer the other? Sapsoon is this barbarian more than you can handle?" asked the Emperor.

At that moment Sapsoon took another tired swing at Brunto. Brunto blocked the sword in defense and repelled with a shot of his own. And the two champions began to battle again. Both of the feathered giants had already suffered many wounds from extensive fighting. Oilaz walked over to the fight, still holding Simon upside down by the ankle. The giant then tossed the man in between the two fighters.

"Let us even up the odds! Sapsoon gets the help from the human," said Oilaz.

Simon looked surprised when Oilaz pitched him a spear. The spear landed near the man within an arm's reach. Simon scurried to pick it up from the hard, dry ground. He clutched the wooden pike in his hand and stood to his feet. But before he had a chance to join in, Sapsoon gave the man the back of his fist sending him back down to the ground. Then the warlord spoke to the crowd.

"I don't need his help. I'll finish this fool on my own!" shouted Sapsoon at the top of his lungs.

Then Sapsoon put both hands on his sword and lifted the blade above his head. With a charge Sapsoon came at Brunto with the sword in his mighty clutches. Sapsoon attacked with fury and rage. The swords clanged and sparks flew. The two Sagans shoved on the blades trying to push each other down.

"You cannot match my strength, Sapsoon," said Brunto

as he pushed the older Sagan away with a grunt.

Sapsoon wasted no time in striking back. The old Sagan swung the blade at the feathered monster with all his might. Brunto blocked the powerful hit with his mighty sword, but as the sword struck the blade it flew from his hand. The sword flew through the air and stuck into the hard ground. Sapsoon's eyes grew wide with amazement.

Brunto could not believe he let go of his sword and struggled to think of his next move. Sapsoon quickly moved in between Brunto and his sword to insure his victory. The power of the blow rang the mighty hands of the master sword-wheeler and sent chills up his spine. Sapsoon then began to boast and gloat in front of the crowd.

"Ha! Ha! Ha! I have him! I have won! Victory is mine!" shouted Sapsoon, lifting his sword.

"Not yet! He must die!" shouted Oilaz as he grinned.

Sapsoon was eager to finish the job. He moved into position to make the kill. Brunto took steps back away from the warlord. Brunto began to realize that there was no way out of it now. Sapsoon sluggishly trotted at Brunto to end his life, but as luck would have it, Brunto backed into his spear he had planted in the ground earlier.

As soon as he felt the wooden javelin touch his back, he reached around to grab it. Just in time he used the pike to save his life. Brunto struck Sapsoon in the shoulder, knocking him from his feet. Sapsoon's sword sailed into the air away from his strong grip. Brunto had shattered the spear when he hit Sapsoon.

Since neither of them had a weapon, the pair then began to beat on each other with their fists trading hard blows. The transfer of weight and power was overwhelming to Simon, who sat there and watched in terrible fear. The battle changed hands many times with neither Sagan able to overtake the skills of the other. Sapsoon began to show some fatigue after Brunto punched him hard in the side.

Both of the Sagans were bleeding heavily. It seemed as though at any moment one of them could fall over dead. They began to stagger around the arena with lifeless eyes. Old Sapsoon was showing that he had a lot of pain in his side by hunching over to the left. It was then that the emperor spoke.

"This is a disgrace! I am ashamed of you both!" shouted Oilaz.

"Give me a sword! Please, I can no longer fight hand to hand!" shouted Sapsoon as he held his side.

"No! Do not give him a sword!" shouted Cassereen.

Sapsoon then began to retreat, staggering toward his soldiers. They quickly surrounded him and gave him a chance to catch his breath. He called for his horse and tried to climb up on the powerful steed. Sapsoon's soldiers begged for him to stay and fight. One of the Sagans even went to his aid trying to rally him back into battle, but the old warrior could take no more of it.

"Get back here and fight!" shouted Brunto as he limped toward Sapsoon's soldiers.

The old pirate paid him no attention and shrugged away. He locked his feet in the leather saddle and turned the tall horse to ride away. One of Sapsoon's soldiers grabbed the reins to prevent him from leaving the challenge. The big bull held the reins tight in his huge hand.

"Do not leave! It is a disgrace," said one of Sapsoon's

soldiers.

"Let me go," said Sapsoon with fear in his eyes.

"Why aren't they enforcing the boundary?" asked Cassereen.

Sapsoon's troops could not believe their eyes. Their fearless leader who had never run from a fight was leaving them. But as tough as he was, the old warlord could take no more pain. Sapsoon took a swing at the soldier who held the reins of his horse, forcing him to let go. As the soldier backed off, Sapsoon nudged the horse in the sides and began to ride away. He hunkered down on the horse's neck protecting his wounds.

"Come here and finish! I'll ring your scrawny neck!" shouted Brunto as he collapsed to his knees.

"I cannot believe this. The mighty Sapsoon has been defeated. Brunto is victorious!" shouted Oilaz.

Magoonagoon

CHAPTER 55
Message of Warning

Brunto's soldiers quickly surrounded their leader to give him aid. They congratulated their hero and helped him to stand with their hands on him. However, the celebration was cut short when the mighty emperor, Oilaz, spoke.

"Bring me the man!" shouted Oilaz.

The Sagan soldiers quickly grabbed Simon by the neck and legs and carried him before the emperor. When they reached a close distance, they tossed his body down at the Sagan's feet. Simon hit the ground with a thud and rolled in the dust with pain in his limbs. Oilaz stepped near to the man and put his large foot on Simon's chest, snapping the ribs.

"Now you have seen what these things are capable of. Look at the dead around us. These men are dangerous vipers that can be used to our advantage," said Oilaz pointing his finger at his troops and spurned the crowd with an evil look. Then he quickly gave out orders to his band of cutthroats.

"Take this man and cut off his ears. Then break his legs below the knee to keep him weak. Place him on the back of a horse and send him on his way. He will return to the Foucinians. He will be the one to tell this tale and give this message of warning," said the emperor.

The soldiers quickly leaped on the body of the man and tackled his strong arms and legs. Simon struggled to free himself from the binds, but it was no use…the Sagans had him overpowered. The huge soldiers snapped the man's strong shins with ease just below the knee while he screamed. Others took hold of the man's head and sliced through the thick cartilage of the ears. In the skirmish, they broke the man's arms and dislocated his shoulders.

When they finished, they put the man on a fast horse and he slumped over at the waist. Simon was unable to steady his shoulders from the broken ribs and his legs ached with wrenching pain as the Sagans forced his feet in the stirrups. Then they pointed the horse in the direction of the desert and gave it a smack on the rear. The horse ran in the night across the void with the wounded man on its back.

As soon as the man left, Brunto called for the red Sagan Sandion to come to the front. Sandion pushed her way through the crowd to meet the winner. Always at her side was the proud fighter Atsuel. When the two of them reached Brunto, he whispered to them regarding what to do with Sapsoon.

"If you want him, go get him. I want him dead!" said Brunto.

The pair of Sagans knew exactly what to do without hesitation. They strode long steps to their horses. Sandion mounted her powerful horse and waited for Atsuel. Atsuel also climbed on his mare and walked her over to Sandion's side. The pair rode off into the cool night. Atsuel and Sandion quickly stalked Sapsoon and arrived at the top of the canyon wall. There they dismounted from their horses, and waited to double-team the old Sagan. Sapsoon had reached the top and was searching for a place to hide where he could lie down and rest. When he met the two killers, he was caught off guard and surprised to see them. The evil pair gave him a second to catch his breath while they slashed their swords against the hard rocks. The iron blades sparked as they struck the stone. Atsuel and Sandion snarled and growled in their Sagan tongues as they stalked Sapsoon. Perplexed and outnumbered, Sapsoon was backed against the cliff. The old Sagan eased back away from their swords. Sapsoon was still exhausted from Brunto's attack and showed a lot of weariness. So seeing his end, he spoke to the pair.

"Have mercy! Let me go! Spare my life!" said Sapsoon.

"Ha! Now when you are at your end do you yield! This is better than revenge! To hear you cry like a whelp and beg for your life!" said Atsuel.

Then the two attacked again with shrewd fighting. At first the older Sagan put up a good fight, but he paid too much attention to Atsuel and Sandion had his arm. The powerful blade had severed the arm clean off, straight through the bone. The old Sagan let out a wail as the sword sliced through. The arm whisked over the side of the cliff as it tossed in the night. The drool dripped from Sandion's beak and her eyes grew wide with glee. The two taunted Sapsoon with swipes from their swords.

Again, Sapsoon began to beg for his life, but it was no use, because the two killers had one thing on their mind. Revenge flooded into their hearts. Sandion drove her sword through the pirate's heart and buried it all the way to the handle. The blade protruded out the Sagan's back and spewed blood. Sandion let go of the handle and stepped back to watch Sapsoon wobble around at the edge of the cliff. With a grin, the old female took both hands and gave Sapsoon a push. The old pirate flew over the edge and fell to his death from the tall bluff.

Magoonagoon

CHAPTER 56

Sapsoon's Lost Chariot

Oliver and Felix traveled across the land alone. When they had traveled a great distance, Felix spotted a silhouette in the darkness that looked like a dragon. When Oliver caught a glimpse of it his spirit was lifted. As the two boys journeyed closer to the object it whinnied at them. Felix gasped at the noise and the two boys proceeded on with caution. When they came close, the object moved and made a rolling noise. The sound sent chills over Felix and he stopped in his tracks.

"Is it a dragon?" asked Felix and Oliver chuckled.

Oliver held up his tusk and commanded it to glow. The

bright light revealed Sapsoon's lost chariot and the horses. The team trotted a few steps and stopped when their eyes adjusted to the ambiance. Oliver whistled for the horses and they came over to the boys. Felix grabbed the bridle of one of the horses and patted his neck.

"It looks like they could use some water," said Felix.

"You're right," said Oliver.

Oliver used his magic to make a gushing stream of water burst up from the ground and they all had a drink. The horses lapped up the cool water and filled their bellies with the refreshment. Then Oliver changed some of the stones into carrots and gave them to the horses. When the horses were finished eating, the boys climbed inside the cart and they rode toward the stronghold.

Magoonagoon

CHAPTER 57

In the Bush

Elsewhere in the night, the horse that carried Simon continued to run toward the center of the desert. It had carried the man on its back to the middle of nowhere, a place where the wind never blows. The dry sand parched the man's throat as the blood dripped from his head. He fell over backward on the horse's hindquarters and lay stretched out as if he were dead. With each step the horse grew closer to danger in the night. For in the darkness lurked a pride of lions on the prowl.

The horse grew winded and slowed to a trot on the cracked ground. The gallop soon turned to a walk and the walk pranced to a stop in the middle of the mudflats. The darkness turned to a twinkle of light as the moon came out from behind the clouds. When its light was shown, the keen eyesight and honed senses of the horse picked up the scent of the pride.

Startled by the reflection of the luminous green eyes around her, the horse called out in fear. Her muscles shook and the hair stood up on her neck as she danced about. The shaking was enough to cause one of Simon's feet to slip out of the stirrups of the saddle. The man fell to the side when the horse sprung up to run. Luckily, his other foot lodged in the leather stirrup, and kept him safe from the lions.

The lions gave chase in the hunt as the man was dragged across the coarse sand. The blood from his ears only added fuel to the chase and tempted the cats. They swiped at the horse's legs and slashed the muscles with marks from their claws. The horse worked to stay alive in fear of those pearly teeth. Nevertheless, deception took her when she ran straight into their trap of death. For ahead in the bushes lay the huge male in wait. When the horse passed the bush, the lion leaped upon her, tackling her. The lion dug his huge claws into her coat and sank in his white teeth. The bite jarred the swift horse and the claws ripped the skin, spilling forth the blood.

Simon's body pitched around from the force and he flipped off the horse like a slingshot. His body soared through the air and passed through the sky high above the cats. The man landed in the thick thorns of the bushes. The pangs sank into the man's back and bit at his neck like snakes. However, the thick thorns gave him protection against the golden hides of the killers.

Through the night there he remained, atop the thorny

desert bush, and out of the lions' reach. When the morning sun crawled up above the horizon, the lions fled to their den. The sun baked down upon the man and cooked the blood dry on his neck. For three days he lay in the bush. Each night the lions would come and roar at him. Then the buzzards circled over the warrior's head hoping to scavenge a meal.

    Simon may have met the torture of death if not for the Foucinian patrol that found him. The Foucinians carried the man back to the stronghold and gave him to Victor. Victor called for others to help him and they carried Simon to the palace where they could attend to his needs. Amelia washed away the blood and cleaned his wounds. After she had finished, they carried him to a bed and laid him down to rest. When the time was right, Amelia woke the fellow with water. Simon opened his eyes and looked upon her. To him she was the most beautiful girl he had ever seen. Simon tried to speak, but the girl touched his lips and gently whispered to him.

    "You are safe now. Rest," said Amelia.

    Several days later the two shared stories and thoughts explaining their journeys. Simon spoke the words of warning from the Sagans and Amelia listened with a heavy heart. When Simon told the maiden how many soldiers were lost, she fell to her knees in agony. The young girl ran out of the room and headed straight for her father. When she reached him, the girl gripped his powerful legs tightly and cried out loud.

    "Stand to your feet and explain what's wrong," said Victor.

    "You must come and hear what this man has said," said Amelia as she cried.

Victor gripped the girl's hand and they walked down to the room where Simon was kept. Amelia took Victor over to the bed and asked Simon to tell him the story. After Victor had heard how many men were lost, he withdrew from the room. He walked down to the fine fountain in the courtyard and there he washed his face and head with the clear water.

Magoonagoon

CHAPTER 58

No Other Choice

Soon all the men in the palace knew of the terrible loss and rumors of what had happened grew. When Victor made up his mind to do something about it, he straightway went to the leaders of the Foucinians. He moved to find Premo and speak to the elders of the tribes. Victor trotted down the streets of marble and entered the main house. In the house he found them eating at the table and quickly he approached the beasts. Prince Marion had arrived only minutes before and he was questioning Premo and the others about the rumors. Victor walked in on the conversation.

"If the Sagans have returned we must act quickly. We

need to make plans at once to secure this place," said Prince Marion.

When Victor came into the room, the stomping of his sandals caught their attention and the burly man moved to speak. But before the hulk opened his mouth, he leaped upon the table and kicked away a bowl. He took his huge fist and beat it against his chest as he began to grit his teeth.

"How can you set here and eat? The Sagans have returned. We should move on them now!" shouted Victor. None of the Foucinians spoke. Only the prince was brave enough to approach him with words.

"Victor? Is it true about the army?" asked Prince Marion.

"Your majesty, they are all dead. Oh! It is terrible! I have received news that hundreds are dead," Said Victor.

"Oh dear, just the lone survivor?" said the prince.

"Yes. They let him live to tell the story. We need to act quickly. My prince, their ships are still on the coast," said Victor privately to the prince.

"Their ships?" questioned the prince.

"We need to go and secure them so we will have a way home," whispered Victor just loud enough for the prince to hear him.

"Indeed! You're right," said the prince.

"Let's leave this place for good," whispered Victor.

Prince Marion's eyes grew wide from the startling comment. The shock only lasted for a moment and shortly after the prince frowned and rubbed his chin to think about it. The prince started to walk away, but Victor grabbed him by the arm. The man pulled the prince out of the range of their ears and he spoke once more.

"Your majesty. It is clear we are on our own. We should have never come to this place," said Victor.

"First, let's see what they want to do. If it is not clear, we will go," said Prince Marion.

Then the prince walked over to the table, placed his hands on the top, and leaned over to look at Premo. He glared at the beast with an angry expression on his face and continued his conversation with Premo.

"Premo what are you going to do about this?" asked Prince Marion.

"What do you expect me to do? They are all dead," said Premo.

"See here! If you don't listen to me now…I am going home," said Victor.

"Premo! Hear this man! If Victor has said that the time is now, this is the hour! Let's attack them before they have a chance to settle in. Let's hit them before they offload their supplies," said Prince Marion.

"All of you! Come with me! Come and see the man who they have sent to us as a warning!" said Victor. Premo stood from his seat and looked hard at the bearded man, deep into his dark blue eyes.

"I don't need to see that fool! Prepare to march! Wolneas! Call for the troops to arm and assemble at the street," commanded Premo.

"We need everyone this time! Not just another hit and run attack! Let's hit them with all we have got! Send out all the troops!" said the prince.

"You leave me no other choice! Go and get old Hob! If you want everyone, she is what you need. But, know this before we get her. You and your men will be the ones to cut the ropes! It will be the men who will set her free!" said Premo, and others followed his lead, administering to their battalions with haste.

The Foucinians opened the huge doors to the dragon's keep. Hundreds of Foucinians pulled and tugged on the massive trailer that carried the giant dragon. She was tied down with thousands of ropes, so many binds that the dragon could hardly breathe. When they rolled her into the light she growled at them and puffed a breath of air out of the large nostrils on her hideous face.

The Foucinians waited until every soldier had gathered near the gate before they made their march. They came out in droves wearing their proud armor and carrying their spears. Vindeen assumed the lead in his swift chariot at the front beside Premo. Vindeen took command of the army and called for the regiments to march to the mudflats. He trotted his horse out in front hoisting up his sword.

The troops flushed out of the gate and formed up into lines and columns. The charioteers led the way. In the middle, marched the archers with their deadly bows and behind them paraded the men. In the back, the bulk of the Foucinian infantry came muscling the trailer that carried the dragon. After the huge cart had passed through the mighty walls, the strong gate was shut.

The host moved through the valley and entered the forest. They headed for the outpost where the mighty Booballet had met his end. The air was cool in the deep woods of the forest and steam rose off the soldiers. The pace of the troopers was fast and they quickly moved out of the woodland into the area before the canyon.

Vindeen ordered scouts to head out front and be the eyes of the lethal force. The lookouts rode out ahead to protect the army from an ambush. When they had traveled a short distance, the scouts came across two young boys who shared a nimble chariot equipped with an iron axle. The wooden cart was drawn by two powerful horses and they were racing straight for the scouts. The riders happened to be Oliver and Felix, who had been desperately trying to find their way to the stronghold.

"Stop! Who are you and where do you think you are going?" asked the scout.

"We are allies headed for the stronghold!" said Oliver.

"The stronghold is empty. Every warrior in the land is right over there. They are just on the other side of that hill," said the scout.

"Permit us to join them then. We need to find the prince," said Felix.

"Go!" said the scout.

Oliver and Felix met the army on top of the hill as they pressed forward into battle. When they reached the Foucinian troops, Oliver stopped the chariot and climbed down from the cart. As the Foucinian procession passed by Oliver and Felix, the two desperately searched the lines for the prince. When they finally found him, Oliver shouted for his attention.

"Your majesty! I have returned!" shouted Oliver, but Prince Marion did not recognize the boy.

"Stand back, boy! What makes you think you can speak

to the prince!" said one of the guards as he pushed the sorcerer down to the ground.

Oliver watched the prince and his guards pass by as he sat there on the ground. For a moment he thought to leap to his feet and use his magic to correct them, but then he remembered that the men had sworn to kill him if he ever returned. The sorcerer smiled as he sat there on the ground and he was glad to remember the possibility of danger. Oliver had recalled the thought just in time, for at that moment Felix was just about to tell the prince about the letter. Just as Felix was getting ready to tell them, Oliver quickly covered the boy's mouth and tucked the letter away from view. At that very moment, all of the sorcerer's friends passed by. They all looked at the boys as they passed by but not one of the men recognized either of them.

"What do we do now?" asked Felix.

"The only thing we can do. Back to the chariot!" said Oliver.

Magoonagoon

CHAPTER 59

Long Live the King

"Wait! I have to give the prince the letter," said Felix.

"You're on your own then. I can't help you," said Oliver.

"Go with me," said Felix.

"I can't let them know who I am," replied Oliver.

"Well, at least wait for me here," said Felix as he jumped down from the cart.

The fellow raced ahead of them to try and speak to the prince once more. He ran past the crowd with a yearning to fulfill his duty. When he reached the prince he called out to him again.

"Your majesty! I have a letter here for you! It is from the princess," said Felix.

"Felix? Is that you? What are you doing here?" asked Victor.

"Oh! Uncle Victor! I am so glad to see you! I have this letter from the princess," said Felix.

"Hold it! What did you say?" asked the prince.

"I have a letter for you sir, it is from the princess," said Felix.

Victor got down from the chariot and walked over to his nephew. The prince eagerly waited inside his chariot. When Victor reached the boy and they met face to face, Victor gave his nephew a hug. After he had squeezed him tight, he patted him on the back and spoke to Felix once more.

"How did you get here?" asked Victor.

"That boy back there brought me here in the chariot," said Felix.

"No. I mean, how did you get to Magoonagoon?" asked Victor.

"I came with the secret army," said Felix reaching out to hand his uncle the letter.

As Victor accepted the letter, he studied it close. When his eyes saw the official seal of the king, his heart began to race. The man held up the letter and gestured to the prince's guardians that it was legitimate. The prince nodded his head, ordering one of his guards to go and collect the letter. Once the man had collected it, the designee took his finger and broke the seal. As he began to read the letter, he spoke to the boy.

"Where did you get this?" asked the guard.

"From the king's messenger," said Felix.

"The king's messenger? Where is he?" asked the guard as he continued to read.

"Before he passed, he asked me to deliver it to the prince," said Felix.

When the guard got to a certain part of the letter he humbly fell to the ground on his knees. The crowd noticed that the guard was distraught at the news and everyone wondered what the message had to say. When the tension had reached a point where things were getting out of hand, the prince got down from his chariot and collected the letter.

The prince looked at the guard, the boy, and Victor before he started to read. After the prince had read the first line and recognized the princess's handwriting, he took his eyes away from the letter to look at the boy again in wonder.

When the prince finished reading, he paused to look away again and shook his head. The prince patted the boy on the head and thanked him for delivering the note. Then the prince handed the letter to the boy and nonchalantly went back to his chariot. Felix looked at the letter and read it.

My love,

I have distraught news to share with you. My father, the king, has passed. We are all deeply saddened by his departure. He has left us after many wonderful years together. I miss you and hope to see you very soon. My darling you and I are now the king and queen.

Long live King Marion
Queen Penelope

The boy's heart began to race. He wondered what to do. Before he had clearly thought, the boy did what his heart told him to, he fell to his knees and spoke to the prince.

"Long live the king! King Marion!" said Felix.

After saying these words the crowd mimicked his actions and proclaimed Marion as their king. The crowd cheered and shouted with glee. After the crowd settled back down, Victor grabbed Felix by the arm and gave him clear orders.

"Get back in that chariot you were in and get to the stronghold," said Victor.

Magoonagoon

CHAPTER 60
I Never Dreamed

"Oliver! Victor ordered me to get back to the stronghold," said Felix.

"He did? Well. I guess I should get you there at once. Come on let's go," said Oliver.

The two boys raced away from the marching army and rushed toward the stronghold. The horses zipped down the hill and within moments, the two had reached the mighty Foucinian stronghold.

"How do you suppose we get in?" asked Felix as the approached the gate.

"I'll think of something," said Oliver. When they came into shouting distance of the wall, Oliver hollered to the watch.

"Open the gate!" shouted Oliver.

"Who goes there?" asked the watch.

"We seek refuge! Please let us in!" shouted Oliver.

The Foucinian lookout went behind the wall where the two boys could not see him. At first it appeared that the Foucinian was ignoring them, but then the boys heard voices at the gate. The voices were followed by a loud sound that must have been the lock. Then the huge door began to slide open. Felix and Oliver watched as the mighty gate opened just enough to allow the chariot to pass through. Felix was expecting the sorcerer to drive the chariot inside, but the fellow never moved.

"Aren't you staying here?" asked Felix as he sadly looked at Oliver.

"No. I am going back to help," said Oliver.

Felix climbed down from the chariot and walked inside the stronghold. Oliver waited until the boy was safely inside and he watched as the gate slowly rumbled to a close. After Oliver confirmed the boy was safe, he lashed the reins and steered the team back toward the battlefield. As Felix stood behind the giant gate and looked up at the towering wall he felt imprisoned and alone. The boy sadly walked through the elaborate gardens of splendor. Felix reached the point where he felt so sad and alone that he almost started to cry. When his eyes started to fill with tears he saw Amelia.

"Amelia, what are you doing here? I thought you stayed back at home," said Felix.

"I secretly snuck aboard one of the ships. Now I wish I

had listened to my father," said Amelia regretfully.

"At least you are safe. I never dreamed I would see you," said Felix.

"Yes. I am so glad you are here with me!" said Amelia.

"Me too, these Sagans are dangerous," stated Felix.

"So are the Foucinians. I am ready to go home," cried Amelia.

Magoonagoon
CHAPTER 61
Hold On

The Foucinians entered the desert void and began to search the terrain for signs of the enemy. As far as the eye could see lay the bones of fallen warriors; numerous were even the big Sagan skeletons, left behind to rot, scattered upon the dry wastelands. Dispersed across the great void also were the remains of many daring Foucinians. The carcasses brought fear to many of the soldiers as they waited for the Sagans to join them in battle. Wolneas brought the battalions to a halt as he checked the lines of warriors with his shrewd calls. The beast called for the trumpeters to blow their horns. They put their horns to their lips and announced their arrival to the sky. The loud battle horns screamed in the ears of the sleepy Sagans.

The feathered creatures were rudely awakened from their fine marble palaces and homes near the coast when they heard the trumpets blow. There in the camp, where they rested in luxury and splendor, Brunto and his band listened to the dreadful noise. Brunto stood to his feet and turned his ear to the sky to listen closely.

"Ha! They want to fight!" shouted Brunto.

"Let's give them one then," said Kounjab.

"Kounjab! You have looked over the humans haven't you?" asked Brunto.

"Ha! Have I looked at them? What a pitiful bunch. Thin, skinny, no meat on the bone. Not a man in the group worth having," said Kounjab.

"I am not talking about eating them you pig. Are there any warriors among them?" asked Brunto.

"Warriors? Ha! There is not one in the lot. I dare say there is not one in all the land," said Kounjab as he watched Brunto hobble off toward the slave holds.

Brunto made his way over to the place where the humans were kept. When he came near to the spot where they were imprisoned, the Sagan noticed a small boy sitting all by himself. The small fellow was resting on the ground with his little arms hugging his knees. The human glared at Brunto with a stare that worried the Sagan. Brunto noticed right away that the diminutive fellow was the one he wanted.

"Who are you?" asked Brunto as he gently pushed the boy's head with his fingers.

"What's it to you?" asked the fellow as he angrily lunged forward at the Sagan.

"Stand up and tell me your name," ordered Brunto.

"I am Emery!" shouted the boy rudely.

"Unlock this slave!" shouted Brunto to the taskmaster, and the Sagan quickly freed the boy.

As soon as the Sagan unlocked the binds and freed the lad, Emery tried to escape. The fellow started to run and may have bolted had not Brunto snatched him at the last possible second. The giant Sagan caught him by the shoulders and tackled the boy with his grip. As Brunto placed his other hand on Emery and got a better grip, he spoke to the fellow.

"You are free from the shackles, but now you belong to me. I will take this one with me," said Brunto as he grabbed hold of Emery's wrist and pulled him to his side.

Brunto drug the boy back to his camp and Emery fought him all the way there. The Brown Sagans were perplexed as they watched their leader walk into their camp wrestling a little boy. Brunto ignored their questions and took Emery straight to his tent. When they reached the abode, Brunto searched for the pouch that he had taken from the goblin. When he found it, the Sagan reached inside and used his fingers to get a pinch of the powder. Brunto sprinkled the magic dust over Emery's head and spoke a spell.

"No longer are you free! Under my command shall you be!" said Brunto with a grin.

Emery rubbed his eyes where the dust had made him blink. Brunto waited to see if the fellow would act any different. The big Sagan lowered his head and studied the lad closely. The

Sagan strained his eyes and looked at him with a disappointed look. Emery frowned and growled at the Sagan for sprinkling his head with the powder.

"Well? Did it work?" asked Kounjab as he studied the lad.

"Hmmh? At least he smells better," said Brunto as he sniffed the fellow.

"Let's eat him!" said Kounjab with a wild look in his eyes.

"All you think about is eating. Go and alert the others. Tell them to prepare for war," commanded Brunto.

Brunto and Emery walked out of the house. The boy was acting a little bit different. The fellow was calm and did not look as though he was going to try and escape so Brunto unrestrained him. The destroyer motioned for Emery to follow him and they moved over to the stables. At the stables they quickly moved to fasten the powerful horses to his prized chariot.

"This will be your job from now on, boy! Watch and study close," said Brunto.

He made sure Emery watched his every move. Brunto backed each horse into place and tied the heavy leather straps in place around the wooden plume. He steadied the pair of horses by placing the yoke in between. Brunto moved quickly to load the chariot with equipment from his tent. Emery stayed right on his heels with every step.

After the chariot was ready, Brunto finished fitting himself with his magnificent armor. First, he strapped on the massive breastplate with the golden trim over the bright yellow sash. It covered the shoulders and had just enough room around the neck. He tied the leather belt around his waist that held the sharp battle sword. Finally, Brunto placed his helmet on top of his head. When he was finished, the band marched out to meet the Foucinians on the mudflats.

When Brunto and his warriors reached the battlefield, they filed into place and waited for everyone to arrive. One by one the other tribes showed up. They all stood with poise, ready to strike at the emperor's command. It was Soociv who initiated the attack. He galloped the big horse out in front of the legions in a steady trot. He paused only for a moment to draw his sharp saber from his leather belt.

Soociv spun his horse around to face the Sagan army. He steadied the horse and peered at the army with his head lowered. Then, in one bold move the feathered man-eater stretched out his neck toward the sun and gave his war cry. The shout carried across the mudflats to the black ears of the Foucinians.

Soociv violently kicked his horse in the sides and headed across the field. The brave soldier rode way out in front of the armies on his own. The rest of the Sagans followed the warlord into battle shaking the ground with their steps.

"Hold on," said Brunto to Emery.

Young Emery gripped the rails of Brunto's famous chariot with all his strength. With a lash from the Sagan's whip the horses leaped forth. The spanking of the reins propelled the chariot across the desert sand. The pair caught up with Soociv in a flash. The iron-axle chariot sped across the cracked earth leaving a plume of dusty smoke behind. As they traveled Brunto instructed Emery to move in front of him and learn.

Magoonagoon

CHAPTER 62
Old Hob

"Cut her loose! Here they come you fools! Let her go!" shouted Premo at the men.

King Marion took his sword and began to hack away at the ropes that held the dragon. Seeing the king move with such urgency caused many of the men to join him. The swords cut the binds and the tight cords flipped away. When the dragon felt the change, she tried to stand. However, the old creature had been bound for so long that her joints were stiff. She snapped her jaws and growled at the men for being so close to her. Old Hob stretched out her arms and legs and the trailer shifted beneath her. When the trailer shifted the dragon grabbed hold of the wood with her sharp claws and growled again.

The men rushed away from her as she broke the rest of the binds. When the dragon stood up the remaining ropes snapped loose and old Hob was free. With one puff, fire consumed fifty men. The red hot flames cooked them to a crisp. She took a step and smothered a group of Foucinians with her deadly breath.

"Get away from her!" shouted the king.

The Foucinians ran away from her and moved across the field in attack. They made their push forward into combat with long steps and wide eyes. Vindeen raced to meet Soociv in contention. The hairy beast lowered his long wooden lance to joust the black Sagan. They converged in fury with thoughts of carnage and massacre. Vindeen planted the pike clean in the center of the giant's chest, knocking him from his proud horse.

Soociv flipped off the back of the black stallion and landed on the hard ground. The pike gave him a hard hit, but his life was spared with the protection of his breastplate. The waves of soldiers crashed together in strife. The shields and heavy armor collided in the sea of dissension.

The dragon snapped and bit a man with her sharp teeth. The man was impaled in the dragon's mouth and he dangled out the side screaming for help. The vile creature coughed out a flame that roasted the fellow's body away. When the dragon stopped, black smoke rolled out of her nostrils. Her forked tongue flipped around in her huge mouth as she roared.

Brunto slammed his spear into the face of one of the

hairy beasts. The mighty Foucinian fell to the earth and his armor struck the ground. The Sagan champion drove the chariot through the crowd lashing the swift trio of horses. He grabbed another spear in his huge hand to reload his mighty arm. Emery feared for his life as he hid beneath the rim of the chariot.

The feathered warrior continued his assault, hurling his long spears into the sea of foes. There was gnashing of teeth among the bloodshed as the Black Sagans of the cavalry raced headlong into the center. The horses trampled the warriors under their iron-shoed hooves.

Brunto and Emery drove through the chaos and rolled toward another chariot in front of them. The charioteer happened to be Oliver. The two chariots almost ran into each other as they dangerously passed. Oliver swerved out of the way and avoided the wreck. Brunto took the brazen spear and struck Oliver across the neck while his chariot flew by. The wooden pike broke in half and shattered at the hilt.

Oliver was knocked from the chariot and he flew through the air. The boy fell right into the hands of one of the big man-eating Sagans. Oliver hit the killer in the chin with his little fist and busted open his own knuckles. The monster tried to snatch the boy, but the clever wizard slipped out of his grip and quickly ran away. The Sagan chased Oliver back into the Foucinian lines taunting him with his sharp spear.

The dragon rose up on her hind legs and leaned back on her lengthy tail. Towering above them she surveyed the war and searched for her next victim. She watched closely for anyone who was foolish enough to come within her reach. As she sat there on her heavy bottom, the dragon took the opportunity to scratch her huge belly.

Brunto and Emery had reached the edge of the fighting and slowed the war chariot down to rearm. At the outskirts of battle, the Foucinians watched as the Sagan's chariot slowly came to a halt. There at the rim, Vindeen made his move. The Foucinian placed an arrow on the string and pulled back on the line. Vindeen took dead aim at the brown feathered Sagan as Brunto reached for another spear. The Foucinian let the arrow go and it climbed through the air. The wooden shaft reached its peak and tumbled to descent. The sharp iron tip struck Brunto on the shoulder blade above the back.

Vindeen hit his mark striking the brown Sagan in the back with his deadly missile. However, the arrow did not pass deep into the Sagan's tough skin. All it did was make the Sagan angry. The big Sagan reached over his shoulder and ripped the dart out of his flesh. The hulk looked through the carnage and warfare to find the assassin who launched the sharp torpedo.

Brunto sighted Vindeen lacing another arrow in his wooden curve. Brunto called to the horses and gave the reins a tug to the right. He turned the war cart around preparing for the assault. In the turn he spoke to the young Emery.

"Take hold of the reins and steady the horses. Run them straight at the beast. Above all, hold the course," said Brunto.

Emery grabbed the leather straps and steered the cart toward Vindeen as commanded. Brunto armed himself with two javelins in each hand from the rack in the chariot. He raised the wooden torpedoes into the air to yell shrewd hate across the field. From the saddle, Vindeen pitched yet another arrow at the behemoth. The arrow soared through the sky and planted its shard deep in the Sagan's thigh.

Brunto shuttered in pain, but remained a fortress. As Emery closed in on Vindeen, the Foucinian turned his horse to run. He jerked the reins of his powerful horse and kicked the ribs of the steed. The horse struggled to reach full speed and was unable to distance Vindeen from the killer. Brunto planted his foot against the back edge of the chariot and heaved one of the javelins with all his might.

The javelins tip drove deep in the lower back of the Foucinian. The wound proved to be deadly as the big fighter slid down the side of the horse. Emery held his course and ran over the Foucinian just as commanded. The cart went airborne as it passed over the hairy beast. Brunto quickly grabbed the reins from the boy and encouraged more speed to catch up with the dead fighter's horse.

It was at that moment when old Hob stretched her wings and flapped them. The bat-like wings lifted her massive body off the ground and the dragon attacked. She was so angry no one was safe. Her deadly flames cooked anyone in its path. Sagans were fried, men were melted and Foucinians charred. The dragon had no mercy. She flew over their heads and continued to rain down flames of doom.

Magoonagoon
CHAPTER 63
Dead

Brunto and Emery had just gotten under way when the dragon swooped down upon them. Luckily, the chariot moved out of the way of the dragon's terrible breath. They both got a little roasted from the heat but managed to escape. The gaps in Brunto's heavy armor let the flames slide in and the heat broiled his skin. With two or three flaps from her huge wings, the dragon soared high into the air. She circled the battlefield once more and then flew away from the fighting.

In the meantime, Oliver's lost chariot rolled around recklessly. The chariot continued to move through the middle of the fighting. Aubrey was battling the giant Sagan Atsuel when the unmanned chariot passed by. The fellow quickly moved to catch the cart leaving Atsuel behind. The legionnaire leaped into the chariot and took hold of the reins. Aubrey smiled as he ushered the chariot up to attack speed.

On the opposite column, Oliver followed the men who had advanced forward into contention. He met the black Sagan Soociv near the center. The black feathered warrior had held his ground at the front without his sturdy horse. Oliver moved to attack the champion by himself, but fell back when he got near the Sagan. The boy raced away to avoid the confrontation.

"You! I remember you! How did you get here? Come here, you little fool! I'll smash your skull!" shouted Soociv.

The beckoning stopped Oliver in his tracks and the scourge brought him back to the front. Oliver called for lighting and the bolts came cracking down all around him. The deadly bolts had eliminated a dozen Sagans around him and knocked Soociv from his feet. The ground smoked from the electricity and all the soldiers cleared out of the way. Oliver rushed to meet the Sagan by himself who lay in disbelief and wonder of the power. Oliver lifted the whale tusk up in the air and called out a spell.

"Up from the dead! Stand to your feet! All who've been killed by this Sagan's defeat!" shouted Oliver.

With these words an army of men came back to life. They stood to their feet and awaited Oliver's command. The sorcerer motioned the whale tusk to the left and incited a charge from the zombies. Then the wizard called for the multitude to come from the right and they attacked. Soociv leapt to his feet and cut the zombies down in droves as they leaped upon him. The surge of attackers almost had him when all at once Oliver's powers gave out. The zombies fell back to the ground dead as before.

Seeing the spell fail, the Sagan leaped at him in attack. The boy was overwhelmed by the power of the blows and he slipped in his tracks. Soociv pushed the youngster around with his bright sword, striking his defenses with precision and accuracy. Oliver proved to be no match for the Sagan champion as the feathered hulk slammed the blade into Oliver's helmet. The leather strap broke loose and flew off the sorcerer's head. Oliver lay on the ground as though he were dead.

Other men drew in close to ward off the monster and his sword but it was too late. The soldiers scrambled to drag the boy's body away, but Soociv sent them running away in fear for their lives. The black Sagan bent down and grabbed the ankle of the boy and lifted him into the air to declare victory. Soociv smiled at the host of men longing for the body and taunted them with words.

"Do you want him? If you want him come and get him," Said Soociv.

The Sagan lifted the body even higher into the air and pivoted around to pitch him behind the lines. The mighty Sagan muscled the sorcerer into the sky and straightway threw the fellow behind the lines. Sadly, no one even knew that it was the sorcerer. The narwhale tusk lay unclaimed on the ground not far from them.

Magoonagoon

CHAPTER 64

Silstra

Victor had been knocked from his horse during the fighting but continued, unarmed at times, to battle. The champion headed for the break in the lines as he made long, heavy strides across the field. Victor armed himself along the way, picking up javelins that had missed their mark. He came across the body of a boy and looked down at him in disbelief. Victor did not know it was Oliver who lay there. The man did not recognize the boy, but he wondered who could do such a thing. Victor bent down and checked to see if the lad was still alive.

A child? Why have they done this to a child? thought Victor.

To the man's surprise the boy did not have a scratch on him. Victor studied the child closer and wondered if he was really dead. The closer look at the body showed no sign of injury. He knew that he could not leave the fellow out in the open. Victor knew that he should do something, but what, he did not know. With the enemy all around him the man thought.

I will hide him somewhere, thought Victor.

Victor picked up the boy's body and carried him over to a dead Sagan and laid him down. The man tucked him beneath the feathers and leaned against the Sagan to hide. After Victor had secured Oliver's body under the feathered giant, he lingered there a moment longer to rest.

Silstra was in the middle of choking an archer to death when he sighted Victor. Silstra dropped the man he had in his clutches and immediately moved on the man's position. From behind, Silstra cleared the dead Sagan with one step and bent down to pick up Victor. The monster gripped Victor with his sharp talons and tightly grasped the man in his hands. As Victor screamed out in pain, the giant rose to his feet and inflated his chest with air to shriek.

"I have him! I have the leader!" shouted Silstra to his comrades.

One of Victor's men tried to save him by sending a wooden pike toward the Sagan. The slender weapon jumped from his hand and Silstra tried to get out of the way. Still the javelin dove into the hip of the murderous Sagan. The pike dug deep into the Sagan's flesh and touched the bone. The big Sagan turned his neck in pain and stumbled a bit. But the large Sagan was not about to drop his prize. Silstra held on to Victor and left the spear in his hip. His forceful hands shook with anger as he squeezed the man tighter.

Behind them, Stratogos and some of his soldiers moved in to investigate. Silstra stretched out his arms and showed off the catch. The mighty Sagan leaned back at the waist and held him up for all to see. Stratogos looked scornfully at Silstra and spoke to him.

"That is not the leader! The leader is not that fat," said Stratogos confidently.

"He is the leader! Look at his cape. This is how you can tell," said Silstra pointing to the embroidery around the edge of the long cape.

"Hand him to me! Let me see him," ordered Stratogos.

"No! He's mine!" answered Silstra selfishly.

"Give him here you fool!" shouted Stratogos.

As the Sagans struggled in a tug-o-war, Victor's soldiers contemplated what they could do to save him. The men circled through the fighting to find a better spot where they could meet. Not far from the capture sight, the men met in a clearing to work out a plan.

"What are they waiting for?" asked one of Victor's soldiers.

"They must be going to take him prisoner," said another.

"We can't let them take him alive!" shouted a man.

"Throw at them all! If it hits Victor at least they won't take him alive!" ordered the officer.

The squad moved into position and fired their weapons at

the Sagans. The wooden missiles drove into the fiends as they pulled and tugged on the man. One of the darts slid through the air and again found its way to Silstra's body. The javelin pierced the Sagan in the forearm just above the wrist and traveled straight through. The wooden pike was buried midway into the man-eater's flesh and was visible from both sides. Silstra let go of Victor to clutch the wound.

"You! You! You idiot! You have maimed my arm and plagued me with injury!" shouted Silstra with hate.

Stratogos was pulling with such force that when Silstra let loose of the man, he fell over backwards. Consequently, Victor's body was set free when the monster fell down. The man rolled away from the danger and quickly looked to arm himself. Victor grabbed a javelin and raced to attack the injured Silstra. Victor threw the pike as he ran, casting the harpoon at the Sagan's head. The halberd fell from the sky and stuck deep in the crest of the Sagan's back. Unarmed, Victor quickly moved to find something else he could use to do battle. He found a sword dropped by a dead soldier and moved to relinquish Silstra of his life.

Victor moved to assault the angry scoundrel with the blade in front of his bulky body. Victor leaped upon the Sagan with fury. He grabbed the monster's neck and took back the weapon. With the sharp sword he stabbed the man-eater deep in the side with the sleek knife. The blade passed through the tunic made from Foucinian skins and pierced through the ribs. There, Silstra fell dead by the hand of Victor.

Magoonagoon

CHAPTER 65
Stratogos

The warfare continued on through the heat of the day. The hot sun baked down its harsh waves of heat. The valor and courage shown by the Sagans that opened the gaping hole in the Foucinian line brought on a massacre. Brunto and Emery flew through the gap on the fast war chariot. Noisop lead the heavy cavalry into the gap to clear the way for the rest. He engaged with Silas and his brother Percival near the edge.

The big bull Brunto rode his fortitude of iron and wood into the multitude shouting shrewd hate and boasting his arsenal of weaponry. The iron-axle chariot sped through the waves of soldiers guided by the steady hand of Emery. The Foucinians gave way, fearing the champion, and parted, quickly rushing to each side. The fighters ducked for cover behind their heavy shields.

Archers threw their arrows at Brunto and his war carriage as he passed, but the fast leaping arrows could not catch up with the wooden chariot. Before the battle, the cunning Sagan had poured the slick whale oil over the iron axle to encourage more speed. The whale oil enhanced the cart beyond all measures, rendering loose and unstoppable speed.

When the foremost foot soldier, Stratogos, entered the break in the lines, many of the fighters fled in retreat. The colossal warrior stamped out many of the Foucinians and sent them running off the mudflats. He grabbed hold of a horse and rider and lifted them both off the ground. The giant took them up over his head and flung them into the men. The horse smashed a group of them killing those underneath.

Stratogos then reached to his belt and pulled his mighty sword. With one whack the monster severed a Foucinian in two. The archers fired upon him hoping to bring him down, but the arrows never penetrated the thick coat of chainmail. Stratogos laughed at the men and scolded them with rude comments.

"Ha! Ha! Ha! Do your worst with those darts! You cannot hurt me!" said Stratogos.

The giant was so large that no one could face up to him. Everyone stayed clear of him and out of his long reach. Aubrey sped by the killer in his newly acquired chariot and threw dirt in his face. The dust choked Stratogos and caused him to sneeze. The crowd was sprayed with snot and Stratogos spoke once more.

"Take that you cowards!" shouted Stratogos.

Aubrey rolled the chariot back around to circle the monster once more. The horses flew by the Sagan and churned up the dust a second time. While Stratogos waved his hands in front of his face to clear the smoky dust, the men attacked him. They hurled their spears and shot their arrows at the giant with the thought to wound him. Stratogos took two steps and cleared the dusty air. With the wave of his sword he laid down seven of them with one blow.

On Aubrey's next pass, Stratogos was ready. The giant slammed his sword down across the hitch of the chariot. The hit wrecked the team and flung the legionnaire out. Stratogos placed his huge foot on the kicking horses and smashed their bones. He peeled away the cart from the leather straps and lifted it up over his head. With a grunt, the big Sagan hurled the cart into the crowd. The chariot bounced and rolled to a stop killing everyone in its path. Then the Sagan made a triumphant display in front of them by beating his huge chest with his fists and roaring aloud.

After everyone had seen the monster hurl the chariot, the Foucinian trumpets began to blow the sound of retreat. The soldiers collapsed the lines and fell back to their rallying point in the forest. The hairy Foucinians all turned and ran with no attempt to guard the rear. Only the tall Wolneas had stayed behind to protect his fleeing race. Even Premo had left. Surprisingly, the mighty Foucinian leader galloped his tall horse out of the wastelands toward the stronghold.

Victor protected and safeguarded the men. He too blew on his trumpet and the men followed Victor into the woods. The men ran as fast as they could to avoid the heavy cavalry that followed. The cavalry gave chase, slashing their hacking swords at the backs of the fleeing soldiers. However, the battle was far from over. They fled to the forest where large and sturdy trees stretched across the bed. The swift Foucinians dashed into the glade walled with its massive trees.

Magoonagoon

CHAPTER 66
Godwin

Near the sight of Oliver's body, Godwin scrambled a few soldiers to fight against the frightening giants. He rallied the squadron and drove them headlong into Sandion and Atsuel. The men tried to surround them as they ran in a circular pattern. Godwin threw his javelin at Atsuel and the pike ricocheted off the Sagan's shield. Still advancing, Godwin reached to his belt and pulled forth his sword to battle. He ran behind the protection of his shield and reared back to strike. Godwin skipped and leaped into the air and swung his sword around to smite the murderer.

Atsuel lifted up his spear and held it out firm to block the attack. The long staff distanced Atsuel from the man as the point struck the leader in the breastplate. Godwin's body continued to travel forward and the punch caused the man to drop his weapons. His sword went sailing forth out of his reach, and his round shield was tossed to the side near Sandion.

While Godwin lay on his back in pain, the others tried to defend their captain. A squad of them attacked Sandion and the rest moved against Atsuel by rushing at the giant in pairs. With one wave Atsuel disabled two more as he swung the spear like a bat. A second pair came at the Sagan's left side as Godwin scrambled to escape the giant's point.

Sandion placed her heavy foot on top of Godwin's shield and taunted the man to come back and claim it. She snapped her beak and hissed at the herald with disdain. A brave soul rushed at Sandion hoping to catch her off guard and was severed by the monster's sword. Sandion proudly laughed out loud at the fellow as Godwin rolled on the ground still trying to recover.

A soldier quickly ran to rearm Godwin with the sword from his own belt. Atsuel stepped toward Godwin with his spear drawn back to kill the man. He stabbed at the hero with great force, and the point grazed Godwin's side. In a flash, he rolled to the side and sprang to his feet. Atsuel reached out and grabbed the man's cape. The Sagan's talons ripped into the fabric as he snatched it in his grasp. The fleeing man was jerked back violently when there was no more slack.

Godwin fell to the ground once more as he was tackled by the towering hulk. As Godwin lay there on his back, stunned from the spike, he gasped for breath. Atsuel quickly snapped the fellow's arm as he dropped down on one knee. The hefty leg of the killer landed right on top of the limb and cracked the bone.

Godwin cried out for help as he lay there in pain and agony. Atsuel readied his spear to strike as he pressed his weight down on the pinned arm. He drove the spear point deep into the hip of the captain, and Atsuel mistakenly forced it all the way through. The spear lodged in the flesh of the man's backside and would not release as the Sagan tugged about.

Godwin's body flipped around dreadfully as the huge Sagan tried to free his point. So seeing the danger, Godwin's men rushed upon the killer, hoping to take him while in distress. Atsuel used the back of his fist to smash the first would-be attacker, and he flew away dead. The next man that came found a similar fate as the giant used his foot to wreck the charge.

From behind, a soldier was able to plant the cold steel of his sword right in the back of the murderer. The shock of the sword's bite forced Atsuel to drop the spear that held Godwin tight. When the captain hit the ground, he tried desperately to crawl away from the danger. Godwin grabbed frantically at the spear that plagued his hip. Blood rushed from the site, and the man felt faint from the shock. The men scurried away from Atsuel and Sandion to reach him. They formed a barrier around their captain and a small group fumbled to free the thorn. As two men gripped the handle to pull, others lay over his body to hold him down.

Atsuel spun around to face the man who had stabbed him in the back with his bare hands. The man slashed his sword back and forth daring the Sagan to chase him. The giant bent down and picked up a dead man's body to use as a weapon. The villain held on to the body by the ankles and swung it around to smash the challenger to the ground.

Behind him, the men had freed Godwin from the terrible point of the spear. They had already helped the Godwin to his feet and rearmed him with weaponry. They had packed the leader's shredded cape down into the wound and stopped the bleeding. At the site where they worked on him, one of his men stumbled across the narwhale tusk. The man quickly picked it up from the ground and handed it to his captain. When Godwin held it in his hand, the wound in his side stopped bleeding and his broken arm was mended. The whale tusk had healed the man of his injuries. The miracle that restored Godwin's health gave all who witnessed a rejuvenated spirit.

Magoonagoon

CHAPTER 67

Dug In to Fight

So the battle continued in the deep wood. The Foucinians had fled deep into the forest with the entrance covered by massive trees. From the forest bed, large and sturdy trees stretched across the wood giving the smaller Foucinians the advantage. Their hearts raced and their spirits were high when they turned to fight.

Brunto and the armed cavalry had no other choice but to stop their pursuit at the forest edge. The wooden chariot and massive horses were too big to squeeze through the trees. The champion drove the chariot in circles shouting obscenities as he waited for the feathered foot soldiers to approach. When the foremost fighters had reached the wood, Brunto pointed to the spot where the Foucinians entered the forest.

After he showed them the way, Brunto and Emery rode back out to the center of the wastelands. The wooden wheels flew across the hard dirt and the war cart left a trail of dust as it rolled across. Brunto commanded Emery to lash the reins and whip the horses. The young lad pushed the horses to their limit steering them into the void.

The Sagans of the cavalry galloped their horses around on the edge of the forest. Many of the Foucinian archers pitched the sharp, pointed arrows at the riders from the tree line. The arrows leaped from the bows and rained into the herd, wounding many. After the pelting, the riders drove away from danger and further from the trees.

The rest of the Foucinian archers had amassed near the skirts of the clearing for an ambush. Aubrey had abandoned his own troops to lead them. He and the Foucinians waited for the opportune moment to fire their arrows from their hiding place. The Foucinians had camouflaged themselves in a ditch with their deadly bows ready to fire. Aubrey ordered them to remain still and be ready to attack. The rest of them moved to the center, in the open, coaxing the Sagans to fight and calling them to war.

A group of Sagans entered the clearing without the others in a bold but foolish move. Two of the Sagans trotted through the swaying trees and rushed to engage the Foucinians that so boastfully called them to war. Not far behind them, another brave Sagan followed the pair carrying his sword. After the three Sagans had moved far enough into the woods, the Foucinians sprung their trap.

Out of a ditch stood many archers with arrows on their lines ready to fire; the eyes of the three Sagans grew wide with surprise. Before they had a chance to run, Aubrey gave the command and the Foucinians loosed their strings. The first two Sagans were pelted and blotted with red blood.

The wooden shards had been thrown from such a close distance that many of them went straight through. Still others penetrated to the bone, calling for screams of anguish. Their screams were soon turned to silence as they fell dead. The Sagan that was trailing behind the others wisely turned to run from the killers in retreat. The men rearmed and fired on the straggler.

Their arrows struck his flesh and settled deep inside. His backside was not protected as well as the fortitude of bronze that dressed his front. The Sagan continued to run through the saplings and reached a point where he was out of their deadly range. The archers moved back to their positions hiding in the ditch. The Sagan limped through the trees, stopping along the way to catch his wind and summon up strength. He had been shot several times in fatal areas by the wooden shards, but moved to warn the others of the ambush. With his dying breath the Sagan spoke to his comrades.

"They…are waiting along a ditch line…with ready bows…" said the Sagan as he collapsed. The others quickly loosened the Sagan's armor to help the Sagan breathe.

"How many are there?" asked one of his comrades.

"It's an ambush! There are too many of them. They have all…all have dug in to fight," said the Sagan.

Magoonagoon

CHAPTER 68
Burn Them Out

Aubrey mocked them from the ditch and dared another to try the gauntlet. The group thought for a moment and decided to call for runners to fetch Kounjab, he was known for his skills in tactics and maneuvers. The rest stood at the tree line poised to attack. They all waited for the Sagan to arrive, the cunning Kounjab.

When the runners returned with him, there were great cheers among the battalion. Kounjab approached the group at the front and was first to speak.

"Why have you called me here?" asked Kounjab.

"The way is blocked by a barricade of archers. They have already taken the lives of three and I fear many more will fall to their volley if we test them again," said the Sagan.

"What do you suggest we do, Kounjab?" asked another.

"We will burn them out! We will set the forest ablaze. The smoke will cover our movements. If they choose to stay and fight…we will let the fires engulf them," said Kounjab.

"If we could somehow encircle their entrenchments we could cut off their route of escape," said one of the soldiers.

"Let us divide into three units, all of which will carry torches. I will take a squad to one side and you will take one to the other. We will set fires to their flanks while the rest of you stand guard here at their front. As soon as their sides are taken by fire, we will move to their rear. We will continue to ignite the tender forest bed until they are surrounded," said Kounjab.

"Send a soldier on a horse to gather torches," said one of the Sagans.

"One of you go! Go to the ships. Go and get some oil and flint from the ships. Get enough for us all. Go quickly," said the Sagan. One of the other Sagans quickly mounted a horse and headed for the ships to gather the supplies.

"In the meantime, I will test their lines," said Kounjab.

Kounjab picked a select group of fighters and rallied to the brush. He moved into the forest and carefully gauged his distance to the ditch. The hulk then took a javelin from his comrade and drew it up high to his ear. The bold Sagan set his feet and reached back to hurl the sturdy wood. Kounjab flung the wooden lance through the trees and it bounced through the air in flight. The wooden pike climbed through the trees dancing and swaying from the force of the throw. The sleek spear took a dive for the ditch and slammed down with a thud. The bolt had slipped through the trees and found its target. A groan came from the ditch where the javelin hit. Kounjab took his talons and marked the ground so they would know how far they could go.

    The Sagan units seemed to have all the odds in their favor as they moved undetected through the brush and foliage. When the soldier returned with the oil and flint, the Sagans quickly set fire to the flank. While they fanned the flames and slowly started the fire, the others kept watch with their weapons. They got a steady ring of fire going and continued to advance toward the rear. In moments, the steady flames built up and began to conger up the black smoke.

    The nightmare had only just begun for the Foucinians in the clearing. The fires soon engulfed the host and surrounded them on all sides. Many of them called for help at the top of their lungs, but no one came to help. The black plumes of smoke sent them on the run to the only escape route. They were chased by the orange and red flames into the mass of Sagan soldiers at their front. To their shock and amazement there was no safe haven.

    Many of them fell to their knees in horror as they gazed into the eyes of the Sagans. There the soldiers from Brunto's tribe stood ready to strike. The largest Sagan initiated the attack, charging into the Foucinians with his sword and shield. The Sagans did not cease until all lay dead on the forest floor.

    Aubrey quickly hid between the bodies and prayed that the Sagans would not discover him. However, they caught sight of the young man and one of the Sagans grabbed his ankle and picked him up. Aubrey tried to slash the Sagan's arm with his sword, but missed the feathered monster as he spun around in the powerful grip. The Sagan quickly grabbed the young man's wrist and squeezed the bone, causing Aubrey to drop his blade.

"The outcome was much different this time, wasn't it, boy? The others will meet a similar fate! It's only a matter of time! This one will be my dinner tonight!" boasted the Sagan.

One of the Foucinians who had survived quickly laced an arrow and fired it at the Sagan. The arrow slammed into the Sagan's shoulder, splintering the very bone. The Sagan dropped Aubrey to the ground as he wailed out in anger. Being free, Aubrey quickly moved to rearm. The young man gripped a javelin in a flash and whirled around to take aim. Aubrey took the point back and threw the stick with the desire to rob the Sagan of life. The pike hit its target near the Sagan's groin, cutting an artery. In the same step, Aubrey grabbed his sword from the ground and killed another, allowing him to escape.

Magoonagoon

CHAPTER 69

The Old Whaler

When all the terror was over in the land of man, Jonathon returned to what was left of his house. The old whaler found his home in ashes. He sat down in front of the entrance and wept for three days. No one dared to try and comfort him. The people just wagged their heads at the man in pity. On the third day, late in the evening hour, the man stood up and entered the charred ruins of his house. Jonathon crossed over the fallen beams and stepped lightly over the hot coals. He made his way back to the largest room and searched through the ashes. Underneath part of the collapsed roof, the man found what he was looking for: the remains of a trunk. Jonathon tore off the lid and tossed it aside. He reached to the bottom of the trunk and pulled out the sword that lay within. Jonathon gripped it tight by the handle and shook with tremors. Now, like his brothers before him, he would travel to Magoonagoon.

Word of Jonathon's departure began to spread all across the land. Other men who had their lives taken away from them, those who felt the same, came in great numbers and committed to go with him. When Queen Penelope found out the men were going she sent some spies to find out whether or not it was true. They secretly pretended to be volunteers and they interviewed many of the men. When they concluded that the assembly was serious about going to Magoonagoon they acted like defectors and left to report back to the queen.

Sadly, many of the best warriors had hastily sailed ahead of them with Simon to the foreign shore. Nevertheless, thousands came from the far-reaching lands of man. They camped on the barren cape where they massed together. Jonathon summoned ship builders and carpenters to build sleek fighting crafts to dawn their journey. It took one hundred days for the craftsmen and artisans to build them.

The city was filled with the burden of the armies. Sorrow and anguish came upon the town. The soldiers grew anxious and impatient, ready to leap into the deep. However, as they waited there on the coast, time made cowards of many a gallant man. Then the days grew long and the wind whipped at their heads on the sandy shore—the very wind that was needed to propel them to Magoonagoon.

Magoonagoon

CHAPTER 70

Zinder-faso

The other legions continued the fight in the forest. The loyalists had entered the deep woods and began to gain ground on the Foucinians. Zinder-faso had managed to kill a host soldiers with his net and three-pronged spear. However, the legionnaire had caught sight of him and rallied a squad of fighters to assault the Sagan. He brought Silas and Percival as well as a host of others against the Sagan. Aubrey was the first to attack, hurling his spear into the feathered monster. The spear slammed into creature's net and dropped to the ground. Zinder-faso grinned and quickly spoke to his adversaries.

"What makes you think you can defeat me, boy? I can see the fright in your eyes," proclaimed Zinder-faso as he laughed. Aubrey answered him by firing another javelin into his net.

"That's two times you have missed. And I see you only have one more javelin," said Zinder-faso boastfully.

The others closed in to face the giant slashing their weapons. Silas moved to spear the giant, but was caught inside of the hulk's mighty net instead. Quickly the Sagan struck him with the handle of his pitchfork and the heavy blow knocked him unconscious. Percival was next to drill Zinder-faso's skill, but his efforts proved fruitless and in vain, for in one stab the Sagan ran him through. Percival was lodged in the center of the pitchfork. The middle prong had pierced the man through the stomach and traveled out the back.

Zinder-faso held the man up in the air and looked at him for a moment. Then, the killer lowered Percival down to the ground and used his huge foot to dislodge him. Percival screamed out for mercy as he slipped off the prong, but Zinder-faso had other plans for him. The Sagan took his huge foot and gripped the fellow's head. The massive foot wrapped around the man's head and with all his strength, Zinder-faso began to squeeze. The Sagan was straining so hard that the foot started shaking. After making a loud cracking noise, the head smashed like a melon, and Zinder-faso turned his attention back toward Aubrey and his men. When Aubrey's soldiers saw the giant turn on them, they ran away as though they had seen a ghost.

"It looks like it's down to you and me!" said Zinder-faso.

Aubrey uncomfortably swallowed and took aim at the Sagan with his javelin. The man let the pin fly from his hand and the wooden weapon jumped into the air. The throw was a perfect shot. The point drilled the giant in the helmet and the hit crippled the feathered warrior and sent him limp to the ground. The legionnaire moved to take the fallen Sagan's three-pronged spear and stab the monster. He grabbed the pitchfork from the Sagan's hand and drew it back to relinquish his life. However, fear filled the heart of the courageous warrior when Zinder-faso grabbed hold of his leg. The Sagan pulled Aubrey to the ground and punched the man in the ribs. Then, the Sagan socked Aubrey in the mouth, shattering his pearly white teeth. Zinder-faso then stood to his feet and picked up the warrior.

    He picked the heavy man high up over his head with both hands. Then the killer slammed the legionnaire down to the hard ground. The tall Sagan proclaimed victory as he picked up his pitchfork. Zinder-faso then began to reach back to deliver a devastating blow. In the meantime, Silas had awoken from the unconscious state and freed himself from the net. The man staggered to his feet with stars in his eyes and mounted an attack to save Aubrey.

    Silas slashed the back of the Sagan's leg, sending him to the ground in anguish. Then, the hero moved away from the Sagan clutching his sword in a poised position. Zinder-faso looked over his shoulder at the wound and put pressure on it with his hand. Bleeding badly, the heavyset Sagan spoke to the man.

    "You got me good. But soon I will have my revenge," shouted Zinder-faso.

    The large Sagan crept forward toward Silas with the intent to kill. He disregarded the bleeding legionnaire and mounted a second assault on his new opponent. Silas took two steps back for every step Zinder-faso took forward. Silas could tell that the Sagan was starting to get faint so he allowed space between them. The man waited until Zinder-faso's weak legs gave out. When the Sagan collapsed, Silas leaped upon the body and buried his sword deep inside the monster's neck.

"No!" shouted Silas when he realized his brother had been killed.

Silas ran to the body of his dead brother and fell to his knees. The fellow was joined by Aubrey and the two grieved at the loss of Percival. However, through the trees more danger approached them from every side. When Aubrey saw the danger coming, he grabbed his trumpet and blew four blasts for help.

Through the fighting many of the fellow's soldiers came to aid. They were greeted by Aubrey yelling harsh words at them as they entered. They moved toward Aubrey near the center and found him guarding Silas. With a bleeding mouth, the wily commander quickly reproached them, and gave out commands to each one. Aubrey ordered the rest of his soldiers to stay behind and protect Silas while he took a squad of men to fight elsewhere.

Magoonagoon

CHAPTER 71
Sandion

Silas continued to grieve at Percival's side through the mess of war. Aubrey's men had him surrounded until Sandion came into the clearing. The powerful female approached them with heavy steps. The appearance of Sandion made most of Aubrey's soldiers retreat. Only a few of the bravest men stayed behind to protect Silas.

With one huge swipe, Sandion made quick work of the fellows. She split the men in half with her huge sword and proceeded to kill Silas. The grieving man turned his sadness into anger just in time to turn and face the monster. Silas lifted his bold shield on one arm to block the killer's thrust. When Sandion hammered the shield, Silas was knocked to the ground. The fall caused the man to drop his long javelin, so he reached to his belt and pulled his sword.

As they fought, Silas was joined by King Marion and his soldiers who came on the scene in perfect timing. The king trotted in with the spear behind his ear eager to fight. His soldiers ran step for step with him in formation. The stalwart man quickly called to the Sagan.

"You murderer! Do you wish to incur my wrath? Toiling with my men in strife? I hope to kill you so that I might feed you to my dogs," said King Marion.

The Sagan grew tense and began to show signs of fear. However, the old Sagan armed herself with courage as she hissed and snapped her beak at the men. The powerful Sagan opened her mouth wide, showing her huge curved tongue. The heavyset Sagan crept back away from them as she rustled the leaves. Sandion then scourged the man with harsh words as she lowered her neck.

"Oh! Royalty! The king! Why have you approached me? You know your attack will be fruitless! I will crown your skull with my fist! I would love to bash it in. Or…have ill thoughts seized you to join with this weakling in the hope of foiling me?" asked Sandion.

"When I leap upon your chest to stab you deep…I hope for you to remember the days of old when you could marshal near the front. Now old age has seized your limbs and your time is at an end," said King Marion.

The handsome man quickly gave Silas orders to move to

the right so he could pitch his spear and make his throw. Silas crept to the right, weary from battle, and moved in on the old female Sandion. The old Sagan waved her sword at the crowd in defense. Mistakenly, Silas moved to assault the huge female by himself. His attack was thwarted by the monster's huge fist. Silas flipped over backward and dropped all his weapons.

As Silas lay there on the ground unconscious, Sandion kept her eye on the king, who had taken up a good position with his javelin primed and ready. King Marion launched his spear at the female with a grunt, and the wooden pike slammed into the Sagan's heavy shield. The tip stuck in the shield, but did not pass through the thick bronze. Sandion loosened the leather strap on her shield to allow it and the heavy javelin to slide off her sturdy arm. The equipment bounced on the ground and settled to a stop.

At that moment, Silas climbed up to his knees and rubbed the place where the Sagan's fist had hit him. The fellow began to grieve again and Sandion glared at the man with a disappointed look. With her back turned to the man, Sandion bent her knees slightly to squat down. Then the disgusting creature emptied her bowels with a loud grunt. Being relieved, Sandion laughed at the man and scratched the ground with her talons like a dog.

Sandion started to drool and pant as she marched straight over to the king's men. She took her sword high up over her head and chopped down on one of the fellows as he cowered away. Another warrior stepped in the way and was able to block the initial blow to protect Silas. The feathered Sagan bashed swords with the man, exchanging sparks. Sandion's hits overpowered the man who tried to protect Silas, and soon she won the contest as the blade cleaved the fellow in two near the waist. Sandion grabbed the upper body and flung it at King Marion. She took the lower body and pitched it at the rest of the king's men.

"You won't have to worry about him anymore! Ha! Ha! Ha!" shouted the killer.

The female forgot about Silas and moved forward to engage King Marion, who was looking to rearm. Sandion sheathed her sword back in the fine belt and walked away from the body to pick up a spear she found on the ground. The bold and valorous king had too much courage to run. If not for the Sagan's weaponry, he would battle Sandion hand to hand. So the vicious Sagan pitched the spear in her hand and moved closer to devour the young man. After she had her fun, the old Sagan stretched the wooden pole back behind her ear in a ready position. Before she threw the weapon Sandion spoke to the man.

"Don't you want to beg for mercy? You paid no attention to my warning! Look there at that fool! He cries still! I warned him! Oh! His poor brother is dead. Boo! Who! Soon you will both join him!" said Sandion.

Sandion threw the heavy spear through the air and it soared about the trees. However, the long pike, tipped in heavy bronze, passed by King Marion's slender body and drove deep into a tree. The man knew he had cheated death, and the king moved to grab the spear from the trunk. He pulled and pulled with all his strength, but could not release the spear. Sandion came at his rear in attack with her sword drawn.

King Marion put both feet on the tree's huge trunk and tugged with all his might. The spear was stuck too deep in the wood and could not be loosed. He turned to find Sandion upon him. The female put away her sliver sword to toy with him.

Sandion smote him across the helmet with her fist, sending him down to the forest floor. The big Sagan kicked him in the ribs with her massive foot, sending his body rolling through the leaves.

"Call out for help, your excellency! See if your comrades will come! You are the king! Where are your vaunts and swagger that once garnished your tongue? What fool is bold enough to come and save you now?" asked Sandion.

The tall Sagan grabbed the king's foot and picked him up into the air. The strong Sagan then tossed the man into the massive tree trunk at their side, knocking the very wind from his lungs. As the king gasped for air, Sandion moved to finish him off. The Sagan grabbed King Marion's neck and choked him with all her might. When the king started to turn blue, the Sagan heard a shout that paralyzed all the muscles in her body.

"Sandion! Sandion! Here am I," shouted Victor.

The Sagan turned to see and to her amazement she noticed that it was Victor. Sandion loosened her grip on King Marion and prepared to battle Victor. Sandion's eyes grew wide with anticipation and drool began to drip from her mouth when she noticed that all the man carried was a short dagger. Victor walked in front of her pitching the knife from one hand to the other. Then he stretched out his arms and gave the massive Sagan a stern look, as if to invite her to tussle. To Sandion's surprise, the man she thought to be dead got up and joined Victor. Silas quickly rearmed and he returned to fight.

"Back for more, are you?" asked Sandion.

While the two men faced off with Sandion, it gave King Marion the necessary time he needed to recover. While Silas taunted the Sagan, the king fetched a weapon from the forest floor. The brave lad was able to find a long bow with one sharp arrow. When the king joined them, they matched up three men against one Sagan. As fast as he could, he laced the string and drew back the bow to fire. With a leap, the arrow flew and shot into the buttock of the Sagan. Sandion felt the sting when the arrow zipped into the flesh and she turned to glance at the wound. That moment gave Silas a chance to attack and he raced to stab the monster. However, Silas ran right into Sandion's fist again, just as before. The Sagan hit the man in the face and Silas rolled over backward and lay motionless, face down on the ground.

"Ha! Tried to get me when my back was turned, did you?" shouted Sandion.

Silas tried to stand, but the man only managed to climb up onto his knees. Sandion drew her long sword out of the sheath and slowly walked toward the man. The Sagan drew the sword back to strike the man while the fellow wobbled in a daze. The king tried to warn Silas of the giant's approach, but it was too late. Sandion lobed off the fellow's head and it pitched to the ground. Victor screamed at the Sagan and vowed to kill the monster. Without a weapon, King Marion had no choice but to run and Victor dared not to face the murderer alone. With a hop and a leap both men were out of sight as they ran in opposite directions. They could hear the feathered female cursing them for running away.

"Come back here, you cowards!" shouted Sandion.

Magoonagoon

CHAPTER 72

The King

Sandion looked in both directions and chose to chase after King Marion. The Sagan called to the king as she raced through the trees. Sandion's long strides propelled her within range of the man's ears. The king looked over his shoulder to see how close the giant was from him and he was startled to see the monster right on his heels.

"You are not fast enough, you fool! I am going to catch you!" shouted Sandion as she laughed.

King Marion knew the creature was right behind him and ready to strike. By chance, the man tripped on a limb lying on the forest floor. Sandion had already decided to leap into the air in an attempt to tackle the fellow. Sandion's huge body soared over the king and the female slid through the leaves on her face.

King Marion leaped back to his feet and headed back in the opposite direction. Sandion shook her head and hissed as she climbed back to her feet. The Sagan dusted herself off and allowed King Marion to have a good head start. King Marion realized his only chance was to retrieve a weapon and fight the Sagan. He knew that Sandion would chase him all over Magoonagoon.

When the king reached the site where Silas and Percival were killed, he searched desperately for their weapons. Through the leaves the man searched without any luck. As Sandion's heavy footsteps grew louder and louder, King Marion scrambled all the more to find anything he could use to defend himself. At the last possible second, the man's hand found the handle of Silas's sword. In a flash, the fellow wheeled the cutlass up to protect himself, deflecting a hit from the female. Sandion had planted a direct hit on the sword and the metal clang echoed through the forest.

"Ah! I am disappointed! I had hoped to sever you in half!" shouted Sandion.

"Too bad! Now! I will avenge the owner of this sword!" said King Marion as he dodged a strike from the Sagan.

Sandion took another swipe at the king and missed. King Marion then returned with a jab of his sword wounding the Sagan terribly. Sandion felt of the spot and scolded the fellow for cutting her. After the giant had glimpsed at the blood, Sandion fixed her hands firmly back on her sword and continued to fight. The king stepped back from the attack and blocked the smooth swipes. Then, all at once the leaves began to rustle all around them and King Marion's soldiers raced onto the scene. Sandion stepped back away from the leader to defend herself from the numerous attackers.

"Now I have you!" shouted King Marion.

"You coward! You were beaten! I would have killed you if these rats had not come to your aid!" shouted Sandion.

The soldiers quickly surrounded the giant with their shields up and swords drawn. Several of the men attended to King Marion and rearmed him with a shield. Sandion's demeanor changed when she counted the men around her. The Sagan lowered her long neck and hissed at the men as they closed in on her. Within moments Sandion was dead as the men leaped upon her. King Marion took Silas's sword and thrust it deep within the killer's belly and left it there.

Magoonagoon

CHAPTER 73
Atsuel

Deep in the forest, Atsuel smashed through the men and Foucinians alike. The Sagan crushed their skulls and severed limbs with blows from his sword. He drove the men to the dirt and rendered many of them maimed and crippled. He made his assault on Aubrey's men, taking advantage of the smoke-filled forest. As he slipped through the ranks of men tackling their lines, Atsuel ran into the group of soldiers. The Sagan slammed into the fighting with fearsome might. Atsuel sent many of them rushing away as they dropped their weapons in fear. The big Sagan cornered a host of them among the tall trees.

The men quickly threw down their weapons and fell to their knees to beg for their lives. Atsuel, the ruthless murderer, had no mercy for them as he cut away at the group of cowards with his cutlass. The killer paused when he caught sight of Warren cowering among them. Atsuel then spoke to him with shrewd words.

"Warren? Why do you cower among these? If Aubrey were here, you would surely be beheaded as a poltroon. Why should I show pity on you? The dog that you are!" asked Atsuel.

"Aubrey may be dead for all I know! Please! Have mercy!" pleaded Warren.

Warren clutched his hands together and pleaded with the Sagan as he shed wet tears. But Atsuel had no time to wait for the man's answer and lobbed off his head with his sword. The silver blade went clear through the spinal cord and through the tough muscle. Atsuel continued his assault on the men blazing his sword. He confronted Godwin and his fearless squadron.

Godwin's men split up into two groups and they tried surrounding the killer. Atsuel grinned as he watched them race around. The Sagan hobbled around in a circle growling and looking for the right fellow to attack. Godwin called for the men to hold their position when they had Atsuel surrounded. The Sagan singled out a fellow and spoke to him.

"You there! You! You are the one I want! Come over here and I will kill you!" said Atsuel.

"I am not afraid of you!" shouted the soldier.

"Oh? You're not are you? Well then get over here and prove it," said Atsuel.

"Silence! On my signal! Cut him down!" shouted

Godwin.

Godwin gave the order and the men raced to kill the Sagan. Atsuel wheeled his sword around and killed a whole group of the men to his right. The soldiers hit him from behind with their sharp daggers and spears. Those that attacked from the left clamored into the Sagan's shield and missed. The stinging Atsuel received in his back side prompted the Sagan to spin around and answer them. As he spun, his shield tackled many of the men in its path. When Godwin realized that the attack was thwarted, he called to his troops.

"Get back! Get away from him!" shouted Godwin.

Some of the men tried to escape but Atsuel chopped them down. All who lingered ended up dead or wounded. The Sagan took a giant step and killed a few more. Soon half of the squad was dead and Atsuel stepped over their dead bodies to reach the others. Godwin came back to protect his soldiers and sliced the Sagan across the groin. The wound stopped the Sagan from advancing further and gave the rest of them time to retreat. As Godwin tried to dash out of the way, Atsuel grabbed the man's cape and claimed victory.

Atsuel took the hilt of his sword and bashed Godwin over the head. The man's helmet protected him from being killed, but the hard strike knocked him out again. Atsuel let the fellow fall to the ground and the Sagan placed both of his hands on his sword to chop the man to bits. The huge Sagan raised the sword high up over his head and arched his back to deliver the deadly blow. Before the Sagan had a chance to chop him, Godwin's soldiers returned to save him.

One of them desperately jumped in front of the captain to

protect him just as the Sagan dropped the sword. The blade traveled clear through the soldier's body and stopped near Godwin's back. Another man threw his sword in desperation and the tip of the blade planted inside the killer's leg. The monster let out a roar and let go of his own sword to pull out the barb. The rest of the men harassed the Sagan and made him forget about their captain.

Magoonagoon

CHAPTER 74

The Queen

In the land of man, the shipbuilders worked day and night fashioning the sleek vessels while the soldiers practiced and honed their fighting skills. They built the seaworthy ships as close to the sea as they could, up near the green surf and misty ocean spray. The sturdy vessels covered the lengthy shore strewn up and down the sandy beach. The carpenters and iron smiths hammered away at their planks. Horses and robust men pulled the wooden beams and painfully heaved the heavy joists across the sand.

When the imminent day of completion came and the

warships were built, Jonathon assembled a meeting, for the day was upon them and it was time to go to war. During the evening the old whale hunter put on his helmet and breastplate and garnished his hip with his sword. The host of them moved to the forefront and Jonathon called for them to set down in the ranks along the seashore. He stood in front of them with his hand on the hilt of his sword. During the twilight of the evening hour, Jonathon spoke to the crowd.

"The Sagans have killed my darling wife! They have taken my sons! They left my house in shambles! I am no longer a man of peace but a man of rage and war! I only think of revenge! I will seek my revenge against the Sagans! Prepare the food and cook the feast! Tomorrow we will sail for Magoonagoon!" said Jonathon.

Saying these things, he dismissed them to their ships. Fittingly, Jonathon ushered the men to eat and drink. After they had their fill, each man laid down to rest. Everyone slept through the night except for Jonathon. The old man could only think of his young boys named by their mother, the oldest Emery and the younger Felix.

During the night Queen Penelope came to the coast with a large group of men. The crowd marched right up to the camp without being noticed. At the outskirts of the camp the large group stood at attention while the queen convened with the king's ambassador. He and the queen argued over how to approach the group. When a determination was made, the ambassador spoke.

"Your majesty, I will go up to the sentinels and request to speak with the leader of the army for you," said the ambassador.

"If you insist on going, demand that the leader of this bunch come out and speak with me," said the queen.

"As you wish," said the ambassador.

The man entered the camp alone and made his way to the perimeter where the guards stood watch. When they saw the ambassador, the sentinels commanded for him to halt. The ambassador wisely stood still until the soldiers approached him. When the guards drew near they questioned the man.

"What brings you here tonight young man?" asked one of the sentinels.

"The queen wishes to speak with the leader of this army. Go and tell the man she has requested it in the name of the king," said the ambassador.

When the sentinels heard this, one of them immediately ran to get Jonathon. The other stood there and watched the ambassador. In a few moments, the guard returned with Jonathon and they met face to face with the ambassador.

"Are you the leader?" questioned the ambassador.

"Yes," answered Jonathon.

"Come with me to the place where the queen is waiting," requested the ambassador.

Jonathon and the fellow walked a short distance and found the congregation of soldiers. The old whaler felt a little uncomfortable when he saw how many warriors stood in front of him. The two men walked inside the formations and found the queen. Queen Penelope greeted the man with a humble request.

"Sir. If you are going to Magoonagoon, I wish for you to take this letter to the king," said Queen Penelope.

"Your majesty, I would be honored to take it to him,"

said Jonathon.

"Good. These men you see before you are the king's elite band. They are yours," said the queen.

Jonathon fell to his knees and humbly thanked the queen with praising words of gratitude. The queen said goodbye to the man and left the scene with her personal escort. Jonathon requested the men to follow him to the shoreline where they could join his army. The elite soldiers silently followed the man into the camp and huddled together by themselves near the ships. The group stationed themselves in an area where they could recline and rest for the night.

When the sun rose above the water and the gulls began to chirp, the army awoke to the startling collection of new soldiers. At first the men were alarmed, but Jonathon explained everything. After he updated the troops the leader commanded everyone to enter the ships. Each man pushed on the heavy beams and splashed the sleek ships into the surf. The lengthy ships slid across the smooth sand and the bow plowed away the water.

In moments, the speedy ships, light and sleek as they were, had easily moved out to deep water. However, the heavier horse carriers and battlements were harder to push. It took fifty men to shoulder Jonathon's ship into the foamy sea. The strongest men put their backs to the timber and slammed their weight against the ships. One by one, they launched each vessel into the hard waves of the ocean. After each ship cleared the beach, they manned the oars and took them out to sea.

The men pulled the oars until they reached the point, then the captains called for them to hoist the sail. They put the oars away under each bench and manned the lines. The strong sail made of thick fabric was doubled and hemmed on each edge. With strong backs, they pulled the stocky ropes and banked off the wind. The warm sun beat down on their skin, tanning each man.

    The winds took the slender ships out to sea and they sailed through the day. The breeze carried them away from their homeland. Jonathon rode the bridge of the paramount ship and steered it toward the front as they crawled across the sea. As dusk came upon them, he called them all to lower the sails and drop anchor. They pitched ropes to each ship so as to pull them in tight. The ships collected together in a mass of wood and rope to drift in the night. Each man kept to his own space as they drank the dark wine and ate the fresh bread. After they all had their fill, Jonathon skipped ship to ship checking each man and ordering them to sleep. Each man would be needed, awake and alert. As the bulky group of ships pitched up and down in the surf the best of them fought to sleep.

Magoonagoon

CHAPTER 75
Cross the Line

In Magoonagoon, the rest of the Sagans had not fared so well. Many were killed in battle, taken in the fight, or left in the trees and fields alone. It was a shocking horror for the Sagans of the Royal Allegiance that would have been worse if not for Stratogos. Stratogos came within range of the men and scared them away with his dominance. He took his huge arms and wrapped them around a giant tree. After the monster roared aloud, he pulled the tree up by the roots and shoved the tree over. The tree came slamming down and Stratogos continued to roar at his enemies as they dashed away. Stratogos chased after them and killed everyone in his path. No one dared to approach the giant Sagan at close range. Many of the men who were too exhausted to run away tried to hide under the leaves and dead bodies.

After Stratogos had cleared the woods of any opponent, the Sagans began to collect around him beneath the trees. When the other Sagans drew near, Stratogos lifted up his head and roared again. The juggernaut beat his fists on his huge chest as he thundered and made cowards of them all. When he was finished, Stratogos growled and took command.

Stratogos sent a fast runner ahead of them to scout the terrain and be the eyes of the moving force. The runner guided the battalion safely out of the wood and back to the barren wastelands. The Allegiance was the first to emerge from the trees weary from battle. As they stepped across the hard dirt, Stratogos bid them all to set down in the ranks. He then spoke to his soldiers.

"Now I will assume command of the Royal Allegiance. I am better than anyone else! Let those who will support me stand behind me," spoke the bold Stratogos.

The Allegiance rested in the lowlands while Stratogos consulted with them. They decided that the weary force had suffered too many losses to enter the forest again. Stratogos ordered the crippled force to move away from the forest edge. The soldiers stood up in the ranks and followed their new commander across the lowlands. They gathered near the wounded at the center of the delta.

Straightway Oilaz and the reserves quickly moved to the center of the wastelands and ordered the remaining troops to return into the forest. The emperor pushed his way into the crowd surrounded by his sword-bearing guardians. The tall emperor looked over many of the Sagans that were hurt and bleeding from gaping wounds suffered during the battle.

"Back! Back into the wood! Follow them into the forest! Don't let them get away!" commanded Oilaz. Then the mighty Jinjo addressed the emperor.

"Chase them into the forest yourself. I have arrows embedded in my thighs and shins! There are many cuts on my arms! My forehead is covered with blood! I see no wounds on you! You have not entered battle since you became emperor! I would be surprised if you remember how to fight. Come out from behind those hooligans and enter the war!" yelled Jinjo.

"Jinjo! Have you no thought?! Do you no longer accept the chain of command? Or is it that you lack respect for your emperor?" asked Oilaz.

"I have no respect for those who do not fight!" yelled Jinjo.

"These are words of treason!" yelled the emperor.

"Ha! Treason! In that case, let me be the first to proclaim independence! Independence from you!" yelled Jinjo.

"Guards! Seize him! Apprehend this fool!" commanded Oilaz.

Moojan and one of his comrades moved to take the bulwark. However, when the pair drew close, Jinjo showed them his sword and ushered them back. Then two other Sagans joined them surrounding the immense soldier. The royal guards closed in around Jinjo to take him prisoner.

"Jinjo! You fool! Why do you defy the command? Do

you not see that you are outnumbered?" exclaimed Stratogos.

At that moment the swift chariot of Brunto approached the gathering. Emery held the reins driving the sturdy pair of horses and Brunto held onto the chariot rim. The war cart approached the group with speed. Brunto took hold of the leather straps and began to steer. The strong Sagan took a hard turn and circled the group, whipping the reins. He encouraged more and more speed with each pass calling to his comrades.

The brown Sagan held his spear in his fist and pumped it boastfully over his head. After he had made several passes, some of the Sagans began to cheer and recognize him. Brunto then brought the chariot to a stop near the gathering. He stepped down out of the chariot with his eyes fixed on Stratogos. Then the brown giant addressed the crowd of fighters with harsh words.

"Why do you hide back here like little teary-eyed whelps?" asked Brunto as he laughed.

The feathered monster bullied his way through the pack of wounded Sagans. The destroyer approached the royal guards and snapped his beak at them. He lowered his neck and began to speak in the old tongues. Brunto snarled and snapped at the guards with a series of clucks and cracks. The powerful Sagan took his hand and arrogantly pushed away Moojan's sword.

"Put your swords away, you fools!" shouted Brunto as he moved next to Jinjo.

"This is not of your concern, Brunto!" stated one of the Sagans.

"It is my concern when swords are drawn against my comrade," said Brunto.

"He is no longer our comrade! He is our foe! A

treasonous dog!" shouted Cassereen.

Brunto gave Cassereen an evil glance as he lowered his long neck and peered at him with one glaring eye. The destroyer once again spoke to the wounded in the old Sagan language. Most of the crowd answered Brunto with cheers and boisterous calls. Brunto drew his sword and began to beat the side of the blade across his breastplate. Then he bent down and marked a line in the sand with his sword. Brunto then addressed the crowd.

"To proclaim Jinjo is treasonous? This must be embarrassing for you! To be marked with treachery?" scoffed Brunto as he walked back over to Jinjo and put his hand on his shoulder.

"Tell them Brunto!" said Jinjo causing Brunto to speak with Cassereen scornfully.

"Jinjo treasonous? Ha! Most noble of Sagans!" proclaimed Brunto as Cassereen began to speak, but Brunto interrupted him with jubilee.

"Hold your tongue, fool! I am not finished!" said Brunto as he pointed his sword at Cassereen and continued to speak.

"Trustworthy he is! Loyal to his very bones! If you search for a treacherous dog look no further than yourself!" shouted Brunto.

"Ha! This comes from a coward and a deserter. Brunto! You should have never come back out of hiding!" said Cassereen.

"Ha! The day you left my army to guard Oilaz was the day you ceased to exist. I have returned to an army that fights among itself. These wounded should be praised for their valor, instead of being scolded by their emperor! An emperor who does not fight! Ha! If Jinjo is considered to be treasonous then I will join him! I have marked a line in the sand to divide us. Who will stay at the coward's side and who will join me? Join me not as your emperor, but as a comrade in arms!" shouted Brunto. Then the emperor let out a shout and jumped down from his horses to approach the line.

"Back down, Brunto! Take back these statements or die!" shouted Oilaz.

"Is there anyone here who will join us?" asked Brunto, ignoring the emperor completely.

The royal guards moved in to kill Brunto, and they might have killed the brute if not for Atlas. He stepped in front of the approaching guards who had their swords drawn to kill. Atlas quickly spoke to the defenders with his chest stuck out.

"I stand for Brunto, and those that oppose him oppose me!" said Atlas.

The royal soldiers stepped back away from the fortress to avoid him. The tall Sagan placed his hand on Brunto's shoulder and tapped his sturdy armor. The big hulk spoke to him in the old Sagan tongues and then moved behind Brunto. Brunto then moved to speak to the crowd.

"Come! Join us all who want! Cross the line and make your stand with us!" shouted Brunto.

A longtime supporter of Brunto was the first to move. He limped over the line covered in blood and stood next to his old friend Atlas. This brought a smile to Brunto's face and joy to his heart. The tall Sagan quickly matched shoulders with Brunto as he stood up straight and tall. Next, to the emperor's surprise, came Moojan as he tore loose his royal sash and threw it to the ground. Once these courageous fighters made their statements others moved to change sides.

However, not everyone moved to Brunto's sturdy side. Not everyone was persuaded to join Brunto's rebellious crew. After all, these were only wounded soldiers and only a small part of the legions. Cassereen and many of the feathered raiders stayed with the emperor. The host was divided almost evenly with half at Brunto's side and half with Oilaz. The small group toiled in the center of the wastelands bartering for separatists and loyalists. The emperor shouted with hate. Oilaz was infuriated with anger and malice and quickly moved to speak.

"Enough of this! These soldiers have made their choice and will suffer the consequences! This is a tragedy for you all. There will be pain, suffering, and death for all those who stand against me!" shouted Oilaz.

He turned to leave as he strode to his horses surrounded by the remaining royal soldiers. Oilaz called for his crew to make ready to move. The wounded troopers loyal to Oilaz moved into formation and they marched toward the forest.

"Ha! Ha! Ha! If it is civil war that you want then you will have it. But you will have it on my terms. You no longer have the sturdy ships at your haven. Nor will you have the same camps on our shoreline…and there will be no food of mine in your bellies! You and your horses will starve and die within a month! All of you who have crossed the line will soon pay the price. Your force will not survive on your own!" said Oilaz.

As the emperor and those loyal to him marched away, Brunto quickly made strategic moves to insure their safety. He bid them all to listen to him speak. He marched among them filling their minds with encouraging words.

"We must move quickly! It is of utmost importance that we commandeer a ship or two if we wish to survive. I need some of you to help me. When we get to the ships I want to steal all the humans," said Brunto.

"The humans? What do we need them for?" asked a Sagan.

"If we are to survive, we will need their help," said Brunto.

"We cannot survive by eating the weak flesh of men. Their meat alone will not sustain us!" said a Sagan.

"No. No. No. We are not going to eat them. We are going to join them," said Brunto causing a murmur among the host.

"Join them? They will never join us," said Jinjo.

"I will persuade them. Leave that to me. I need some volunteers to go and reach the others in the wood and bid others to join our side. There are those among the legions that will join us! Likewise, there are those that will oppose us!" said Brunto with urgency in his voice.

Moojan quickly volunteered to take a group of fighters to rally supporters. The rest of them agreed to go with Brunto and help him to carry out his plan. Brunto climbed on the wooden chariot and bid Emery to speed him to the coast.

They moved toward the fleet anchored in the deep harbor and moored on the sand. The curved vessels cluttered the shoreline with their masts reaching for the sky. There were many for the taking, but Brunto moved to take the fastest. Now they were on their own and nothing for them could be certain. Those who joined Brunto were taking a great risk.

Magoonagoon

CHAPTER 76

Eugene

In the deep woods, charging from the left, a group arrived on the scene to help Godwin, hoisting javelins in the air. The group simultaneously threw the barrage of pikes and they dove right into one of the Sagans, killing him instantly. The squad followed the javelins to the site of the dead villain, and they rearmed. At the helm was Eugene with his vigor.

The fellow raced to defend Godwin and his countrymen who looked to be at the mercy of Atsuel. He gave direct commands to get between the captain and Atsuel. The soldiers ran and leaped to the divide. There they held javelins up to deflect an attack from the feathered monster, so others could tend to his wounds.

Atsuel cursed the group and dared them to attack. He stared down at the host and glanced around for the leader. As he hissed and wagged his head, the Sagan caught sight of Eugene. The men lined up to throw the javelins just as before. Atsuel picked up a dead man's body and pressed his way through the war to seek out Eugene. When he drew near to the man he spoke.

"Call off these men and let me claim my prize!" said Atsuel.

"He is not dead! Only wounded!" shouted Eugene.

"Why do you let him cower away? If he needs time to recover, you can take his place!" said Atsuel.

"Very well! If that is what you want!" said Eugene as he ran toward the giant.

Eugene rushed at the creature with his short sword drawn and his shield ready. He was able to set his heels down near the killer and block a direct hit from the Sagan. Atsuel swung the dead body at Eugene to kill him. When the body struck the man's shield it made a dreadful noise.

Atsuel looked at the limp body that hung in his grasp, and studied the mangled carcass. He noticed the head was cracked open and the eyes had dropped out. This disgusted the Sagan and made him mad enough to throw the body at the enemy. The body soared just over Eugene's head and landed near Godwin. Seeing the men tend to Godwin made Atsuel respond with angry words.

"Look at him lying there! He is not wounded! Direct him over here and I will battle you both with my bear hands!" shouted Atsuel.

The voice carried over to Godwin and the man struggled

with his own troops to get back to his feet. The man staggered around as he tried to shake off the dizzy spell from the bash he took to the head. They tried to hold him back, but the man could not be governed. He climbed to his feet and scampered to Eugene's side. There the two convened and decided on a plan of attack.

In moments, they took to fighting as the pair ran together at Atsuel. The long-armed killer boxed the first man right in the face as he approached. Eugene clipped the Sagan as he passed and blood rushed at the monster's side. Atsuel put his hand on the wound to stop the bleeding, and cursed the man that struck him.

Godwin lay in front of the monster unconscious. The whale tusk had fallen out of his belt and lay on the ground next to him. Atsuel reached down and grabbed the plume of the man's helmet to pick him up. Godwin's limp body stretched out as the strong Sagan picked the fellow up from the ground.

"Hmmh? Dead!" said Atsuel as studied the man only for a moment, and then he pitched him down.

Turning around he found Eugene rearming with a different weapon. He had put away his sword and found two javelins to hoist at the brute. As the captain readied to throw, he spoke to Atsuel with jubilance.

"This one is for Godwin!" said Eugene as he flung the pike.

The javelin flew straight and zipped into the Sagan's hip, right above the thigh. The point buried deep in the creature's muscle. Atsuel screamed out in pain as he tried to pull it out. Godwin woke to the sound of the shrieking voice and he scurried to rearm.

Atsuel ripped the javelin out of his flesh and steadied it in his hand so he might use it. Eugene fired the second javelin at the Sagan and the point glanced off the forearm. Atsuel chuckled as the spear bounced on the ground, and as it started to roll away he picked it up. The mighty Sagan took both the spears and broke them over his knee. The giant discarded the halves by tossing them to the ground. Then the creature snarled with an evil grin and spoke to the men once more.

"I said that I would fight you bare-handed and still I am not dead! Can two not defeat me? Come here and let me snap off your head so I can rid you of this world!" said Atsuel.

Godwin had enough time to regain his strength and approach the Sagan for a second attack. He rushed at the killer just as before and dared the Sagan to strike. The monster swung his heavy fist at the man's head with the intentions to knock it loose from the shoulders. This time Godwin was ready, the man swung his sword at the right time and lobbed off the monster's hand.

"My hand! You have maimed me! Oh! No! You have! You...you...you...viper! I will kill you!" said Atsuel.

As he dropped to his knees the Sagan cursed the men around him. Godwin stepped back away from the giant. The man almost tripped as he scrambled to get out of the way. Yelling obscenities, the Sagan tried to snatch him, but the giant fell on his face. Then, with Eugene's direction, his soldiers lined up in front of the monster. On his command the soldiers launched their spears at him in unison. Many javelins zipped into the Sagan at the same time killing him instantly.

Magoonagoon

CHAPTER 77
Who Is There

The nights were long and cool for Jonathon and his soldiers as they traveled across the sea. The amazement of morning came just when they began to rest. The heralds called for each man to stand to his feet and loosen the thick ropes. They pulled up the massive stone anchors and used the long wooden oars to separate and push the vessels apart. After each ship was free, they sailed again, catching the wind and the current.

They sailed through the deep and through the green sea spray. For many days they held the same routine sailing all day and grouping the ships together at night until they reached the halfway point, a small island, just a bit of sand along the way. They moored the wooden boats on the sands and dove into the surf.

Every man moved to the island and climbed out of the water on the shores. They took goats and many loaves of bread to the beach and fed each man. They bedded down on the sand and slipped into sweet sleep. Little did they know that the island was the refuge of Ruffio the castaway. The Sagan walked among the trees and steered clear of the dangerous men unnoticed.

Through the night he hid in the darkness away from the fires of the camps. When the sun shone warm rays on their heads, Jonathon went to each man and ordered them to the ships. The rudders plowed through the sandy bottom as they scooted away from the jetty. As the boats crawled away from the Island, Ruffio left with them. He swam beneath the waves so he would not be seen and latched his sharp talons onto the huge beams of the rear ship.

The bulkhead was soon out of sight as they jumped the waves across the horizon. They sailed during the day and pulled the ships together each night. The stars guided them across the deep. The men charted them on the wooden decks under torchlight near the rudder. They mapped the way and studied the charts of old closely. When the sailors predicted the arrival within one day, Jonathon knew he should meet with his officers to discuss the landing.

That night, Jonathon called for a meeting. He took maps and called for the heralds to come to his ship. The leader sent his men away to the other ships so they could have privacy. Little did they know the clever Sagan had stowed away onboard and slipped unnoticed into the meeting. The proud man spoke to the leaders.

"I have gathered you together to discuss the landing. How do you propose we land?" asked Jonathon.

"We should circle the island at a safe distance and come ashore unnoticed. We would be fools to invade the camps of the Sagans straight from the sea," said one of the men.

"Well spoken, old man, but where do you suppose they are? We have never seen their position. Nor do we know if our ships can avoid the rocks around the point that are charted on this map," said another.

"I know where the Sagans are, they have moored their ships near Sree," said Ruffio.

To the men's astonishment, the voice startled them and caused even the bravest of them to tremble. The soldiers leapt to their feet with ready swords to fight whatever spoke to them through the darkness. Into the night the old whaler directed his speech to question whether or not this spy was friend or foe.

"Who is there? Why are you listening in on this meeting? I have sent everyone away so that we might meet in private without disturbance. Who is there?" asked Jonathon.

"It is I! Ruffio!" said the Sagan as he poked his long neck into the light.

All the men clumsily leaped back away from the creature. Some of the bravest of them ended up cowering on the ship's deck. The quick shift from one side to the other rocked the boat. As the vessel moved in the water, it frightened the men all the more. With their swords drawn the men began to interrogate the Sagan.

"How did you get aboard?" asked Jonathon.

"Please! Please! I did not mean to startle you! I am unarmed! I wish to strike a bargain with you. Now, because of you, I will return to Magoonagoon," said Ruffio.

"Not if I have a say! Throw him over the side!" shouted one of the men.

"Wait! Wait! Let's see what he knows!" said Jonathon.

"How do you know the location of the Sagan ships?" asked another man.

"Because I have been there. Look here…Roll out your maps! I will give you a lesson," said Ruffio as he pointed to a man. The man retrieved the scrolls and sat the maps down on the table in front of them.

"See the pass and the jagged rocks. If you move closely around the point and keep the island on your port side, the waters are deep and the current is shy," said Ruffio.

"He lies!" shouted a man.

"We know of your kind, Sagan! We know of your double-crossing ways!" shouted a man.

"There is no bargain!" shouted another.

"Let's slit his throat and throw him over the side!" said one of the captains.

"See here! We have no choice but to believe him!" said another man.

"Yes I agree," said a man's voice.

"Hold it! Hold it! Mark the spot on this map and you shall live," said Jonathon to the Sagan.

Ruffio hobbled over to the table where the map laid. The Sagan lowered his long neck and studied it closely. After he found the place that he wanted to mark, he looked around at the men. Before he took his sharp talon to scratch the mark, he spoke to them.

"You said I would live. You did not say you would let me go," said Ruffio.

"If your mark proves to be true, we will let you go," said Jonathon.

"What assurance do I have?" asked Ruffio.

"You have my word," said Jonathon.

"Why should we let him go? If we don't kill him, the Sagan should stay with us!" said one of the men.

"I said the Sagan will live and that we will let him go, if he gets us there safely, why should it matter to you?" asked Jonathon.

"If you release him, he will go and alert the rest of his kind of our landing," said one of the officers.

"He stays with us! Tie him down!" shouted a man.

"You're right! Bind him! Double the ropes! We will take our chances! I might have other plans for this stowaway!" said Jonathon as the men struggled with the Sagan.

"Please! Have faith! There is no need for these ropes! I will make a mark. I will not forsake you!" pleaded Ruffio, but the men tied the thick ropes around him.

So they tied up the Sagan and wrapped his beak shut. Then the heralds took the plan to their own soldiers in their own ships. When the morning sun rose, they sailed the ships again, ever stretching closer toward Magoonagoon. When they reached a certain point, Jonathon took his ship to the front and led the convoy of sleek vessels around the way. The ships followed his lead as they cut through the surf.

"Land ho!" was the word from the lead ship.

They approached the island and met the easy current and each ship lowered their sails. Each man took an oar and they dipped the wooden paddles into the salty sea. They pulled the ships through the shallows and slipped around the island unnoticed. They passed through the colorful but shallow reefs and they landed on the shores undetected.

First, the best of them secured a foothold on the beach while they moored the ships on the sand. Then each man did their duty to unload the hulls that carried the bounty of weaponry. They carried the heavy armor ashore and tugged the horse ships high on the beach with huge ropes. Then they carried the heavy equipment and the lofty poles of the shelters. The men took Ruffio ashore and drove stakes in the ground to hold him. The men tied the creature down with the ropes and made doubly sure the Sagan was secure. Last they carried the thick and heavy tents high over their heads to keep them dry. Jonathon quickly appointed sentries to guard as lookouts and ordered a group to arm themselves.

Magoonagoon
CHAPTER 78
I Beg You

Jonathon sent those who were armed out on patrol to scout the terrain. On their way out of the camp they spotted Ruffio sneaking off the sea coast. The Sagan must have somehow broken his binds. The men had tied him with thick ropes and left him on the beach. Somehow Ruffio was able to get free from the binds and was desperately running for his life. The Sagan ran across the sand and escaped.

The Sagan muffled curse words at them as he left. Ruffio raced to find Brunto. The men could have caught him on horseback. They could have chased him with the chariots; instead the soldiers watched the Sagan flee. They stood there in wonder as Ruffio continued to shout back at them. One of the captains almost called for a squad to chase him down. The man watched Ruffio run toward the desert and started to laugh.

"Look at him go! He looks so silly," said one of the soldiers.

"What is he saying?" asked another.

"Should we go after him?" asked a man.

"Let him go. He's only one Sagan. He doesn't matter," said the captain not knowing the Sagan was immensely valuable to Brunto and could have been used in negotiations.

The rest of the men armed themselves strapping their limbs with weaponry readying for attack. When the patrols returned from their search, Jonathon marshaled them to war. Some stayed behind to stand guard and watch the ships. Others moved on foot to the lowlands, marching in long strides. The heralds led the men at the front, ushering them to combat. With heavy strides they entered the wastelands and they moved hastily to find King Marion and the others.

Brunto had commandeered two ships and stole away all the humans just as he had planned. The leader had sent half of the humans and half of his soldiers to move the ships to a new location on the east side of Magoonagoon. He and the other Sagans had decided to move the rest of the humans on foot to the rendezvous point. He worried that keeping them all together might bring on rebellion. Since there were so few Sagans to oversee the men, there was always the possibility that the men might overpower them. The group had already crossed the wastelands and was marching toward the sea. Little did they know they were running right into the angry army of men. Emery was the first to spot the attackers as he drove Brunto's chariot. The young boy's eyes grew wide when he heard the trumpet blast. Emery held his tongue and said nothing to warn the Sagans as they slowly staggered into the striking distance of the mob.

Brunto caught sight of the men as they trekked into the void. Relentlessly the band of men approached with heavy feet. The feathers stood up on Brunto's neck with excitement, for the droves of men covered the landscape as their long spears and bright shields clanged on their way. Brunto gazed at the horde in amazement. With wide eyes he brought the horses to a stop and pondered what to do.

We have already covered so much ground on foot. This band of mine is too weary to run. There is no way we can fight. What will I do? wondered Brunto.

Brunto knew that he and his comrades would soon be dead. They were outnumbered, weary, injured and alone. He knew that unless he did something to negotiate with the angry mob it would only be moments until they would be captured or killed. In a bold move, Brunto grabbed Emery's wrist and spoke to his group.

"Quick! Each of you! Take hold of a man and hold him!" shouted Brunto to his soldiers.

Emery was perplexed at Brunto's order. The boy did not know what to think as the Sagan squeezed tighter. The Sagans snatched as many humans as their arms could hold. They wrestled with the spirited ones who tried to get free. Most of the men were still chained and they had no chance of escape. However, a few of the humans were not shackled and they had a chance to flee. Brunto pulled Emery closer to his side and picked him up in his arms. He enfolded the lad under his huge arm and glared at the humans who managed to escape. He watched them run across the delta to meet the approaching force. Emery could tell that the pending danger had shaken Brunto's confidence, but he did not understand what the Sagan was doing.

"What are you doing? Put me down!" shouted Emery.

"Listen well! If you wish to live! Hold on to your humans! Use them to save your life! I will ride out to meet these fools and try to negotiate. Wait here and hold these men as hostages! Wait for my return!" shouted Brunto to the crowd.

The humans who had managed to escape from the clutches of the Sagans raced to join the army of men. When they reached the marching group they rejoiced. As Brunto drove the chariot out to meet them he realized the doom. He knew that approaching them would be suicide and sheer death. Nevertheless, the Sagan held on to the young boy as if he were his lifeline. Emery tried to get free from the monster by kicking and screaming, but the Sagan had him locked under his arm. The boy tired from the struggle and decided to give up. Emery rested beneath the Sagan's arm and looked ahead as they rolled closer to the army.

Neither Brunto nor Emery knew that the boy's father was at the front leading the men in attack. However, as they drew closer, Brunto could sense something was wrong. He looked at the young boy and noticed tears streaming from his eyes. Emery's eyes grew wider still as the came closer to the ranks. So Brunto spoke to the brave lad.

"Are these your people?" asked Brunto.

"Look there! There is my father!" said Emery.

"Your father?" asked Brunto.

"Yes. He has come for me," said Emery.

Knowing this information, Brunto squeezed the boy tighter as they approached the horde. He slowed the pace of the proud speed horses to a gallop and began to turn them. Brunto drove them around to the side exposing the left wheel to the army of men. Soon he brought the chariot to a stop and he held the boy's waist firmly under his arm.

Jonathon caught sight of his son and was consumed with joy to see him alive. He stepped out in front of the men and ordered them to stop marching. The men slowed down and stopped just as Jonathon commanded. Jonathon walked toward the chariot and pitched down his javelin and unbuckled his round shield. He took off his helmet and pitched it to the dirt. He loosed his fine belt that carried his silver sword and let it fall. Jonathon moved toward the Sagan. It was then that Brunto spoke to the man.

"Halt! I order you to halt! That's far enough, old man!" shouted Brunto as he stepped out of the chariot.

Jonathon clutched his hands together and fell to his knees in front of the feathered monster. Tears of joy began to flow from the old man's face as he gazed upon his son. The old whale hunter began to plead and speak for his son's life.

"Please! I beg you! Give me my son!" said Jonathon causing Brunto to pull Emery even closer to his fat belly.

"Be still!" whispered Brunto to Emery as he drew his sword and pointed it at the fellow's side.

"What are you doing?" asked Emery as Brunto looked at the old man scornfully.

"Do as I say. I am not going to hurt you," whispered Brunto as he put the tip of the sword against the boy threatening his life. Then Brunto spoke to the man with harsh words.

"Old man! You have traveled across the sea to kill me! You know nothing of me or my kind! But...let me be the first to tell you...make no mistake about it! I am your true enemy! This boy used to be yours. Now he's mine! I have offered him a way to survive and have taken an oath to protect his life," said Brunto.

"Give him to me and we will spare you and your soldiers," said Jonathon.

"Ha! If I turn loose this boy, your soldiers will attack in defiance of your command," said Brunto as he laughed.

"No! No! They will not attack. I give you my word. Please! I beg you!" said Jonathon as the tears came forth.

"Old man! Old fool! I will not release the boy," said Brunto.

"Coward! Using a boy to save your own skin!" shouted Jonathon as he stood to his feet in anger and rage. Brunto placed the sharp sword to the boy's side and spoke once more.

"I will keep the boy. With me he will live. The soldiers behind me are wounded and weary. They too have hostages! On my order they will execute them," said Brunto.

"Cowards! All of you! Hiding behind hostages!" shouted Jonathon.

"My soldiers are no threat to you and your armies. Leave us be, and your son will live!" said Brunto with the sword aimed at Emery.

"You! Take him? Give him to me! You fool! Look at the

host behind me! You are dead! Give him up!" demanded Jonathon as he grit his teeth in anger.

"Have it your way!" said Brunto, drawing back the sword to strike.

"No! No!" said Jonathon, falling to his knees once again.

"Father! Please! No! Please no!" shouted Emery from underneath the huge Sagan's arm.

Brunto put away his sword and stepped back into the cart. He then put one hand on the reins and held Emery with the other. Brunto then tapped the reins to start the young ponies. The horses started to prance away, but he pulled them to a stop once more. He was too proud to let the old man have the last word in the matter. Brunto turned to speak to the old whale hunter.

"Remember this, old man…above all things. Listen well! All of you! Remember who I am! So from this day until that…Remember your enemy! I am Brunto!" boasted Brunto to them all as he whipped the reins against the nimble ponies.

Emery and Brunto whisked away to the Sagans. Jonathon watched his son ride away with the Sagan and longed to hold him. The old man stood to his feet and was quickly surrounded by his comrades. In the distance, the Sagans slowly tracked out of sight. Jonathon watched them go as he wept and cried aloud.

"Who among you is the most courageous? For the task I have for him requires a heart of iron," asked Jonathon and for a moment none spoke, they only looked at the ground and around the host.

"I will go after them!" said one of the men.

"Give him a horse!" said Jonathon, pointing to a soldier.

The soldier stepped off his horse and led the brown mare

over to him. The man mounted the mare with two steps and pranced her around the foremost. He made the horse's chin touch its muscular chest as he pulled the reins tight. The soldier looked to Jonathon for guidance. Jonathon quickly spoke to the man, giving him stern orders.

"Track them down and follow them to their camp. Find out where this monster will be keeping my son," said Jonathon.

The man kicked the ribs of the fair mare and galloped off to track the young fellow. The others quickly gathered Jonathon's armor that he had pitched to the dry dust. Like good servants, they returned his shield and weapons. After he was armed, he checked the men with harsh words and ordered them back in formation. When the lines were in form, they marched inland, toward the forest. As they marched away Jonathon wondered.

He said he has taken a vow to protect his life. He vowed that Emery will live. Why would he do that? wondered Jonathon.

Magoonagoon

CHAPTER 79

Reunion

Jonathon's men marched to the tall trees and followed their commander to the front. When they arrived at the forest edge, they met the black smoke from the blazing fires. Jonathon caught sight of the feathered foes as they battled among the trees. The old man quickened the pace as he strode to a swift stride. The legions of Sagans held the high ground.

The Foucinians held on by a thread with the help of Victor. He checked the center lines and held them in place, bidding them to fight. They were ready to break as they fought hand to hand with the foremost. Victor was ready to call for retreat when he caught sight of the old whale hunter. His spirit leaped out of his body when he saw his brother.

Jonathon and the men entered the tree line at a steady pace. Their armor clanged and rattled through the trees as they came on in hate. Victor's eyes grew wide as he watched his brother speed through the trees. The Sagans caught in the middle began to realize their time was up and their lives over. The Sagans were trapped in the midst of the battle and the men closed in. Jonathon inspired them all to go faster by running at full speed through the trees.

The men crashed into the Sagans, smashing their might and dominance. A host of feathered giants fell to the leaves as the waves of men came crashing in. Some of the Sagans were caught in the crossfire of spears and arrows. The old whaler and his soldiers quickly leaped over their massive bodies to continue advancing. Jonathon strode to the front, calling each man to follow him into war.

The remaining Sagans quickly became surrounded by the host of men. The group hoped to have their lives spared as they surrendered. However, the old whale hunter had harsh words for the feathered killers.

"Take no prisoners!" shouted Jonathon to his men.

The soldiers closed in on the giants boasting their heavy weapons. The Sagans fell to their knees and began to beg for their lives, calling out for mercy. One of them reached to his fine belt and pulled his sharp dagger out of hiding. The old Sagan waved the knife back and forth in front of the men hoping to discourage their assault.

In mere moments, the men finished off the feathered

Sagans, and the soldiers moved to meet their fellow men. Victor closed in on Jonathon with his hand upon the hilt of his sword. The brothers took heavy steps through the thick foliage and debris. Victor approached the old man like a lion who moves to track and rival another who had stumbled into his territory. Jonathon stood still with his hand upon his sword. The two men came chest to chest for the reunion. Each man looked scornfully at the other under their proud helmets. Their armor bumped together as they met under the tall trees. Victor was the first to smile and finally the brothers embraced. After they hugged, Victor was the first to speak.

"Oh! I never dreamed you would come!" said Victor.

"Is this Jonathon? Is this the same Jonathon, who scorned his younger brother for traveling to this land? The same man who pledged to stay out of the war. Why have you come?" asked King Marion.

"Your majesty. I have come to join you. These men have come from our shores to reclaim our sons and daughters," said Jonathon. King Marion then grabbed the wrists of the old whaler and smiled.

"Together! Against the heathen! An army of man!" said the king.

"Your majesty! Some of these men you may recognize! They are from your late father-in-law's elite band. They have been sent to you along with a letter from the queen," said Jonathon as he pulled out the letter and handed it to the king.

The king opened the letter and started to read the message. The cheerful expression on his face turned to a concerned look and then his face blushed red. When he finished reading the letter, he shook his head and smiled. After the king took a deep breath he spoke to the crowd.

"I am going to be a father!" said the king and all the men cheered.

"An heir to the throne, your majesty," said Jonathon and the men cheered again. After they settled, King Marion held up his hand to speak.

"Look around us! I see only man in the wood. The Foucinians have fled, leaving us alone. This has been the tale of our story. They used us to carry their heavy burden. We will not return to their stronghold. They have proved to us that we are here alone. I will not stand for it any longer," said the king as he took the shard of truce and pitched it to the ground.

"Come to our ships. Each one of you. Every man is welcome. Let it be known now and forever that we are united. Let it be known to all that every soldier will obey your command my king," said Jonathon.

"Long live the king!" shouted a voice from the crowd and the congregation cheered.

"To the shore! Back to the ships!" shouted the king and the men cheered once again.

Victor looked down at the shard and all at once the man remembered. He fell to his knees in a panic as the crowd around him stirred. Victor crawled to grab the shard from the ground where the shuffling feet of the crowds pressed. When Victor finally grasped the broken spear he burst into tears and yelled out.

"Amelia! Oh! Amelia! What have I done? What am I to do?" asked Victor.

Since the order had already been given to march, the noise and hustle of the crowd muffled the man's plea. As the crowd dispersed, Victor called out for help again and the petition found the ears of his men. They moved to the herald quickly and picked him up from the ground. Victor was crying and sobbing so bitterly that the soldiers did not know what to think. In a few moments, Aubrey was able to piece together what the man was mumbling and figure out what was wrong.

"His daughter! The others! The wounded! They are still in the stronghold! Oh! We must tell the king. We have to tell Jonathon! Felix is with them!" said Aubrey.

Magoonagoon

CHAPTER 80

Ask For My Son

Victor was delusional. Aubrey ordered the men to take him to the ships. Out of the wood, Aubrey raced to warn King Marion and the others. When he reached the swift ships where they were camped, the legionnaire hunted for the king. He found the king's tent under heavy guard. King Marion had ordered his soldiers to encircle his tent and not allow anyone to pass. Aubrey was stopped by the watchmen and ordered to leave. Desperately, the fellow began to shout to the king.

"My king! My king! You must come quickly! I fear we have made a terrible mistake!" shouted Aubrey.

"Go away!" shouted one of the guards.

"Get out of here! The king is not to be disturbed!" shouted another.

"No! I must see him!" shouted Aubrey and the disturbance caused the king to come out of his tent.

"Who is there?" asked the king as he scratched his head.

"Your majesty! It is I. Aubrey!" shouted the legionnaire.

"What is it? What do you want?" questioned King Marion.

"Victor is deeply troubled. His daughter is still in the stronghold," said Aubrey.

"Call the assembly!" ordered the king.

In the evening hour, the vast assembly gathered. When Victor reached the assembly, he moved through the ranks to search out his brother. He found the old whale hunter consulting with a soldier by the water's edge. Victor walked in on the conversation as the warrior spoke.

"The Sagans have grouped not far from here. I watched them as they set up a camp along the beach. As I spied on the group, a ship moored on the sandy beach and a second squad of Sagans jumped into the surf. I hid between the rocks and watched yet another ship approach. I started counting them...but then, to my surprise, there with them on the beach, were humans. Hundreds of them! We need to go and get them," said the man.

"Good! You have done well. We will alert the king and organize at once. We will go straightway to these ships and get him," said Jonathon.

"Hold on, brother! I have made a terrible mistake," said Victor.

"What could be more important that recovering these men? My son is with them!" asked Jonathon.

"I have abandoned Amelia and Felix back at the stronghold," said Victor.

"What? Felix? You have seen him?" asked Jonathon.

"Forgive me, brother! I sent him to the stronghold before the battle. They are both there in the stronghold. My dear Amelia is there! Your son is there too!" said Victor with tears in his eyes.

Hearing this Jonathon fell to his knees; then he cried aloud with his hands in the air. For now he knew that both of his dear sons were alive. His heart fluttered and his legs became weak when he heard the news.

"He is alive! Oh! Dear God, he is alive! I thought him to be dead. Killed by the murderous creatures," said Jonathon with tears of joy.

"Yes. He is alive," said Victor.

"Alive! Oh! I cannot believe it!" said Jonathon.

"You must forgive me. I left him there along with the others. Now he is inside the walls with our former allies," said Victor.

Oh! Who do I go after? Why must I shoulder such a heavy burden? thought Jonathon.

Jonathon shook his head and deliberated the problem. He thought for only a moment and crawled over to his brother and placed his hands on his feet. Then the old man spoke to his dear brother, the foremost fighter, the burly man of war.

"If you have love for me, go to them and ask for my son. I beg you. Take whosoever you need," appealed Jonathon.

Magoonagoon
CHAPTER 81
The Golden Trees

Victor moved quickly to pick the men he trusted most to travel with him to the Foucinian stronghold. After he gathered his soldiers he quickly went on his way. His only hope would have to be that the Foucinians would welcome them inside. There he would seek out Premo the great Foucinian leader. Victor then gave out orders to his men.

"Go and get four chariots for the journey," commanded Victor.

The soldiers quickly went to the equestrian ship where they had the stallions tied. The men carefully prepared the rigging and latched the horses to each chariot. They supplied four horses for each rig. The set up would give them the speed that they would need to get there quickly. On one hand the horsepower was a tremendous benefit, but it was hard to control. To keep the horses from taking off required three men to hold them back. After Victor and his team entered the chariots, the soldiers rode across the desert. Victor led the way, striding the four horses along the void. Hurriedly, the group took the four chariots and rigs to bring back every prisoner.

They rode through the Rocky Pass and entered the mudflats on the swift horses. The sun was beginning to set and the twilight began to smile on them. They rode hard and straight to avoid any patrolling Sagans to the rolling hills where the grass grew high. When they reached the crest of the last hill, they passed the remains of the old outpost that was destroyed by Sapsoon. The black timbers and chard remains lay across the ground in rubble.

As the company passed the ruins, a man spotted a patrol of Sagans in the distance and stopped the convoy. So Victor decided to take the squad around and avoid any confrontation. The riders turned away from the danger and headed toward the sacred golden trees. There the frogs chirped their songs in the night. When they reached the beautiful orchard, they were met by Foucinian sentries.

As they trotted the horses near the golden glade, the guards stopped the riders with their long spears with sharp points. The Foucinian guard ordered each of them to dismount. Slowly the patrol of men obeyed the hairy guard's orders, all but one man. Then the burly man of war also stepped down from his chariot. There from the edge of the wonderful trees, he spoke to the hairy beast.

"It is I. Victor," proclaimed Victor.

"Why do you approach the golden trees?" asked the Foucinian.

"We wish to slip through the back gate and find our way to the house of Premo," said Victor.

"I do not recognize some of these men in your company. I cannot allow you to smuggle foreigners into our city," said the Foucinian.

"That is fine. Let me go alone," suggested Victor.

"Go. But the others must stay here to await your return," said the Foucinian.

Magoonagoon

CHAPTER 82

Wolneas

Victor gave the reins of his chariot to Eugene and trotted through the beautiful trees. As he entered the orchard they began to glow with wonder. He slipped through the golden foliage and entered the secret passage at the back of the city. As the burly man made his way to the gate, he was stopped yet another time. Serpano, the heavyset hunter, ordered the man to stop. Victor quickly stopped in his tracks to heed the mighty beast's warning.

Victor stood still near the back entrance to the great city. Serpano moved through the trees and peered at the man with his scary eyes. The beast's hairy coat of fur was intertwined with his bright silver armor. Serpano approached the man with caution for he could not quite make out his face. When he drew near, he recognized his comrade and greeted him with inspiring words.

"Either you are foolish or you have a heart of iron, old man," said Serpano as he pointed his long spear in Victor's face. Under his helmet, Victor's brow grew angry.

"Get that spear out of my face," said Victor.

"Oh! Victor! I couldn't tell that it was you! The darkness has clouded my eyes and judgment. Why have you come this way? Why have you approached the back gate?" asked Serpano.

"The front gate was blocked with foe as I met a convoy of Sagans on my way," said Victor.

"Were you followed?" asked Serpano.

"No. The convoy was a great distance away," said Victor.

"Go ahead, old man! Pass on through. But, let me be the first to warn you. Premo is dead. He was your last tie to our truce," said Serpano.

"Premo? Dead?" asked Victor.

"It is still a mystery. Wolneas was appointed before he passed. Or so he says," said Serpano.

Wolneas? wondered Victor.

"You once saved my life. That is why I tell you this. Leave this place now while you still can. Wolneas knows of your desertion and he is displeased. He plans to kill you. The men you left behind are doomed. He claims them as his property," said Serpano with a smile on his face.

Victor shook his head and slipped through the gate. He walked down through the tunnel that secretly leads to the city. He walked along the marble street and passed the spray of the fine fountains. Along the way he passed many a decadent warrior. Many of the hairy beasts had shed their fine armor from their bodies as they lounged around in luxury. The hairy Foucinians peered at him like wolves with evil, green, glowing eyes. Still, the old man strode through as though he were in his own territory. Without fear or concern, he walked toward the house of Wolneas. One of the Foucinian warriors caught sight of him and quickly called out.

"You have a lot of nerve, old man! To come here after deserting us!" said the Foucinian.

Victor glanced at the old beast scornfully, but paid him no attention. The man continued his journey through the city with his hand upon the hilt of his sword. The crest on his helmet cut through the streets like the mast of a heavy ship ripping into a bay. Victor quickened his pace a bit when he passed the hard veterans of the Foucinian legion. The wily man approached the dwelling of Wolneas with caution, for his guardians stood with ready weapons near the front of his magnificent house.

Heavily armed protectors met him near the door holding their heavy spears. Victor had no choice but to stop at their command. The man could sense the danger in the air. He knew that he was no longer welcome there in his old abode. After he was recognized by the guardians, the tallest of them, Hawasaw, questioned the man.

"What do you want, Victor?" asked Hawasaw.

"I need to speak with Wolneas," said Victor.

Hawasaw looked over his shoulder at one of the others and motioned for him to tell Wolneas. The Foucinian returned after only a moment's time and bid the old man to enter. Victor met eye to eye with Hawasaw on the steps as he moved toward the door. After the two looked intently, Victor entered the well-lit house.

Victor approached the brute as he sat at his large wooden table. Wolneas bid the man to sit down on the wooden bench and he offered him food and drink. But Victor declined the hospitality and moved to speak.

"I have come for the others. I will leave with them at once," said Victor.

"The others?" asked Wolneas as he supped from his cup.

"Yes. They are here. Do not pretend to forget them. I have come for them," said Victor.

"You have a lot of nerve! You enter our stronghold alone! And you approach my table with demands. It should be a request you know…after abandoning us," said Wolneas.

"Where are they?" asked Victor.

"These men are prisoners. Soon they will be judged and condemned. There is nothing more to be said," said Wolneas as he slammed his heavy fist down on the table.

Victor peered across the wooden table at the hairy Foucinian with angry words ready to leap from his lips. However, the man held his tongue with clenched teeth and waited for the beast to calm. Instead, Wolneas grabbed the thick table edge and tossed it easily with his huge arm across the room. Seeing he was outnumbered, Victor kept his cool and for that matter kept still in a cold, stiff position.

"Get out of my house!" shouted Wolneas as he pointed to the door.

Victor moved slowly and cautiously to the exit. Then he

stopped in the doorway and made a bold move. He turned around to face the Foucinian and he stared at the beast with sorrowful eyes. For the man had been betrayed. He paused for a moment with the thought to battle them all then and there. There in the doorway he reached to his belt, but instead of pulling forth his sword, he took hold of the broken shard of truce that the king had discarded. Victor had salvaged the shard and hoped it could be used to bargain with.

When he took it in his powerful grip, the man pulled it from his belt causing all the Foucinians to flinch. Victor held it up at eye level and showed it to everyone in the room. Trumped with the old oath, Victor gave it a wave with his hand as if to say all bets are off. Then the burly man pitched the broken spear down at the Foucinian's feet.

"That truce died with Booballet. Oh! By the way! Why don't you stay for dinner tonight? We are having a feast! Know this before you go old man. Tonight they die. Tonight we will feast on your men! My best soldiers will fill their bellies with your kinsman! Their life is doomed!" said Wolneas.

Victor began to grit his teeth in anger and every last one of his hard muscles clenched in his body, popping the bones. The man fought hard to keep his composure from the shrewd comments. Nevertheless, the man turned and walked out of the house. He could barely control his rage when he heard the hairy beast call for his soldiers to fetch the cooks.

Victor took his massive hands and rubbed his face to ease the stress. As the old man continued to walk along the marble street, he clenched his stocky hand near his collar on his golden breastplate's edge. He tried to think of how to free them all.

Victor thought to turn around and to go after Amelia and the others by himself. He knew that he had to do something to save them from the killers. Even though the man was an army of one, he could not contend with all the Foucinians alone. He stopped in his tracks and wondered.

If not them, me, thought Victor.

So the old man turned around and quickened his pace back to the Foucinian's house. He strode heavy steps to the doorway with his hand tight on the hilt of his sword. Then, the man did what few would ever even think of. Victor moved to appeal to the Foucinian.

"Wolneas! Hear me!" shouted the man. Wolneas and the others came forth out of the house.

"I told you there is nothing more to be said," said Wolneas. Then Victor moved to speak.

"If there is a price to be paid, then take me! I am the one you want! Let them go!" said Victor.

"You would trade your life for theirs?" asked Wolneas.

"Yes! Gladly!" said Victor.

"Then give up your sword! Lay down your weapons and surrender!" said Wolneas.

"No! Let my eyes see them go free. Then I will give up my sword," said Victor.

"Ah! A hard bargain! Still, I wonder if you will keep it. How can I trust you?" asked Wolneas.

"You have my word," said Victor.

"Well then I will have some insurance. The boy. The boy who is with them. He looks like you. I dare say he is your son. I will keep him and let the others go," said Wolneas.

"No! They all go free," Said Victor.

"He stays!" shouted Wolneas.

Victor took a giant step forward and wondered if he should just try and battle them all. Even though the Foucinians had him outnumbered and surrounded they dared not approach him without Victor first giving up his sword. Seeing that he was outnumbered nearly thirty to one, he reconsidered the deal.

"Do we have a deal?" asked Wolneas.

What am I to do? thought Victor.

"After I give up this sword you will let him go as well," said Victor.

"Done!" shouted Wolneas.

Then, keeping his end of the bargain, Wolneas called for others to go and release the prisoners. A group of troopers moved to usher the captives out. Felix was brought before Wolneas and within moments the deal was done. The captives were released and they quickly moved toward the back gate. Amelia passed by her father and looked deep into his teary eyes. She raced over to him and they embraced.

"Go child. Do not let them think you are mine. I love you," whispered Victor.

When the girl finally let the man go, she dashed out of sight and never looked back. As the last prisoner moved out of sight, Victor conformed to his enslavement. Victor loosened his belt and let his sword fall to the ground. In that instant the Foucinians captured him and Wolneas ordered for the burly man to be scourged. Felix kicked and screamed for the Foucinians to let him go and he wrestled himself free. The boy raced down the street to catch the others and quickly darted out of sight. The

Foucinians stripped Victor of his armor and horsewhipped the man. As Victor lay there bleeding, he muttered a few words that found the ears of Wolneas.

"Soon he will come for me and you will be dead," whispered Victor. It was then that Wolneas realized that he had made a terrible mistake by setting the captives free. He then spoke clear orders to his soldiers.

"Capture them. The others! They are not to leave this city," said Wolneas.

"Get them!" shouted Hawasaw.

The hairy beast gathered a throng of troops and moved to apprehend them. In their haste they had no time to adorn armor. With sharp weapons the beasts moved to re-arrest them. Felix had caught up with Amelia and the others near the secret passage. He found the men scolding Amelia for crying.

"You must be quiet!" shouted a man.

"Don't you know we are trying to sneak out!" said another just as Felix arrived. The boy quickly put the men in their place.

"Unhand her you fool! Don't you know she is the reason you are alive! He came to save her! We owe our lives to her!" said Felix as he took the maiden by the hand and spoke comforting words to her.

"Don't cry. Your father has saved us all. He is a true hero. Since he has saved me, I will protect you with my life," said Felix as he bowed his head.

"I don't understand. Why do they want him? I thought we were helping the Foucinians?" asked Amelia.

"I don't know why they want him, but we are still in

danger. Let's stay together and walk quickly toward the opening. We still have to get past the guard," said Felix before they entered the secret passage.

The soft spoken words had convinced the girl to calm down. As the group pressed into the darkness, they found Serpano asleep with his big head against one of the thick tree trunks. His terrible snoring sounded like a growling bear. The men crept by him and Amelia was hesitant to sneak past the beast. If Felix had not been holding her hand, she never would have gone by him. They each had to step over his huge legs that cluttered the passage. Felix wisely grabbed Serpano's spear that lay near his grasp.

After they passed by Serpano, Felix gave him a smile and a nod as if to say farewell. Quietly, they slipped into the golden trees in their entire splendor. The captives rushed out of the grove and met the charioteers. When the group reached the chariots they were welcomed by the waiting men.

"Quickly! Get in the chariots!" said Eugene.

"Where is Victor?" questioned Aubrey.

"He traded his life for our freedom," said one of the men.

"Hurry! They are right behind us!" said Felix.

Hearing the news, Aubrey jumped down from his chariot and instructed the men to go on without him. Somehow the man thought he would go rescue Victor on his own. Hawasaw and his troops funneled through the back gate and swept into the trees with ready swords. Aubrey dashed at them with the confidence of a hundred men. The Foucinians came on with heavy footsteps and met him ten to one.

Magoonagoon

CHAPTER 83

To Escape

Eugene had started to ride away when he saw Aubrey make the daring move. He noticed that all the other chariots had left and Aubrey was attacking them on his own. In desperation, Eugene made the decision to help him. Eugene ordered the men in the chariot to wait for him and he too entered the trees to fight. He rushed at the commotion with his sword drawn to ward off the beasts. Eugene met up with Aubrey and advanced on the Foucinians with two hard blows of his cutlass.

Hawasaw and his escort came on in fury with murderous shouts and thundering calls. One of the other Foucinians moved in close to engage the men in hand-to-hand combat. Eugene blocked his swing with his weapon as he moved in a defensive position. The other Foucinians then staged their attack on Aubrey, wheeling about, glancing blows.

Eugene ran his sword straight through the Foucinian's hairy side and the blade stuck between the ribs. The man pulled with all his might to remove the sleek steel, but the blade was stuck. Hawasaw, seeing the unfortunate slip, struck the man across the helmet, sending the fine headpiece flying off into the trees. The loud clang alarmed the men who were waiting in the chariot just outside the grove. The fellows were so frightened they thought about leaving without Aubrey and Eugene.

Aubrey smashed into the host with his mighty armor and heavy weaponry. He clipped the tall beasts down with his arsenal of weapons and his bare hands. The legionnaire slammed Hawasaw to the ground when he struck him near the heart with his well-made javelin. In a flash, he had the arm of another with his sword. Soon every Foucinian that chased after them was dead.

So Eugene moved to retrieve his helmet and after he placed it back on his head he quickly moved to call Aubrey to retreat. Aubrey had already made up his mind to enter the stronghold and rescue his friend. Eugene called to the man as he ran into the danger.

"Aubrey! Don't go! Come back!" shouted Eugene.

Eugene raced through the leaves and searched for the men who were waiting for him. When he found them, Eugene jumped into the chariot and watched intently to see if Aubrey would return. As Eugene waited, he could hear the rustling sound of shuffling feet. Just in time, Aubrey strode out of the trees and leaped into the chariot to escape as droves of Foucinians came from the trees hoping to capture or kill them. The men dodged the swift spears that flew at their heads and lashed at the racehorses to flee. The hooves thundered along the trail and sped the men away. The men had traveled a great distance when they heard a frightening noise behind them. Three Foucinian charioteers had burst out of the gates to give chase. Wolneas himself joined the pursuit in a sensational chariot. The hairy beasts whipped their teams and beckoned more speed on the open range.

      Aubrey was the first to spot the interceptors as he looked back over his shoulder. As the Foucinians raced ever closer with every fleeting stride, the man borrowed a spear from the rack and made plans. He jumped up on the rail of the chariot and steadied his feet. The fellow waited until he had good balance and leapt onto the back of the outside horse. Aubrey secured his hands on the leather straps and used his knife to cut the horse free from the rigging. In moments, the horse was loose and the fellow peeled away to fight.

      Aubrey steadied the lengthy weapon in one hand and pulled on the reins of the horse to make her stop. The mare slid to a halt and almost tripped from the command. Eugene rolled away from the legionnaire and dashed away to catch up with the other men. The leading Foucinian charioteer bounded toward Aubrey with intentions to run him over. The legionnaire ushered his horse directly at the helm of the center chariot.

      Aubrey continued on, planning to commandeer a chariot of his own. As the legionnaire persisted in direct line of the center chariot, he switched hands with the spear. He grabbed the reins with the hand that also held the spear and reached to pull his knife. Slowly and gently the man pressed his knife into the neck of his own horse. The blade cut right into the artery of the animal. With only a sight jerk the mare continued to gallop at a steady pace toward the center chariot. Without hesitation the chariots approached with dangerous speed.

As the dangerous team drew near, the blood loss began to take its toll on Aubrey's horse. The mare stalled only a bit until she trotted into close range. Then, just as the man had planned, the animal collapsed beneath him. Her head went down first and she folded under the man. Aubrey had anticipated the fall and he planted the point of his spear down in the ground in front of him to vault over the oncoming foe in perfect timing.

The Foucinian charioteer never slowed down as his team passed over the fallen horse. The horses leaped and stammered over the top of the mare as Aubrey whisked above. Luckily, the man's leg snagged in the rail of the cart and kept him from falling out. Aubrey's other leg slammed into the chest of the driver and the sheer momentum flung the Foucinian out the back. The poor beast flipped and tumbled in a cloud of dust as the chariot sped away.

The other Foucinian in the chariot dropped his bow and wrestled the man. The two grappled and fought each other intensely. The chariot raced out of control and turned a sharp corner at high speed. When the cart tipped up on one wheel, the Foucinian was cast out. The hairy beast slammed into the dirt and the deadly force caused his body to go limp. Aubrey quickly struggled to free his leg and grab the reins of the loose cart. The man grabbed the straps just in time to regain control of the chariot. The hooves rumbled and thundered toward the persistent enemy.

Being one of the best charioteers to ever live, Aubrey was able to catch the Foucinians in no time. He drove the cart so close to the Foucinian's chariot that the wheels almost touched, Aubrey abandoned his chariot and leapt into the opposing chariot with his sword leading the way. The initial punch knocked one of the Foucinians out. The blade met the other hairy Foucinian warrior and drove deep into his body. The brute tried to fight death with his last fleeting breath, but the sword sent him on his way. Aubrey kicked the beast out of the cart and took hold of the reins. In complete control, the man raced into attack formation with the goal to sting the lone Foucinian charioteer.

When Eugene had looked back at the pursuit, he noticed that Aubrey had eliminated all but one of the chariots. So the man decided to turn his chariot around and help him. The horses bellowed as they made the turn and the dust churned up in their wake. When the team straightened the wheels, Eugene ushered them up to full speed.

When Aubrey reached the Foucinian, the hunter became the hunted as they bumped and traded scuffs. Every move that Wolneas made Aubrey countered. The legionnaire squashed the assailant's horses and they locked together as they bumped. Headlong they ran, toward Eugene, who approached from the opposite direction. Ever fleeting strides took the three chariots forward to an inevitable collision. A moaning sound came from the horses and a terrible crash followed.

The horses knotted and wrinkled together, pinching men and crushing the wooden carts. Wolneas was thrown from the wreckage a great distance, and the men were cast aside. Not a single man or beast stood from the crash. Each of them lay in agony from the jolt. When the dust settled, the first to stand happened to be the Foucinian. He gripped his knees as he mustered enough strength to rise. Bleeding and desperate, Wolneas struggled to take advantage of them.

The beast found a weapon and moved to strike. Wolneas picked up a spear and limped to finish off the injured men. Hobbling forward into the site of the wreckage, he first spotted Aubrey, who was crawling toward his sword that lay just out of his reach. Wolneas quickly shuffled and advanced on the legionnaire threatening him with evil words.

"Crawl on your belly like the worm you are, boy! For you have met your doom!" said Wolneas.

When the Foucinian reached the man he drew back the spear to kill. Aubrey wisely turned over to face the beast, where his armor could protect him. The spear point slammed into the legionnaire's breast plate. The metal met the tip of the spear and rung the man's bones. Then, to the Foucinian's surprise, the man answered his attack with a swift kick. As Wolneas prepared for another assault, Aubrey stretched out to get his sword, but it was just out of his reach. As Aubrey struggled to grab the handle, he called out for help in desperation.

"Eugene! Save me!" yelled Aubrey.

"He cannot save you, boy! You are dead!" said Wolneas.

Then the hairy beast wounded the legionnaire with the spear point. The hit was not direct, but it was enough to pierce the man's side. Wolneas kicked the man away from his weapons and again the Foucinian tried to kill him. Once more the

Foucinian managed to wound the legionnaire. All the while Aubrey shouted at the top of his lungs for his comrades to save him. In the frenzy the man clutched his helmet and slung it into the face of the evil beast. The helmet busted Wolneas directly in the snout. The glancing blow gave the man enough time to grab his sword.

With the sword in hand, the legionnaire stood to his feet. Even though Wolneas could distance himself from the man with his spear, he dared not try. The beast backed away in fear and gestured with a stabbing motion as he stepped. When he put enough space between them and felt comfortable with the range, he spoke to the man once more.

"I will remember you, boy! We will meet again! It is just a matter of time!" said Wolneas.

Then the beast hurled the spear and ran. The weapon had no chance of hitting the legionnaire or anyone else. The swift Foucinian fled like the coward he was to live and fight another day. Aubrey moved to attend to his comrades that lay strewn amongst the wreckage. Eugene awoke after the man jarred him and the two searched for the others under the debris. Sadly they found them pinned beneath the rubble.

Magoonagoon
CHAPTER 84
Anyone

Amelia and Felix rode in the lead chariot hanging on to the rim. They passed the watchmen that were positioned as lookouts along the front and drove to the center of the encampment. The group jubilantly returned with relief. When they dismounted from the chariots the crowd began to question them.

"Where is Victor?" shouted a voice from the crowd.

"Where are the others?" shouted another voice.

"They are behind us! Battling the Foucinians who chased us all the way here," said Felix.

The former captives answered all their questions and the news of their return finally made its way to Jonathon and King Marion. Jonathon ran to meet them and when he saw his son, he fell to his knees. The two embraced and the old whaler was so happy that the boy had returned safely. So there on the ground he buried his head in the boy's shoulder and wept.

Everyone rejoiced and the crowd was so cheerful. Every person who was rescued received special care. Still, questions and rumors stirred throughout the camp. The people waited anxiously for Aubrey and Eugene to return. An audience formed near the edge of the camp and the congregation of soldiers was filled with speculation. They began to wonder if the men would come back. At nearly midnight, a shout came from the crowd.

"Look there!" shouted a voice from the crowd.

Aubrey and Eugene entered the camp and all eyes were upon them. The two men hurriedly walked into the mob. The congregation congratulated them as they walked through. The crowd patted them on their backs and cheered for the homecoming. Before they stopped, Aubrey pushed the hands away and spoke to the multitude.

"Let me go! Where is King Marion?" asked Aubrey as he fought their praising cheers.

Aubrey pushed his way through the crowd. As he shuffled through the gathering, they continued giving him congratulatory remarks and he battled the many hands that tried to embrace him. Through the rush, the legionnaire demanded to speak with King Marion at once. Jonathon was shocked at the legionnaire's request, but when he caught sight of the expression on Aubrey's face, he knew that he should join them.

Aubrey's demeanor was different than all the others who had returned safely. Jonathon wondered why the man was so angry in such a joyous time. Aubrey continued walking toward the tent where they could meet privately. Jonathon was still enjoying the time with his son and held on to him a bit longer.

"Aubrey. You are wounded! Let's get you to the doctor," said Jonathon.

"No! We do not have time!" shouted Aubrey.

"What do you mean? What is it, my friend?" asked Jonathon.

Aubrey placed his hand on the old whaler's shoulder and ushered him into the tent. Eugene followed the two into the well-made tent, for no man would dare give him an order. Jonathon never let go of Felix's hand so he too entered the tent with them. The four of them went in and stood in the center of the shelter. Then Aubrey spoke to the old whaler.

"We must move quickly. We still have time to save him," said Aubrey.

"What? What do you mean?" asked Jonathon.

"He is in great danger. The evil beast took him as payment for the others. He is still there within the walls. Imprisoned," said Aubrey. Outside the tent, the crowd began to shout out questions.

"Where is Victor?" asked a voice.

"Where is Victor? Is he dead?" asked another.

A cold look came to Jonathon's face and the old man grew angry. He thought only for a moment, long enough to make the decision, and sent each man to rally their troops. As they left to tell the others, strength left the old man's legs and he laid down on the bed. As he lay there on the bed, the old man was encouraged by his son.

"What is going on here?" asked King Marion.

"Your majesty. The Foucinians have imprisoned Victor," said Aubrey.

"A prisoner of war?" asked the king.

"Yes my king. What are we to do?" asked Jonathon.

"Do we know if he is still alive?" asked King Marion.

"No your majesty. But if we move quickly we might be able to save him," answered Aubrey.

"Go at once. If there is still hope, I will not stop you," said the king.

Then, Jonathon did what some men do in difficult times; he lost all hope for his dear brother. Jonathon was filled with rage and anger, but deep within his heart he knew that there might not even be a chance to save him. The wind howled in the night as the soldiers readied the troops among the tents. The old whaler remained in his tent to regain his strength. During that time his mind was changed and the revelation came to the old lion in thought.

I will go, and I will go alone, thought Jonathon.

So Jonathon marched to find King Marion and ask him to order the soldiers to stop assembling. The stars were hid behind the clouds and the west wind blew hard on their backs bending the large palms. The old man found King Marion and told him the story. The king shook his head in doubt, but agreed with the decision not to rush off and try and save him without careful planning. Jonathon quickly moved to find Eugene and Aubrey and call them off for the night. He found them at the front of their lines marshaling their men into formation and calling to the ranks. When Jonathon saw them, he spoke to each man.

"Do not send your troops against the foe tonight…not for my sake. Let us hold off until tomorrow. What good would it do to approach the fortified city? We cannot fight an effective battle against the tall walls and battlements. I have already lost hope for my dear brother…the beasts have taken him and now we fight a two-front war," said Jonathon but the legionnaire was quick to answer him.

"We will enter in through the secret passage. All these soldiers need is a captain or leader to point out the way. We still have time to save him! We will go after him tonight," shouted Aubrey.

"I beg you. Wait until the morning," suggested Jonathon.

"We stay here tonight!" said King Marion as he walked into the argument.

"No! I will not give up! Anyone! I beg you! Is there anyone brave enough to volunteer to go with me?" asked Aubrey.

"Please. Apprehend this man and calm him down," said Jonathon. Troops came from every direction to detain the delusional legionnaire.

"No! Please! He is right! Why won't you help him?" cried Amelia.

"My troops will not lie down in sleep. We will remain ready throughout the night to engage them," said Eugene.

"No. Let your soldiers rest for I will not change my mind again. Let your men sleep so that their minds will be ready for battle. We will pray that the old man can make it through the night," said Jonathon.

"He traded his life for these here! He saved your son! What manner of man are you?" questioned Aubrey.

After he spoke those words, Jonathon looked at Aubrey with a disapproving look. All the man could do was shake his head. Jonathon stayed only for a moment more, and then he turned to leave. As he walked away Aubrey continued to plead with him and the others. Aubrey spoke with such inspiration that he almost had them convinced that there was no other way. King Marion himself was ready to join the man, but he hesitated to speak for just a moment and Aubrey spoke again.

"Are you men? How dare you call yourselves men! If you don't go, I call you cowards!" shouted Aubrey.

Aubrey flew mad, screaming at the whole lot and calling them names. He flung his helmet at the crowd and cursed at his own men for cowering. Plenty of men would have joined Aubrey, if he would have just waited a moment longer. When no one volunteered, the legionnaire did the unthinkable; he pulled his sword and threatened their lives.

Aubrey knew, just as the words came out, that he was wrong. Still, the man held firm in his position and waited for someone to speak. He turned his head and searched with his eyes looking for a glimmer of hope. He glanced at Godwin, but the man looked away. Aubrey glared at Eugene and his lip began to quiver. When he glanced at King Marion, he could see it in the fellow's eyes and knew that he was alone. Without support, the legionnaire slowly lowered his sword and sat down on the ground in disbelief.

A short distance away, Jonathon beheld the fellow

grieving. He rubbed his face and scratched his head as he digested what he had just witnessed. Jonathon headed back to his tent where he posted guards at the entrance. He gave the lookouts strict orders not to let any man enter. There he rested with his son and Amelia. It was during these moments when the old man consulted with the two. They spoke about the entrances to the city and shared wonderful thoughts. When Felix and Amelia fell asleep, the old man covered the boy with a blanket and gave him a kiss on the forehead. He patted Amelia on the shoulder as she slept. There in the tent, the old whaler remained until the camps became still and quiet. Jonathon waited patiently until all was calm and then he made his move.

Magoonagoon

CHAPTER 85
Go To Freedom

There in the tent Jonathon prayed. The man knew in his heart what he must do; he did not need the legionnaire to tell him. Jonathon would go alone in the night after his brother. If he was going to be called a man, Jonathon knew that was exactly what he must do. Victor would do the same thing for him. As the nightfall lingered on, he made preparations for the journey.

While Felix and Amelia slept, Jonathon slipped off his armor and took loose his white tunic where he would not be seen. He gently took his knife to cut the fine tunic at the seam and made a strip the entire length of the garment. Jonathon used the linen to gird his loins as he tied the wrap tight around his waist. Silently he moved to the back of the tent and tossed his fine leather saddle underneath. Then, he grabbed his round bronze shield and passed it through with care. Last of all he took the well-made sword, the same sword he had pulled from the ruins of his home, and slipped underneath.

After he had done these things, he himself passed beneath the canvas. The old man stayed low to the ground and began to sneak away from the guards and soldiers. Jonathon crept through the darkness to the stable ships where the horses stood in sweet sleep. The old whaler approached the horses with caution and care. He found his mighty steed among the sleeping chargers, on the far end of the line. In a flash, Jonathon loosened the straps of the mighty war horse and moved him to the end, near the surf, where none could see.

The old man could hardly draw a breath in the night in fear of being caught. So he moved quickly, for he feared far worse for his brother. Jonathon pitched the fine leather saddle across the back of the speedy horse. After he positioned it in place along the hefty stallion's spine, he buckled the strap along the belly. When the leather was snug and tight the old man mounted the animal.

The old whaler then began his journey with haste, for he knew above all things that he had little if no time left. He rode the horse softly around the camp away from the soldiers and out of sight. When he reached a point where it was safe, he let the horse run. The magnificent stallion stretched out his legs and pumped its powerful neck. With every stride the powerful hooves punched the earth. He rode through the blackness with sorrow in his heart.

As he crossed the desert the sky once more began to rumble. The whaler's teeth began to chatter as the cool air ran across his skin. The man began to fear when he passed glowing eyes in the night that could have been wolves, lions, or lurking demons.

What have I had done to merit such a heavy burden? wondered Jonathon.

When the old whaler caught sight of the gate, he trotted the horse into the trees. For if he was to enter the gates he must have a plan. When he reached close range he dismounted from the fair stallion and hitched it to a skinny tree. Jonathon approached the wall, peering across the landscape for guards.

He tracked along the perimeter searching for a way to penetrate the castle. The old man encircled the tall walls searching and searching until he had almost given up hope. He passed the columns and pillars made of fine marble and he studied the beautiful statues of the greatest Foucinians. When he went back to his horse, he found the entrance through the golden trees. Jonathon slipped through the grove with caution and readiness.

As he snuck through the trees, he stepped upon a red serpent with bright scales. The viper took its sharp pits and laid a strike upon the man's heel. The red snake locked its jaws down tight on the ankle and began to pour in the deadly poison. Jonathon held the pain between his white teeth and chopped the serpent in half with his bright sword. The teeth lost their grip and the snake fell away from the sword's bite.

The viper pitched about among the leaves as it coiled to

death. However, the deadly snake had already made its terrible mark on the heel with its sharp fangs. So Jonathon continued on to the entrance with the deadly venom in his veins. He entered the gate without opposition for all the Foucinians were asleep inside their stronghold. His nerves began to dance and his heart began to race as he continued on. The man's lips and tongue began to tingle as they grew numb.

Some may have looked at the snake bite as a bad omen, but it never crossed Jonathon's mind. The old whaler moved along the marble streets to the center of the city where he hoped to find his brother. Along the way he repeatedly looked at the wound from the viper that bit him. He passed many a gallant soldier's house along the way as he snuck through the village.

He staggered along the streets like a drunken sot, in and out of consciousness. Jonathon passed along the houses trying to keep his feet in stride. He came to a beautiful fountain and dipped his hands in the clean water and splashed his face. The cool water took away the dizziness for a moment and allowed the man to continue. He started to go on, but Jonathon stumbled back over to the fountain and washed his head once more. The cool water covered his thick grey hair and woke his sleepy eyes. So the man moved on to find the place where Victor was kept. Jonathon knew that if Victor was still alive, he would be under heavy guard.

Drunken and dazed from the snake's venom, Jonathon pressed on to find his brother. He began to sweat and breathe heavily as the ankle began to swell. Quietly, the man slipped through the streets as he darted through shadows looking for cover. Jonathon looked for the place where a prisoner might be kept.

The old man crept behind the wall to avoid the dangerous Foucinians lurking nearby. He stopped to rest near a house where the lights were still on and sat beneath the window. As he rested, the man heard voices and laughter.

"Look at him! How proud he was! Now he is broken!" bellowed one of the Foucinians.

"Get him out of here, I have seen enough! Take him to the dungeons!" said one of the Foucinians.

Jonathon knew that it was his brother they were speaking of. He hid in the shadows and listened as the shuffling feet scurried in the house. Jonathon rubbed the wound on his ankle and heard the wrestling commotion. The sounds painted a picture in his mind of severe cruelty. Rattling chains tingled on the floor and a thump followed. Then, the only noise was the dragging slip across the floor.

Out of the house they went, dragging the man. His clothes were tattered and torn. Blood dripped from his limbs. His face was mangled. The fellow had been beaten so badly that he did not look human. Around his neck, the man was shackled with an iron collar. Looped and bound to it was a thick chain. It was stretched as tight as it could be and led the man like a dog.

The Foucinians around him used staffs to prod and urge him forward. However, the switches that lashed the fellow did nothing to speed his travels. Victor slipped behind the Foucinian that dragged him as limp as a rag. The beast struggled to drag the man and had to pause often to catch his breath. When he stopped, the others would also rest from the constant beating. Their sticks were stained red with the man's blood.

Jonathon carefully followed them down the street, staying out of sight. He kept his distance, until the beasts reached the entrance to the dungeons. When Jonathon saw them enter through the passage, he moved quickly to spy on the sentries who guarded the entrance.

One of the Foucinians fled down the steps that fell from the doorway. The others kicked the man down the flight and his body rolled all the way to the bottom. The beasts followed the man closely and quickly regained control of the leash. Victor moaned from the pain and sighed a deep breath.

At the entrance, Jonathon made quick work of the sentries. They were not prepared for the attack and both of them dropped dead with swipes from his knife. The old man waited for a moment to make sure no one was alarmed, and then he too entered the dungeons. Down the steps he tracked, over the fresh puddles of blood.

Jonathon could see the torches ahead of him and he sped toward them with unexplained strength in attack. In pursuit, Jonathon prepared for assault by lifting up his sword and shield. The first Foucinian he met was easily toppled as he stabbed him right in the back. The other one tried to smack the man with his staff, but the blow was deflected off the fellow's shield.

One of them scampered back against the wall in defense, while Jonathon headed for the leader. The Foucinian had dropped the chain and pulled a sword to battle the man. Jonathon rushed at the beast and blocked a strike with his shield just as before. The point of the blade zipped into the Foucinian's belly and the man pressed it deep into the flesh.

Seeing his comrades dead, the last Foucinian tried to run

for help but the old man stepped in his way, and cut off his escape. The beast swung at the man's head hoping to kill him. However, the beast missed and hit the wall, shattering his weapon. Jonathon leaped at the hairy monster and cleaved the Foucinian near his neck. A second strike took the beast's life as he fell to the floor.

The old man laid down his weapons and dove to the side of his younger brother with his strong hands. He gripped Victor in his arms and tried to get him to respond, for he feared him dead. Jonathon woke the man with his powerful grip as he lifted the husky body from the floor. As Jonathon held him tight, Victor moaned and acknowledged that he was still alive. The bloody man rubbed his eyes and strained to see.

"It is you! You came for me! I knew you would come! It did not take long for you to come!" said Victor.

"Yes. I am here. I have braved the host of Foucinians with no thought for my own life," said Jonathon.

Victor embraced the old man around the neck and his spirit rose as he shed tears of joy for the greeting. He started to speak, but Jonathon quickly covered his mouth as he coughed. Then Victor listened as Jonathon whispered in his ear.

"Listen to me. I am near the end. For I will not be with you long. You must go to freedom. Listen close for death may be near to me. Get out the gate and through the golden trees. My horse is not far from here. He waits for you there. Amelia is safe. Go after her. She is waiting in my tent. There my son also awaits your homecoming. Take him as your own…tell him this is my wish," said Jonathon as he fell back from the dizziness.

"No. I will not go without you," said Victor.

"But you have to. It is up to you to lead the men," said Jonathon as he struggled to breathe.

"We will go together. I am not leaving you here," said Victor.

"Do you want the Foucinians to have us both? My eyes are fading," said Jonathon.

"What has happened to you? Why? Why are you at your end?" asked Victor.

"There is no time. Listen to me! Please," pleaded Jonathon.

"Please come with me," said Victor.

"I have one more wish. You must grant it. Promise me you will save Emery. He is alive. I have seen him. He is prisoner to a Sagan named Brunto. Please save him," pleaded Jonathon.

"I will. I promise," said Victor.

"Take my weapons and go! Go to freedom! Goodbye, my brother," said Jonathon as he lost consciousness.

Victor slowly lifted up his eyes and realized what he had to do. He wrapped the long chain around his shoulders and picked up his brother's weapons. With a sniff he obeyed his wishes and quickly carried out the orders. Victor hobbled up the stairs and out of the dungeons. He moved down the street as quickly as he could. When he met the door step of Wolneas, he prepared himself to attack. The brave man entered the house with the ready sword and leaped upon the hairy Foucinian as he slept.

The man forced his knife deep into the beast's side and pressed his shield around the Foucinians neck to choke away his life. Wolneas struggled to breathe as the man pressed and pressed. As Victor pushed his weight on the beast, he could see the fear of death in his eyes. Wolneas tried to get up, but Victor stuck him again with the knife, taking the beast's life.

Victor began to get dizzy, for he had taken such a fierce beating earlier that night. He sat on the floor beside the bed for a moment to shake off the spell. Then he hid behind the doorway, for the man was sure that others had heard the commotion. After he shook off the daze, he moved to find his way out. With his back to the wall, Victor took a deep breath and just before he left the room, he mumbled these words.

"God. Help me," said Victor as he burst out of the house.

He passed through the city and through golden trees undetected. He steered by the guards unnoticed and the man limped toward the exit. There Victor found his brother's powerful horse. So the steed raced back toward the sea with the warrior on his back.

The man left the stronghold of the Foucinians, and traveled to freedom across the desert. Through the night the old man cried for his brother with each step forward. As he journeyed, the stars slipped out from behind the thick clouds. An eerie sense crept over the land as he traveled across the desert. With his brother's help the man had escaped doom.

Magoonagoon

CHAPTER 86

Forgive Me

Victor rode across the desert throughout the night. When the morning hour came, the horse staggered into the camp. The man was stopped by the sentries and guards at the perimeter. They ordered him to halt for they could not identify who he was. The Foucinians had beaten him so severely that they did not recognize the old man. After questioning him, the sentries allowed him to pass, and the burly man rode his brother's horse into the camp. He trotted the stallion over to the tents and fell off the horse to the ground.

Aubrey scrambled to help him and gripped Victor in his arms. The legionnaire looked at the man with wonder and surprise. A host of others ran to aid Victor and they carried him to his tent. On their way, Victor spoke to them in his delusional state.

"He is gone! Oh! He is gone!" said Victor over and over.

Jonathon's men questioned the whereabouts of their leader. Some of them had already concluded that Victor was speaking of Jonathon. To their dismay the thoughts were confirmed when Aubrey asked him who he was speaking about.

"Jonathon! He is dead!" said Victor as they entered the tent.

There Amelia cared for his wounds and nursed him. He lay in the tent for three days and no man was allowed to enter. When he finally emerged, Victor went to the sea and waded out in the ocean. For most of the day he stayed out in the surf and no one was brave enough to approach him.

Later that day, Victor called for Felix to come to his tent. The young boy obeyed the command and came to the tent as soon as he received the message. Felix entered the tent and collapsed down on his bottom to the coarse sand. Victor walked over to him and gritted his teeth while twirling the hair in his beard.

The little fellow did not know what to expect from the man so he waited for him to speak with anticipation. Victor continued to stand there and look at the boy in silence and the man began to cry. Felix's first thought was to be puzzled at the action, then his eyes filled with tears too and he felt sad. Victor hung his head low in front of the little boy and began to sob. Then inside the tent, silence took command of them both. After a moment, Victor broke the calm when he spoke sorrowful words.

"Forgive me. He is gone. I am the reason. Forgive me…I could not save him," said Victor.

He paused for a moment to look at the disheartened boy and the spit dripped from his bearded chin. The wind took it and pitched it to the sand as Felix stared at him with watery eyes. The man dropped his head once more to erupt words of promise and value to the youngster.

"Forgive me. Let not…this mistake…that I have made drive a wedge between us. Please, let me welcome you to my family. It is just Amelia and me. Please. Stay here with us and join our family. I will care for you and protect you as my own. Take thought of this promise I have made," said Victor.

Magoonagoon

CHAPTER 87
A Familiar Face

The next morning, a familiar face returned to the shores of Magoonagoon. Julian landed his ships on the western tip of the island, not far from the Sagans. He set foot on the land and looked intently at the landscape. Julian took a hard look around and spoke to his officers.

"I swore that I would never return to this place. Now I am here," said Julian as he sighed.

"What are your orders sir?" asked the officer.

"Shields up! Move out!" shouted Julian.

"You heard him! On your way!" shouted the officer.

He gave the command to his heavily armed soldiers to march. They shuffled their feet and followed their commander down the beach. Julian's chin was held up bravely as he rode his horse beside them. They quickly approached the Sagan ships with their swords drawn and their shields up. When they reached the ships and passed through the homes the men discovered the ruins to be empty.

When they reached Jinjo's ship Julian ordered them to stop. Then the mercenary set out to find any sign of the feathered raiders. He looked for tracks of departure and any possible evidence of the direction they might have traveled. He found heavy tracks from the sharp hooves of the cavalry heading toward the canyon. Julian sent out a team of scouts to find them.

The man shouted angrily for the rest of his men to head out. The soldiers traveled to the entrance of the canyon and found the dead lying everywhere. They tracked further to the forest where he found it burning with columns of black smoke. Still, his men marched on to find their financier and carry out his plan. They traveled further into the wood with confidence.

There in the deep wood Julian found the massacre of men on the forest floor. There he found still more Foucinians dead among the leaves. He came upon Zinder-faso's carcass among the foliage and trotted his horse over to his massive body. Julian leaped down from the horse to examine the body close. The old Sagan had suffered a deadly blow to the neck. Many of his black feathers had fallen loose from the skin.

Surely no man could have done this? I had better be prepared to change sides, thought Julian as he kicked the old body of Zinder-faso.

As Julian studied the dead Sagan something caught his eye. There on the ground in front of him was the sorcerer's magical tusk. The mercenary grabbed hold of the tusk with both hands and hugged it with glee. He glared his eyes and wondered if any of his soldiers had seen him pick up the weapon. Then he carefully slid the whale tusk down in the quiver with his arrows. Julian mounted his horse and pressed on to find Soociv.

"Look there!" shouted one of the officers.

Up ahead of them, the officer spotted a Foucinian on a horse trotting down the trail toward their position. So the mercenary gave orders for his archers to be ready with their bows. They laced their lines with arrows and set the string tight to fire. Julian lowered his hand and gave the command for the bowman to shoot. The arrows leaped to the sky and dropped all over the rider. The arrows zipped into the Foucinian and toppled both the horse and rider to the ground.

The soldiers continued on into the dangerous territories of the Foucinians without caution or fear. The stately professionals marched in unison with quick steps. When they drew near to the river, Julian's scouts returned with a report.

"There was no sign of them. It is so quiet I believe they are all dead," said the scout.

"Head east! Toward the sea!" said Julian.

"Move at once!" shouted the officer.

Julian kicked the ribs of the steed to hasten the journey and find them. Behind him the horse pitched up dirt and a cloud of dust as she galloped. When they approached the ocean, he ordered his men to set up defensive positions while he would ride on ahead to search. So Julian galloped the steed further east to the shoreline. When he reached the coast, Julian turned north and continued his hunt. He kept a close look upon the horizon for any of the marching patrols.

Julian checked the horse and kept it in line as he bounced along the beach. Then to the mercenary's surprise he spotted a mass of smooth warships moored in the sand ahead of him on the beach. As soon as the mercenary spotted the ships in front of him, he was stunned to see hundreds of men all around them. Julian was so fearful of being noticed by the guardians and sentries who were on duty that he wheeled his horse around violently. Unknowingly, the quick move caused the whale tusk to be flung out of the quiver. As the horse turned, the magical tusk sailed through the air and jabbed down in the sand.

Julian was shocked at the size of the army of men. He never dreamed there would ever be that many men in Magoonagoon. He was in a dreamlike state of confusion. His eyes saw thousands of men down the coast. As far as the eye could see there were men preparing for battle. After Julian thought about it, he realized he was on the wrong side. The mercenary sped back toward his soldiers and took a deep breath as he kicked the ribs of the horse to encourage more speed. The horse carried him inland, away from the shoreline and back to his soldiers.

When Julian reached his group, he ordered them to march north toward the Rocky Pass. The men strode long strides and stretched their legs toward the pass with unmatched speed and power. When he reached the high rock walls, they slowed down at the orders of the leader.

"Go to the top and wait for my signal!" shouted Julian.

At the entrance of the Rocky Pass he found the war. Julian found his financiers fighting the hairy Foucinians. He caught sight of the Sagan he was looking for among the grey stone walls. Julian galloped the steed into the harsh fighting and he drew his sword to fight. At the front he called to Soociv.

"Soociv! I have arrived," yelled Julian.

"It took you long enough! You said you would be right behind me! Where are your troops?" shouted Soociv.

"Look to the hills. They are right over there," said Julian.

"Set up a defensive position and hold here! I will call for you when ready," said Soociv.

"They will only move to the sound of this trumpet and they will only move after I have negotiated payment," said Julian.

"What are you doing? Deploy your troops at once!" commanded Soociv.

"From the looks of things I have arrived at just the right time," said Julian with great enthusiasm.

"Set up your defensive position at once!" shouted Soociv.

"You know, they don't do well without payment. I will need a lot more money to continue," said Julian.

Soociv stepped down off his horse with heavy feet. Julian kept himself in the saddle and held his reins tight as his horse tried to run from the monster. With his chin held up high, Julian prepared to negotiate with his rather large employer. Once Soociv had moved close enough to hear Julian's voice clearly, the old mercenary carried out his plan.

"These men are ready to earn some of your money, but they could just as easily march back to our ship," said Julian.

"Julian! Deploy your men! We need them to guard our back," said Soociv.

"First we must settle on a price. I will not enter into this tussle until we come to an agreement. I do not work for free," shouted Julian.

"Name it!" shouted Soociv.

"A thousand score!" said Julian.

"Done! Get them!" shouted Soociv, gnashing his beak.

"Where should I send them?" asked Julian.

"Do not test me! Move them to the rear! Look there! See them! They are in danger! Look there at the Sagan in that chariot. Take your troops and defend him!" shouted Soociv.

"That one there with the human boy?" asked Julian.

"Do what I say, old fool!" shouted Soociv as he stared down at the mercenary with an angry brow.

Julian raced up the hill back toward his soldiers. As he drew near to them, the man blasted his trumpet and signaled them to move. Instantly, the troops sprang into action following their leader toward the rear. The mercenary drove the soldiers straight for the Sagan in the chariot and commanded them to engage with another toot from the trumpet.

Magoonagoon

CHAPTER 88
You're Human

As Julian and his soldiers entered the fight, the men had to avoid Brunto and his chariot. Brunto had closed his eyes because he thought they were going to kill him. In moments, the group had swayed the momentum back in the Sagan's favor. To Brunto's amazement, the men were on his side. They had joined him. Brunto circled the chariot around in another pass to make sure his eyes were not playing tricks on him. After he was sure that they were helping, Brunto spoke to Emery.

"Are these your people, boy?" asked Brunto.

"No. I don't think so. I have not seen them before," said

Emery.

Brunto rolled the chariot over to Julian and brought the cart to a stop. The Sagan handed the reins over to Emery and stepped down out of the chariot to confront the man. Then, the mighty Sagan clenched his fist and drew it back as if to strike Julian. The man squinted his eyes and tilted his head to receive the blow, but to his surprise Brunto struck a Foucinian with his hard fist saving Julian's life. Julian had not seen the Foucinian attacker approach him from behind. Then, Brunto picked the man up from off the back of his horse and placed him in his own chariot with Emery.

"Direct your men to follow my command. Drive this boy back out of range. Keep him and my chariot safe," said Brunto.

At the chariot, Brunto gathered weaponry from the cart's floor. He took three javelins and his long spear out of their tightly fitted clamps around the chariot rim. Then the warrior draped his shoulders with the fine leather belt that carried the bright sword and the well fashioned dagger. So the feathered monster armed and readied himself for battle. When he was well equipped, he sent Emery and Julian away.

Emery cracked the whip and sent the horses forward with a leap and the two sped away from the battle. Julian blasted five toots on his trumpet signaling instructions for his men. As Emery drove the team of horses and lashed them with the whip, the mercenary made plans to change course. The mercenary thought to trick the lad at first, with clever tact and wit. However, knowing the fellow was just a child, the mercenary decided to just overpower him.

Julian grabbed the reins from the lad as he nudged him to

the side. Emery was puzzled and wondered why the fellow had taken such action against him. Emery frowned at the mercenary with a disappointed look, and rested on the rim to await an excuse. However, Julian ignored the boy and drove the team in a different direction. Knowing that they were traveling the wrong way, Emery spoke to him.

"Where are you going? The camp is back over that way!" said Emery.

"We are not going back to the Sagan camp. I am taking you where you belong! Back to your people! Back to the men!" said the mercenary.

"The men? Are you mad?" asked Emery proving the goblin's magic powder had worked.

"Have you forgotten that you are a boy? You're human! The Sagans are our enemy!" said Julian.

"Our enemy? Then why are you helping them?" asked Emery.

"For the money!" said Julian.

The mercenary's speech was interrupted by the boy's foot. The little lad planted his heel in the middle of Julian's belly and launched him out of the chariot. The mercenary rolled on the ground and settled face down in the sand, not knowing what had hit him. Emery continued on driving the team when he reclaimed the helm.

Emery lashed the reins and swung the chariot back around in the direction of the mercenary. When he came near, Emery noticed that the mercenary was out cold. The fall must have given the man a hard hit to the head. Julian rested in the same position when the chariot passed by, still unconscious from the fall. Seeing the man, Emery was alarmed and thought to himself.

What manner of man is this that can change sides in such a way? With the Foucinians before, and now with the Sagans, now he is on his way to the men? wondered Emery.

As fast as he could, the boy raced by, putting the mercenary behind him and distance between them both. Emery knew that he should follow Brunto's orders as he had commanded, but the skirmish changed everything. Emery wanted to hurry back and report the occurrence to Brunto. On his way back, thoughts raced through his head.

Now is the time. Why don't you escape? I can run back to my people. That fool is right! I can escape, thought Emery.

He slowed the team down and contemplated what to do. The magic spell had some control over his thoughts, but not enough to keep him from doing the right thing. He struggled with the idea to run, but something deep inside ordered him to stay. Emery tried to shake the magic spell, but his thoughts tried to trick him.

Am I any different than that man back there? Have I changed sides? How can I do that? How can I join these monsters? I was with the men before but now I am with the Sagans. contemplated Emery.

In the moments that passed by, as the boy weighed his options, the Foucinians converged upon him. The beasts attacked him from all angles and cut off his escape. They surrounded the chariot and closed in on the fellow. Emery gave the horses a hard lash and squatted down below the rim. The team had somehow managed to escape, but they propelled the boy deep in the heart of the battle he had left only moments before. When he reached the dense crowd, Emery had to steer around the dangers in order to reach Brunto and the others. Along the way, many adversaries tried to snatch him. The Foucinians hurled things at his head hoping to clip him off the cart.

Brunto then checked his fighters among the horde and called for each of them to join him. He stood up tall and stuck out his feathered chest covered in bright golden defense. Brunto arched his neck and let out a mighty roar as he bent over at the waist. The high-pitched sound continued as he swayed his neck back and forth and from side to side. Then the destroyer began to stride hard into battle.

He glanced to the left and then to the right as he strode through the challengers in the droves. Nevertheless, none approached him. They parted like waves of the sea, cowering away from the Sagan and hiding among the host in fear of death. So the hulk trotted through the foremost with his head high and his sword ready. Brunto severed the lines of the swift Foucinians and crippled their armies at the front. He passed the deadly archers who took aim at his chest as they knelt on one knee, but not one dared to let loose of the pointed pikes in fear of the killer. Instead they held their pikes on the lines as the foe passed through the realm. Brunto's eyes grew wide with rage as he engaged the enemy alone without the protection of a shield.

Still, one archer loosed an arrow as the feathered giant passed in front of them. The arrow flew and the sharp point landed in the back of Brunto's thigh. The Sagan let out a wail and a deep sigh of pain. Brunto turned to attack the arrow-throwing beasts. So, in defense, the other archers let loose of their arrows in a smooth volley. They too found their place of rest in the giant's limbs as the sharp points dove into the feathers and skin.

However, the points only prolonged their lives for a little longer as he advanced on their position. Brunto slashed them with his sword and spilled their loins with his sharp, pointed spear. The wounded fighter scourged them with his weapons until they were rendered useless, and then he took out the rest of them in hand-to-hand combat.

The Foucinians dove on him with spears in hand and sharp pointed javelins to take out the tall murderer. Brunto repelled the beasts with his bare hands as he crushed the skulls of many with hard punches from his fists. After a while the huge Sagan began to tire from the continuous waves of attackers. He sluggishly fought on among the beasts in strife and turmoil.

Soon the Foucinians took the upper hand with their weapons and battlements. They struck him to the ground with concussions and pulses from their spears. Then at a decisive moment Emery showed up and circled the chariot around Brunto to save him. When Brunto fell to the ground, he snapped off some of the slender arrows and drove others deeper into his feathered body. He lay stretched out on the earth suffering from the harsh wounds. In the moments that Emery circled around Brunto, others came to help their commander with quickness and haste. Julian's men also came to his aid near the Sagan's side. The soldiers put their shields up and formed a protective barrier around him. Others helped him to his feet for they could not carry the Sagan on their own.

The group was able to get him out of the battle and away

from the danger. With the help of his comrades, Brunto collapsed into the chariot with Emery and the boy drove him all the way to his tent. The hulk called for a soldier to mount a horse to fetch Komoras from the fighting. So the fighter obeyed the commands and trotted a horse after Komoras. The others got Brunto into the tent and laid him down. Controlled by the magic spell, Emery moved quickly to gather fresh water and a dry cloth to catch the blood.

So the feathered monster lay down in the tent to rest from the skirmish. After a while the soldier returned with Komoras. The soldier pointed the way to the tent. Komoras entered the tent as he threw open the fabric of the tarp entrance. The old veteran moved to Brunto's side and began to assess the wounds. He counted the arrows and the total came to fifty. Then, he counted the other wounds and began to lose track. So the old warrior Komoras gave Brunto potions to sooth the pain and started his work.

He called for a few of them to set some irons in the fire and to heat them. They quickly obeyed the orders as they marched out of the tent and plunged the pokers into the flames. The iron rustled up the embers and sent the ashes flying in the sky. When the fires cooked them red, Komoras commanded the soldiers to take the strongest ropes from the ships and tie him to the table. They hastily obeyed the commands and gathered the robust ropes and tied down the huge Sagan.

When they were done, Komoras ordered the soldiers to double the binds. They looped the sturdy ropes around Brunto's limbs and fastened them with secure knots. When the Sagan was pinned, Komoras began to pull out the deadly fangs. He took his time jerking the sharp points so to keep from tearing the skin, and each time they prodded the holes with the hot pokers. Brunto arched his back and wailed thunderously from the table.

Near the end of the surgery, Brunto broke the binds from one of his legs and kicked away the doctors. They called in others to subdue his reproach, and they fastened him back down. They continued throughout the evening and into the night until the wounds were all treated. Komoras poured wine into the wounds and covered them with oil. When Komoras was finished, they let Brunto rest. He slept for three days without food or drink and rumors spread through the camp that he was dead.

Magoonagoon

CHAPTER 89

Instruction

    A few days later Brunto was able to walk. He emerged from the tent and went and laid down in one of the old Foucinian healing pools. The Sagan kept to himself during the time he needed to recover and his only visitor happened to be Emery. Emery waited on the Sagan's every need. He fetched him food and water. He made the trips to see Komoras to get the medicines and potions for Brunto's wounds. Within days, Brunto was feeling good enough to do other things. Every moment Emery was there to help him.

    How can such devotion be in a human being? puzzled

Brunto.

So Brunto set out to train the boy. Brunto instructed the lad the first day with the staff and rod. Emery dodged many of the quick jabs and lightning-fast strikes from the old Sagan, but some still found their place of rest on his young bones. Emery suffered many bruises from the taps. Then during the evening hour, Brunto had Emery fetch a rope the length of seven or eight hands. Brunto took the rope in one hand and the staff in the other. He showed them both to the boy and spoke once more.

"Watch closely, little one. Take warning of the rope…but remember the staff," said Brunto as he flicked the rope as a whip.

Emery nodded his head and readied himself for the oncoming attack as he set his feet shoulder-width apart. So, Brunto whipped the lash and swung the rod at the same time. The young lad concentrated on the rope and felt the hard wood against his ear. Brunto laughed for a moment, for he could not help it. Then he turned both the rope and staff in his wrists upright to show them to the lad. Then he spoke words of teaching.

"Look at these. Study their character. Which of these will cause the most damage to your frail body?" asked Brunto.

Emery said nothing. Instead the boy frowned in anger at the Sagan. Seeing this Brunto tapped him with the rope and it wrapped around his waist. Brunto then took it back away from Emery and swung the staff with quickness. The rod split the hip and rang the bone to bring pain to the boy's waist. So Brunto dropped his head in disgust and shook it in disappointment. Then the distraught Sagan spoke inspiring words to the teary-eyed youngster.

"Enough! Today's hard work is finished. Let us move on to better things," said Brunto as he rose to his feet.

The process continued each day until the evening hour and each day the boy learned more. Brunto added new techniques and challenges to each session. The brown Sagan stressed the fundamentals that he bestowed upon the lad. When Brunto felt that the young boy was ready, he taught him how to use a spear.

He started at the water's edge within a stone's throw of the curved bow of his ship. Brunto took the spear and began the instruction by pointing out the target on the fourth rung of the mighty planks and timbers of the boat. First, and most important of all, he showed Emery how to set his feet in the correct position and how to properly balance his weight. He positioned his feet to propel the harpoon's point into the planks of the ship.

The recovering Sagan lifted the lance high above his shoulder and balanced its weight in the center. He pitched the spear up into the air twice to feel its weight on his arm and get the correct grip, closer to the point. When he was ready, he showed Emery how to take the spear back, way behind the ear, and how to bend at the waist. He fixed his eyes on the target and hoisted the spear into the air.

The lance bounced in flight as it carried over the waves. The point of the pike slammed into the timber with a jolt and the force made the pole swim, shake, and shimmer about. Brunto put his hands on his hips and nodded his head with pleasure to see a perfect bull's-eye hit in the center of his target.

Brunto gave Emery another pike to hurl, but pointed him away from the ship. For it was too great a distance for the young lad across the surf to the ship. So he took many tries at the water's edge with little instruction from Brunto. Emery was beginning to understand and receive the knowledge that was given to him. As he pitched the spear along the sea coast, Brunto began to take pride in his young student. Brunto took the spear away and let him practice inland near the center of camp.

In the ensuing days and weeks Brunto began to recover and return to full strength from his wounds. The wounds healed and his power came to him after time took its toll. The scars made his skin like iron and his body like stone. Still, there was grumbling and fussing among the Sagans for the return of their leader. Rumors stirred among the host of them that the old feathered monster was growing soft. Many of them took resentment and bitterness toward him for not participating in the battles of the war.

"Look at him. All he does is spend time with that human. Why doesn't he come out and fight?" asked one of the Sagans.

In those days, he continued to train his apprentice. Brunto showed Emery the sword and taught him its worth. At first they used sticks of the right size and weight, but the boy kept breaking them. Emery was progressing so quickly that Brunto thought it might be time to instill the sword and test the lad. So they took swords and marked off a space to practice with their sharp points. The two engaged in fencing and maneuvers with the points of a cutlass.

To Brunto's surprise the boy was steady on his feet and quick to defend and attack. For days and evenings they continued to practice the art of the sword, for its worth was far greater than other weapons when war was close and hand to hand. So they continued day after day until Emery's skills grew greater still. Then on the last day of instruction with the sword, Emery wounded Brunto.

It was an accident that Brunto could not foretell. The wound was only a slight cut on the Sagan's hand along the bones. However, its mark was by far the boy's greatest achievement. Emery had become dangerous.

Emery dropped the sword in fear as Brunto sniffed the blood on his wrist. The old Sagan checked his anger for this was his doing. Then, Brunto scratched the huge feathers on his chest and gathered the right words to say.

"Ha! A victory! It is a victory for you!" said Brunto.

Magoonagoon

CHAPTER 90

The Hitch and Wheel

Emery smiled at Brunto and the two continued their practice. When they grew weary, they sat down to rest in the circle. Then, as they sat, Brunto taught him the tricks of the blade and what the slight twist of the wrist could do in a moment's time. He spoke the old tongues into the boy's ear and Emery understood. Amazement came to the Sagan when the lad spoke old words of the feathers.

Hearing this Brunto was inspired to continue at a quicker pace and accelerate the boy's teaching, but he used restraint for things of importance that cannot be rushed. Brunto decided to use the rest of the goblin's magic powder on the human prisoners. He dusted each of their heads just as he had dusted Emery's before. He chanted the same saying to mimic the same spell and get the same result.

Nevertheless, the time had come for Brunto to rejoin his comrades in battle, for they had begun to snarl and scoff at him. The very next day he joined them in combat on his sleek chariot of war. Seeing him on the field, the Foucinians cowered away and gasped in fear. Brunto took them on at the front as Emery steered the war cart with ease. The upper hand quickly changed back into the Sagan's favor as he stomped the horses at the front and checked the lines with his javelins. The Sagan crippled their backs and slew a host of challengers without fear. The pair rolled along at the center as the horses danced about and Brunto crushed the Foucinian lines.

Without warning a long spear became lodged in the spokes of the masterfully built carriage and wrecked them. They both tumbled in the sand and dirt of the wastelands and Brunto was stepped on by the horses. The large hooves had pranced across his huge head and knocked him out cold. Emery was unharmed and leaped to his feet. Seeing the wreckage Brunto's soldiers drew back in fear.

Emery vaulted to protect the body of his teacher as he took the mighty sword from Brunto's belt. The sword was too large for Emery to fight effectively but the hairy beasts were all around them. The men who had been dusted with the magic powder rushed to protect Brunto because they were hypnotized by the magic spell. The Foucinians came from all angles with their ready spears and sharp swords. The hairy beasts rushed in to overcome them. Emery dodged their throws as the wooden spears zipped by his head.

In an instant, the beasts were upon him with their weapons, but he and the men held them off. Emery used the teachings he had learned from Brunto to disable many of them. In fact, he challenged them with his bright sword as they attacked. Like a true warrior, he slashed at their advances and laid a host of them down. Still, the Foucinians came on in disbelief and wonder with their heavy weapons. In an instant, he had killed three, but still they came.

Emery drove the sword into their bellies and across their necks with precision and tactical speed. Two came at him with a net and pitchfork with the desire to snatch him. However, he had separate plans for them as he dodged the net and the hairy fingers. Emery slashed the sword and in a second he severed the hand from the one's limb. The other stabbed at him with the fork and nearly caught his side with the sharp points. Emery saw it coming and avoided its bite.

So he and the men who were under the spell continued to fight off the oncoming horde until Brunto awoke. When the Sagan stood to his feet, they cowered away from the pair. Then they fought to salvage the chariot and each side pulled on its loose parts with hesitation and fear. The Foucinians took one of the wheels and the smooth iron axle of immeasurable value. Brunto was able to grab the hull of the cart and the straps of the fine ponies. Emery grit his teeth and strode after the other wheel with little care for his own safety.

The Foucinian lines broke and scattered in a woven pattern as they took quick strides to flee. Their swift legs took them far away from the battlefield. However, as the Sagans regrouped and picked from the spoils of armor and weaponry, the very ground began to shake and rumble. The Sagans raised their necks and straightened their crooked backs to gaze upon the horizon. As the rocks danced upon the hard floor at the base of the canyon, the flags of man emerged.

The Sagans leaped to converge in the center and rally to arms. Emery stayed with Brunto and took up other weapons that he picked from the ground. Brunto marched in front of his fighters. Emery rolled the heavy wheel over to Brunto and gave it to him to use as a shield. Brunto used the hitch as his sword and prepared to battle. The strong hulk raised the hitch and wheel to marshal the group back into the thrash of battle.

On the other side, Victor directed each man into combat. As they approached, He stepped off the horse to stride with the fighters at the point. Victor darted at Atlas and matched what appeared to be a small dagger against the long blade of the hulk's sword. Victor met each blow with the small bit of steel. After a while, Atlas took the upper hand, and smashed his huge fist across Victor's burly face. The hit lifted the man off his feet and knocked loose both his sword and the fine helmet from his head. The leather strap broke and the headpiece spun around on the ground like a top. Victor rolled around on the ground in agony and blood gushed from his chin.

Magoonagoon

CHAPTER 91

Atlas

Victor dodged the killer's sword as he attacked above him. He rolled to the left and then back over to the right to miss the sharp point. The blade struck the sand and dirt as the Sagan swung recklessly about. Just in time, Victor's fingers touched the bright sword that he dropped a short time ago. When the fingers touched the hilt he took hold of the handle and turned to meet the blade. The two swords met with a spark and the fighters engaged in more grappling. The warriors took turns countering and defending each attack.

Atlas slammed down on Victor's sword with great force.

The bolt of the quick strike broke the blade in two and crushed the cutlass down to the hilt. Victor's eyes grew wide with surprise and shock. As the old man shuffled back out of the killer's range, he shook his head with skepticism and wonder. Atlas took his sword up over his head with both hands to strike. Victor dove to the side and the chopping blow missed his body. Atlas growled at the man and prepared to swipe at him again.

As fate would have it, others stepped into their leader's aid at just the right time. Eugene moved to Victor's side and gave him a replacement sword and a round shield. So Victor moved on Atlas again when the crowd subsided. Atlas took up his challenge again with a jubilant roar and wave of his hand.

Victor and Atlas fought with epic force and uncommon strength. Victor claimed a small victory as he sliced at the murderer's thigh with a quick jab and flick of the wrist. The dark blood spilled out with pouring drops of pain and hurt. Atlas became enraged with anger and came back with a full motion coil, a swing with all his might.

As the blades clashed once more, Victor's sword gave way from his hand as it cracked in two. So a second time the giant had broken a sword in Victor's hand. The blade was indeed too powerful in the arm of such strength. The fragments flew away from the man's hand and tossed over the heads of his fellow companions. The men rushed in to save Victor from the killer once more with their shields up. Atlas hammered them with bashing waves of force. As the men dragged their captain away from the Sagan, Atlas hurled harsh words at the man.

"Run away, coward! Twice you cheated death and twice your soldiers saved you! Come back and fight!" said Atlas.

Hearing this, Victor ordered one of his soldiers to give him a sword that he could use against the giant. So the soldiers let him go and his fine sandals carried him to the thick of the fighting where the huge Sagan stood. Victor ran headlong toward the monster where he was greeted with the hard knuckles of the Sagan's long reach. The old man flipped over backward from the hard blow. Atlas put his hands on his hips and leaned back as he laughed at the man.

Victor's soldiers rushed at the Sagan and Atlas decapitated one of them with his smooth blade, casting the head and helmet across the field. The others moved to protect their commander as the murderer shuffled around them in attack. So they pulled Victor to his feet and dragged him away from the Sagan a third time. Through the host they drug him as he passed in and out of consciousness. They took him away from the heavy clash of battle to the rear where they splashed water on his head.

Then the old man's head began to pound as the blood began to gush over his forehead. The man awoke in ill accord as he stumbled to his feet and cursed. Victor rubbed the spot where the Sagan struck him and scratched his head as he moaned. Then the old man called for the quickest of his soldiers to fetch him a new helmet to place on his head. The youngster swiftly obeyed the orders and went through the fighting to find a helmet suitable for his captain.

The young man found a gold helmet that was lined with the soft wool. So he took it up and ran back to his captain with the fine headgear. Victor placed the helmet upon his head and tightened the smooth leather strap under his chin with the bronze clasp. With a leap his smooth leather sandals carried him back into the fighting once more. His soldiers followed him as he raced through to the front and foremost of the fighting. It began to rain with huge drops falling from the sky.

Opposite from Victor, on another side of battle, Brunto smashed and cracked the backs of the men as they rushed upon him. He still carried the wooden hitch and wheel from his broken chariot. He used his weapons to lay down many would-be attackers as they tried to kill him. Brunto conquered them and left them for dead as he battled. He swung the hitch around and the mass of men fell in front of him. Through the battle he took many a wound from the men, but he returned them threefold.

The battle continued as the conflict rose and the hard rain dropped on their heads. When the men could suffer no more casualties, Victor called for retreat as he blew the trumpet. The flag-carrying soldiers turned around and raced away from the field.

The Sagans let them go for they were weary. Brunto ordered the host of them to gather the spoils of weaponry and armor from the field. The Sagan soldiers collected all the armor and bright weaponry of worth to the nearby ships. The rain began to let up and the hard drops turned to mist as they walked back to the ships. The Sagans made countless trips to and from the ships carrying well-made tools of war. Countless treasures were left by both the Foucinians and men as they fled.

As the Sagans worked, the young boy Emery gathered up the pieces of the fine chariot that lay strewn across the field. He rolled the finely crafted wheels and dragged the heavy timbers into a pile. He found the long hitch that Brunto had thrown at the fleeing men and he collected the leather straps that lashed the swift horses. The young man found all of the pieces and placed each on the pile near the ships. Emery felt weary and tired as he finished his work and sat at the base of the pile.

As the young lad sat on the hard ground the pieces of the chariot began to rumble and the ground began to shake once more. As the boy turned his head upon the horizon, he spotted Oilaz and the loyalists running at them. Like a rushing wind they came on in fury with long spear points and bright shields. The war turned to Sagan against Sagan as Brunto and his soldiers scrambled for their weapons once more.

Emery hid under the remains of the fine chariot he had collected and watched the attack with wide eyes. It became disturbing and surreal with the Sagan riders tumbling in and smashing away at bone and flesh. Brunto found a favorable weapon that was left on the field so he took up the sword and ushered his weary force back in attack.

Oilaz drove his soldiers into the thick lines as he led the force into battle. Brunto could not keep his soldiers together so they broke and gave way running for their lives. Oilaz joined the fighting and he took them as they ran. He was surrounded by the royal guard and they rushed to the ships. The fighting grew fierce and hand to hand, with steel finding bone and the sand soaked red. Arrows flew and the ground shook as the feathers took to fighting. The war came to the coast near the rushing waves, and the shrill noise made it sound as if it were all a dream.

Brunto's army fled from the ships, abandoning everything when they left. Oilaz and his troops chased after them. The humans that were shackled in chains screamed out in horror. They called out for help and longed for someone to free them. Only Brunto had remained to protect the fine ships from the blazing torches. Hearing their cries, the Sagan took his giant hands and lifted the massive post that anchored them to the sand. He pulled the pylon out of the ground and tossed it aside. The iron band that was wrapped around the pillar slid off the pole and fell to the ground. With the band free from the pole, the men raced away. Brunto had made possible their escape.

Brave as he was, Brunto stood alone near the ships. He arched his tremendous back and the feathers rose up on his broad shoulders as he stood to protect their navy. However, Stratogos moved to engage Brunto with a full coat of mail. Seeing the juggernaut rushing upon him, Brunto prepared for the worse by screaming out his battle cry as a warning.

Magoonagoon

CHAPTER 92

Captured

Stratogos gripped his long sword and arched his back and neck to the sky. With a shriek and a loud screaming babble, he yelled at the top of his lungs. Brunto stepped back into the sea with his head hung low. The giant was weary from the continuous battle, and he yearned to elude the predator. Brunto shrugged away from the huge juggernaut, but he dared Stratogos to come near with a taunting motion from his sword.

Oilaz and the royal guard had been in pursuit of Brunto's fleeing army, but they returned to the scene with drool dripping from their beaks. The crude mob desired revenge and they dismounted from their horses quickly to have a part in the inception. With squinting eyes and open jaws they prepared for his demise. Their tongues drooped from their mouths as they snarled and hissed. Without any comrades to even out the count, the rebellious Brunto was in great danger. As the angry mob collected on the water's edge, Oilaz was the first to speak.

"Have you ever seen such a weary fellow? Where have your followers fled? Do they want to see their leader destroyed? Come forth from the sea and meet your doom!" shouted Oilaz.

"Ha! Dishonor and disgrace on you all! I dare even the best of you crows to come near! For that goat will be the first to lie down!" shouted Brunto with a shaky skip in his voice.

"Back! All of you! He is mine!" shouted Stratogos as he wheeled around to his comrades.

"Don't be a fool, Stratogos! We will take him together!" said Oilaz.

Stratogos snarled and grunted at the others with a look of hate. That look was enough to scare them away. Then the juggernaut turned to face Brunto alone. The others stood by as he splashed into the surf on his heavy feet. He spit at Brunto and snapped his pointy beak twice. The monster relieved himself in his competitor's direction. With his posture arched backwards, the urine flowed from his body, as he laughed aloud and shouted obscenities. The crowd of Sagans joined the villain in laughter as he continued his attempt at humiliation.

Brunto was unfazed by the gesture and he prepared for battle with disregard for the Sagan's actions. With their crooked backs bent, the two Sagans circled in the shallows daring one another to make a move. Brunto declared a victory before they began to fight, shouting words of warning to the twenty-four-footer. After the taunting ended, Stratogos moved to attack. Through the waves he came with his arms stretched out. He swung his sword around with such strength and fury, the wind changed direction.

When the blades hit, the noise was broadcast all over the land. Then Brunto took a swing and rang the chime once more. With each swing and each hit, the champions grew wearier. The two battled and battled until they were so fatigued, they fell over in the surf. As they dropped beneath the surface of the water, Oilaz spoke to his troops with a sense of urgency.

"I want him alive! Drag them out of the waves! He will be a valuable prisoner!" said Oilaz.

The Sagans entered the ocean to retrieve the two giants and they struggled to get them ashore. They pulled Brunto in by the neck and he slid over the sand limp and unconscious. They took better care of Stratogos, as they pulled him ashore by the chainmail. With the pair safe from drowning, the crew parted their garments and seized the loose armor. Their helmets were snatched away first, and a frenzy followed. The giants were picked clean of every possession they owned.

The group took advantage of their own comrade as he lay helpless on the beach. Stratogos moaned once as they turned him to steal his prized chainmail and his cape, which was decorated with golden stars. They pillaged the bodies until they could only come away with glossy feathers. It was at this moment that Oilaz called for them to stop. As the two lay there motionless, the emperor spoke.

"Apprehend him! Bind his hands and ankles. Take loose the cart from that chariot and tie him to that hitch! We will drag him back as our prisoner!" said Oilaz.

So the Sagans obeyed his orders and bound Brunto to the team of horses. Brunto lay motionless with his neck stretched out across the sand. His comrades were nowhere in sight. Only the brave human, Emery, had stayed behind. Out of sight and hidden beneath the wreckage of Brunto's chariot, the boy watched them tie the mighty Sagan to the horses.

One of the Sagans lashed and lashed at the horses to propel them forward. The animals screamed from the pain and struggled to a slow start. The pulling force towed the heavy giant over the sand. Along the way the Sagans scourged Brunto and mocked him with snapping beaks.

Emery watched from his hideout as the team pulled away with his teacher. From beneath the wreckage he wondered what to do. The chance had come to escape from bondage and return to the humans. Yet he felt a need to help his teacher and save him from the hands of the murders. As the boy hid in the shadows, he pondered deep thoughts in his head that only the goblin's powder could have invented.

They have captured him. Oh! What do I do? I cannot leave him. After all he saved my life. But who am I to free him? I am just a boy. If he is to be in bondage and at the mercy of those murderers, what chance do I have at saving him? thought Emery.

When the enemy traveled out of sight he crawled out from beneath the wreckage and looked in both directions. He raced down the coast with fleeting steps away from the giants.

With inspiration he fled to find his own kind, longing to embrace his father. His little heart raced as it beat in his chest and fluttered with excitement. Down the coast the lad ran and his spirit soared, until he reached the charred and smoking ships that Oilaz had burned. There the boy stopped in his tracks and his heart sank.

Emery's eyes were fixed on the front of one of the burning ships. His eyes locked on the spear that lay buried in the planks on the bow. It was the very spear that Brunto had pitched; it was the unclaimed bull's-eye that he had abandoned after the morning practice. It stood there as an indication of the time he had been in bondage. He pictured his life before him.

Now the lad was liberated and he could return to the men. Still, the spear watched him as he gently walked past the ship. It marked the skyline like a monument and seemed to call out for the lad. There Emery slowed to a trot and contemplated the situation. Emery scratched his head and thought for a moment.

I will follow the enemy into their territory and free my teacher from captivity! thought Emery.

He entered the surf and climbed up the side of the ship. As Emery reached the spear and clutched it in his hand, he took the plunge into the sea. As he battled the waves to reach dry land, Emery struggled to climb ashore. His only hope would have to be that it was not too late to save Brunto.

Magoonagoon

CHAPTER 93

Emery

Emery tracked the Sagans along the shoreline until he came upon the mountain of feathers that lay strewn across the beach. The massive body of Stratogos, stretched out over the sand, wet, dilapidated, and defeated. He was not dead, only abandoned by his comrades, who had hastily gathered up the spoils and fled. The feathered monster was obtunded and oblivious to any danger.

The young lad rushed to relinquish the life of the outstanding Sagan. While Stratogos lay defenseless, Emery's eyes found something that lay partially hidden by the gritty soil.

The lad dropped the spear and promptly gripped it with a sense of eagerness. From the moment he grabbed the handle, the boy knew of its power. It was the whale tusk, the sorcerer's trophy.

It must have been dropped by the sorcerer during a skirmish, thought Emery.

He had found the treasure that the wizard carried with such great pride. He pulled it from the sand and held it up to see. The slight noise of the tusk being pulled from the sand was enough to wake the huge creature. Stratogos opened only one eye to peer at the young fellow and shut it back when he saw him turn. The Sagan lay there motionless, in ambush and waiting.

Emery remembered the training he had received from Brunto and steadied his footing in attack. He tracked toward the Sagan with determination and stealth. His intentions to exterminate the feathered giant were stalled when the Sagan rolled over and grabbed the little fellow's wrist in one swift move. Emery did not anticipate the monster coming to life and was startled by the abrupt change.

Stratogos squeezed the boy's tiny wrist and the whale tusk fell free from his grip. Then, for fun, the giant picked the boy up and squeezed the wrist tighter. From the great height, Emery cried aloud for help. Stratogos began to laugh as he toyed with the young man's emotions. Then, the Sagan dropped him to the sand. With his other massive arm he gripped the boy's neck and tackled him to the ground. There he placed his hand on Emery's head and braced his own weight against the boy's skull.

The huge Sagan pressed his weight on the youngster's body as he climbed up to one knee. The heavy load would have killed him if not for the cushion of sand beneath. Still, the agony and pain was hard for the boy to bear. As the monster laughed, he shoved the skull; as he compressed and constricted, his arm shook from the strain as he squashed. Tighter and tighter Stratogos clutched, until he heard a shout from the distance that made his own bones tingle.

Down the beach came a voice so decisive and stern that it caused the killer to pause. The shout beckoned the giant and insisted for him to stop. Stratogos peered down the beach at the advancing foe with his grip ever tighter on the boy. When the foe tracked into clear sight, Stratogos let loose of the boy and stood to his feet. The giant reached down and picked up the spear that lay at his feet. He kicked some sand over on the boy, as if to say that he would deal with him later. Emery tried to dig his way out of the hole that Stratogos had tried to bury him in.

Racing down the coast was King Marion and his elite band of soldiers. His soldiers were still in formation and they were armed with bright weaponry. In three or four steps the king called for the troops to align themselves in attack positions. The troops transformed from marching formation into a spread pattern. The transformation itself was enough display of force that it sent chills over Stratogos and the boy. The king stuck his arm out stiff in front of him as he ran to command more speed. The wave of his sword swept the swell of men forward. The surge ran violently toward the enemy.

The troops sped across the sand and raced toward Stratogos. The mighty wave of soldiers collapsed on the giant with a crushing blow. Soon after, the king was upon him with his gleaming armor. His beautiful helmet and decorated cape accentuated his extraordinary talents. The king leaped through the air with his sword leading the way to finish the killer. The monster braced for impact when the king leaped at him. Stratogos gagged from the wounds he had already received and spat blood from his mouth. Without his chainmail to protect him, the men were able to wound the Sagan.

With a sweeping motion Stratogos's neck arched with a violent scream. King Marion's direct hit to the giant's lung stung him precisely in the area that hurt the most, causing the Sagan to drop the spear in his hand. In the same moment, another soldier's blade found the bone and chopped at the Sagan's flesh. The stab alone should have killed the giant Sagan, but the monster was able to fling his arms out and free himself from the attackers. The juggernaut waved his arms and repelled the soldiers with a scream. King Marion ordered his troops to surround the giant and they followed the command. With quick thinking the king gave the order for them all to attack at once.

The men raced to the Sagan in unison. The men began to sting Stratogos with their sharp swords over and over. For the moment, the powerful Sagan was at the mercy of the king's men and could do nothing to stop them. Then, all at once, the giant started swatting at the men and a great number of them fell dead. Stratogos reached down to the ground and filled his huge hand with sand. The giant flipped the handful directly at the attackers and the sandy grit caught the king and his soldiers off guard. The sand entered the king's eyes and rendered him defenseless. King Marion quickly moved back out of the way to avoid the killer's reach. He hustled to remove the sand from his eyes and regain his sight. It was at that moment when the king called out to his soldiers.

"Retreat!" shouted King Marion but the elite band would never retreat. They would fight to the death to protect the king.

Stratogos approached the king while the young man was still cleaning his eyes. With clear advantage, the Sagan made a move, drilling the king in the face with a hard punch. The king rolled around in the sand for a moment, and then he climbed back up to his feet. As the king staggered around wiping his eyes, his soldiers ran at the monster in waves. One of the men took a full swing at the giant's knee cap and cleaved it with his sword. The others stood between the king and Stratogos. One by one the Sagan killed them as he desperately tried to reach the king.

Emery watched as the Sagan took out the entire band. The boy was afraid of the giant, but he too moved to protect the king. While Stratogos moved in, the lad searched for another weapon to use against the enemy. All the boy could find was a sword that had been discarded by one of the soldiers. Emery picked up the sword from the sand and ran into the fight. As he advanced, Emery watched Stratogos backhand the king and send his helmet flying. The king toppled over in the dust and gasped for breath. With the sword gripped tightly in both of his hands, Emery raced at the giant's back.

His little feet slid to a stop a short distance away from the Sagan. Emery took the sword up over his head and coiled backwards to prepare for a big throw. With all his strength, Emery threw the sword into the air and the blade planted deep into the monster's spine. The point slammed into the innards and released the thick red blood from the wound. Stratogos dropped to his knees and the ground shook when he landed. The juggernaut wobbled around for a moment and fell on his fat belly. There the giant remained like he was made of stone. The murderer was brought down by the young boy.

The king lay unconscious on his back, shaken from the hard hit that Stratogos had given him. He laid there snoring and talking in his sleep. Emery ran over to the king and grabbed his sword. He picked it up from the ground and turned to face his competitor. In an instant he had lifted the heavy sword over his head to eliminate the enemy.

Stratogos was paralyzed from the blow to the back and lay there motionless on the sand. As he stood near the giant's ghastly head, he reached for the sky with the sword in both hands. With one whack the sword lobbed off the Sagan's head and it rolled over in the sand. The fellow reached down and grabbed the short feathers on the crown of the skull. Then Emery got an idea as he lifted the head up.

The boy used the cape of the sleeping king for a sack and placed the head within the pouch. There he collected as many of the Sagan's black glossy feathers as he could pluck, for if he was to enter the enemy's land, he would have to have a disguise. It would have to be a clever, camouflaged cloak that would mask his identity. He would use the feathers to conceal his pale skin and make them into a suit or throw that he could wear.

As Emery was leaving, his eyes caught the sight of the whale tusk again. It lay there on the ground unclaimed. The youngster collected the tusk and when he gripped it in his hand he was filled with glee. The boy pitched the sack carrying the awful head over his shoulder to leave. The lad left the snoring king behind and traveled back to the burning ships. He moved down the coast to a place where he could make preparations and create the disguise. Near the waves, the boy found an abandoned campsite. The place was ideal for the boy to make his arrangements.

With the burning fires of the ships aiding his search, the boy found what he was looking for. It was a deep cauldron with thick iron sides that rested on top of a heap of kindling. The wood was dry and the pot was empty, so he immediately dropped his sack and proceeded to fetch some water. He found a small bucket and ran to the ocean to fill it up. After several trips to and from the ocean the fellow had filled the kettle to the brim.

Emery flung the bucket into the darkness and it smashed against something that made a terrible noise. He cringed at the awful noise and shook his head in disappointment. Then he stood in silence for the longest time, entertaining the thought that he had drawn the attention of a thousand enemies. Seeing that nothing foul had come from the incident, the boy continued as he hummed a little tune.

The boy found his sack and reached inside to claim the ugly head. With a fling, the head splashed down in the water and it bobbed up and down only for a moment, before resting in the depths of the kettle. Then, the lad used the magic of the whale tusk to start a fire beneath the pot. The water soon reached a boil as the bubbles popped and spewed. That night, the fire cooked and simmered the head until the meat came away from the bone. Beneath a blanket of stars, the boy made himself a trophy, a helmet, which would be his triumphant crest. When the skull cooled from the intense heat, Emery placed it on his head, and the boy became a Sagan.

Magoonagoon

CHAPTER 94

The Rescue

All night, Emery worked on his disguise. When he was finished, Emery armed himself with the sharp, pointed whale tusk and covered his head with his new skull helmet. He clothed his body with a tunic made from the king's cape and the glossy black feathers of the late monster. Like a king, noble and wise, the lad set out to rescue his teacher. With only the thought of freeing him, the boy set out alone.

He traveled over to the ruins, where the dreadful Sagans were camped. Emery used the skills that he learned from Brunto to track the enemy. He felt an obligation to save the Sagan, even though he was not of their kind. It was though he was betraying his own people to save him, for he was free to return to the armies of man. The goblin's magic powder had full control of him. The fellow was determined to pursuit the enemy and aid his instructor at any cost.

The path before him was set, and to return from the ruins would mean he must cheat death. With the tactics of stealth and sleuth, the boy slipped into the forgotten city early that morning. The Sagans were still sleeping from the drunken mess the night before. The trickling fountains gave the boy freedom to sneak about undetected. He passed by the dangerous loyalists and crept past the emperor's sect. He journeyed past their homes and lodgings in the shadows with tender steps. When he passed by the stables, the boy wondered if his teacher was dead.

Emery searched by the streets and gardens. He looked near the entrance at the west gate, and he combed all over the city. He climbed the steps to the once stately Foucinian sepulcher. From the highest point he peered over the ruins to see if he could spy Brunto. He found him with a keen eye, down at the foot of the stables in the filth and slop.

Brunto's strong hands were bound tight and his ankles were chained together. In the sewer and in the waste of the animals the giant lay, disgraced and degraded. He dangled upside down from a lynching post, where his head would be forced to rest in the excrement. Brunto had been beaten to a point so near to death, his wounds and abrasions had already begun to rot. His upper beak was broken off and lost from his face forever. One of his eyes had been put out and it dangled from the socket by a thread.

Emery moved swiftly and discreetly to his teacher's side under the cover of darkness. Like a condemned man with no regard for his own life, the boy advanced toward the prisoner. No other creature in all of Magoonagoon could have been so brave. It was if he was born for this purpose and lived only to rise to this occasion. The soothsayers would be befuddled to know that a human boy would enter the ruins alone.

When the fellow reached the dreadful body of the besmirched Sagan, he removed his skull helmet so that he would be recognized. Then the lad held his breath from the stench and stepped into the waste. His feet sloshed and mired in the excrement and the ripple burped up a vile smell. The lad almost vomited from the fume and he gagged at the reeking stink.

Emery slipped in the muck to the side of the defiled body. When he came near, the boy reached out with the handle of the whale tusk to nudge the Sagan in the ribs. The tusk reached the distance and Emery tapped the Sagan to see if he might still be alive. The giant came to life as he was startled from sleep, and he rose up in the marring mess. In one motion, the Sagan snatched the whale tusk away from the lad and prepared for battle.

It was at this decisive moment, when Brunto realized who the small stature was. With one scowling eye the monster looked up at him. Brunto dropped the tusk and reached down to grab Emery's wrist. The giant felt his heart race; like a traveler who returns to his homeland after many years, his spirit soared in the night. Tears dripped from the little fellow's eyes when he watched Brunto try to climb up from the sludge. So the young lad was the one to speak, and he whispered with a soft voice.

"Brunto. I have come to rescue you. I have come to save

you. Here is the sorcerer's magical tusk. Let me free you from your binds and we will leave this place together," said Emery.

The lad touched the tip of the whale tusk to the shackles and freed the Sagan's arms. With his strength exonerated, Brunto moved to break the chains that bound his legs. The Sagan had to lift the weight of his massive body up to reach the binds at his feet. He moaned and strained to reach the top of the lynching post and grab the chains that hampered his feet. From an upside-down position, the brute took hold of the shackles with a mighty grip, and he pulled on the irons with all his might.

The metal stretched and weakened, and in seconds one of the links gave way. Then the nightmare unfolded before Emery's eyes. The leg which was broken hung in the shackle as the other slipped free. The sudden jerk from the intensity of the weight shift caused the bone to sheer in half and mangle the leg. A terrifying noise came from Brunto's throat. It was a dreadful noise of agony and the sound traveled out in the darkness.

Emery leaped on the Sagan's neck and forced his head under the murk. The Sagan struggled for a moment and bubbles burst at the surface from the shouts of cursing underneath the bile. When the bubbles ceased, the lad freed the neck of his teacher and helped his head return to the surface. The clamor was loud enough to alert any enemy who was in range, but they were all so drunk from the wine that they took no thought of the noise. Now silent, the giant dangled by threads of tendon and skin in a torturing position.

Emery knew he must act quickly if he was going to save Brunto from certain death. So the boy took the tusk and painstakingly climbed up the body of the giant until he could reach the wound. He held onto the leg with one hand and drew back with the whale tusk in the other. Then with one decisive blow he severed the leg in half. With the leg free, the giant splashed down in the stagnant cesspool. Again the noise was loud enough to wake the enemy, but the drunken fools slept on.

    The boy helped the giant struggle to stand and he stumbled about in the slime on his wobbly foot. The huge Sagan whimpered from the pain as he jerked and hitched. His posture was so slumped that he looked to be four or five decades older than what he was. His huge talons that once steadied his foot had been torn from the flesh. His beautiful feathers had all been plucked from his skin. The few that remained dangled from the bleeding wounds. The bone protruded from the skin where Emery had clipped him below the knee and cut him free.

    As the pair scuffled from the mire, the drool dripped from the giant's lower beak. It was the only fragment on the monster's face that had endured the terrible scourging. His long neck hovered low to the ground as he leaned against the small fellow. The terrible smell of the spoil reeked from his body. The enemy had ransacked his frame and left his disposition frail and weak. Brunto collapsed to the ground and Emery quickly attended to him. The boy found a rope and used it as a tourniquet to keep the Sagan from bleeding to death. After he was finished, Emery picked up his trophy, the skull helmet, and placed it on the head of Brunto.

    Brunto stood back up on his single leg and hopped back over to the lynching post. The Sagan put both hands on the lynching post and ripped it out of the ground. Using the post as his crutch, Brunto wrapped the thick chain around his neck that held the amputated leg to begin the journey out of the enemy's territory. The two of them hobbled through the dangerous ruins at a hurried pace. Soiled in slop and shaking from the strain of holding up the giant, everywhere Emery turned, he found peril. They scurried through the city and fumbled over the landscape.

As the sun began to rise, the giant Sagan lumbered through the streets on one leg leaving a trail of blood to boot. Brunto wondered why a human had suffered to enter the enemy's land and risk death in order to save him. No Sagan would have done as much as the lad. No Sagan would be used as a crutch, no, not one. Brunto pondered the idea.

Where are my comrades? Those who dare to spit at the enemy? Where are the giants that prevail with such strength? They have not come to the rescue. This is a mere child that has come into the dominion of evil to save me. The strength that lies in his tiny body is far greater than any Sagan. If so much bravery is found in such a small sprite, then what sort would be found in an adult? thought Brunto.

Brunto paused for a moment and gazed down at the small fellow that held him up. The ideas that came to him brought about a new sense of fear—fear that plagued him and made his body tingle from head to toe. Distress came over the monster when he began to realize that the Foucinians were not to be the most feared. No, on the contrary, the humans were.

Magoonagoon

CHAPTER 95

Regroup and Recover

King Marion awoke to find himself alone on the beach. The king sat up from the grit and rubbed his sore head tenderly. Under a blanket of stars the man peered to search for the enemy in every direction. There in front of him laid the slain body of Stratogos. The monster's head was missing along with many of his glossy black feathers. King Marion scratched his chin in amazement as he stared at the body of the former adversary.

How could this be? Where are my soldiers? thought the king.

The king wondered what could have happened during the moments he had laid there unconscious. After he shook his head, the king stood to his feet and moved to retrieve his helmet. The headpiece had a dent in the side of the glorious gold. It had been bent from the devastating smash to the head the fellow received from Stratogos. He fiddled with the dent and tried to pop it back out as best he could. Then the man donned the headpiece and fastened the leather strap.

Sadly, as the king looked around he found every one of his faithful guardians dead. He fell down on his knees and cried for them. He shook his head in disbelief as he counted all the bodies. When he was able to stand, he searched the ground for his weapons. As King Marion walked along the beach he thought that he heard a voice speaking to him.

In the distance, King Marion heard voices, and he scoured the sand for his weapons. In the darkness, the king searched for any sort of weapon to arm. When his hand found a sword, the king rejoiced. He leaped up on top of the dunes and discovered the blazing torches that illuminated the faces of many Sagans. To the king it was just another group of Sagans. To him it was the enemy. They happened to be part of Brunto's band, and the war party was arguing audibly. The king listened closely as one of their scouts returned from a patrol.

"They have seized him!" shouted one of the Sagans.

"Oh! Say it is not so! We are doomed!" shouted another.

"Let us return to the others! We must rejoin them at once!" said Kounjab.

"Ha! Return! There is no way to return, you dolt! We are on our own now!" shouted Jinjo.

"Without Brunto we will surly die!" said Iipkam.

"Shut your mouth, you featherless fool! Brunto is not

dead! Only captured. If we band together, we can go and retrieve him. Let us discuss tactics and strategy to rescue our leader," said Jinjo.

"He is dead! They will not let him live! He is surely dead by now," said a Sagan.

At that very moment Emery and Brunto staggered near to the camp. They came down the coast resting along the way. When they heard the voices, they stopped in their tracks and Brunto instructed the boy to go ahead of them and spy on the group. If it was the enemy, they would be killed. All they could hope for is that it was their comrades, who had regrouped after their defeat.

Emery approached the dunes with caution and the boy anticipated the worst with the whale tusk drawn in attack. Brunto stayed behind and collapsed to the grit with a heavy thud and a growl. He laid there defenseless with no protection. Ahead of him, Emery slipped through the sand and surprised the eavesdropping king. King Marion was caught off guard and struggled to defend himself from attack.

"Who goes there?" asked Emery in a quiet voice.

"King Marion," said the king softly.

"Get out of here! Don't you know you are in great danger? What are you doing here?" asked Emery.

"I don't really know what I am doing. Who are you? Show yourself," ordered the king.

"Get out of here at once or I will be forced to yell for help," whispered Emery.

Emery forced King Marion to run and saved his life. Outnumbered, the king had no other choice but to run down the coast away from the danger. So the boy let the king go and resolved to fight—or join—him another day. At the top of the dune, Emery lifted his head up over the hill to spy upon the danger. To Emery's glee, the band happened to be his own, and he climbed on top of the hill to make sure they were all comrades. He made out the voices and searched for their faces. The boy's spirit soared when he saw them there before his eyes. He listened to them argue for a moment longer until he could no longer contain his exuberance.

The boy raced back to get Brunto. When Emery reached the giant, he found him lying there on the ground in an unconscious state. Emery tried to wake him and tell him the exciting news. However, the Sagan was so tired he would not wake up. Emery grabbed the skull helmet and headed back to greet the others. In a flash, the boy was back on top of the dunes. Then, he spoke to the crowd of Sagans as though he was a king.

"Ho! Comrades! I have returned with him! Come forth and help me carry him! For he has many wounds and is in need of care!" said Emery.

The crowd of Sagans shuddered away in fear of the voice. From their standpoint they could not see who spoke to them; they could only see a shadowy figure in the shape of a Sagan. With the skull helmet and feathered cape on, the boy resembled a Sagan with the likeness of one of them. Standing at the pinnacle of the hill with the whale tusk drawn, the youngster frightened the giants and sent many of them on the run. So again the boy spoke to them from the mound with a boastful twang.

"Do not be afraid! It is I! Emery! Think well ere you speak of me again, for I have returned!" said the fellow as he raised the wand.

    The Sagans all climbed the hill with their weapons drawn to face whatever trick or trap was before them. However, when they reached the top they discovered their ally. Seeing their leader down below, they rushed down the slope after him and gathered around the giant. They picked him up from the ground and carried him to the safety of their gathering where they could regroup and recover.

Magoonagoon

CHAPTER 96

Discipline

Many days later, Simon had finally gained enough strength to emerge from his quarters. The man slipped through the canvas, opening and batting his eyes at the shining sun. The poor fellow had been recovering from his wounds that had been given to him by those villainous Sagans that dreadful night. Simon scratched the sides of his head where ears used to be. He growled a low rumble and chewed on his lip while studying the soldiers around him.

Victor's men looked at him with their lips snarled and their teeth tight. Simon held his head up high and walked through them like a winter wind. He nodded at a few of them while he searched for their leader. The men seemed to scurry out of the man's way as though they feared him. They scattered as if he were a ghost, and they dared not greet the man with salutes or waves. No, they spurned him until he came near to the doorstep of Victor's tent. Then the sentries at post followed his every move as though he were a phantom.

When Simon reached the doorway, the wide-eyed centurions hastily moved to prevent him from entering. They held their spears out like gates that would hold back ten men and stopped the man in his tracks. Simon looked at them in the eye and frowned at them both with slanting eyebrows. The man held out his hands to show them that he was unarmed, but the gesture made little difference to them. Simon called to the man through the opening.

"Victor! You sent for me!" said Simon.

"Ho! Men! Let him pass! This is the man I told you of!" said Victor as he met him at the entrance.

"Yes! I am fully recovered and ready to join you!" said Simon as he saluted.

Victor came out into the open and bid the officers to gather the heralds so he could speak to them. Immediately, the officers rushed to gather the men, and they returned after a short time with them all. The scruffy crowd of battle-hardened veterans moved into the closure, and Victor bid the host of them to sit down. Then, without delay, Victor spoke to his captains in high spirit.

"Look now! Each man! This is the man who will replace him," said Victor as he pointed to Simon.

"Tell me what you speak of," said Simon softly.

"This is the leader of that band of volunteers! The leader of the night attack! He is the only survivor! Don't you remember him riding into our camps bleeding and bruised," said Victor as he placed his hand on the man's shoulder.

"Ho!" the men shouted and honored him.

"This man has returned to us in a dire time. Jonathon's men have been without a captain for too long. This man is a trooper of valor and bravery; he will fill the position. Let him have full command of my brother's men," said Victor.

"Please. Keep me from them no longer. Show me the way to their camp! Allow me to meet them at once," pleaded Simon in anticipation.

So the new leader strode to meet his troops with Victor and they found them still grieving by their tents. The soldiers were in complete disarray, with the majority of the ranks tipsy and drunk. Their horses were loose from the stables and the chariots were being taken out by the ocean's tide. Their armor was scattered along the sand and the exalted flags of the legion draped over the ground. The officers lay soused upon the beach. It was conduct that was unbecoming, and it was behavior that should never be practiced by the pacesetters.

Simon frowned at the sight of those drunkards and cringed at the thought of leading this ragged band. Still, the man moved to correct his officers and set things straight. He rushed over to the leaders and scorned one of them with his hands, smacking the young fellow across the face. The drunken youngster wanted to fight back, but he had the good sense not to. When he leaped to his feet, the officer caught a glimpse of

Victor. Forthwith, Victor addressed the crowd with a disgusted look upon his face.

"Ho! Hear me! All of you! This is the man! Look at your captain! Join him! He is the one I spoke of! The leader of the night attack! Obey him as you would Jonathon. Look to this man. Look to Simon," said Victor as he placed his hand on Simon's shoulder.

"Simon! Command is yours!" said one of the officers.

"Credit to you. Is this mess yours?" said Simon.

"With much regret! The burden is great as you can see. The men are drunk with wine and lethargic. They have wasted the last few days in a dense blur," said the officer with his head hung low.

"Get this mess cleaned up! I will not have disorder!" shouted Simon.

Then the unit staggered to their feet and sloppily commenced cleaning up the camp. Simon approached the officer he had struck and ordered him to stay at his side. The fellow took a glimpse at his missing ears and shuddered at the wounds. The officer followed Simon and Victor into the tent and they entered through the canvas. Inside he spoke to the officer in private.

"How long have you been an officer?" asked Simon.

"Two weeks. The last four officers have been killed," said the man.

"What is your rank young man?" asked Simon.

"Second in command," said the officer.

"Second in command? I will not have this squadron weakened by discredit from my officers. Your actions call for discipline. The punishment will be forty lashes," said Simon, hoping to evoke a response.

"I will have your orders carried out at once," said the officer.

"Very well. You may go," said Simon.

The officer departed from the tent and went to make the arrangements. Simon sent for food and drink and bid for Victor to stay and rest a while. With the request, Victor moved to speak.

"This man is an officer. Is it wise to correct him in front of his men?" asked Victor.

"What other place do you suggest? This man serves as an example. He will pay for his conduct and pass on the discipline," said Simon.

"I do not know this man, but I know he is still grieving. Exonerate him and dismiss the charges," suggested Victor.

"The charge will not be dropped. This man will meet the criterion for an officer or he will be replaced. The punishment will be carried out in plain view of the men. Others will follow until there is order," said Simon.

"Is there nothing more to be said?" asked Victor.

"Victor. If you want me to govern this squadron, let me do it in a way that demands compliance. These men are grieving. I know. But this is a time when they need direction, leadership, and structure. The officer will profit from the sentence. I promise. He will counter from the punishment and excel as a pacesetter," said Simon.

After a splendid meal, the two chatted about other things and they turned their attention away from the problem. They discussed trivial things which induced laughter. Then, at the moment when all of their thoughts hushed, they were interrupted by a visitor. He entered the tent unannounced and summoned the immediate attention of the captain. The soldier was breathing deeply and was sweating profusely. When he spoke, the men began to tremble.

"You must come at once! They have gone too far! The officer has had enough!" said the fellow.

Simon stood to his feet and slammed his fist on the table before him. The strike shook the plates and bowls. The man put on Jonathon's armor and prepared to go and speak with them. Simon had his mind made up that he would not be undermined by his squadron. He trekked out of the tent and headed toward the shouting crowds. Victor accompanied him on his way and the two moved to quell the flogging. When they arrived on the scene, they found drunkards and sots at the helm.

In his first charge to business, Simon took direct command, pulling his sword and calling for them to cease. The men who carried the whips ceased and dropped them in fear. They looked at him as if he was a ghost. In the armor, he appeared to be Jonathon reborn. Under the helmet he found a like countenance. The stately gear made him look just like their old hero.

No, he was not the man, but at that moment their drunken perspective led their minds to believe it as so. He ordered the officers to cut the man down from the post and to restore his tunic. Then the prosecutors became the debtors when they rightfully took the man's place. In that instant, he restored the garrison and returned them into service. He had the fellows horsewhipped and stopped it at an appropriate time.

Still, there were those who paid him no mind. They laid

down in the sand and sopped up the wine. They laughed at the spectacle before them and cursed. They threw their bottles at those who lethargically worked. Simon tried desperately to make corrections and quell the surging drunks, but those who at first answered their captain soon joined the others in rebellion.

A coordinated effort from the drunken men soon became the prevailing choice for the majority. Simon raised his sword at them and fruitlessly shouted out commands, until he began to sob and cry aloud. In a moment of madness, he almost killed a drunken sot, but he recovered just in time. He returned his sword to his belt and retreated to his tent in disappointment.

Simon had expected to single-handedly foil the rebellion and restore order to the camp. However, the man could not control the exceeding tide that immerses even the loyal when a mob is formed. As he walked away, the drinking continued, and the shouts of slander and defiance plagued his departure. Verily, even Victor could not direct them. Victor was dispirited from the events, and his heart ached for his newly instated herald.

Magoonagoon

CHAPTER 97

Never

Victor walked down the coastline and gazed up at the heavenly starlight. As he looked up, he caught a glimpse of a shooting star streaking past. The star zipped across the darkness and disappeared in a flash. As the man walked further away from the shouts and slurs, he put the uncontrollable mess behind him. Victor shook his head after thinking of Simon and wondered if he had made the right decision. In the night he thought to himself with many qualms.

Will this man be able to govern these men? Surely he will have their respect. His persona demands it. The drunken fools are out of order and I may have to send my own men to control them. It truly is a mess, thought Victor as he looked up at the stars.

At the edge of his own encampment, where the sentries stood guard, the unarmed man began to hear footsteps in the night. Without warning, he met the attacking Foucinians. With a zip and a tear a spear stuck into his shoulder and sent the burly man tumbling back. Numerous Foucinians sprinted into the camp aspiring to catch them off guard.

Ashamed and alone, Simon had rushed after the leader for advice. He was going to tell Victor the truth. Simon was going to tell him that he was fake and never at any time was he a great warrior. Instead, the man acted instantly to defend Victor. Victor was wounded and his life may have been taken if not for the quick actions of Simon. Out of the darkness he came with his sword drawn to shield the body of the wounded man. Simon called out for the others to fortify the garrison and rally the others to fight. The surprise of the attack had shocked Simon's men, who were at rest near the fires in sobering light. The Foucinians took the upper hand by killing and wounding a multitude of men. Only those who managed to find arms endured, all the others succumbed to the beasts.

Serpano, the new Foucinian commander, had cunningly positioned himself back away from the initial wave of the attack. The blitz was intended to be a hit-and-run assault, and the barrage had appeared to be a success. They had wounded Victor and butchered many of Jonathon's old-hand veterans. Simon had battled, outnumbered and alone against a superior force. He began to fatigue when he found himself encircled by the enemy.

The host of Foucinians barked and shouted as they closed in on the pair, claiming that it would be doom for them both.

It might have been just a coincidence or it could have been fate, but at the last moment a savior came riding on a sleek chariot. The charioteer sped headlong into the invading beasts with his wheels ripping through the sand. With his sword drawn and his team racing, the man cut down and ran over a host of them. Victor and Simon were delivered from the menace, when the charioteer barreled past them.

At least for the moment the duo avoided capture, but the momentum had taken the charioteer to a great distance past the enemy. He rolled past them as quickly as he came and in the distance he took some time to turn around. In his absence, the host returned with their jabs and snarling snouts; they moved on Simon as Victor tried to stumble away. Still, they came with their long spears in hand wishing to snare the fellow.

In a cloud of churning dust, the charioteer made an attempt to turn around. He yanked on the leather straps and the force seemed to throw the horses back in the direction of the assailants. The man lashed the reins and encouraged speed with every rap. With the enemy sighted, the driver zoomed toward their positions. Victor and Simon looked on hoping to spy the driver and be rescued. When he made his second pass, the men ratified their initial thoughts. The man, their redeemer, was Aubrey, the legionnaire. The young fellow smashed them a second time with a decisive blow. The Foucinians started to scatter and they fled from the battle. At their rear waited Serpano to impede their retreat. The hairy beast stood there like a blockade to stop them. He marshaled them back into the fight for another charge.

The poor Foucinians followed him only for a short distance until they turned to flee once more, leaving the beast all alone. There on the coast the Foucinian made his final stand. In front of the legionnaire the beast raced and he called out taunts of swagger. From the chariot, the young fellow spotted the vile beast and he aimed the horses right at him.

All the other Foucinians had fled with cowardice, and they had left their leader alone. The beast was in a bleak situation and his only thought was to make a final triumphant stand. Aubrey pulled on the reins of his chariot and stopped his team from advancing any farther. He put away his sword and grabbed one of the short javelins that rested in the cart. When Serpano saw the fellow change weapons he shouted to him.

"Boy! Are you that afraid of me? Why do you switch to long-range weaponry?" asked Serpano.

Aubrey paid the beast's comments no mind as he set the smooth lance correctly in his hand by pitching it into the air and catching it at the right moment. The time was right for attack and the legionnaire lashed the team. As he gripped the reins tight, he approached the spirited Foucinian with rushing hooves. The horses punched the ground with their smashing steps as they advanced on the lonesome enemy.

Serpano raised his shield to protect his upper body and prepared for the worst. Aubrey raced directly at the beast with intentions to run him over if he missed with his throw. When the man was in range, he let the dart fly and it leaped from his hand with a whisk. The javelin flew at Serpano and struck him right in the center of his shield. The lance deflected off the face of his round shield and toppled to the ground.

Still, the horses thundered at the beast with heavy steps. When the horses reached the Foucinian, Serpano carefully maneuvered to avoid ruin by rolling out of their dangerous path. As he rolled in the dust, he tried to cripple one of the wheels on the cart by slashing at them with his sword, but his attempt failed miserably. The cart rolled by and the Foucinian champion leaped to his feet to flee only to find himself surrounded by Aubrey's squadron of angry men.

The men encircled the beast and trapped him within a perimeter. He cautiously looked for an escape route with turns and twists in every direction. He paced back and forth until he came to the realization that there was no refuge. He proceeded to curse the men and dare any of them who wished to advance upon him. The circle of men shrank down to a close distance before they decided to stop.

Serpano shuddered at the thought of being captured and held prisoner. He cursed the Foucinian cowards who had left him behind in their retreat. The beast swung his weapon at the crowd and promised to punish any of the would-be attackers. He carried on in a fit of rage until he heard a voice he recognized in the distance. It came from the rearmost with such a still purpose.

Wounded and bleeding heavily Victor pushed his way into the arena. He held his shoulder with his hand and pressed a cloth against the wound. The cloth had already been soaked red from the pouring gash. On his own power, Victor stepped into close range of his adversary. Victor spoke to him with a certain distinctive magnitude.

"An old friend! I pity you. Why have you pressed to find

this end? You have hurried to your death. You and I were once allies in this war, and now we are enemies. Just the same, toss away your weapons and we will take you prisoner," said Victor.

"Old friend? Ha! Old fool! We were never friends! I will not surrender to any of these dogs before me! No! Never will I surrender!" said Serpano as he spat at the crowd.

"This is your final opportunity! Surrender or die!" said Victor.

"Ha! If that is what I am faced with, I will take as many of you with me as I can!" said Serpano.

At that moment, a soldier moved into the center of the chaos with purpose and design. He was one of the few armored men with his distinctive protection. At first glance, some thought it to be Jonathon, back from the dead. Others pressed and shoved to see what the man might do. He walked in front of the beast and stood with his posture erect. His weapon was not drawn. It dangled in his belt at his side. The man only leered at the beast in a lazy fashion with his hands on his hips. Yet, in his eyes there was a glooming stare that proclaimed doom.

The beast's jaws looked as though he was chewing away at his own tongue. He almost lunged at the man with the thought that he might take him. Then, with the odds clearly stacked against him, Serpano decided to back down. He pitched down his shield and threw away his sword to surrender. Quickly, some of Aubrey's men moved in to subdue him. The beast was captured and taken without trouble. The escort huddled around him and kept him tame.

Aubrey's squadron wondered who this man was that stood so near to the beast without his weapon in hand. They wondered why he had such gall, and each of them studied him close. He looked to be Jonathon's ghost, appearing in the flesh to haunt them, he must be an immortal who fears not of death. No, he was not a ghost; it was Simon, the newly appointed herald, who had convinced the Foucinian to relinquish his sword. Without pulling his weapon, without saying a word, the man took him single-handedly.

Magoonagoon

CHAPTER 98
The Badlands

Brunto and the rebel Sagans had decided to cross the narrow span of ocean that separates Magoonagoon from the badlands. They had forced some of the human prisoners to carry Brunto over the great distance. The Sagan had sustained death only by the magic dust from the goblin's bag. But even the dust could not save his leg. For the time being, the powder had only saved his life.

Brunto would not have been able to make the journey if not for the doctor, Komoras, who stitched the nub of the severed leg. He had sawed away the shard of bone that protruded horribly from the skin, and sewed the wound shut with some twine. The bleeding had stopped, but his body was so severely beaten that the doctor predicted his death within days.

They had moved to a new area where they felt safe and secure at the very edge of the wastelands. With a boneyard of death all around them, they pressed on past the skeletons of old. As they moved further north, the group had to cross the Narrow Pass to get into the badlands. They marched through the hot splashing mess and traveled further from the dangers until they peered upon the flat rock.

The men carried Brunto, with their backs in constant burden. He was strapped to a plank of wood that must have come from a hull of a mighty ship. The large beam was stout and true, heavy enough itself, without the Sagan on top. He spanned the entire length of the plank and sagged the thick wood so much that it looked as though at any moment it would break.

In the center of the boiling tundra, there rose a mighty plate of rock, which withstood the erosion of the sloppy soup. It was higher than the hot tar by only mere feet, but it was exemplary to sustain their needs. When they saw the cresting island the pioneers selfishly moved to claim the ground first. When the men that carried Brunto looked up to see everyone else racing toward the place, they stopped dragging the body through the mess. The giant sunk in the tar and within a few moments disappeared into the bubbles with a gasp of air. The men battled the sinking mud themselves and they struggled to stay above the quagmire.

Forsaking him, the Sagans all climbed upon the oasis and selfishly skirmished for space. Many of the men were trampled and marred in the muck by the monsters rushing to the rock. Still, there was little room on the stone and the Sagans selfishly pressed and shoved to claim a spot. Not one of them dared to give up his spot on the sheltering island. The place cursed them and deprived them of rest. For the dominate ones strained to keep their spot, and the more they struggled the weaker they became.

Emery searched through the murky hot water to recover his teacher. The lad had to submerge his little frame deep in the muck in order to try and feel him. He sloshed all around the area where he saw the giant go down, but could not locate him. He poked and prodded with the whale tusk and could not seem to find him. He called out for the Sagans to help him, but they only whispered and schemed to take a place on the stone.

The humans who had not been marred beneath the waste watched the boy search from their positions nearby. The Sagans waited anxiously for any of the humans to come near the rock. The Sagans sat there huddled together in groups snickering, murmuring, and planning to eat any of them if they came within their reach. The lad called out to them as he sunk down in the soup. He gasped for air and struggled to stay atop the bubbling tar. Then the lad touched a lump beneath his feet that felt as solid as a sturdy mountain. He grabbed it with his foot and climbed up on the mass. From the top of the mound the lad called out to the Sagans.

"I have found him! Come and help me! He is here!" shouted Emery.

The majority of the Sagans ignored him. Yet there were a few Sagans who sympathized with the lad and wanted to see their leader pulled from the waste. However, they sat on the rock in silence and not a single one of them moved from his spot. The frustrated lad shouted at them in anger, which did little good to convince any of them to help. So the boy shook his head and gripped the tusk tightly in aggravation.

At the last moment possible, the thought came to him to try his hand at magic. He had watched the sorcerer summon up countless spells and send them from the tip of the wand. So Emery lifted the tusk and closed his eyes to concentrate. Then the young fellow waved it around in a circular motion and called out with a shout.

"Up from the slop! Bring this Sagan to the top!" said Emery.

The tar began to bubble and the soup boiled, until the monster rose up from the mud. The congregation that rested on the slick rock leaped to their feet and watched as the body floated up from the bottom. The hot tar had cooked his wounds and destroyed the infectious cuts and abrasions. The goblin's dust must have sustained him, for he was still alive and breathing. When the others saw that he was still alive and awake they ran to him and carried him to the center of the island. There the slick rock became Brunto's refuge.

All around them the bubbling spew of the hot geysers sputtered and gargled. Emery sat on top of the giant while he rested through the night. The wind began to howl and nip at their necks, and when the moon climbed over the hills its bright light showered their eyes and filled their senses. It was at that moment when Emery moved to speak to the host. He had some urgent and pressing news that he knew would be important to them. So he stood upon his teacher's belly and from the peak, the young fellow drew their attention. Late that night he spoke in the Sagan tongues.

"You must not be so self-centered! This is your friend! Your comrade! You left him to die! For a cool place on a rock! You should be ashamed! I will scoff at you some more! This is the reason for your defeat! You are not united! You do not wish to succeed!" shouted Emery.

"Silence! You are not one of us! What right do you have to ridicule us?" asked Jinjo.

"If you do not band together you will soon die! You let your leader sink to the bottom of this waste while you fought for a place on this stone! Shame on you all!" shouted Emery.

"I was wrong! I will admit that! I should have helped him," said one of the Sagans.

"Yes, you should have, and so should the rest of you. In my hand I hold a great power and it can be used to persuade all. Swear your loyalty now! Swear to Brunto or die!" shouted Emery.

At first the Sagans scoffed and murmured among themselves making plans to devour the boy. Then Emery convinced them that he was serious by killing one of the Sagans that hungrily crept toward him. A bolt of lightning leapt from the tusk and fried the Sagan to a crisp. When the Sagan fell dead, the host shouted and called out to the lad. Each of them pledged to forever protect him and their leader. From that moment on, they honored him and gained respect for each other. It all came from the human boy, who taught them things that they never understood. In a day's time, the youngster had rescued his teacher and united the host.

Magoonagoon

CHAPTER 99

Back To Life

The same day, a trumpet blast sounded that echoed all across the land. The blast found its way to the ears of the dead sorcerer where his body lay beneath the body of the giant Sagan. When the second blast was sounded, the wizard opened his eyes. His magic powers had somehow brought him back to life. Oliver wrestled with the carcass that lay piled up on top of him and wiggled his way out.

The sorcerer slipped out from beneath the Sagan's body and climbed to his feet. His body was back in the form of a man. He dusted off his clothes and looked for his helmet and the narwhale tusk. The man found his helmet under the giant leg of the dead Sagan, but the whale tusk was missing. So the sorcerer armed himself with a discarded staff and set out to find his people.

The sorcerer traveled along the hills and discovered how treacherous the ground really was. Along the way he passed a few patrols from both sides and he disguised himself as a lion, an eagle, and a deer. After a long and exhausting journey, under the cover of darkness, the sorcerer returned to his comrades. However, he knew that they would not welcome him, for they still held the grudge against him for the trickery that almost killed Victor.

So he slipped into the camp unnoticed, and snuck by all of the sentries and guards. He passed by all of the officer's tents and found himself at the doorstep of Victor's tent unscathed. At the entrance he changed into a mouse to slip by the posted sentries. He slipped into a hiding place and eavesdropped on the conversation that came from inside. He could hear the muffled questioning and the strange sounds of an inquisition. The sorcerer knew that it would be better to meet with Victor alone, but the information he possessed was far greater than the risk.

Into the center he slipped, and there the magician transformed back into the image of the man they knew. In their presence he stood, kingly, dashing, and confident. The wizard was unarmed, but his charisma alarmed the officers of the legion. His sudden appearance flabbergasted the audience and left them stunned with disbelief.

"Oh! You're alive! Thank God you're alive!" said Victor but the others drew their swords to fight the wizard and they lashed out at him with anger.

Godwin was the first to scorn the sorcerer with cursing and abusive threats. Others in the room wanted their chance at him and they gathered in front of him with intentions to repay him for what they thought was wrongdoing. Still, the sorcerer remained calm, with his hands at his side. When the situation looked as though it might turn violent, Victor intervened with calming words.

"Ho! Men! Stand down! This is a returning friend. He has completed a great mission that will bring us intelligence," said Victor.

"Ha! This goat has been promised the edge of my sword if I ever saw him again! Here he is. Oh! What a fool you are to return," said Godwin.

"Stand down! The things of the past are over. This man tricked you to prepare for a mission. He has done nothing wrong. Let me be the judge here," said Victor as he stepped between them.

"Victor! He tried to kill you! This man is a traitor! Do not grant him immunity. He will turn on us again; just as before, let us not forget what he did to you. The man stabbed you. I remember it well. Do not be a fool. This man is evil," said Eugene as he moved forward with his sword.

"Eugene. I have not told you that this man tricked you. He fooled us all with his magic. All the commotion he caused in the Foucinian stronghold was my own doing. I asked him to make the scene. It was by a purposeful design that those things took place. From that day until now he has been in the realm of the Sagans, studying for their weaknesses and pinpointing the leaders as a spy," said Victor.

"Forgive me, Oliver. I had no idea. This plan was well coordinated and executed. Please except my complements," said Godwin as he curtseyed.

"Old friend! You have returned! It makes me very glad to see you again. Let me hear of everything you have seen. Tell us! What news have you learned from them?" asked Victor and the officers and leaders listened for the magician to speak.

With these very words, the king burst into the tent. He had an angry expression on his face and appeared to be in a terrible mood. The men in the room looked him over and realized that something was terribly wrong. His raiment was torn and the king was dirty. The soldiers had never seen him in those conditions before. The king walked right past them and they cleared out of the way. He walked over to the center of the room and spoke to them with an ill tone.

"Why have you not been out searching for me?" asked King Marion as he waited for an answer, but not a one of them spoke.

"My lord?" questioned Victor.

"Not a single one of you even knew I was even gone. Did you? Which one of you could be so bold?" asked the king expecting an answer.

"My king!" said Victor trying to give an explanation, but the king interrupted him and let them all have it.

"I will not punish you as much as I really should. For I am a king and not a man," said King Marion.

"Oh! My king! Please forgive me!" said Victor.

"Victor. You are relieved of command," said the king.

Magoonagoon

CHAPTER 100

Surrounded

King Marion told them of the Sagans headed for the badlands and he called for the legions to arm. He sent the officers and heralds to gather their troops and ready the march. They could sense the relevance in the timing. King Marion ordered them to go to the badlands where they would surround the enemy.

The men scurried about fulfilling their duties and following orders. King Marion appointed guardians to stay and watch over the ships. The charioteers tended to their horses and lashed the carts to their teams. Within a few moments the entire legion was ready to march and the drum beat set the pace. They rumbled to a shaky start and crawled toward their destination at an eager pace.

King Marion rode in a chariot near the front guiding the way. The king continuously watched over his shoulder at the ensuing army. They proceeded north, where the most deadly war was fought. It seemed the danger lurked in the place still, like a haunting ghost bound by thick chains. They tracked with the legion nipping at their heels. Aubrey was right behind them, with his swift horses, the fastest in the human army, and the most prized.

So the force reached the crossing point, and they could see across the ocean into the badlands. Rotting carcasses and bones strewn across the ground let them know they had found the forsaken place. The ground began to bubble and spew beneath their feet. The hot spray melted on their skin and burned their flesh. The toughest of them took the pain and continued without even so much as a whimper.

When the force reached the flat rock, they discovered signs that the Sagans had been there. The trackers looked at the signs and determined which direction they might have gone. When they reached a conclusion, the king convened with the leaders on top of the flat rock. The group worked out a strategy for how they would deal with the Sagans once they caught up to them. King Marion sent scouts in every direction to pinpoint their location. When one of the scouts returned, he spoke.

"I found them. They are not far from here," said the scout.

"Show us the way," said King Marion.

On the way to the enemies' camp the force spread out as they had planned. Each of the heralds took a force, and the army broke into seven different pieces. The plan was to surround the Sagans and hope to take them by surprise. To seize such a tiny force would be no problem, if the foe was a small band of humans. However, these creatures were giant killers with the longing for death and destruction.

The squads departed and picked up the pace to attack. When they came in sight of the camp, the plan worked as intended and they converged on the foe with haste. Just as they had planned, the force surrounded the camp and held their ground. The king had instructed the host of them to wait at the edge of their perimeter for his signal. Quietly the force held their positions until the man gave the command. The lookouts of the Sagan force must have been asleep, for the guards never alarmed the others. Instead, the men snuck right up to them with silent steps and overwhelmed them with their numbers.

Like an old wolf that howls at the moon, a giant Sagan warned the others. He stretched out his neck as if he wanted to reach the stars and then began his loud siren. With his mouth open wide, and his slender tongue wiggling, he blared out the shout that could have been heard for miles. The noise traveled from his mouth and ventured to the ears of his comrades.

Emery ran to the center of the camp where Brunto lay. There the recovering Sagan was stretched out on his belly. His amputated leg ached and shot deadly bolts of pain through his wounds. The boy approached the giant with caution for he moaned terribly and he shivered and shook with convulsions. Emery tried to wake the feathered giant and nudged his side to free him from the nightmare. The nudge startled the Sagan from sleep and woke him with astonishment.

The Sagan leader yawned and snapped his crippled beak at the lad as he tried to wake. The giant shut his one good eye and with a growl laid his head back down on the ground to rest. There flat on the dirt the giant fell into a deep sleep, for the potions had taken their toll leaving him helpless and groggy. He struggled to breathe with a whimpering snivel, for the drugs were so powerful that his system was almost shut down.

In seconds, the giant was in deep sleep and cared not for the world around him. A second time Emery shook his teacher to ask for direction, and the Sagan woke in the same manner. He snapped his broken beak and yawned a bit, until he opened his only eye halfway. His long neck lifted off the ground and Brunto turned to find the fellow near his side. This time he recognized the little lad and he spoke to him with a sleepy voice.

"What is it, child? Why do you bother me while I am trying to sleep?" asked Brunto.

"An army of men approaches! Thousands of them! They have us surrounded! What should we do?" asked Emery with desperation.

Brunto opened his eye wide for a moment and then shut it in order to think. He tried to swallow, but his mouth was so dry he could hardly speak. He reached up and felt of his broken beak and touched his splintered mouth. Then he scratched the back of his neck and whispered in the Sagan tongue softly. He looked over his shoulder and peered on the danger as it moved ever closer. The giant placed his hands on the ground and coaxed his arms out in order to lift his body. With a painful jolt he failed and struggled even to move. It was at that very moment when all the retreating Sagans converged in his presence.

The broken champion was too groggy to fight or for that matter, to retreat. The drugs that Komoras had used to perform the surgery had crippled his limbs and kept him numb from reality. So as the old champion lay there, he thought of a plan, a maneuver that would have to work or it would denote the end. Realizing his position he called for Emery to come close and he whispered something in his ear. It was too quiet for the rest of them to hear, and it was in the old language, which was hard for humans to discern.

Armed with the knowledge from the old teacher, the boy leaped upon the hulk's body. From the peak the young fellow called to his Sagan comrades and the prisoners alike. Gripping the magical whale tusk in his hand, the youngster called for them to gather around him.

The humans converged on the remaining Sagans with their sharp, pointed weapons. They closed in on the group like an angry mob clamoring and clanging with rushing steps. Defeated and discouraged, the Sagans huddled around their leader. They hunkered down and shuddered away from the attackers. Their feathers rose up on their backs and flared like the hair on the neck of a frightened dog. There in the shrinking center the rebel Sagans awaited their doom.

ORDERING INFORMATION

If you have enjoyed

Magoonagoon

and would like to purchase a copy for a gift

please visit:

https://www.createspace.com/3758636

or

http://www.amazon.com
key word: Magoonagoon

Made in the USA
Lexington, KY
20 June 2012